W9-BUH-243

Other Titles by Karen White

flight patterns

KAREN WHITE

BERKLEY
New York

BERKLEY
An imprint of Penguin Random House LLC
375 Hudson Street, New York, New York 10014

Copyright © 2016 by Harley House Books, LLC
Readers Guide copyright © 2016 by Penguin Random House LLC
Excerpt from *The Night the Lights Went Out* copyright © 2017 by Harley House Books, LLC

ISBN 9780451470928

The Library of Congress has cataloged the hardcover edition of this title as follows:

Names: White, Karen (Karen S.), author.
Title: Flight patterns/Karen White.
Description: New York City: New American Library, [2016]
Identifiers: LCCN 2015047815 (print) | LCCN 2016001086 (ebook) |
ISBN 9780451470911 (hardcover) | ISBN 9780698165861 (ebook)
Subjects: LCSH: Families—Fiction. | Homecoming—Fiction. | Self-realization
in women—Fiction. | Self-actualization (Psychology) in women—Fiction. |
Domestic fiction. | BISAC: FICTION/Family Life. | FICTION/Contemporary Women.
Classification: LCC PS3623.H5776 F58 2016 (print) |
LCC PS3623.H5776 (ebook) | DDC 813/.6—dc23
LC record available at http://lccn.loc.gov/2015047815

New American Library hardcover edition / May 2016
Berkley trade paperback edition / March 2017

Printed in the United States of America
1   3   5   7   9   10   8   6   4   2

Cover photograph © Maatman / Shutterstock Images
Cover design by Rita Frangie

To my mother, Catherine Ann Sconiers,
who instilled in me a love of fine china.

acknowledgments

One of the best things about writing a novel, besides sharing my stories with readers, is the lovely people I meet along the way who are so incredibly generous with their time and knowledge. I learned so much while writing *Flight Patterns*, and I'd like to thank those who helped me with everything I didn't know, and who made the learning a real joy for me.

Thank you to the lovely people of Apalachicola for your warm kindness and generosity in sharing your love for your beautiful hometown—especially Caty Greene at the Apalachicola Municipal Library and Susan Clementson, both of whom allowed me to borrow their names for the book. Thanks, too, to Kathie Bennett of the Magic Time Literary Agency, who introduced me to both of these fabulous women.

Thanks also to beekeeper James Rish for teaching me everything I needed to know about harvesting tupelo honey in the Florida swamps, and to Florence Love for your patience with all my endless questions and for allowing me to invade your backyard for several hours while you showed me your bees and how it all works. I appreciate your lending me your name and your dangling bee earrings for the beekeeper character in the book.

Since I don't speak French, I owe a great deal of gratitude to the French-speaking friends who agreed to translate for me—Luke McCracken, Alicia Kelly, and Nicky and Mathieu Limousi. Any mistakes are completely my own.

And, of course, a huge thanks to my amazing team at NAL/ Berkley and Writer's House for the incredible support you give to me and my books.

Last, but by no means least, thanks to my sister-in-law and "research buddy," Claire White Kobylt, who tagged along with me on my first visit to Apalachicola and happily jotted down notes as we drove through the tree-shaded streets studying the architecture and learning the history of this incredible town. And to my first readers, talented writers, and BFFs, Wendy Wax and Susan Crandall, for reining me in and keeping me far from the ledge.

flight patterns

prologue

"The keeping of bees is like the direction of sunbeams."
Henry David Thoreau

—NED BLOODWORTH'S BEEKEEPER'S JOURNAL

SEPTEMBER 1943
PROVENCE, FRANCE

Dead bees fell from the bruised dusk sky, their papery bodies somersaulting in the air, ricocheting like spent shells off the azure-painted roof of the hive. Giles straightened, breathing in the heavy scents of lavender and honey, of summer grasses and his own sweat. And something else, too. Something chemical and out of place in his fields of purple and gold. Something that made sense out of the bees lying like carrion for the swarming swallows above.

"*Ah! Vous dirais-je, maman,*" sang his three-year-old daughter with her clear, perfect voice from her perch on an upturned bucket, unaware of the sky or the bees or the tremor of fear that shook the breath from his lungs.

"*Colette, calme-toi,*" he said, putting his finger to his lips.

The little girl stopped singing and stared up at her father with a question in her dark eyes. He had never asked her to stop before.

Keeping his finger to his lips, Giles closed his eyes, listening. A low hum escaped from inside the hive, quieter now, a volume dial turned low on a radio. A sign to any beekeeper that something was wrong. The queen had died, perhaps. Or any of the dreaded parasites—mites or beetles, even—had invaded the hive, taking over an entire population and killing them.

Or the entire colony had become aware, even before Giles, that the one thing he'd hoped and prayed would never happen was now waiting with open arms on his doorstep. And the bees had chosen a sudden death instead of a long, lingering passing.

He strained to listen, wanting to hear beyond the sound of the bees and the circling birds and his own breathing. There. There it was. The gurgle and thrum of multiple engines. Not cars. Trucks. Large trucks to transport as many people as possible, a slow convoy climbing its way through the small farms and vibrant fields of Provence.

It was inevitable, he supposed. As soon as the Germans had invaded the free zone in southern France the previous November, there was nobody to protect them. Not even a puppet government. His chest expanded and contracted as a cloud of dust and cut hay churned up by the trucks' tires drifted over the winding dirt road in the far distance like poison descending on the valley.

He thought of the family now huddled in his barn, in the small room he'd created beneath the hidden trapdoor covered with bales of hay. A mother and father and three small children, the woman's belly swollen with a fourth. He hadn't even asked their names. These families came and went so frequently that he'd stopped asking. It was easier that way, later. When he'd learn that some hadn't made it over the mountains to safety it was better that he hadn't known their names.

Giles cursed under his breath. Three days before, when the cobbler had sent his new assistant, he'd known. He'd seen the way the young man's eyes had darted about the barn, taking in the tidy table and bench pushed against the wall. The way the cobwebs had been swept out of the corners of the rafters. The neatly stacked tools, carefully placed. All signs of a woman's touch, yet Giles's wife had been dead for three years. Yes, Giles had known even then. And the bees had known, too.

Half an hour. That's all he had before the trucks reached his farm, saw the brightly painted beehives and the stone house where his family had lived for almost two hundred years in the shadow of the château. Before they reached the barn and started moving the hay. His nostrils flared as the exhaust fumes overtook the sweet scents of his beloved fields, and he turned abruptly to Colette.

"C'est le temps." He picked her up, her warm breath on his neck, and began to run.

She started to cry before they'd even reached the barn, her sobs already hiccups by the time the family had crawled from their hiding place and begun their escape across the lavender fields, their shadows chasing them through the rows of purple.

In the kitchen at the back of the farmhouse he removed the small leather suitcase that had been Colette's mother's, packed the same day he'd decided he could no longer be a bystander. Carefully he took the teapot from the hutch, where it had been nestled between its matching cups and plates, the feel of the china fragile beneath his rough hands, as he remembered his dead wife and how she'd loved beautiful things, how she'd loved to set the table and eat from the delicate plates. The china set had been a wedding gift from the château to his grandparents, a thank-you for his family's years of service.

He wrapped it in a small towel and tucked it carefully amid Colette's clothing inside the case, then lifted the little girl into his arms again, pressing his forehead to hers. "It will be all right, *ma petite chérie.* Madame Bosco has promised to look after you until I return." He lifted the suitcase and began walking swiftly from the house toward the neighboring farm. The Boscos were a large Italian-French family with seven children of their own and had not asked him why he might need to leave his daughter for an unspecified amount of time. It was better they did not know.

"Non, Papa." Colette's bottom lip quivered, but he dared not slow or look behind him.

He pressed her blond head against his chest as he walked faster, seeing the lights of the stone farmhouse, white sheets flapping on the clothesline like a warning. The door opened before he reached it. Madame Bosco's large, round form filled the doorway, the light illuminating her. A young girl, dark haired like her mother but slender as a reed, peered out from behind madame.

"Go back inside," the woman said to the girl. "Keep your brothers and sisters away from the door." She waited until her daughter had left, the girl stealing a glance over her shoulder only once. Madame Bosco turned back to Giles. "It is time?" she asked, her voice low.

Giles nodded, holding Colette even tighter, knowing what a terrible thing he was asking the child to do. And how this very scene must be playing out again and again all over the burning fields of Europe. A chorus of children's cries and parents' despair that fell on parched earth and thick air that smelled of burning things. The wailing might be heard, but no one was listening.

He touched his lips to Colette's sweat-soaked forehead and tearstained cheek, breathing in the scent of her one last time. "You are my heart, *ma chérie*," he said, holding her small fist tightly in his own larger one, replaying something they did every night. "And only you can set it free." He opened his hand and wiggled his fingers like petals on a sunflower. Even in her misery, the little girl remembered her part and opened her own hand, the small fingers slow and heavy.

"Remember this," Giles whispered in her ear, the folds and curves as delicate as a flower. "Remember you are my heart."

Before he could change his mind, he handed Colette to the welcoming arms of Madame Bosco. There were tears in her eyes as she held the sobbing child. "We will keep her safe until you return. We have already instructed the children."

Giles nodded, remembering her mother, as he stroked Colette's blond curls. He slid a postcard from his pocket and handed it to madame, his thumb obscuring the foreign stamps. The edges were torn and frayed from having been held and read so many times, the image of the beach with impossibly white sand engraved in his memory. "If something happens, let my friend know. His name and address are on here. If I can't find you, I will go to him." He paused for a moment. "Keep it hidden. It will be safer for you that way. No questions."

Madame Bosco nodded and he felt the trembling in her hand as she took the postcard. "I will pray that I will put this back in your hands along with Colette when this is all over."

He gave her a solemn stare. "I hope God listens to your prayers. He hasn't listened to mine in a very long time." Lifting the suitcase, he set it inside the kitchen door. "Be careful with this. I have wrapped something precious inside, something of her home and family. Please keep them both safe."

One last time Giles pressed his lips against Colette's soft curls. "*Au revoir, ma chérie.* I will come back for you; I promise. However long it takes."

The little girl looked up at him with her mother's eyes, large and dark. She reached for him. "*Ne va pas, Papa!* Don't leave me!" She struggled to release herself from the woman's grasp, her legs kicking frantically.

"Be safe," madame said, her own eyes damp. "Until we meet again."

He touched her arm and pressed it, grief like cement filling his throat. With one last glance back, he turned in the opposite direction from his farm and began to run. He heard his daughter sobbing as the sky cast out the light, and imagined he could hear the sound of dead bees hitting the parched earth, lamenting the passing of all that was good.

chapter 1

*"The bee collects honey from flowers in such a way as to do the least
damage or destruction to them, and he leaves them whole,
undamaged and fresh, just as he found them."*
St. Francis de Sales

—NED BLOODWORTH'S BEEKEEPER'S JOURNAL

Georgia

APRIL 2015

NEW ORLEANS

Memories are thieves. They slip up behind you when you least
expect it, their cold hands pressed against your face, suffocating. They blow icy-cold air even on the hottest days, and pinch you
awake in the middle of the night. My grandfather had once told me
that memories were like a faucet you could turn on or off at will, and
that after I got to be as old as he was, I'd have figured out how it works.
Maybe I just wasn't old enough, because my memories always had a
way of getting stuck in the "on" position, flooding my mind with images
and snatches of conversations I'd rather not relive.

Perhaps that explained my obsession with old things, with antique
clocks, armoires, and shoes. My fascination with ancient books filled with
brittle paper, with mismatched china pieces, and with old-fashioned keys

and their corresponding locks. It was as if these relics had been left for me to claim as my own, to make up a past devoid of my own memories.

Old china was my favorite. It allowed me to live vicariously through somebody else's imagined life, to participate in family meals and celebrations, to pretend to be a part of a bride's place-setting selection. Experiences from somebody else's life, but definitely not my own. Despite, or probably because of, my family's well-grounded belief that I was born to founder, I'd discovered a vocation I not only loved but was actually good at. I was an expert in most things antique, a sought-after consultant, and proof that it's possible to become someone different from the person you once were. The person everybody expected you to still be. If only I could have figured out how to turn off the memories, I might have been able to sink comfortably into the new life I'd created from old china and discarded furniture.

I dipped a cotton swab into the cleaning solution and dabbed at the intricate scrollwork of the padlock on my desk. The silver shield-shaped lock with grained bar-and-diamond-embellished trim had been found in a box of old horse tackle in a barn in New Hampshire at an estate sale. Mr. Mandeville, my boss, and owner of the Big Easy Auction Gallery, had grudgingly let me go. I had a good eye and an even better instinct about these things, and after eight years of my working for Mr. Mandeville, he'd finally started to agree. I would study the history of a property and its owner when an estate sale was announced so that I could look at pictures of boxes stacked in an old barn or pushed against the walls of a humid attic and know what treasures I'd find.

I wouldn't say that I was particularly happy, or as successful as I'd have liked to be, but there was nobody in my life to ask me whether I was. Nobody to hold up a mirror to make me see whom I had become, or to see the person I'd been who had never really believed she could be anything more than ordinary. My mother had once told me that she didn't know that particular sorrow, the sorrow of being ordinary. But I did. And I relished it, if only because it made me not her.

I opened the large bottom drawer of my desk, listening to the clink and slide of dozens of mismatched keys and padlocks I'd collected over the years, my hope of finding a matching key and lock one of the stupid little games I played with myself. I'd just grabbed a fistful of keys when I heard the front door of the building open, the bell clanging ominously in the empty space. It was Sunday, the offices and gallery below were closed, and nobody was supposed to be there. Which was precisely why I was there, unconcerned about the vintage jeans with frayed bell-bottoms that sat a little too low on my hips, flip-flops, a 1960s tie-dyed T-shirt, and hair pulled back in a ponytail that made me look about ten years old.

"Georgia?" Mr. Mandeville called up the stairs. The gallery was an old cotton warehouse on Tchoupitoulas, and every word bounced and ricocheted off the brick walls and wood floors unencumbered by rugs or wall coverings of any sort.

I stood to let him know where I was, then froze as I heard another male voice and two sets of footsteps climbing the stairs.

"Georgia?" he called again.

Knowing he'd probably seen my car in the small parking lot behind the building, I sat down behind my desk, hoping to at least hide my flip-flops.

"I'm in my office," I shouted unnecessarily, their footsteps coming to a stop outside my door. "Come in."

Mr. Mandeville opened the door and stepped through, then ushered his companion inside. The tall ceilings and windows dwarfed most people, including my boss, but not the visitor. He was very tall, maybe six feet, four inches, with thick and wavy strawberry-blond hair. As a person who studied objects of beauty for a living, I decided that's what he was and didn't bother to hide my scrutiny.

He was lean but broad shouldered, the bones in his face strong and well placed, his eyes the color of cobalt Wedgwood Jasperware. As they approached, I stood, forgetting what I must look like, and allowed my gaze to rove over the full length of him like I would a Victorian armoire or Hepplewhite chair. I'd started to grin to myself as I realized I must be one of a very small number of women who'd compare a handsome man to a piece of furniture.

He must have caught my grin, because the man stopped about five feet from me, a pensive look on his face. It took me a moment to realize that he was studying me with the same examination I'd just given him.

I sat down quickly, chagrined to know that I wasn't as immune as I believed myself to be.

Mr. Mandeville frowned slightly at me seated behind my desk. I knew he had issues with my insistence on solitude and working long hours. He was a family man who thrived on noise and bustle and the adoration of his employees and extended family. But he'd never had concern over my manners. Until now, apparently.

"Georgia Chambers, please meet a prospective client, James Graf. He's come all the way from New York City to see you. He was so excited to meet you that he made me bring him straight here from the airport." He sent me an accusatory glare as we both understood my lack of a cell phone meant he hadn't been able to give me advance warning.

James tucked a parcel under his left arm to free up his right as he extended his hand toward me. I half stood, painfully aware of my low-slung jeans. "It's a pleasure to meet you."

His hand was large and swallowed mine in a firm handshake. I slid my fingers from his and sat back in my chair. Turning toward Mr. Mandeville, I asked, "What's this about?"

"James is in the process of settling his grandmother's estate and came across a set of china that he believes might be valuable. He Googled china experts and found your name."

The visitor continued. "But I couldn't find a phone number for you, so I reached Mr. Mandeville instead. I offered to e-mail a photo, or speak with you directly, but he explained that you prefer to look at pieces in person, to hold them to get a real 'feel' for them. And that an e-mailed photo is something you've never considered working with."

He said it without the usual derision I was accustomed to hearing when people learned I had yet to move into the twenty-first century.

"She also declines to use a cell phone," Mr. Mandeville added.

The man looked at me with assessing eyes, and just for a brief moment I thought that he might understand why a person would choose to live surrounded by other people's things.

Then he said, "I couldn't imagine."

He was right, I knew. But I could almost believe that I'd seen something in his eyes that seemed a lot like longing for a world he hadn't even known existed.

"Do you know anything about antique china, Mr. Graf?"

"Not a thing, I'm afraid. And please call me James."

I nodded, taking in his well-tailored suit and Hermès tie—possibly vintage. He wasn't a Jim or Jimmy, had never been one. He was mid-thirties, but had a youthful air about him that didn't seem like a Mr. Graf at all. He looked like a James who sailed a lot and was probably on the rowing team at Dartmouth or Yale or wherever up north he'd gone for undergrad. His hair was a little too long for the Wall Street stereotype, but I would've bet my collection of Swiss watch parts that he belonged to the fast-paced financial world of constant texts and two cell phones to manage the craziness.

He narrowed his eyes and I realized that I'd been too busy cataloging him to be aware that I had been staring again. Flustered, I slid the items on my desk to the side, then reached for the brown corrugated box. "May I see?"

"Of course." He handed the small square box to me, and I placed it in the center of my desk.

I picked up ivory-handled scissors—from an auction in Louisville, Kentucky—and slit the single layer of packing tape that held the top flaps in place. He'd carried it on the plane, then, not entrusting its safety to anyone else. I imagined it must mean something important to him. He'd said it had belonged to his grandmother.

I began sifting Styrofoam peanuts from the box. "Did you eat from this china when visiting your grandmother?" I wasn't sure why I asked, why I wanted to know more about the life of the inanimate object I was unwrapping.

"No," he said, almost apologetically. "We never used it. It was kept in a place of honor in her china cabinet ever since I can remember from when I was a little boy. She'd dust all of the pieces and carefully return them to their spots on the shelves, but we never used it." There was a note of wistfulness in his voice, a hint of loss and longing I wasn't wholly convinced was about his grandmother or her china.

"It's Limoges," said Mr. Mandeville, as if to validate his presence. He was a great businessman, and had a fond appreciation for beautiful and expensive antiques, but what he knew about fine porcelain and china could fit onto the head of a straight pin.

My eyes met Mr. Graf's—James's—and we shared a moment at Mr. Mandeville's expense, distracting me enough that I almost missed the white handle of a teacup emerging from the sea of Styrofoam.

Using my thumb and forefinger, I gingerly lifted it from the box, then sifted through the remaining peanuts and found the saucer. "It's Haviland Limoges. Haviland and Co., to be exact—not to be confused with Charles Field, Theodore, or Johann Haviland Limoges."

I felt Mr. Mandeville beaming at me. "I told you she was good."

James leaned in closer. "You can tell that without looking at the bottom?"

I nodded. "You can tell by the blank." I ran my finger along the scalloped edge of the saucer. "That's another name for the shape of various pieces in the pattern. I can tell by the edges of this saucer that it's probably blank eleven, which is a Haviland and Co. shape. It's evident by the scalloped border with embossed dots along the edge. It's very similar to blank six thirty-eight, but because I have the teacup, which is completely different in both blanks, I know for sure it's number eleven."

The visitor smiled. "I had no idea it would be this easy."

I tried not to sound smug. "That's actually the *only* easy part in identifying Limoges china. David Haviland, who founded Limoges in 1849, never saw the need to put his pattern names on the pieces he manufactured—that's why there isn't one on the bottom of your teacup." I held it up to prove my point. "Which becomes problematic . . ." My words trailed away as I studied the brilliant colors of the pattern, noticing for the first time the bee motif in bright gold and purple, with fine green lines and loops showing the trajectory of the bees in flight as they danced along the scalloped edges of the saucer. It was extraordinary and unique. *So memorable.*

I looked up to find both men watching me, waiting for me to continue. I cleared my throat. "Which becomes problematic when you learn that since the company was founded it has produced almost thirty thousand patterns under five different Haviland companies on several continents."

"Do you know this pattern?" James asked, and I got a brief whiff of his cologne. Something masculine. Sandalwood, I thought.

I shook my head. "I don't think so." I flipped over the teacup, seeing the familiar Haviland & Co. marking. I swiveled my chair and reached for the bookcase behind me and pulled out a thin book with a spiral binding, one of a six-volume set. "But if it's been identified, it will have been given a Schleiger number and will be cataloged in one of these books."

"And if it's not in there?" Mr. Mandeville asked.

"Well, it could have been a privately commissioned pattern, or such a rare one that it never made it into the catalog. Mrs. Schleiger was a Nebraskan trying to fill holes in her mother's set of china and was appalled at the lack of pattern names on most of the Haviland china, and did her best to identify as many as she could—hence the name 'Schleiger number.' But the scope was too great to include every pattern ever created."

I leaned back in my chair. "There are other Haviland identification books we can refer to if we don't find it in the Schleiger volumes, but I've rarely had to dig that deep. The Schleiger books are pretty comprehensive."

"So there's a chance you won't be able to identify it or determine its value?" he asked.

"Not necessarily, but it will take some time. It might not have a pattern name, but there are other ways to determine its origin, and through that a more exact value. For instance, floral patterns were popular in the 1950s, and there were distinctive patterns from the Art Nouveau era that can help us pinpoint the time period the china was first made. Although I must say I can't really identify a time period where insects were the 'in' thing. I'll need to double-check, but I believe the blank was in use in the second half of the eighteen hundreds, so that would be a place to start."

I picked up the cup and ran the tip of my finger over the bees, so lifelike that I could almost imagine their buzzing. "This pattern is so unusual. If it was mass-produced, there will be more out there, unless it wasn't popular and had a limited run. Even harder to find would be if it was made on commission." I looked up at Mr. Mandeville. "Well-known artists like Gauguin, Ribiere, Dufy, and Cocteau actually designed several patterns for David Haviland. If this is one of theirs, it could be very valuable."

"But wasn't Haviland Limoges meant for the American market?" Mr. Mandeville asked, beaming. I'd had to explain that factoid to him many times and was glad to know it had stuck. "And if Mr. Graf's grandmother was from New York, perhaps you could start by looking at the local retailers there who sold Limoges."

"Yes, but the Limoges factories were in France, so it wouldn't be unheard-of for a French customer to commission a set of china. And that might be like looking for a needle in a haystack." I ran my fingers along the end of the teacup again, a reluctant memory stirring.

James turned the catalog around to face him and began thumbing through the pages with a frown on his face. "So to identify the pattern, you have to look through each page to see if you recognize it."

"Pretty much," I said, wanting to explain that I loved the minutiae of my work, the mindlessness of flipping through pages that took enough of my concentration that my mind didn't have to wander down paths it wasn't allowed to go.

"I could help," he offered, his blue eyes sincere.

I shook my head quickly. "I'm sure you have to get back to New York. If you allow me to keep the cup and saucer, I'll fill out the necessary paperwork for insurance purposes. . . ."

He straightened. "Actually, I've taken a leave of absence from my job, so I have as much time as it will take. I wasn't planning on heading back until I have some answers."

"And he's already promised that we will handle the auction of the china and the rest of his grandmother's estate if this search proves fruitful," Mr. Mandeville added, giving me a hard look under lowered eyebrows.

I studied the bees again as they swirled around the pieces of china, their wings stuck in perpetual movement. *So memorable.* I had a flash of memory of my grandfather in his apiary, my hand in his as we walked down the rows of hives, the bees thick as they darted and spun around us, and how I hadn't been afraid. And then I remembered Birdie finding me in her room, rummaging through her closet for something vintage to wear, finding instead something entirely unexpected, something that had made my mother so sad that she had to go away again. Something that had made her put her finger over her lips and make me promise to keep it a secret. It was the only thing my mother and I had ever shared, just the two of us. And so I had.

"I think—" I said, then stopped. I wasn't sure I wanted to mention that I thought the pattern seemed familiar, that I might have seen it in my childhood house. Because, even after all this time and all that had happened in the intervening years, I didn't want to give my mother another reason to be disappointed by me.

"What do you think?" prompted Mr. Mandeville.

"I think," I said again, "that I may have seen this pattern before. Or something very similar." My eyes settled on Mr. Mandeville. "On a soup cup I found in my mother's closet. My grandmother was a bit of a junker—always collecting stray bits of china and knickknacks, which is probably where it came from."

"Good," said my boss. "Then all you have to do is go home and bring it here so we can compare."

I frowned up at him. He'd been urging me to go home to see my family for years now, not understanding how people related by blood could be separated for so long. As if being related meant permanence and acceptance, two words I'd never associated with my family.

"I really don't think that's necessary. I'll call my grandfather, ask him to look for it and ship it here if he finds it. Or maybe he can just take pictures and send them. That might be enough to compare it with this one. It wouldn't be necessary to physically hold it to see if it's the same." I indicated the cup I still held in my hands, almost feeling the thrum of the flying bees through my fingertips.

"If it is the same," asked James, "what might that imply?"

"That the pattern could be mass-produced, which will mean it's not worth as much as a custom one." I ran my fingertips along the edge of the cup, trying to remember that day in my mother's closet, trying to see again the pattern of bees. Trying to remember what it was about it that had sent my mother away again. "Although I'd be pretty surprised if it were mass-produced. I've seen thousands of Limoges patterns before, but never anything like this. It's rather . . . unique."

"I'd prefer to see it in person," Mr. Mandeville said. "That way we won't make any mistakes." He cleared his throat as he turned his attention to James. "We're very particular here at the Big Easy. We like to make sure we're one hundred percent correct when assigning values."

"I'll call my grandfather," I repeated, my higher voice sounding panicky, and I hoped they hadn't noticed.

Mr. Mandeville frowned. "But if the piece doesn't turn up, I want you to go look for yourself. You're very thorough, Georgia. It's what makes you so good at what you do." His frown morphed into a fatherly smile that made him look like an executioner holding an ax.

I felt James's presence beside me, watching me closely, making it impossible for me to tell my boss exactly why I hadn't been back to Apalachicola in ten years.

"I'm sure your family would love a visit from you, too," he added.

Impotent anger pulsed through me, forcing me to close my eyes so I could focus on breathing slowly to calm down, just as Aunt Marlene had shown me when I was a little girl and the world had stopped making sense. *Breathe in; breathe out.* The air whistled in through my nose and out through my mouth, sounding more and more like the drone of hundreds of angry bees as I tried to force the word "no" from my lips.

chapter 2

A bumblebee, if dropped into an open tumbler, will be there until it dies, unless it is taken out. It never sees the means of escape at the top, but persists in trying to find some way out through the sides. It will seek a way where none exists, until it completely destroys itself.

—NED BLOODWORTH'S BEEKEEPER'S JOURNAL

Maisy

APALACHICOLA, FLORIDA

Maisy Sawyers followed her mother to the back porch. She peered into the late-April morning sunshine toward the backyard and the apiary, the air sweet with the scent of sun-warmed honey and filled with the low drone of bees. She stiffened at the sight of a bee flitting above her mother's gold hair. Maisy hated the little flying insects almost as much as her grandfather, mother, and half sister, Georgia, loved them. Maybe it was because they loved them so much.

She spotted her ninety-four-year-old grandfather wearing only a long-sleeved shirt and baggy dungarees on his tall, thin frame, walking down the middle of his ten bee boxes, five on each side. He was getting ready to move eight of his hives into the swamps around the Apalachicola River, where the white Ogeechee tupelo trees were beginning to blossom. There was only a small window of time between late April and early May when the trees bloomed, and if a beekeeper wanted the much-sought-after pure tupelo honey, he had to make sure his hives were in the right place at the right time.

Turning to her mother, she said, "It's still pretty cool outside and there's a nice breeze. I thought we'd sit in the shade of the magnolia for a bit if that's all right." She watched her mother as she considered. By all estimations, Birdie was most likely in her mid-seventies, but looked a decade or two younger, owing in part to good genes and an almost fanatical aversion to letting any sun on her skin.

Birdie tilted her head to the side and began to sing, her voice still as clear and pure as a girl's. It wasn't a song Maisy knew, but that wasn't a surprise. Her mother had studied voice since she was a child, accumulating a repertoire that spanned decades and styles. And it had been the only sound she'd made for nearly ten years.

Maisy followed her mother down the steps from the back porch and then through the yard of sandy soil and sparse grass toward the majestic tree that had held court over this part of the yard since she and Georgia were little girls.

Her thoughts skittered over memories of her half sister, something she rarely allowed them to do, and she wondered whether Georgia remembered the tree and the old swing—gone since Hurricane Dennis—or thought about her home at all. Or the people she'd left behind, frozen in time. In the nearly ten years since Georgia had left, nothing had really changed. More tourists and construction on St. George Island, more fishing regulations and fewer oysters in the bay. But Maisy had remained, along with their grandfather and mother, and her memories of a childhood that were incomplete without including Georgia.

"Mama!"

Maisy turned to where her nine-year-old daughter, Becky, stood on the back porch in her bare feet and pajamas. "The phone keeps ringing."

"Who is it?"

"I don't know—they hang up before I can answer. Caller ID says it's from a number starting with five-oh-four. They didn't leave a message. Do you want me to wait by the phone and see if they call back?"

It took a moment for Maisy to find her voice. "No, Becky. That's all right."

Becky returned to the kitchen, letting the screen door slam shut behind her.

Birdie stopped singing and Maisy knew that she'd heard, too. Had understood what it meant. Maisy's mother was a conscientious objector to her own life, but that didn't mean she was unaware of it swirling around her.

"That's New Orleans," Maisy said unnecessarily. Georgia never called the landline, just in case Maisy happened to answer it. Maisy knew her sister had monthly conversations with their grandfather, and that he initiated the call from the old black Princess phone in his bedroom.

Birdie and Maisy watched as Grandpa began walking toward them from the apiary, his slow movements confirming his age. His mind was as quick and agile as that of a man of half his years, but his body had already begun to betray him with stiffened joints and an irregular heartbeat.

The faint ringing of the telephone began again from inside. Knowing it would continue until she answered it, Maisy left her mother and ran back to the house. She grabbed the kitchen phone, the long cord that was so knotted and kinked now that it reached only about three feet.

"Hello?" Something buzzed by her head and she jerked back as the bee darted past her and up toward the ceiling. *A bee in the house means there will be a visitor.* Her grandfather's bee wisdoms seemed imprinted on her brain no matter how much she wished she could erase them.

There was a brief pause on the other end of the phone. "Hello, Maisy? It's Georgia."

Like she needed to introduce herself. Like Maisy wouldn't know the voice almost as well as she knew her own.

"Hello, Georgia." She had no intention of making this any easier. The bee buzzed past her again, and Maisy turned toward the wall and retrieved the flyswatter she kept on a nail. If that damned insect bothered her again, it would be the last thing it would ever do.

"I need to ask a favor."

I'm fine—thank you for asking. "Is this about that soup cup?"

A pause. "Yes. I guess Grandpa told you then. He didn't remember it, but said he'd look for it. He said he didn't find it."

"Well, then. It must not be here." She held the phone to her ear, listening to her sister breathe.

"I'd like you to look," Georgia said finally. "To make sure."

"It's not here," Maisy said quickly. "I helped him look, and we were very thorough. We even looked in Birdie's closet and didn't find it. I thought he already told you that."

She pictured Georgia's lips tightening over her teeth, clamping her mouth shut. Grandpa used to say it made her look like an oyster unwilling to give up her pearl. It was an expression Georgia always used when pitting herself against what she was hearing and what she wanted to hear. An expression that was usually reserved for interactions with their mother.

"He did," Georgia said slowly. "It's just that this is pretty important, for a potentially very big client. . . ."

"Well, I'm sorry we can't help you." Maisy was thinking about whether she should think of something innocuous to say or just hang up when Georgia spoke again.

"I guess I'll be coming home, then. To see for myself. It's not that I don't believe you—it's just . . ." Georgia paused, and Maisy imagined that closed-oyster look again. "It's just that my boss is insisting on it. It's for what could be one of our biggest clients, and there's a possibility it could be from a very rare and valuable pattern. He wants to hear from me that it's not there."

Panic filled the back of Maisy's throat like bee venom. "But you promised, Georgia. You *promised*." The last word was mostly air.

"I know. But that was ten years ago. Things are different. *I'm* different."

"How do you know that, Georgia? How can you really know that? This is not a good idea."

There was a hint of something in Georgia's voice. Resignation, maybe? Or was it more like anticipation, the hum of bees approaching a summer garden? "I'm sorry, Maisy. I have to come."

Maisy relaxed her jaw, aware she'd been grinding her teeth. "Will you be staying here?"

"No," Georgia said quickly, as if she'd already anticipated the question. "I'll probably stay at Aunt Marlene's. I don't want things to be . . . awkward."

"Lyle and I are separated. He's living at his parents' old place until we figure things out." Maisy wasn't sure why she'd said that, why she wanted to advertise her biggest failure. Maybe it was simply the old habit of needing to share all her heartaches with her sister, as if they were still children and life hadn't happened to them yet.

"I know. Grandpa told me last time I called. I'm sorry."

Maisy closed her eyes for a moment, considering the word and how useless it was, how much it resembled a teaspoon bailing out a sinking boat. "When will you be here and how long will you stay?"

"I should be able to get there by Monday. What I need to do shouldn't take more than a few days." After a moment in which neither of them spoke, Georgia asked, "How's Birdie?"

"The same. And you don't need to pretend you care just because you're coming home."

"I didn't say I cared. I just asked how she was."

Silence. Then, "How's Grandpa?"

"The same. You'll see them both, I expect, when you're here."

"Of course," Georgia added quickly, almost as if to convince herself. A longer pause, and then, "And Becky? How is she? Is she in third grade this year or fourth?"

"We'll see you when you get here," Maisy said as she gently replaced the telephone into the cradle.

"Who was that?"

Maisy turned to find Becky standing in the doorway, her blond hair still tousled from sleep, her bare toes peeking out from too-short pajama bottoms and polished in different shades of orange and purple.

"That was your aunt Georgia. She's coming for a visit."

"The same Aunt Georgia who always sends me birthday and Christmas presents?"

"Yes." Maisy didn't say any more, although it seemed as if Becky was waiting.

"Have I ever met her?" Becky's eyes, so dark they seemed almost black, peered back at her intently.

"Once. When you were a baby."

"Daddy said I'm not supposed to mention her to you."

Maisy stared back at her daughter, wondering whether her expression was as guileless as it seemed. "Did he? Well, your aunt Georgia and I don't get along, is all. We had an argument a long time ago and she left. That's pretty much all there is to it."

"What was the argument about?" Becky leaned against the kitchen counter, as if preparing for a long story.

You. "I don't remember," Maisy said. "Maybe if you had a sister you might understand how one can drive you crazy more than anyone else in the world."

"I *wish* I had a sister," Becky said.

The bee chose that moment to land on the phone's receiver. Without thinking, Maisy brought down the flyswatter. When she lifted it, the bee slid to the floor, completely still.

"Did you kill a bee?" Becky asked with the same sort of drama one might use if a person had unexpectedly died.

"It kept buzzing around me. I was afraid it was going to sting me."

Becky pried the swatter from Maisy's hand, then used it to pick up the dead bee. "A bee in a house means a visitor's coming. But if you kill it, the visitor will bring bad luck."

Maisy watched as Becky carefully carried the small corpse to the back door, then flung it into the grass. She rehung the swatter on the doorjamb before facing her mother. "Do you think that's t-true?"

Becky stuttered only when she was nervous or upset, and Maisy felt worse for causing that than for killing the bee. "Of course not, sweetie."

Becky stared at her for a moment. "I'll g-go get d-dressed."

Maisy listened as the creaks in each step marked Becky's slow path up the stairs.

When Maisy returned to the backyard, bringing her mother's wide-brimmed straw hat, her grandfather had pulled up a worn lawn chair next to Birdie. To any bystander, it would look like they were having a two-way conversation. But as Maisy approached, she could hear her mother humming a show tune as her grandfather talked about the recent heavy rains and how they might affect the upcoming tupelo honey harvest.

"I thought you might want this," Maisy said as she set the hat on Birdie's head, adjusting it just so. Even at her age, Birdie was a vain woman, protecting the beauty she'd been famous for. Her skin, sheltered from the sun by an overprotective mother since she was a child, had few lines, and her dark eyes hadn't faded to a lighter hue. Every morning she painstakingly applied her makeup, purchased on regular trips into Jacksonville she made with Maisy.

Since Birdie no longer communicated in normal ways, Maisy was often asked how she knew what her mother wanted. People didn't understand that she'd had a lifetime of studying her mother, trying to decode her. Trying to understand how a woman with no maternal instincts could have hoped to raise two daughters. Trying to piece together the woman her mother had been before her life had jolted off the rails one final, permanent time ten years before, sending her into a dark place from which she didn't appear to want to return.

The clues were everywhere in picture frames around the house of the beautiful Birdie in various costumes from school plays and regional theater productions that had been her life for most of her youth. They were there in the thick photo albums stuffed with old Polaroids of her mother with her first husband, handsome in his army uniform before he left for Vietnam in 1965, and then of Birdie holding baby Georgia in a christening gown. It had only recently occurred to Maisy that there weren't any photos of her own father, Birdie's second husband, or more than the requisite school photos of herself. It almost seemed as if they were an afterthought, a failed attempt at a second chance.

Maisy sat down on the ground near her mother's chair and leaned against it. She remembered other times here, under this tree, other spring mornings before the Florida sun scorched the earth and burned the skin. When she and Georgia had been as thick as bees in a hive. If only she didn't know how badly it hurt to be stung.

"Georgia's coming home for a visit," she announced without preamble. "Just for a little while. She said she wants to make sure for herself that the soup cup you and I looked for isn't here. She says her boss needs her to make sure." She wanted to add that the real reason was because Georgia didn't trust them to do a thorough job. But then that would mean that Georgia *wanted* to come back to Apalach, and they all understood why that couldn't be true.

"The soup cup?" her grandfather repeated, an odd note in his voice.

She sent him a sharp look, wondering whether he could have already forgotten. "Yeah—remember? Georgia called you the day before yesterday and we looked all over the house for it. You said it was probably just another stray piece of junk Grandma brought home and we got rid of long ago."

He regarded her steadily, but his eyes were empty, sending a cool shudder down her spine. *He's ninety-four,* she reminded herself. *That's why he doesn't remember; that's why his eyes are so blank.* But there was something else, something behind his eyes. Something he didn't want her to see.

Maisy looked away, toward the house that held so many memories that she sometimes imagined she could hear the old nails and joists at night groaning with all the secrets they contained, and thought again of Georgia, and how she was coming home to the place she'd promised she'd never return to.

chapter 3

"Even bees, the little almsmen of spring bowers, know there is richest juice in poison-flowers."
John Keats

—NED BLOODWORTH'S BEEKEEPER'S JOURNAL

Georgia

The wooden floorboards complained like the bones of an old woman as I walked from the small kitchen in the back of my shotgun cottage straight through to the front room, where my dining table sat littered with china catalogs and reference volumes. I sat down in the rustic farmhouse kitchen chair I'd found at a garage sale somewhere between Mobile and Pensacola and placed my steaming cup of coffee on the coaster beside my notebook. A classic jazz standard drifted from my circa-1980s clock radio, the dial permanently stuck on WWOZ FM 90.7. If I ever decided to listen to different music, I'd have to buy a new radio.

After rolling my shoulders, I returned to volume two of the Schleiger books, my eyes already feeling the strain from looking through the first one. It was harder because I didn't have the cup and saucer to reference, and I had to go on memory. Not that I really needed to stare at them to remember. The pattern seemed to be imprinted on the inside of my eyelids, like the light from a camera flash.

I wasn't procrastinating about leaving. Not really. I felt sure that Maisy was desperately looking through the house one more time, as eager as I was to find it and probably for much the same reason, and would find the piece of china so that I wouldn't have to go down to Apalachicola.

The 1880s wooden school clock chimed eight times on the wall behind me just as a firm knock sounded on the front door. I sat back in my chair, deliberating on whether I should answer, when the knock came again, followed by a male voice. "Miss Chambers? Georgia? It's James Graf. I'd like to talk with you."

I looked down at my clothes, mortified to realize I was still wearing my pajamas, albeit vintage silk men's pajamas from the twenties. I'd half risen from my chair, ready to dash to my bedroom, when he called through the door again. "Just five minutes of your time—I promise."

With a sigh of resignation, I went to the door and unbolted the six locks that laced it like a corset. James was dressed in khaki pants and a long-sleeved shirt rolled up at the sleeves, and he carried a bag that looked suspiciously like the ones from the Maple Street Patisserie that I usually brought to work.

He held it toward me like a peace offering. "Mr. Mandeville said you were particularly fond of the chocolate croissants, so I stopped by on my way over."

My stomach rumbled as I smelled the pastries inside the bag, and tried to remember the last time I'd eaten. It was always this way when I was lost in the hunt for a singular piece of a collection, an unbroken lid, a missing key.

"Thank you," I said, hesitating only briefly before I took the bag. "I thought you'd be back in New York by now."

James smiled, and I liked the way the sides of his eyes crinkled easily, as if that meant he smiled a lot. "I need to ask a favor."

I stepped back into the room to allow him to enter. "I don't have a lot of time. I was hoping to get through one more Schleiger book before I head out of town."

I motioned for him to sit at one of the mismatched chairs around the table, then excused myself to get coffee and plates. When I returned, I found him examining the small collection of antique locks under glass in a vitrine in a corner of the room. The collection was added to only when I matched a key to a lock, leaving a lot of empty space on the royal blue velvet cushion I'd placed inside.

"Nice collection," he said, looking up. "Who would have thought that something as utilitarian as a lock could also be so decorative?"

"That's why I collect them," I said, setting down a steaming cup of chicory coffee on the table, then placing two mismatched plates of Meissen china next to them. "I've always thought that creating and appreciating beautiful objects is what sets us at the top of the animal kingdom."

He sat down, his blue eyes quietly appraising. He slid the chair out to accommodate his long legs before picking up the bag and opening it, then offering it to me. He selected a croissant for himself, then sat back in his chair, his head tilted. "Miles Davis?" he asked.

I smiled. "Either it's a big favor and you've done your research, or you know your jazz."

He shrugged. "I'm a recent convert. I find it very soothing."

His noncommittal answer lifted my antennae. "Life pretty rough right now?" I asked. I was prying, but I couldn't stop myself. There was something unsettled about him, something *missing*. It took all of my willpower not to reach over and shake him to see what came loose.

"You could say that," he said carefully. "I live and work in the city. There's a reason they call it the city that never sleeps. It's just a bit . . . much for me right now." An unconvincing smile crept across his face.

I took a sip of my coffee, trying to tell myself that it was time to back off. But knowing when to quit had never been one of my virtues. "What do you do for a living?"

"Real estate development. It's my father's firm. My sisters work for him, too, in various capacities."

"Sisters?"

His smile was more genuine this time. "I've got four. I'm the youngest."

"I'm sorry," I said, before I could stop myself. Before he could question me, I quickly changed the subject, skirting around the subject of the favor he needed to ask. Whatever it was he needed, I was pretty sure I didn't have enough left in reserve to give. "Have you inventoried your grandmother's china? It's important to know if it's complete."

"What do you mean by complete?"

I sighed, reminding myself that he was a male and wouldn't necessarily know what a place setting was. "Do you know how many dinner plates, bread-and-butters, soup cups?"

"Oh, you mean place settings? My oldest sister thought I might need to know this, so we counted everything together. There are twelve mostly complete six-piece place settings, with just a few pieces missing here and there."

"Any serving pieces?"

He looked at me as if I'd stopped speaking English.

"Ask your sister and let me know." I pinched a bite of my croissant, suddenly seeing a younger version of my mother's face as she pressed her fingers to her lips.

"That's good, right?"

It took me a few moments to realize that he'd asked me a question. "Yes, of course. The more complete a set, the more valuable. Unless somebody is trying to match pieces to an existing set, most clients are looking for something already complete."

He took a bite out of his croissant, then wiped his hands on a napkin. His assessing gaze returned to me. "I'd like to come with you. Down to Apalachicola."

I stared at him for a long moment, wondering whether he might be joking. But his eyes were earnest, pleading almost. I looked down, shaking my head. "Absolutely not. That is an incredibly bad idea, for lots of reasons, the main one being that I don't need your help."

"You said yesterday that maybe you've seen the pattern before, in your grandfather's house. Was it just the one piece or were there more?"

I wondered for a moment whether he hadn't heard me, or if he had a lot of experience arguing with his four sisters and was deliberately ignoring my protest. Annoyed, I said, "I only saw the one piece, and I only saw it that once. My grandmother probably found it in a shop some- where and purchased the single piece because of the pattern since my grandfather is a beekeeper. She might have thought that he would appre- ciate the bee motif. And both my grandfather and sister have already looked for it and not turned up anything. Obviously it's going to be a wasted trip for me, and there's absolutely no reason why you should—"

"But somebody in your family might know where the piece came from. And there could be more," he pressed.

I took a quick swallow of my coffee, scalding my tongue. "There could be, but I'm sure I would have seen other pieces if they existed. I lived with my mother and grandparents in their home for most of my life."

"And the piece you found was a plate?"

It was my turn to scrutinize him, to study him as I might a scarred and dusty console, its secrets buried under a century of dust and neglect. There was more to James Graf than a bored businessman searching for the provenance of his grandmother's china, something hidden beneath the patina of thick, wavy hair and dark blue eyes.

I took my time tearing off another bite of my croissant, then slowly chewing. "No. It was an individual soup cup." The memory of it made me temporarily forget why he'd come, and what he was asking of me. I spoke slowly, remembering. "A bee had been painted beneath each finger hole, and I recall thinking that they looked so real that they would sting if you put your finger too close." I met his eyes. "I wish I'd thought to turn it over at the time to read the marking. Sometimes an importer would add his own stamp to the bottom of china pieces, which can make it even more attractive to a collector. It would also tell me if it was part of your grandmother's set or not. Going on my memory of the pattern, I'd say yes, but it's not definite." I straightened. "Not that it matters. The soup cup is gone or my sister and grandfather would have found it. I'm only going as a courtesy to Mr. Mandeville."

He took a sip from his coffee, a frown on his face as he stared into the cup.

"It's chicory," I said in apology. "It's all I drink, but I probably should have asked. People who aren't used to it say it's like drinking dishwater."

James smiled, and I saw again the creases on the side of his face that seemed so out of place with the serious man I'd first met. "It's fine, really. An acquired taste, probably."

He set down his cup and sat forward, his fingers tapping restlessly on the table. He was looking around the small room, at the collections of random items that had found a home with me. Even the lamps on either side of the Victorian couch were made from mismatched candlesticks. Ever since I was small, I'd been attracted to unwanted objects, ordinary items that held some purpose or beauty if one cared to look close enough.

With a serious look, he said, "I know my request to come with you to Apalachicola is an odd one. And I really don't want to bribe you with my business to get you to agree. As I've already mentioned to Mr. Mandeville, my grandmother's estate could be very lucrative for you both."

That smile again, and I wondered whether he knew how devastating it was, and how it had begun to make his case long before he'd spoken.

He continued. "I want you to know how . . . important this is to me. How much I need to immerse myself in this search."

"You were close to your grandmother?" I softened toward him, thinking of my own grandfather, imagining I could feel the warmth of my hand in his, smell the scent of sweet honey that seemed to saturate his skin. I thought of how much I missed him, and how our separation had hurt us both.

"I was. She'd been suffering with dementia and in a home for the last eight years, so her death was not unexpected. But that's not why I'm doing this." He tightened his hands into fists and then spread them wide on his knees. "I already mentioned that I've taken a leave of absence from my job. I'm in desperate need of a . . . distraction."

My spine stiffened. "My job isn't a 'distraction,' Mr. Graf. It's a serious business that takes all of my concentration, which is why I do it alone. Your presence would be a distraction for me. I haven't been home in a long time, and there's a reason for it. If I have to go, I'd rather go alone."

He regarded me closely. "Do you have a lot of skeletons in your closet, Georgia?" He wasn't obvious about it, but I'm sure he'd noticed the shadows under my eyes, and was wondering how somebody so ordinary could have any spectral skeletons.

More than I can count. "My answer is no, okay? I'll leave some catalogs with you so you can go through them and see if you can find the pattern, if that would make you feel better, and you can be part of the search. We'll meet when I get back, and compare notes."

I stood and began clearing the table, and noticed how he stood, too, out of courtesy. I imagined his mother or grandmother or sisters having taught him that, or another female in his life. Maybe he was married, then. He didn't wear a ring, but not every married man did anymore. As proof, I had a collection of discarded wedding bands in a shadow box in my bathroom, displayed like trophies.

He picked up the coffee mugs and followed me into the kitchen, placing them carefully in the sink. He looked out the tall window and into the yellow clapboard side of my neighbor's house, his hands gripping the edge of the sink. "I suppose I could make good on my threat to take my business elsewhere, but I really don't want to."

"As much as I'm sure we'd regret it, I'm equally certain that we'd survive."

James turned around and faced me, his eyes unreadable. "I'm just not sure that I will. I was looking for an excuse to get away from my life for a while when my sister suggested I find out more about my grandmother's china. I've recently suffered a personal loss, and it was either this or check myself into a mental hospital. I chose the china."

I looked at his perfect face and form, his intelligent eyes and capable hands, and felt the old bitterness arise in me. "What happened? Did your girlfriend leave you?"

Something flickered in his eyes, but he didn't look away. "No, actually. My wife died."

He said it so matter-of-factly, with no emotion, but I felt his words like a fist to my stomach. "I'm sorry," I said quietly, identifying now the regret I'd seen in his eyes when we'd first met.

"Do you understand, then?"

I nodded slowly, wishing that I didn't know the need to hide myself in ordinary objects that had managed to get lost along the way. "Yes," I said. "But . . ." I thought of my grandfather and Birdie. And Maisy. All the unfinished business I had left behind. How I wasn't ready to face it again, especially not with an audience.

"You won't even know I'm there," he pressed. "Unless you need my help looking at catalogs or moving large boxes in the attic." He gave me a small smile that did nothing to erase the pain in his eyes. "And I won't make you tell me anything that you don't want to share."

I almost laughed. "That's not what I'm worried about. It's a small town. People will make it their business to tell you everything you want to know, and a good part of what you don't."

A genuine brightness lit his eyes. "I'm from New York. I'm very good at rebuffing people."

I sighed, knowing I'd lost more than just this argument. "Fine. I'll let Mr. Mandeville know. I was planning on leaving tomorrow and will stay with my aunt. There are a few hotels and B and Bs in town and I'm sure you can find them online. I'm thinking two days, tops."

"That's better than nothing," he said.

"And I'm still hoping to get a phone call from my sister to let me know she's found it and we don't have to go. She's as eager to keep me here as I am to stay." He didn't ask me to explain, and I was glad to know he'd been serious about not making me tell him anything I didn't want to share. I led him to the door. "Thanks again for the croissants."

"You're welcome. Thanks for letting me come along."

I pushed away the swelling of regret I felt rising like bile. "Nine o'clock sharp. Be on time, because I won't wait."

We said good-bye and I closed the door before I could change my mind. I shut my eyes for a moment, remembering my mother's face as she pressed her finger to her lips, took the small cup from my hands, and told me to keep a secret. I imagined now the buzzing of the bees painted into the china, held down by my years of silence. And how I was getting ready to finally set them free.

chapter 4

He who would gather honey must bear the sting of the bees.

—NED BLOODWORTH'S BEEKEEPER'S JOURNAL

Georgia

I was carrying the box of china catalogs out to my car when a taxi pulled up behind me at the curb, a good twenty minutes early. It meant James had taken seriously my threat to leave without him, or he was naturally punctual. Since he'd grown up with four sisters, I could only imagine the sort of friction that must have caused.

"Let me help you with that," he said, rushing toward me as the taxi pulled away.

"I've got it," I said, lowering the box into the trunk, sounding peevish. I was disappointed that he'd really shown up, and angry with myself for allowing it. But even after tossing and turning all night, I hadn't come up with anything else to stop what only promised to be a massive train wreck. I'd tried to explain it to Mr. Mandeville when I'd spoken with him the previous day, but I couldn't without going into specifics. And that was something I was not yet prepared to do. It was like standing on the beach staring at an oncoming wave, knowing sooner or later I was going to get wet.

"Wow. Is this your car?" James stood back to get a better look at my white 1970 Cadillac Coupe de Ville convertible, his expression like that of a ten-year-old boy who'd just been given a new bike.

"It was my grandmother's. My grandfather gave it to me when I got my driver's license at sixteen."

He nodded appreciatively, taking in the bright chrome bumpers and the angular fins on the back. "I was going to offer to pay for gas, but now I'm thinking that I can't afford it."

I surprised us both by laughing. I didn't want to enjoy his company. But my learning about his wife had formed a tentative bridge between us, a loose connection of loss and memories. It wasn't that we wore badges on our sleeves announcing our emotionally crippled status. It was more a wariness shown in the eyes that only the fellow wounded could recognize.

I sobered quickly. "I like a big car so that if I pass any garage sales along the way and find a stray piece of furniture, I can bring it back with me. And I always stop." I sent him a pointed look, a last-ditch effort to make him change his mind.

"Sounds like fun," he said, returning to the curb and picking up a leather duffel bag. "I travel light, so there will be plenty of room for any garage-sale finds." He tucked the bag next to my own small suitcase in the voluminous trunk, as if to emphasize the fact that even if I found a giant chifforobe, it would still fit.

"Did you bring the teacup and saucer?"

He nodded. "Packed securely in my bag." He studied me again with those blue eyes that seemed to miss nothing. "I like your outfit." I figured a man with four sisters would probably be used to noticing such things and wouldn't think twice about saying it to somebody he barely knew. But still I felt pleased.

I flattened my hands against the bright floral fabric of the A-line dress. "Thank you. It's vintage. Circa 1960." I was about to tell him about the great vintage clothing store I frequented on Royal Street but stopped myself in time. I wasn't comfortable with relationships with the current and living, and didn't want to invite any interest.

With no further distractions or reasons to delay, I returned to the house to lock up. As I slid behind the steering wheel and stuck the key in the ignition, I said, "Just don't expect to drive her. Nobody but me is allowed."

"Good. Because I don't know how."

I slammed my foot on the brake, making both of our heads snap back. "What?"

"I mean, I know how—I took lessons so I could get a driver's license—but I've never owned a car. I've never needed one—way too complicated to park them and to navigate the city, especially when there are so many other options."

"But what if you want to get out of the city, drive to the country or the beach for the weekend? Do you rely on your friends?" I was remembering my own childhood in Apalachicola, where the most popular kids were those with a driver's license and a big enough car. My nose and cheeks stung with remembered sunburns from visits to St. George Island, my trunk full of coolers and all of us pooling our loose change for gas.

He cleared his throat. "We, uh, had a driver for those kinds of trips. My mother said she felt better knowing we weren't behind the wheel, so it worked out for us."

I looked at his neatly pressed knit shirt and Rolex—definitely not vintage—and couldn't picture him shirtless and sitting in the sand with a beer bottle raised to his lips and singing along to an AC/DC song blaring from the open doors of a pickup truck. And that was a good thing. The more uncomfortable he felt in Apalachicola, the sooner he'd be ready to leave.

I put the car into drive and pulled away from the curb. "So if I have a flat, I'm on my own."

He held up his phone. "That's what this is for. Help is only a call away."

I resisted an exaggerated roll of my eyes. "Assuming your battery hasn't died and there's cell coverage in the middle of Alabama, which is never a guarantee. Which is why I know how to change my own tires. And have on multiple occasions."

"I'm impressed. You're pretty petite. I wouldn't think you'd be strong enough."

I met his gaze. "People aren't always what they appear to be."

He faced forward again, staring at the pocked asphalt on St. Charles Avenue as we merged into traffic heading toward Carrollton. "I know," he said. "I just need reminding every now and again."

I wanted to ask him what he meant, but was glad of my increased speed and the sound of the wind rushing into the convertible that prohibited conversation. The car still had its original radio, so our choice of music was limited to whatever we could pick up on AM or FM. We sped east on I-10 toward Florida, barreling down the asphalt, each of us lost in our own thoughts.

He spent a lot of time tapping into his phone, his fingers quick and agile. I wasn't a Luddite, and could even admit to myself that some technology—like computers and the Internet—were actually good for business. But that didn't make me want to have a cell phone. A cell phone meant that I could always be reached by the people I'd left behind. I had a landline in my house that I used to call my aunt and grandfather, but I didn't have an answering machine or caller ID. It made my life simple, and I liked it that way.

After a brief stop for lunch near Mobile, where we ate at a Chick-fil-A because he'd never been to one, and during which we stayed on safe topics of conversation, like the weather, we continued across the panhandle, exiting the interstate to Highway 98 heading south along the white sandy beaches of the gulf. We detoured onto Highway 30, which ran parallel to 98, hoping to run into a roadside sale, but I was disappointed. Mostly because I'd been eager to see whether James's enthusiasm about garage sales had been genuine.

I'd grown up on the coast and had taken for granted the beauty of the blue-green water and tall pine forests, the salty breezes and thick, humid air that never seemed too hot to me. Even in New Orleans, too far inland to smell the tangy air of the gulf, the steaming days of August only made me homesick. Homesick for what had been, not what was there now.

"That looks like snow," James said, reminding me of his presence. We were crossing a bridge near Panama City, allowing us a glimpse of the tall dunes that cupped the iridescent water of the gulf like protective hands.

"It's sand," I said impatiently. The closer we got, the tenser and more agitated I became. Angrier at myself. I didn't want anybody with me to witness the humiliating return home, and snapping at James was the easiest recourse for my personal misery.

"I'm sorry," I said. He wore sunglasses, but I imagined his eyes full of understanding, which only made me feel worse. His wife had died recently, yet I was the one holding on two-fisted to my own losses that were mostly self-induced and almost a decade old. Such self-involvement reminded me of Birdie, adding to my shame.

He rested his head against the back of the seat as if to go to sleep.

"You shouldn't have come," I said quietly, the words torn from my mouth by the wind rushing through the car. *I shouldn't have come,* I thought. I was acting as if ten years could be stomped beneath my feet like flotsam, as if promises meant nothing and memories were short. I found myself torn between wishing this visit were already over and holding on to the hope that ten years really was long enough.

The two-lane road stretched out in front of us between tall stands of pines, the small beach towns of the Forgotten Coast—Mexico Beach, St. Joe Beach, Port St. Joe—like knots in the ribbon of asphalt. The scents of seaweed and raw fish crept into the car as we approached the Apalachicola River on 98, the smell alerting me that I was home long before we reached any recognizable landmarks.

The original city plan of wide streets and squares had been modeled after Philadelphia, although that was where the resemblance ended. I'd always been proud of that fact: that our little city had managed to keep its unique Southernness despite its origins or the devastation of fires, hurricanes, and war.

"Are we here?" James asked, his voice audible now because of my slow speed.

I understood his confusion. We hadn't yet passed the single

streetlight in town. The only clue that we were nearing civilization was the appearance of a Burger King and a Piggly Wiggly, as well as a corner lot filled with garden statuary for sale that was as familiar to me as the back of my hand.

"We're here," I said, feeling an odd sense of pride mixed with trepidation. I took a left on Eighth Street and pulled up onto the grass alongside Chestnut Cemetery to put the car in park. After a moment's hesitation, I turned off the ignition and pulled out the key, not sure how long this might take.

"Why are we stopping?"

I stared through the iron fence of the old cemetery, seeing the funerary art that had managed to become a tourist attraction for those visiting Apalachicola or passing through on their way to St. George Island. I'd always known it as the place where most of my ancestors had been buried for the last two hundred years. In more recent years, a little girl named Lilyanna Joy had been laid to rest beneath one of the towering oaks that huddled over the tombstones with bent limbs. There were no more interments in the ancient cemetery, hadn't been in a long time, but an exception had been made because there was just enough room in our family plot for such a small coffin.

"I needed to catch my breath. I'd feel better if I had a game plan."

He slid off his sunglasses and I could read the amusement in his eyes. "A game plan for seeing your family? Are they that difficult?"

I loosened my death grip on the steering wheel, focusing on getting the blood flow back into my hands. "Not so much difficult as . . . damaged."

He nodded as if he understood, but he couldn't. Not really. "Has it been a long time since you've been here?"

I leaned back in my seat, focusing on pressing my shoulders against the leather. "Almost ten years."

He was silent for a moment, as if trying to remember what he'd promised about not asking questions. "Is there anything I should know before we go any farther, so that I don't say the wrong thing?"

"I don't think we have enough time for that," I said quietly before glancing at my 1953 Bulova watch and subtracting fifteen minutes to arrive at the actual time. It was another one of the stupid games I played with myself, this one meant to keep me punctual. "It's four o'clock, which means you can check into your hotel room. Why don't I drop you off there now? That will give me time to head over to my grandfather's house and break the ice, and at least let me warn them that you're here and that they need to be on their best behavior."

He raised his eyebrows.

"I don't think they'll throw anything or shoot anybody, but I promise that it will be awkward. My sister and I don't get along. And our mother—Birdie—is . . ." I searched for the politically correct word for crazy, quickly discounting all the words my aunt Marlene had used to describe her sister-in-law. "Not in her right mind," I said, deciding on something ambiguous enough that he could draw his own conclusions. "She doesn't speak anymore, although we're pretty sure she hears and understands everything that goes on around her. She just chooses not to involve herself. Oh, but she does sing."

James was silent for a moment. "Or I could go with you, to deflect some of the awkwardness. And I'm a big guy. I could even deflect a blow or a bullet if necessary."

He said it lightly, but I didn't think he was joking.

"Why would you do that for me?"

"Because it's my china that's brought you down here."

"True," I said ungraciously. I sighed, ready to admit the truth that had been niggling my mind ever since we'd left New Orleans. "But I needed to come back eventually. You just sped up the inevitable."

"So let me come with you. I can check in later."

I frowned. "Why are you being so nice to me?"

He was serious again. "Because I come from a large family that I only really learned to appreciate when I had to face the worst thing I've ever had to face in my entire life." He smiled softly. "Isn't home supposed to be the one place where they have to let you back?"

Despite myself, I felt part of my mouth turn up. "I've heard that. I guess I'm about to find out if it's true."

I pressed my foot on the brake and stuck the key back into the ignition. "Just promise me one more thing."

He faced me with an expectant expression.

"Promise me that you won't listen to anything my sister, Maisy, says about me."

"Are they all lies?"

I turned the key in the ignition. "Sadly, no. Most of the things she says are true."

chapter 5

*The male drone's sole purpose in life is to mate with the queen. The
successful male will die during the midair act, and the unsuccessful
drone will be kicked out of the hive to starve to death.*

—NED BLOODWORTH'S BEEKEEPER'S JOURNAL

Maisy

Maisy looked up from where she sat in the study of the old house,
grading papers. The sight of Georgia's Cadillac convertible
didn't surprise her. She'd seen it often enough during her girlhood at
its place at the end of the driveway that it was what she dreamed of
when she imagined her sister finally coming home.

She held her breath, listening. The sound of the bay through the
window screens facing the back of the house seemed to intensify, as if
it had been holding its breath, too, and was finally allowing an exhale.
Maisy had even imagined during those long years of absence that the
house had contained an air of expectation, each room she entered feeling as if someone had just exited.

She stood, then methodically slid her chair under the desk, as if
by slowing her movements she could postpone the inevitable.

She found her grandfather and Birdie in the living room watching
one of the twenty-four-hour cable news stations, a woman with bright

blond hair and impossibly white teeth saying something about gas prices and spring break. Birdie's eyes were focused on the heavy Victorian wood paneling on the wall behind the television. Maisy often wondered what her mother saw inside her head, and if it really was so much better than the reality of the life that swirled around her. Despite visits to numerous doctors, and a drawer full of prescription bottles, nothing had ever helped. Her mother had simply decided to check out, a constant condemnation of the family that had failed to interest her enough.

"Georgia's here," Maisy said, letting them know so they could take over the homecoming and allow her to escape upstairs.

Her grandfather's hands clutched the arms of his chair as a deepseated smile settled over his face. "That's good news." He turned to Birdie. "Georgia's home. Isn't that good news?"

Her mother continued to stare at the wall while Grandpa switched off the TV and stood, the process taking longer than even a few short months ago.

"I'll be upstairs, checking on Becky's homework," Maisy said, already backing out of the room. She'd made it to the bottom of the carved wooden balustrade—with two bite marks still on the edge of it from a lost bet she'd once made with Georgia—when she heard a male voice from the other side of the front door. Curious, she paused, and by the time she'd made up her mind to run up the stairs, she'd already seen the watery image of her sister through the stained-glass sidelights and knew she'd been spotted. She waited to see whether Georgia would turn the handle, as if she thought of the monolithic Victorian house as still her home.

Instead, there was a light tap on the door. Maisy glanced toward the living room, where she heard her grandfather trying to cajole Birdie into leaving her chair. With a sigh of resignation, Maisy moved to the door and pulled it open.

The first thing she noticed was that Georgia hadn't changed at all. Still breathtakingly beautiful. Still small and delicate-looking, her blond hair straight and shiny, her dark brown eyes not lined by makeup that she didn't need anyway. She wore a ridiculous floral-print dress that dwarfed her, made her look insufficient and vulnerable, two things she knew her sister wasn't. Maisy wondered whether that had been the intended effect.

"Hello, Georgia." Maisy's gaze moved behind her sister, looking at the tall man with the piercing blue eyes for the first time. She stared at him a moment longer than necessary, trying to place him. He wasn't the type of man Georgia had always been attracted to. This man was attractive, but not in the broad-shouldered, long-haired, overtly sexy way that had always annoyed their mother and turned Georgia's head. And she was pretty sure Georgia hadn't slept with him. Not yet, anyway. It was in her sister's eyes, a look that was devoid of shame and self-recrimination.

"Hi, Maisy." There was an odd note of expectation and anticipation in Georgia's voice. After an uncomfortable pause, she said, "This is James Graf." Georgia stepped aside to allow Maisy a better view of the stranger. "He's the client I mentioned on the phone."

Maisy wondered at Georgia's story, even imagining her to have made it all up just so she'd have an excuse to bring in a buffer; somebody to deflect the blows. She just as quickly dismissed the thought. Georgia was impervious to hurts of all kinds—both those she inflicted on others and those intended for her. She'd always known how to shed arrows the way ducks shed water, walking away unscathed and unconcerned with the carnage left behind.

Maisy nodded at the man and was about to step back to allow them entry when James held out a big hand to shake hers. "It's a pleasure meeting you. Georgia has said a lot of good things about you."

Maisy caught a sharp glance Georgia directed at her companion, but he didn't seem to notice. He stepped back to look at the Queen Anne Victorian house, with its wedding-cake-white trim, hipped roof, and asymmetrical round turret on its left side, taking in the bay, side yard, and apiary. She and Georgia had always called it a castle, the wide expanse of water behind the house their personal domain. It sat on the bay side of Bay Avenue, a wide vista of water visible from every window at the back of the house, the front with its circular drive of crushed oyster shells welcoming visitors.

"This reminds me a lot of my grandmother's home on Long Island. A real architectural masterpiece." He smiled broadly at her.

"Thank you," Maisy said slowly, warming slightly. "So, you're from New York?"

"Yes. Born and raised. You have a very beautiful town here."

She glanced at her sister, waiting for Georgia to fill her in on the full story and reason for the visit. As expected, Georgia was looking past her.

"Georgia." Grandpa came up behind Maisy, Birdie clinging to his arm, her long red nails digging into his sun-darkened skin. He opened up his free arm. "Welcome home."

Maisy pretended not to see the moisture in her grandfather's eyes as he hugged Georgia, or the way Birdie stared at her oldest daughter like a princess at a tiara. She was about to excuse herself and head upstairs when Becky burst out of her bedroom and ran down the stairs.

She skidded to a stop. "Aunt Georgia?"

Georgia looked at the young girl and it was almost as if the two were staring at their own reflections: both small and delicate-looking except for their determined jaws and a way of looking at a person that made you know they were paying attention.

Their grandfather released his hold on Georgia. "Sweetheart, this is your niece, Becky. You haven't seen her since she was just a little thing."

Georgia stepped toward the girl. "Becky?"

Becky answered by throwing herself into Georgia's arms. "I'm so glad to meet you! Mama said it would be a snowy day in hell before you ever showed your face in Apalach again."

James coughed into his hand as their grandfather frowned and said, "Watch your language, young lady."

Georgia's hands fluttered like uncertain butterflies before enveloping Becky in a hug. "It's good to see you," she said, her voice thick. "It's been a very long time."

Becky looked into her aunt's face, their eyes almost level. "We're practically the same size."

"Yeah. I noticed that." Georgia's voice broke and she swallowed hard.

Maisy took hold of Becky's arm and pulled her away from her aunt, trying to tell herself it was Becky's use of a banned word that was getting her sent back to her room. "That's enough, young lady. Go upstairs and finish your homework. I'll call you when it's time for dinner."

Becky resisted. "Is Aunt Georgia staying for dinner?"

"No—" Maisy began.

"Yes, I think I will," Georgia interrupted before turning hesitantly toward James. "If there's enough for two more."

"Of course there is," her grandfather said, reaching out his hand toward James to shake. "I'm Ned Bloodworth."

"Nice to meet you, sir. James Graf. I'm a client of Georgia's, and I'm afraid I've intruded on your family reunion."

"You're not intruding," Georgia and Maisy announced together, equally grateful for his presence.

Maisy glared at her sister before facing the visitor. "You're not intruding, Mr. Graf. We're having lasagna, so there's more than enough for all of us. We'd love to have you stay." She'd included Georgia in the "we," knowing they both welcomed the buffer of a stranger at the dining table.

Birdie stepped forward, and for a moment Maisy thought her mother was trying to get a better look at the newcomer. But then Birdie flipped her hair over her shoulders and smoothed her yellow sundress as if to accentuate how small her waist and how rounded her bosom still were. Something like annoyance flickered in Georgia's eyes. It was the one thing they'd always had in common, a shared disdain over their mother's behavior in front of a good-looking man.

"Hello, Birdie," Georgia said, not moving closer to hug her or offer a kiss on the cheek, and Birdie didn't seem to expect it. "It's good to see you."

Birdie's gaze slid over to her daughter, lingering on the high cheekbones and strong brow that were so much like her own. So much like Becky's. But like a child quickly having lost interest in a new toy, she returned her gaze to James, who was making heroic attempts not to notice her scrutiny.

"James Graf, this is my mother, Susannah Bloodworth Chambers Harrow. But everybody calls her Birdie."

Georgia must have already told him about their mother, because he didn't offer his hand. "It's a pleasure to meet you, Birdie. You have a beautiful home."

Her eyes drifted past him, to a spot behind his shoulder. Without a word she left the room, sending one last glance over her shoulder toward him. A hummed melody drifted back, and it took Maisy a moment to determine it was "Try to Remember" from *The Fantasticks*. It was a favorite of Birdie's, and Maisy had once looked it up and found that *The Fantasticks* was the longest-running musical in the world. But it hadn't explained why her mother was the way she was. She'd never bothered to look anything up again.

"What do you know about bees, James?" Grandpa asked. His face was serious as he said this. Beekeeping wasn't a commercial enterprise for him, but it was more than a hobby, too. He always made sure people knew this from the beginning. Maisy had learned as a child that her grandfather's bees were his way of figuring out life and all of its complexities. *There are no problems in life that can't be solved by studying the ways of bees.* He'd said it so often that for a while she actually believed it. Until life became too unruly to be explained by buzzing insects whose behavior always seemed single-minded at best.

James's smile was genuine. "Not very much, sir. But I'm always willing to learn."

Georgia sent him a worried glance, but James just grinned.

Grandpa put an arm around the younger man's shoulders. "Maybe there's a beekeeper in you. The world needs more of us, because bees are dying out. Did you know that Einstein said that if bees disappeared off the face of the Earth, man would only have four years left to live?"

"No, sir. I hadn't heard that." With a backward glance at Georgia, James allowed the old man to lead him toward the backyard, leaving Maisy and Georgia alone, the air swirling between them with unspoken words.

"She's beautiful," Georgia said softly.

Maisy straightened, trying to rein in the anger that always seemed so near the surface. "Becky is a bright girl who is great at math and a starter on the girls' basketball team. We don't focus so much on physical appearance. You of all people should know why."

Georgia swallowed back something she wanted to say, as if she'd been practicing this reunion and knew what she needed to do to make it go right. As if a person could practice something as messy and haphazard as the wind.

"Let me help with dinner. Can I fix a salad?"

"I don't need your help, Georgia. It's been a long time since I did, and I don't expect to need you anytime soon." Maisy turned toward the kitchen, wanting to put as much space between her and her sister as possible.

"I'll set the table," Georgia said. It had always been the chore they'd taken turns with, along with the cooking. They'd gradually taken over all household chores for their grandfather, who'd taken care of them since their grandmother's death, when she and Georgia were in their tween years. It had never occurred to any of them to expect Birdie to help, because their grandmother had always done everything for her daughter, had doted on Birdie to the point of making Birdie seem helpless. Their grandmother's death hadn't changed that at all.

Maisy and Georgia had gamely gone along with the illusion of Birdie as a delicate butterfly until they'd reached the age, as all girls do, when reason and reality crept up like a flood tide, leaving behind drowned dreams and possibilities in its wake. Maisy had forged ahead with acceptance, but Georgia couldn't, finding instead an odd bitterness. If Maisy had to name a precise moment when the two of them had begun to drift apart, she would have easily said it was when they both opened their eyes wide enough to see their mother as she really was.

A crash from the dining room sent Maisy scurrying out of the kitchen to find Georgia squatting over a pile of shattered white china.

"Sorry," she said, straightening. "This was on the bottom of a stack and I thought I could pull it out without breaking anything. Don't worry—it's not valuable. It's an inexpensive Japanese brand, which doesn't have a high collector's value. But I'll replace it anyway."

"Why would you be pulling china from the back of the cabinet?" Maisy stepped closer, her eyes widening in recognition at the broken pieces. "That's from my wedding china."

Georgia looked chagrined, an expression Maisy had rarely—if ever—seen on her sister's face. "Sorry. I was looking for something. I could only see the edge of the platter and I needed to see the rest of it."

Maisy retreated quickly to the kitchen to retrieve a broom and began sweeping up the remnants of the large serving platter, stabbing at the small pieces. "I told you—we've already looked for that stupid cup. It's not in there."

Georgia grabbed the handle of the broom, and after a brief tug-of-war, Maisy let it go. "I know. But I thought I recognized the pattern but on a different piece. I was mistaken." She pushed the broken china into a small pile, every movement precise and measured. You had to really know Georgia to see this side of her, this side she'd always kept buried underneath the wild and carefree girl and young woman she'd shown to the outside world. Maisy was just never sure which one was the real Georgia. At least not until Lilyanna.

"You weren't supposed to come back." Maisy's voice cracked on the last word.

Georgia leaned the broom handle against the corner of the room, angling it precisely so that it wouldn't fall. "It's been a long time, Maisy."

"Not long enough." Georgia flinched, but it wasn't enough to make Maisy stop. "And you promised."

"I already told you—I'm not the same person who made that promise. And it's not like I came here on a whim. I can see now this was a big mistake, and I will leave just as soon as I can." She took a deep breath, like a nurse preparing to plunge a needle into a child's arm. "I just realized that even if you didn't find the cup, Grandma might have bought other pieces in the same pattern. It's an unusual one, and if I find more of it I can assume it wasn't a custom pattern—which would affect its value. But I won't know for sure unless I can hold another piece in my hand, and see the marks on the bottom."

"I'll take off a few days from work to go through every nook and cranny in this house to find whatever it is you might need. Anything to make you leave first thing tomorrow morning." Maisy's jaw hurt from the effort it took to hold back all the words she wanted to hurl at her sister.

Georgia stared back at her, her eyes sad. "Don't be ridiculous. I'll be as quick as I can and then I'll leave. Don't think I want to be back here any more than you want me here."

Keeping her voice calm, Maisy said, "Stop being so selfish. There are people who could be hurt. Do you ever think about anybody but yourself?"

Georgia's shoulders slumped, for once making her appear as petite as she really was and not strong at all. "I'm not here to hurt anybody."

Maisy turned back toward the kitchen, stopping to slam her fist against the heavy mahogany door frame. The handle of the broom made a slow dragging sound down the wall before bouncing off the chair rail, then slamming against the wood floor. Neither one of them moved. "Why did you have to come back and mess everything up?"

She felt Georgia shrug behind her. "Because it's always been the one thing I do best."

Maisy left the room, already planning to search again for the china on her own. Hopefully they'd find it soon so Georgia would be on her way back to New Orleans before anything else broke, shattering into so many pieces that could never be put back together.

chapter 6

*The telling of the bees was a traditional English custom in which bees
would be told of important events in their keepers' lives, especially deaths.
The hives would be draped in black as they were told the name of the
deceased. If the custom was omitted, then it was believed a penalty would
be paid, that the bees might leave their hive, stop producing honey, or die.*

—NED BLOODWORTH'S BEEKEEPER'S JOURNAL

Georgia

Dinner was as stiff and awkward as I imagined showing up at a
wedding in a bathing suit and flip-flops might be. Grandpa
chatted about the heavy rains that might impact the harvest of his
precious tupelo honey, while James asked appropriate questions about
Maisy's students and Becky's basketball techniques. Even Becky was
silent except for occasional "yes, ma'ams" and "no, sirs," making me
wonder whether she'd been prewarned by her mother about bringing
up any subject that might cause an argument. Which basically left
nothing of any substance to talk about. This allowed us all to ignore
the pink elephant in the middle of the room, holding in its trunk ten
years of absence and questions that nobody seemed to want to ask.

Although Maisy had indicated for Becky to sit at the opposite
end of the table from me, Becky had moved her glass of milk to the

setting beside mine. I loved having her there, loved her scent of soap and shampoo, loved looking at her chipped nail polish and the way her fine hair escaped her ponytail. I felt Maisy watching us, as if anticipating my leaning over to whisper a secret in Becky's ear. I didn't, of course. All I would have wanted to say was, *I've missed you.*

Maisy cut Birdie's food into bite-size pieces, as she'd probably once done for Becky, and the way our grandmother had also once done for Birdie. Our mother was physically capable of cutting her food, but sometimes the best way to handle Birdie was the path of least resistance, which usually meant doing everything for her. She picked at her food, eating only a small portion of what was on her plate, and took delicate sips from her water glass, her gaze focusing only when it rested on James.

As soon as dinner was over, Maisy and I stood simultaneously and began clearing the table, each of us eager to be done. She brushed away my offer to help clean up, and I just as quickly declined Grandpa's invitation for dessert and coffee on the front porch, using our long drive as an excuse and promising we'd be back the following day to begin our search. Becky had to be pried from my side by her mother citing math homework. She hugged me tightly and made me promise to see her the next day.

"I'm t-taking tennis l-lessons. You c-can come see me p-play. Daddy says I'm really g-good."

I hadn't heard the stutter before and looked up at Maisy. Calmly, she said, "Sometimes Becky has trouble getting her words out when she's excited or upset."

Maisy looked at me with accusation, as if I were responsible for the tension that was thick enough to be felt by a young girl. "I would love to, Becky. However, I'm on a deadline with the project and I need to get back to New Orleans as soon as possible. But I promise to see you before I leave."

Becky had looked so disappointed that I kissed her forehead and then wished that I hadn't, because it reminded me of the last time I'd seen her and had pressed my lips against her delicate skin. I turned away abruptly, and headed toward the door.

Grandpa walked us out onto the porch to say good-bye, the flickering gas lamps outside moving shadows over his face. "I'm sorry we couldn't find what you were looking for. But I'm glad you came anyway." He spoke quietly, and for a moment I thought I heard something in his voice, something that reminded me of a man on a ledge in a movie I'd seen recently. Something that sounded a lot like despair.

I touched his hand. "Me, too. But I'll be here for another day, at least. I'm going to look through everything again just to make sure you and Maisy didn't miss anything in your search, and also see if I can find any other pieces in the same pattern. It's hard to imagine there would only be that one soup cup."

"A soup cup with bees on it. Like I said, I'm pretty sure I've never seen it before," Grandpa said, stroking his chin, the bristling sound louder than the buzz of the night insects. He turned toward James. "Where did your grandmother get her china?"

"We really don't know. She said it was given to her by her mother, but that's all we know about it. It was kept in my grandmother's china cabinet ever since I was old enough to remember."

"I found the cup in Birdie's closet, but Maisy said it's not there anymore. I just can't imagine what it was doing there in the first place. She wanted me to keep it a secret for some reason. I guess it would be pointless to ask her about it now."

I thought I saw something move in his eyes, but it must have been the porch light. Then he smiled. "Our Birdie—always so dramatic. I bet it was a prop from one of her shows that she took as a souvenir." He stepped out of the shadows, and his face appeared normal again.

"Maybe," I said. "I'll wait until Maisy is at work before stopping by tomorrow, so maybe about ten?"

He surprised me with an embrace, his worn flannel shirt soft against my cheek, and for the first time since my return I thought about the last time I'd had close human contact: a warm embrace. A kiss. It reminded me again of the good things that I'd left behind along with the bad.

"I always knew you'd come back, Georgie."

"Like a honeybee," I muttered into his shirt. "No matter how far they go, they always manage to find their way back to the hive."

He held me tighter. "They say the same thing about the truth, don't they? How it always finds its way home."

I pulled back, aware of James listening. "I'm not here to dig up the past."

He looked confused for a moment, as if he wasn't sure who I was. "But you are," he said softly. His eyes searched mine in the darkness, and they were clear again, reminding me that he was ninety-four years old and that momentary confusion wouldn't be that unusual.

"I'll see you in the morning," I said, stretching up to kiss him on the cheek.

James shook his hand and we said our good-byes before heading down the walkway to the car. We sat in silence for a long moment, my headlights illuminating the newly sprouted redbud trees that had always lined our front walk.

"Are you sorry you came yet?" I asked.

He didn't hesitate before answering. "No. I enjoyed meeting everyone, especially your grandfather and his bees. Everybody was very kind to me, although I did sense a bit of . . . tension."

"Tension? That's one way to put it. I sometimes wonder if Birdie is the only one who's got it right, opting out of the unpleasant realities. Maybe I should try it sometime, except I'd need to find someone who wouldn't mind cutting my food, and I don't think Maisy would volunteer."

"How long has your sister taken care of Birdie?"

I looked away, watching how hundreds of little insects danced in the two round beams of light from the headlights. "Since I left."

"So your father doesn't take care of her at all?" He held up his hand. "I'm sorry. Never mind. I'm intruding."

I rolled my shoulders, trying to release the tension. "Yes, you are. But after forcing you through that dinner, I probably owe you an explanation. My father died when I was small."

"That must have been hard on your mother, losing her husband while they were young."

I gave a hard laugh. "Not exactly. He survived Vietnam but couldn't survive losing Birdie when she divorced him. He shot himself the day she married Maisy's dad."

There was a short pause before he spoke. "I'm sorry."

"No, I'm sorry. I shouldn't have told you. It's just . . ." I shrugged. "You're safe, I guess. Like a stranger on a plane. You don't know any of the players, so you can't take sides."

"I know you."

"No, you don't. And hopefully we'll be gone from here and you'll be on your way back to New York before you're any the wiser."

He pulled out his seat belt and buckled it, the sound like an accusation.

"Look, I forced myself on this trip, so if you need to vent, I'm a good listener. You can tell me anything. Remember, I'm like a stranger on a plane."

"Be careful what you wish for," I said, pulling away from the curb. "Because there's a lot more where that came from."

I headed toward Water Street and the Consulate Suites where James was staying to drop him off. After he pulled his bag from the trunk, he stood by my car door. "Since you don't have a cell phone, how can I reach you?"

"I'll be staying at my aunt Marlene's—my father's sister. Everybody knows her number. She's in a house on Ninth Street near Avenue E, but has a business in Two Mile—the area of town exactly two miles from the center of Apalachicola. Not very creative, but it works. Anyway, we passed it on the way in. Everybody knows where Marlene lives because she has lots of her product samples in her front yard."

He raised his brows in question. "What kind of business?"

"Lawn and garden statuary. Yes, exactly what you're thinking. Except her goddesses, gods, and sea creatures have been dressed for modesty while they're waiting to be sold. Marlene's Marvelous Marbles is the name of her business."

"I'm thinking I'm missing out by staying here instead of with your aunt."

"Staying with Aunt Marlene may be even more of a distraction than you're looking for."

His smile faded. "Can I ask you a question?"

"You can ask, but that doesn't mean I'm going to answer."

"Fair enough." He paused for a moment, weighing his words. "Did your father really kill himself because he'd lost your mother?"

I didn't want to answer, and even thought that I wouldn't. But there was something in his eyes, something in the way he asked me, that made me think he was trying to make sense of an event in his own life.

I breathed in deeply, the air thick with the scent of salt and spring blooms, remembering the night my grandfather came to my room and took my hand and told me that my daddy had gone to heaven—even though according to overheard gossip that wasn't necessarily where we'd find him. "He didn't leave a note. But Aunt Marlene said it was because my daddy loved my mama like fire loves dry wood. They couldn't live with each other, but they couldn't live without the other, either. They'd been divorced for a year, but I guess as long as she wasn't married, he thought she was still his."

I leaned back in my seat and looked up into the clear night sky, the stars so bright I thought that if I reached far enough I could touch them. "What's so sad is that my mother never stopped loving him, no matter how much she didn't want to. I guess it's true what they say."

"What's that?"

"That the heart wants what the heart wants."

His steady gaze considered me for a moment. "My wife was shot in a random mugging. On a random night on a random street corner."

I winced, hearing the raw note in his voice and wishing that I hadn't. "Why are you telling me?"

He shrugged. "I'm not really sure. Maybe because I felt I owed you. But maybe because it made me think of your father, and how unexpected her death was. Sort of like a suicide without a note. It's a hard thing to work through."

I watched his face and knew there was more, but I didn't press. I told myself it was because I didn't want to know any more about him or his life except the provenance of his grandmother's china. I already knew what a complicated, messy life was like, and I'd gone to great lengths to simplify mine.

I turned away for a moment. "Yes, it is." He shifted on his feet and I faced him again. "I'll pick you up at nine fifty tomorrow. We'll head to my grandfather's house and ask Birdie if she remembers anything about the soup cup. I'm expecting we won't get anywhere there, so be prepared to go through some closets and even the attic. And if that turns up nothing, then we can spend the rest of the day looking through Limoges catalogs. Bring your laptop. I find sometimes looking on the Internet at old Limoges ads can help with identification, too."

"Sounds good." He kept a hand on the door over the lowered window, preventing me from pulling away. "I like what you said before. About the heart wanting what the heart wants. That explains a lot."

He stood back without saying more and lifted his hand in a wave, a sad smile on his face. I watched him for a moment in my rearview mirror, wondering what he'd meant and angry with myself because I cared enough to want to know.

〜〜

It was almost as if my car didn't need directions to Aunt Marlene's. Although I'd grown up in my grandfather's house—except for a brief stint living with Maisy's father for the two minutes Birdie had been married to him—I'd spent much of my time with my father's sister. She'd never married, calling the various statuary and her pack of mutts that yapped around her heels her family. They didn't ask her to do anything for them and never talked back—two advantages over a husband that she wasn't willing to trade in. Unless the man looked like Pat Sajak. She was a lifelong *Wheel of Fortune* watcher and usually came up with an answer long before the contestants did.

The daughter and sister of oystermen, she was whipcord thin but strong enough to help haul in a net or stand for hours shucking oysters—which is what she did throughout high school and into her twenties until she'd saved up enough to open her own business. Her skin was lined and weathered from years spent outdoors in the Florida sunshine and, according to Birdie, looked like it could be used to reupholster a couch. Or fix a flat tire. Despite having my daddy in common, they'd never been friends, but it had never seemed to bother Birdie that I always chose my crusty aunt over her.

Strings of small clear lightbulbs wrapped around trees and strategically placed poles, illuminating crushed-shell-covered paths and the unsellable remnants of concrete statues of cherubs made to look like marble and a local artist's interpretation of Greek gods and goddesses, along with a liberal dose of commercial and mythical creatures. The most remarkable of these included a small replica of the Loch Ness Monster, swimming in its spot on the sandy soil between Poseidon and Ronald McDonald. Despite painting Nessie purple and putting her front and center for years at her business, she'd yet to find a home. Feeling sorry for Nessie, Marlene had brought her to her house to rule over the other rejected statuary in her front yard. I remembered climbing on her as a girl, having the scars on my knee to prove it.

The house was a nondescript structure that had probably been built around the 1920s and added onto over the decades without any thought to form or design, including the paint color, which had always been the same Pepto-Bismol pink. It was odd and quirky, but as long as Aunt Marlene was there, I considered it home.

The bare bulb over the front door flicked on as I parked the car in the mostly sand driveway, and Marlene stepped out surrounded by a yapping entourage of four dogs of varying sizes and indeterminate breeds. She wore her usual uniform of T-shirt, denim shorts, and flip-flops, and just the sight of her made me want to cry.

"Is that you, sweet girl?" Although she'd given up smoking two decades before, she still had that smoky rasp that would always give her away. Her unadulterated and unapologetic Southern accent was as pronounced as ever.

"It's me, Aunt Marlene," I said, grabbing my bag, then running to be embraced by the woman who'd always been more of a mother to me than the woman who'd given birth to me. The dogs ceased their barking when they saw that I wasn't there to attack and began earnestly sniffing my feet and legs, one of them brave enough to saunter over to my car and pee on a tire.

She pulled me inside the house, the dogs following faithfully on her heels, bringing me back to the small kitchen with the same linoleum floors and lime green Formica countertops that I remembered. The dogs flopped down on the floor beneath the table, tongues lolling. "Let me look at you." She held me at arm's length, where we studied each other for a moment. She still wore her hair long and curly and dyed black, along with the thick blue eye shadow and false eyelashes that I'd figured out as a teenager looked right only on her.

"You look even more tired than the last time I saw you." She came to New Orleans with a group of her friends every Mardi Gras and shared all the news from home, including what my grandfather omitted from our frequent phone conversations. Gently she pressed the pad of her thumb under my eyes. "You got more purple circles than Saturn. Having problems sleepin' again?"

"No more than usual." I smiled. "I'm guessing Grandpa called you?"

She pulled out a green vinyl chair, the foam stuffing held in check by strategically placed strips of duct tape, and indicated for me to sit. "He did, but he didn't have to. Half the town's called to let me know you were back."

I rolled my eyes. "Great. So much for hiding under the radar."

"Sugar, this is Apalach. There's no such thing as hiding here; you know that. Besides, don't you want to see your friends?"

I shook my head quickly. "Not really. Most of my friends have moved away, and the ones who stayed are mostly people I don't want to stay in touch with. Besides, this is a business trip."

She reached into her harvest gold–colored refrigerator, where rope and duct tape had been formed to replace the broken handle, and pulled out a pitcher of sweet tea. Without asking, she poured me a tall glass and then one for herself before placing both on the table.

"Business, huh? Then who's that nice-looking young gentleman with the expensive shoes?"

I took a sip of tea and stared at her for a moment, knowing it was pointless to ask her where she'd gotten her information. She knew everything about everybody, had even known things about me before I did. Like the time I'd been expelled from school for punching Dale Cramer in the nose for teasing my little sister about her crazy mother. It hadn't occurred to me until later that we shared the same crazy mother. All I knew at the time was the sight of my sister huddled in a corner of the playground while Dale taunted her with words she didn't even understand.

"He's a client. We're on the hunt for a china pattern."

"Sounds fascinatin'." She winked so I'd know she understood what it was like to be passionate about something other people didn't get. "Maybe he'll want a little lawn ornamentation to take back with him as a memento."

"I'm sure he'd love that, but he lives in New York City and I doubt he has a lawn."

"That's a shame." She grinned and winked again, and I felt a real smile cross my face.

"I've put fresh sheets on the bed and clean towels for you in the bathroom. You know you're welcome to stay as long as you need to."

"It shouldn't be more than a couple of days to find the china or give up."

"That's not what I mean." She reached across the table and put her roughened fingers on my arm. "Maybe it's time to set old rumors to rest. People 'round here say you bolted, leaving Maisy the burden of caring for your mama and grandpa."

"That's not true, Aunt Marlene, and you know it."

"Yes, I do. And Maisy does, too. But you girls have had a lot of time to grow up. To put things in perspective. To understand that the past can't be changed, but it can be accepted." She leaned back in her chair. "You're both old enough to pull up your big-girl pants and move on."

I thought of what my grandfather had said after I told him that I wasn't there to dig up the past: *But you are.* I looked down at my hands. "I wish it were that easy. I left because I wasn't a good person, Aunt Marlene. And everybody knew it. Leaving was a lot easier than staying, and I've always been particularly good about taking the easiest path."

She reached over and patted my arm again. "I know what you gave up, sugar. And what you left behind. There was nothin' easy about any of it. But Maisy's your sister, and you once meant the world to each other. Just like me and George. That kind of bond can't be broken—even if it needs a little glue now and again."

I stood, my legs sticking to the vinyl seat, and took both of our empty glasses to the sink, promising myself I'd wash them in the morning. Aunt Marlene had never had a dishwasher or any intention of getting one, thinking it was a symbol of the growing laziness of Americans.

"I'm tired. I think I'll turn in now."

Marlene stood, too, and surprised me by cupping my head in her hands. "You look so much like your mama—and that's not a bad thing, no matter what you think. Nobody can deny she's a beautiful woman. But that's where the resemblance ends. You wasted all those years trying to be different, and all you had to do was be yourself."

I pulled away, angry and embarrassed. "I told you—I'm not a good person, and I don't deserve Maisy's forgiveness."

"Oh, sugar, you're so wrong. You're the best kind of person. The kind who's smart enough to know when to bend so she won't get broken. Your mama was never strong enough to figure that out."

"I'm going to bed," I said again, turning away from her.

"Good night, darlin'. Sleep tight, and don't let the bedbugs bite."

Despite myself, I grinned, remembering that from my childhood good-night rituals. "I'll try," I said. "Good night."

I sat in the dark on the narrow bed in the small room at the front of the house, watching the moonlight creep stealthily between the statues, altering the ground so it resembled a silver sea with the hulking shadow of Nessie keeping watch over us all. I stayed there for a long time thinking about what Aunt Marlene had said, and how far a person could bend until she snapped in two.

chapter 7

*When a hive is invaded by a wasp, the bees cluster around the
intruder and fan their wings to make it 117 degrees, knowing that
wasps cannot survive temperatures above 116. This is the ultimate
act of survival, as the bees will die if the temperature reaches 118
degrees.*

—NED BLOODWORTH'S BEEKEEPER'S JOURNAL

Maisy

Maisy watched impatiently as Birdie moved her manicured finger
over the rows of neatly arranged lipstick tubes in her dressing
table drawer, hesitating slightly over individual colors before moving
on again. She wasn't usually this indecisive, and it most likely had
everything to do with a return visit from Georgia and her client, James.

At this rate, Maisy would never make it to work, and Becky
would be late. Again. It never ceased to surprise Maisy how Birdie
could still control the entire household without ever uttering a word.

She crossed her arms tightly over her chest to prevent herself
from grabbing a lipstick and forcibly applying it to her mother's rose-
bud lips. Maisy had worn the same shade for years, and sometimes
wondered why she even bothered at all. Habit, most likely. One
couldn't emerge unscathed from living with Birdie and Georgia for as

long as she had. She'd begun wearing makeup early, in a misguided attempt to fit in with her mother and sister. But Maisy had always felt too tall, too dark, her feet too large. Like an ostrich among doves.

And then there'd been Lyle, and she'd felt beautiful for the first time in her life. But even that had been temporary. She turned her back on Birdie to stare out the window. The circular view encompassed the bay at the back of the house, along with their grandfather's apiary on the side, and the driveway and wide front yard that abutted Bay Avenue.

Birdie had the largest bedroom: the room in the turret that had seemed so magical to Maisy and Georgia when they were small, playing Rapunzel or other fairy tales, where Maisy always played the prince because she was so much bigger than Georgia, even though she was almost four years younger.

Growing up, this had been Maisy's whole world, and unlike her mother and sister, she'd been content to picture herself right there, standing in that turret, for the rest of her life. And here she was now, exactly as she'd always wanted. Yet all she wanted to do was scream.

She spotted her grandfather in his apiary, a lawn chair pulled up near the first row of hives, his back to her. He did this sometimes, Maisy knew, to work out a problem. "Unraveling life's knots," was how he described it. Something about the hum of the bees, their regimented work schedules and the irregular flight patterns of their small, striped bodies and the incessant flapping of their wings held answers to life's complexities, according to him. To Georgia, too. But to Maisy, bees were just annoying flying insects, much like mosquitoes or cockroaches, with nasty little stingers on their backsides. She'd been stung too many times to believe them to be anything but pests.

A loud clattering brought her attention back to the dressing table. Unhappy about being ignored, Birdie had taken out the lipstick tray from inside the drawer and thrown it on the ground, scattering the shiny tubes on the rug.

Maisy looked down at the mess and then at her mother's petulant expression and pulled her cell phone from her skirt pocket before hitting the first stored number. Lyle answered on the first ring. As a patrol officer, he was usually not too far away.

"I'm going to be late. Can you pick up Becky and take her to school? I have no idea how much longer I'll be." It had been her decision to teach at the high school in Eastpoint across the bay rather than at the ABC charter school that Becky attended on nearby Twelfth Street. Maisy thought it would help Becky to be more independent if her mother didn't teach at the same school. It had made things more complicated, but Lyle had supported her, even though he didn't necessarily agree. It was one of the things that she loved about him, the way he always put family unity first.

"I'm on my way," Lyle said, then hung up.

Maisy ignored the hurt of his abruptness as she bent down and began retrieving the tubes of lipstick, making a mental note to deny purchasing another color until these were all used up. Like she really would. Like Maisy would finally decide one day to stop trying to win her mother's affection.

She heard a car door shut outside and she stood, wondering how Lyle had gotten there so quickly. Peering out into the driveway, she was surprised to see Georgia's Cadillac, an hour and a half earlier than expected. "Georgia's here," she said. "With James."

Her mother brightened, and immediately selected a lipstick. Maisy dumped the loose tubes in the drawer and moved toward the door. "I'll meet you downstairs. I'll have your coffee waiting."

But Birdie wasn't listening, instead slowly smearing the lip color over her lips, humming to her own reflection.

Maisy met James and Georgia in the foyer. Her sister wore a white lace dress that looked like it came straight out of *The Great Gatsby*. Maisy had once shared Georgia's love for vintage clothing, allowing her sister to select things for her to wear. She'd loved the way she'd felt, thinking she looked pretty, like her sister. At least until their mother had told her that Maisy was too tall and big boned like her father to look good in any of the delicate silhouettes from previous decades. Maisy had always resented Georgia for lying to her, for making her believe she was something she could never be.

"You're early," Maisy said, not bothering to hide her annoyance.

"I'm sorry," James said. He was carrying a small box that he set carefully on the hall table before removing a china teacup and saucer and placing them next to the box. Maisy wasn't near enough to see it closely, but it looked like bees flitting around the white china background. She repressed a shudder, wondering why anybody would want painted insects on dishes that held their food.

"That's my fault," James continued. "I've become a bit of an insomniac, so I spent most of the night Googling various china Web sites. I found a museum of antique china in a small town in Illinois. I thought we should contact them, and wondered if Georgia knew anybody there. I couldn't wait to tell her."

Maisy could tell that Georgia was more amused than annoyed, and that surprised her. She hadn't seen her sister in so long she thought Georgia would be a stranger to her, that her emotions would be off-limits. But she wasn't. How could she be? Their grandfather used to say that they were like oysters from the same bed, clinging together despite the vagaries of the tides. Their girlhoods had been spent dreaming fearlessly together in the house on the bay. Before Maisy learned how Georgia liked to discard people like used linen, and that they weren't so much alike at all. But Maisy could never forget that her first memory was of her sister's face peering over her in the crib, Georgia's name her first spoken word.

"At least he waited until seven o'clock to call Marlene's to tell me," Georgia said. "Although he could have called earlier, since I was awake. I'd forgotten how quiet it is here at night. I kept waking up, thinking something was wrong."

"If you had a cell phone, I could have texted you so that you'd have known to call me when you were ready," James said matter-of-factly.

She sent him a withering look. "It would still be an hour earlier in Illinois. I doubt anybody would be in at the museum answering phones."

"Remind me to tell you sometime why she doesn't have a cell

phone," Maisy blurted out. She wasn't sure why she'd said that, thinking it probably had to do with lingering resentment over the incident with Birdie and the lipstick.

Georgia stared hard at the floor, while James only raised his eyebrows, making Maisy wonder how much he'd been told—or warned about—by Georgia.

James cleared his throat. "Anyway, I went for a run, and it was still early, so Georgia took me to Dolores's Sweet Shoppe for breakfast. So we're already fed and ready to get started."

"Get started with what?"

Their grandfather emerged through the back hallway from the kitchen.

"Looking for the china piece I remember seeing in Birdie's closet. The soup cup with the bee design," Georgia said, her face brightening at the sight of their grandfather.

He paused, breathing heavily, as if he'd just run all the way from the apiary. "Yes, well, good luck with that. Right before she got . . . sick, Birdie went on a huge cleaning-out and remodeling phase. You remember that, Georgie, don't you? It was right before you left."

Georgia's face had stilled, and Maisy knew she remembered, too. Remembered their mother's reaction when she'd heard rumors about a movie being filmed in Apalachicola, and how the actors and director might need housing. Maisy wondered, too, if Georgia remembered everything else about the summer of '05 and the double hurricanes of Katrina and Dennis, the external storms matching those going on inside their house. Or the moment their mother went up to the attic and had to be brought down in a catatonic state by their grandfather. Probably not, Maisy thought. Georgia was very good at brushing her hands clean of a messy past.

"Yes," Georgia said, her voice strained. "Birdie made it through the downstairs closets and cabinets, but stopped when she was halfway through the attic. I always thought . . ." She stopped. "I figure I'll ask her, see if I can get through to her. . . ."

Whatever else she was going to say trailed away as Georgia's attention focused on the stairwell behind her. Turning, Maisy saw Birdie standing on the landing, a delicate hand poised on the banister, her hair swept up in a French twist, her pink silk shantung suit decidedly retro but still glamorous. She looked so much like Grace Kelly that Maisy almost went to her to put her hand on her arm, to let the others know that despite appearances, Birdie meant to be taken seriously.

But there was something about Birdie's face, the way her jaw trembled and her eyes shifted, that made Maisy aware that she'd heard their conversation, had understood most of it. And maybe even comprehended that Georgia wanted to ask her a question and even expected an answer.

Grandpa stepped forward, and Maisy smelled his sweat, and noticed that beads of perspiration were slipping down his nearly bald head. Two bright spots of red had erupted on his cheeks as he walked toward Birdie. "You look beautiful, my dear. As always."

Birdie looked at her father's outstretched hand and then up to his face, and for a horrifying moment, Maisy was sure her mother was going to cry. After a moment's hesitation, Birdie stepped down into the foyer, grasping Grandpa's hand and moving into the center of the group.

"Good morning, Birdie," Georgia said quietly. James must have said something, too, because Birdie turned her head to smile at him. But there was something brittle about her, something glasslike, at risk of shattering. Maisy tried to remember what they'd said that might have upset her, but was distracted by the sound of tires rolling over broken oyster shells in the driveway.

Taking her mother's elbow, Maisy began leading Birdie into the kitchen. "I'm going to get her breakfast. When Becky comes down, tell her that her dad's here to drive her to school." She'd barely made it halfway across the foyer when there was a brief knock on the door before it opened. Lyle stood on the threshold in his uniform, seemingly as surprised to see everybody as they were to see him.

"Sorry," he said, taking off his hat. "I didn't expect . . ." He stopped, his gaze resting on Georgia. And then he smiled, and Maisy felt the old longing, the old hurt. Her own inadequacies. The old anger.

Lyle and Georgia had always shared a special friendship, one that had excluded Maisy, made her feel like an intruder. Despite their claims that they were strictly platonic, Maisy knew Georgia too well, and couldn't completely erase all doubt that there was even one unrelated male in town her sister hadn't slept with.

Maisy pulled on Birdie's arm to leave, but Birdie remained where she was, a silent spectator to what promised to be a good show.

"Hello, Lyle," Georgia said, her head tilted like that of a little girl choosing which hand holds a surprise. "It's good to see you."

James reached out his hand toward Lyle. "I'm James Graf. A client of Georgia's."

Nobody said anything as they shook, making Maisy wonder again what Georgia had told James, and whether he was aware of the role he played; whether Georgia had to beg him to come with her, to deflect all the stares and under-the-breath comments that were bound to come her way regardless of how short her stay was supposed to be.

"Lyle Sawyers. Pleased to meet you." Lyle took in the stranger with what Maisy had used to joke were his "cop eyes." They were light brown, just like an actor's on one of the police shows they used to watch together when they were in high school and they were supposed to be studying.

"Daddy!" Becky came down the stairs quickly.

"Hey, squirt," he said with the same grin Maisy had fallen in love with the first time she'd seen him at the Seafood Festival, when they were both too young to know what love at first sight meant.

"Daddy." Becky groaned unconvincingly as she allowed Lyle to hug her to him with one arm.

She pulled away to fling her arms around Georgia. "Hi, Aunt Georgia. I made a list of all the things I want to show you, and it will take at least four days. Can you stay that long, at least?"

Georgia bent her head over Becky's, their hair blending so that it looked like it came from the same head, and it felt as if Maisy was watching Birdie and Georgia again, the hurt of exclusion like a sharp jab to her chest.

"I wish I could, sweetheart. But I have to get back to work. And so does Mr. Graf. Maybe soon, though, okay?"

Becky's entire body radiated disappointment. "But I already told B-Brittany Banyon that you were here for a v-visit and she wants to meet you. She said her d-daddy knew you in high school."

Maisy put her hand on Becky's shoulder to remind her to take a deep breath, aware of Georgia's stiffening, seeming to be struggling for something to say. Oblivious, Becky said, "I'll b-bring her home after school and you can meet her then. M-maybe you can tell some embarrassing story about her d-daddy."

While Georgia struggled for a response, Maisy asked, "Do you have your homework?"

"Yes," Becky answered. "And my tennis racket. I don't need a lunch because I'm buying today." She smiled brightly, looking so much like her aunt and grandmother that Maisy's heart broke a little more.

"All right. I'll see you after school." She smiled, and Becky gave her a long hug, as if she knew her mother needed it.

Lyle opened the door, then turned back to Georgia. "How long are you staying?"

"If everything goes as planned, we hope to leave tomorrow."

Lyle nodded slowly. "Well, don't be a stranger," he said with that same slow grin, and Maisy looked away.

"Nice to meet you," he said to James before heading out the door toward his patrol car with Becky tucked beneath his arm.

Maisy pulled on Birdie's elbow, desperate to get away, knowing she'd have to call in late so that her class wouldn't be in her first-period classroom without their teacher. But Birdie resisted, pulling her arm free.

Grandpa sat heavily in a hallway chair, his skin blotchy still from the heat outside. He clutched his hand and Maisy could see the pink welt near the wrist. He'd been stung, which, considering, was a rarity. He'd always told them that he knew how to communicate with the bees, knew how to walk among them without their bothering him. Had always said that you knew when you'd made a mistake when you allowed yourself to be stung.

Maisy moved toward him, wanting to get him into the light so she could take the stinger out, then stopped. Both she and Birdie watched as he lifted the teacup and saucer James had placed on the table by the chair, holding them up at eye level, his eyes wide and blue behind the thick lenses of his glasses.

Birdie took a step toward him, and Maisy thought Birdie was going to say something, could almost hear the air move in anticipation. Her grandfather's eyes flickered up for a moment, meeting Birdie's, and then, as if in slow motion, the saucer dipped and the teacup slid in an avalanche of china. Everything seemed suspended for a moment, every breath, every heartbeat, even the ticking of the anniversary clock on the hall table where the cup and saucer had just been stopped as if the Earth had suddenly decided to rotate in the opposite direction.

Then everything was sound and spraying china and shouts. And then their grandfather slid out of the chair like a vanishing man in a magic show, collapsing in a pile of loose clothing. He landed on the bright white shards of broken china, clutching at his chest while Birdie screamed and Georgia knelt on the crushed china, trying to place his head in her lap. Maisy grabbed her phone, misdialing 911 twice until James calmly took it from her and dialed correctly, speaking with authority.

Birdie knelt next to Georgia and slid a large piece of the saucer from under her father's elbow, staring at the flying bees, whose flight pattern appeared interrupted by the jagged break. She began rocking back and forth, keening softly and seeming unaware of the deep cut on her thumb that dripped bright red drops of blood onto the pink silk of her skirt.

chapter 8

In cooler climates during the winter, the male drones die while the sister bees cluster around their queen, fluttering their wings to keep her warm until spring.

—NED BLOODWORTH'S BEEKEEPER'S JOURNAL

Birdie

There is a curtain inside my head like one would see on a stage, dividing what is allowed to be seen, and hiding what is not. I know it's there because I hung it in place ten years ago, when I chose to live on the performing side of that curtain, to smile and pretend and to act. To keep that curtain down so I would not see what lay behind it. Some people would call it cowardice, but it's how I've survived all these years. My mother made sure I knew how to act and how to sing and be pretty, but not to face my fears or be strong. Part of me wants to lift that curtain, to peer behind it, to face what's lurking in the darkness. But I'm not strong enough yet. So I watch, and learn, and wait for that thread of light to appear between the closed curtains, images flickering like a movie projector.

I think I saw a glimmer of the light today. It started with the vividly colored bees, and then the delicate china they were painted on. I knew them, somehow. Knew what it felt like to hold that delicate cup between my fingers. A flash of memory filled me for a moment, and I held my breath as I stood on the stairway in front of Georgia and Maisy and my daddy, remembering, seeing the images of memory flash behind the drawn curtain of my mind.

I am very small. I know this because I am swinging my legs from a chair and they are far from the floor. It's a kitchen, with large black and white square floor tiles and the delicious scent of bread baking in the oven that makes my mouth water. I know I will get a thick slab soon, with cool, melting butter slathered on top, and although I'm not hungry, my stomach rumbles.

The kitchen door opens and my father steps in, smelling of the sun and warm air and honey. He reaches for my hand, and leads me outside to show me something in the hives and I go with him eagerly, the bread and butter forgotten.

My hand is small inside his large one, and I feel the familiar calluses. I tell him that if we are ever running somewhere in the dark, I'll still be able to find him by touching his hand. I know I've said something funny because he laughs.

It is nearly nightfall as we approach the hives, and I imagine all the worker bees inside, their long day's journey over. A few still linger in the sticky evening air, little guards hovering, buzzing around our heads in warning. But we don't get stung. It's as if they know us, recognize us as part of their world. And I love this world. This house and my father and the hives are all I know, and it is all I want to know. I feel the sun on my face and my bare legs and I am happy.

I want to hold on to this memory, the way summer clings to warm days while autumn tugs at her sleeves. It's a little slice of sanity I've been denied all these years. Doctors have tried to label my condition, classify it to make it worth the money they are paid to diagnose me. But they can't fix me. Only I can. I'm like a china plate that's been fractured into too many pieces, and I think I'm getting too old to care enough to glue them all together.

When I met George I thought I'd found the one thing that could make me whole again, would take me back to that place where I'd felt so happy. But for all things irreparable, fixes are temporary.

Like most of the boys in Apalach, George grew up along the water of the bay, the son and grandson of oystermen. They called their skiff the *Lady Marie*, after George's grandmother. When it became his, he called her *Birdie*.

I loved George, loved how he could make me forget things. How we shared a secret, just the two of us. I loved him as much as I hated him, but our love was the brick wall we broke ourselves against. It was like I had to keep hurting myself just to know that I could still feel, hoping that it would wake me from my nightmares. To keep me from the dark places that clouded my memories. Even back then I sensed the dark curtain behind me, pregnant with all the untold secrets I didn't want to know.

I thought having children would chase away the darkness. And it did, for a while. When I held both my daughters in my arms I was back in that farmhouse, my hand in my father's, and I was happy again. But only for a little bit. Until the dark places came back and took over.

I wish I could tell Georgia and Maisy that I love them. That none of this is their fault. But I kept thinking about my father and the warm summer night and my hand in his, and I couldn't stop trying to remember what happened next all those years ago when I was so small.

That's why I threw the lipsticks on the floor this morning, trying to make my mind go back to the happy part, trying to focus on the colored tubes rolling on the rug and onto the wood floor.

Maisy practically hummed with anger, but I welcomed it, wanted it, because that's what I need to crawl back into that person I became whom I don't really recognize. She's not me. She's the person I play so no one looks too closely. Somebody once said that life is a stage. And it's true. We all have our parts to play. Mine is the crazy woman who thinks she's always on a stage. The truth would be so much harder to know.

I want to tell this to my daughters, to make them understand. It would be easier for them if they understood it's all my fault. That I need to hide from my memories to protect myself. Like now. I'm remembering the bees and the hives and the house, but then he holds up the teacup and saucer and all of a sudden the curtain lifts a little and light floods inside my head, and I can't make it stop, because of the noise of the breaking china and Maisy shouting and Georgia's look of sorrow. And suddenly a part of a memory comes back to me and I'm sliding like that teacup from the saucer, except I can't break because I'm already broken.

chapter 9

A bee flies to thousands of flowers to make only a spoonful of honey.

—NED BLOODWORTH'S BEEKEEPER'S JOURNAL

Georgia

Someone tugging on my empty coffee cup brought me abruptly awake. It took me a moment to remember I was in a waiting room at Weems Memorial Hospital and that my grandfather had suffered a stroke. I looked up into James's blue eyes and relinquished my cup, remembering him bringing it to me hours before.

It had been James who'd thought to run out the door after handing the cell phone to Maisy to speak with 911, thinking Lyle wouldn't have gone far and could probably transport Grandpa to the hospital faster than waiting for an ambulance.

I smiled ruefully up at him. "Thank you. For everything. I guess it's too late for you to change your mind about coming with me."

He placed the empty cup on a table, then lowered himself into the chair next to mine, stretching his long legs in front of him. "It's certainly been a lot more exciting than I imagined it would be."

I glanced across the room, where Maisy sat next to my mother. Birdie had her eyes closed, her head resting on my sister's shoulder, the bloodstain on her skirt turned the color of rust. I remembered Maisy bandaging our mother's hand as Lyle left the house with our grandfather, Birdie letting go of the broken saucer only after Maisy promised that she'd leave it on the table and not touch it.

I rubbed my face, feeling as if we'd been in Apalachicola for weeks instead of just a day. "I'm sorry about your teacup and saucer. The saucer has a clean break, and I have a source who can fix it so that you can't even tell it was broken. But the teacup . . ." I stopped, remembering the splattering of china as it exploded on the floor. "I'm afraid it's not fixable."

"Don't worry about it. I've got eleven more, and if it makes you feel better, I'll even commission you to find a replacement. But for now, you've got other things to worry about."

Becky, who'd been allowed to miss school, came back from another trip to the snack machine with a candy bar and a Coke and returned to her seat next to mine. She'd hardly left my side since we'd arrived at the hospital, and I wondered whether Maisy minded. "How's G-Grandpa?" Becky asked, her voice quavering.

She raised her hand to take a sip from her Coke can and I noticed her fingernails. They were bitten to the quick, the cuticles jagged and torn. I felt somebody watching and I looked up to find Birdie's eyes focused on us, taking in what I was seeing, her gaze almost challenging. *You can always tell a lady by her hands,* I remembered her saying to me after spotting my own ruined nails at the dinner table. I'd kicked Maisy under the table to warn her about keeping her own hands in her lap, but she'd misunderstood and had started howling because I'd kicked her.

I'd heard the stutter, and I wanted to say the right thing, wanted to reassure her. I tucked Becky's hair behind her ear, recognizing the gentle curve of it, the silky feel of the blond strands, and for a moment the words were stuck in my throat, and I remembered the last time I'd seen her, tiny and pink and bawling. And I thought of all the years between in which I'd thought nothing had changed. But of course it had. She'd grown older. We all had. Just not any wiser.

I smiled. "He was lucky your dad got him to the hospital so quickly. That saved his life. And we're lucky, too, that we didn't have to go to the hospital in Panama City, because a very good neurologist happened to be here this month. Grandpa's still very sick, though, and they're going to need to keep him here for a little while."

She looked at me with worried eyes. "What about his b-bees? He was supposed to m-move the hives next weekend to the swamp."

I looked over at Maisy and met her eyes for a moment. "I'm sure we'll figure out something. I know your mama will know what to do."

"But M-Mama hates bees. You p-probably need to stick around to m-make sure they're all right until G-Grandpa gets better."

I felt the panic rise in the back of my throat. "Oh, sweetheart, I can't. I need to get Mr. Graf back to New Orleans so he can fly home to New York. And I've got work. . . ."

I stopped, watching her face. The set of her jaw and the way she'd narrowed her eyes and tucked in her chin was so much like Maisy when she was preparing an argument that I wanted to laugh. "So you're j-just going to t-take off again?" I would have made a bet that she was quoting her mother verbatim.

I was acutely aware of James next to me. "I never 'took off,'" I said, feeling the need to defend myself in front of him.

"But G-Grandpa needs you. The b-bees need you." She put her hand in mine, and I felt the raw, jagged edges at the tips of her slender fingers.

James stood and I knew he was looking at me, but I couldn't return his gaze. "I'm going to get some more coffee. Does anybody need some?"

Nobody said anything and I shook my head. "No. But thanks."

I looked at our clasped hands, then up at Becky's eager face. Her expression was open and honest, nothing hidden.

"I can come back," I said hastily. "As soon as I drive Mr. Graf back, I can return until Grandpa is better."

"You w-won't," she said matter-of-factly. "If you l-leave, you won't come b-back. M-Mama told me that last night, so that I w-wouldn't be hurt. I just didn't b-believe her."

My emotions ricocheted between hurt and obligation, shame and hopelessness. How could I explain now the choices Maisy and I had made, and the promise to never regret them? I put a hand on her arm, meant to calm her, to remind her to take a deep breath. Just like I'd seen Maisy do.

Maisy stood and walked toward us. "We can manage fine without her, just like we always have." She took the almost empty Coke can and the half-eaten candy bar and placed them on the table by Becky's chair. "Come on, Becky. Let's go get some real food. We can bring something back for Birdie and Aunt Georgia."

I met Maisy's gaze. "I've been thinking. About Grandpa's stroke, and how unexpected it was. And how he was looking at the teacup when it happened. Do you think that's what caused it?"

She frowned impatiently. "His stroke was caused by a burst blood vessel in his brain. And probably from his high cholesterol and blood pressure. If surprise had something to do with it, I would say it had more to do with your visit and not some stupid teacup." She held out her hand to Becky. "Come on—let's go get something to eat."

Becky walked slowly to the door with her mother, then paused before running back to me, cupping her hands around my ear to whisper. "B-Birdie wants you to stay." She pulled back and I stared at her in surprise. Her teeth—small, white, and straight—worried her lower lip, her eyes trained on the ceiling as if she were trying to remember something she'd memorized for a test. Then she cupped her hands around my ear again and whispered, "She n-needs your help."

She pulled away, then ran to Maisy, who was watching me closely with the same narrowed eyes I'd just seen on Becky. I stared at the empty space where they'd stood long after they'd left, wondering whether Birdie had really spoken to her, or if Becky simply had a vivid imagination.

My gaze shifted to Birdie, who was staring out the window across the room, humming something low and toneless, and I thought about Grandpa's bees, and how he once said that it made sense for bees to always flap their wings, because if they didn't, they'd fall to the ground and die. But people weren't like that, our constant movement just a distraction from the things we couldn't bear to face.

"Birdie?" I called, almost expecting her to turn to me with clear eyes for the first time in almost a decade. I wanted to believe that Becky wasn't making it up, that Birdie talked to her. But if that were true, what did it mean? And did I really want to know? My short visit home was turning into quicksand, and the more I struggled to extricate myself, the stronger the pull to keep me stuck.

Birdie continued her soft, monotonous humming, reminding me of a funeral dirge, and I wasn't sure why, but it made me want to cry. Something had happened to my mother almost ten years before and I'd been too wrapped up in my own life to pay attention, to watch as the threads were spun and knotted around her too tightly for me to be able to pick them apart and set her free.

I stood quickly and rushed to the doorway, wanting to tell Becky that I would be back, that it was time to fix things before it was too late. I nearly ran into James, causing him to splash coffee onto the floor and on his shoes.

"I'm so sorry," I said, clutching at his arm, not completely sure I was apologizing for the coffee. "But I need to stay a little longer. To make sure my grandfather is going to be okay. I can drive you to the airport tomorrow, but I'll come right back. And I'll continue searching for your grandmother's china pattern."

His eyes searched mine. "I don't need to go back. Not for a while."

I dropped my hands, understanding. "You're running away." I didn't mean it as an accusation, merely a statement of fact.

He nodded. "I need to keep moving."

I thought of the bees again, their incessant wing flapping keeping them aloft. I met his gaze. "Sooner or later you're going to have to find a place to land." I began walking away, my sandals slapping the linoleum floor.

"Have you?"

I felt the anger in the back of my throat, stinging my eyes. I wanted to turn back and yell at him, to tell him yes, that I was so much better now, and that all those years of being gone were worth it. But then I thought of my grandfather and Becky, and Maisy and Birdie and all that I'd missed, a photo album full of blank pages.

Everything has its price. I stopped with my back to him, trying to recall who'd said that, remembering it had been Aunt Marlene as she'd helped me pack my small suitcase and I'd told her what I'd done.

I kept walking, feeling his gaze on my back until I pushed through the glass door at the front of the building before running down the front walkway and out into the fresh air saturated with the scent of salt water. I gulped the air into my lungs, tasting it along with all the memories it brought back to me.

"Georgia?"

I spun around and saw Lyle approaching me from the parking lot. "Are you all right?"

I nodded. "I just needed to be outside. I'll be fine in a minute."

"How's your grandfather? I was coming to pick up Becky and was hoping for good news."

Finding a smile, I said, "He's okay, considering. And thanks to you. You saved his life."

He shrugged. He'd never been any good at accepting compliments. "I wouldn't have been there to help if James hadn't come running after me." He leaned a little closer. "Is everything okay?"

I tried to pinpoint just one of the things that tickled my brain like crawling insects. "Yeah. It's just . . ." I met his gaze. "I think I'm going to stick around for a little while. At least until I know Grandpa is going to be okay."

His brown eyes were warm. "That's probably a good idea. I guess with your job you can work remotely."

A corner of my mouth turned up reluctantly. "Assuming I owned a laptop and cell phone. But James has both, so I'm not worried. And my boss is one of those annoying family men who thinks I should want to spend time with my own family. I haven't asked yet, but I know I can stay as long as I need, with his blessing."

"Good," he said. "But that's not all, is it?"

Like Maisy, he'd always been able to read my mind, which was probably why we'd never become romantically involved. That and the fact that he'd loved my sister since the moment they met. I looked him in the eye. "Has Becky ever said anything to you about Birdie talking to her?"

"A few times. But I just thought that was her being dramatic, making up stuff to suit her point of view, if you know what I mean. She's definitely inherited the flair for drama."

I looked up at the impossibly blue sky. "That she has." Glancing back at him, I said, "She's a great kid. You and Maisy have done a really good job."

"Thanks. That's mostly Maisy's doing. She lets me be the fun parent while she's the rule maker and enforcer. Can't say that's fair, but it just seemed to work for us. Until recently, anyway."

He shifted his feet, rubbing the soles against the cement, and I noticed how his hair had begun to thin on the sides, and how his face showed lines and shadows I didn't remember.

"How about you, Lyle? Are you doing all right?"

"Yeah, I'm fine. Just trying to work things out with Maisy. Figure out what we're going to do." Our eyes met for a long moment. "I miss you."

The stress of the last few days seemed to be compounded by those three simple words, and to my horror I felt my eyes well with tears. Lyle reached out his arm and hugged me to him, pressing my face into his shoulder, and I gave in to his warmth.

"You can come back to stay forever, you know. People who matter don't care what happened years ago. And the people who do care don't matter." He patted my back in comfort, the gesture making me want to cry even more. I didn't deserve it.

"Not Maisy." I sniffed.

"You know how to fix that," he said softly.

I thought for a moment how right he was, how all I had to do was quite simple, really. Like unpainting a portrait stroke by stroke. But we wouldn't be left with a blank canvas with which to start over. I would still have my pride and Maisy her resentment, with enough of each to sink a ship.

"Why have you never blamed me?" My voice was muffled in his shirt.

He didn't even hesitate. "Because I know you. Because I know the person you really are."

"But Maisy is my sister." As if that relationship were like an eraser on the end of a pencil, correcting all mistakes. Grandpa had told us that when we were little girls, and we had always believed it. Until a sunny afternoon in early July all those years ago, when Maisy and I had stopped believing in anything at all.

We both looked up at the sound of the front door opening. Maisy stood holding it open for Becky to walk through, and I spotted James behind her watching us with a blank expression. I stepped away from Lyle, realizing how it might look.

Leaving Maisy's side, Becky ran toward us, throwing her arms around us both in a group hug, then standing back to smile. I couldn't look at Maisy, so I allowed my gaze to stray behind her, where I met James's gaze. I realized that I'd have to explain a few things to him if we were planning on staying any longer.

Ignoring me, Maisy approached Lyle. "I've already called Becky's teachers and they'll have her missed work ready to be picked up at the end of the school day. Please make sure you go through all of it to make sure it's done. And no pizza for dinner. She's been eating mostly junk food all day, and she'll need something nutritious."

"Mama!" Becky moaned. Lyle kept his expression serious, but I was pretty sure he and Becky would be eating pizza for dinner.

Maisy turned around and headed back toward the hospital door. "Grandpa's awake and he's asking for you," she said over her shoulder to me as she brushed by James and continued inside.

I said a quick good-bye to Lyle and Becky, then followed Maisy into the building. I made to move past James, but he took hold of my arm, stopping me.

"I can go find your aunt Marlene's house and start looking through the catalogs you brought with you. Or I can stay here at the hospital. My sisters say I'm a good referee."

"What makes you think I need a referee?"

He raised his eyebrows in response.

I wanted to tell him that I didn't deserve his kindness, that if he knew everything, he'd be on the first flight back home. And that I was just fine on my own, not just because I'd grown used to it, but because it was what I preferred now. Relationships of all kinds were messy, untidy things, like balls of twine full of knots that never knew how to unravel properly.

But James wasn't looking for a friend any more than I was. Maybe that made him safe. Maybe that made me take his hand and pull him along with me down the corridor, feeling like I'd been tossed overboard and he was the only thing keeping me afloat.

chapter 10

*Honeybees communicate with dance instead of words to tell other
bees in the hive where to find food or a new home or to warn of
approaching danger. It's a complicated dance of turning in circles and
bisecting precisely calculated angles, and understood only by bees
and those who bother to pay attention.*

—NED BLOODWORTH'S BEEKEEPER'S JOURNAL

Maisy

Maisy woke up the following morning to a quiet house that
smelled of coffee. She'd taken the day off from work, planning
on spending most of it at the hospital, and hadn't set her alarm. Still, she
was surprised to see it was past nine o'clock and that she hadn't moved
from her position in the bed since she'd passed out in it the night before.

She quickly slid to the floor, throwing on a robe over the T-shirt
and boxers she usually slept in, then padded barefoot across the hall to
Birdie's bedroom. The door was open, and there was no sign of her
mother in the bed or adjacent bathroom.

Feeling slightly panicked, she ran down the stairs and into the
kitchen, halting abruptly on the threshold. Birdie, fully dressed and
adorned with makeup and jewelry, sat at the table taking tiny bites of
scrambled eggs from her plate. Georgia, in jeans shorts full of patches

and a tie-dyed T-shirt—both looking as if they'd barely survived the seventies—had her hair pulled back in a ponytail. She stood at the stove flipping pancakes, wearing no makeup and looking no less beautiful.

"You're here early," Maisy muttered as she stumbled toward the coffeepot.

Georgia kept her focus on the pan in front of her. "Yeah, well, you stayed so late at the hospital that I figured I'd get Birdie out of bed and breakfast started before you got up."

Maisy was silent as she poured her mug to the brim, then took a sip, needing fortification if she had to speak with her sister. She recognized the mug, with its chip near the top and the letter "M" formed from the outlines of three mermaids. Its twin, except with the letter "G," sat on the counter next to the coffeemaker, half-full of cold coffee. Maisy hadn't seen the mugs in years and figured Georgia had had to dig pretty far back in the cabinet to find them.

"Birdie usually takes her breakfast on a tray in bed," she said ungraciously, eyeing their mother over the rim of her steaming cup.

Georgia's gaze flickered over at her for a moment. "I didn't ask. I just told her that I was making breakfast and to come down when she was ready."

There was no hint of smugness, but Maisy felt annoyed all the same. As if taking care of Birdie were as easy as telling her the way it should be. As if after all these years Birdie wasn't still playing favorites.

"How did she get dressed?"

Georgia slid a spatula under a pancake and carefully turned it over. "I imagine she did it herself." She turned to face their mother for a moment, as if she actually expected her to say something. Focusing her attention on the stove again, she said, "I'm soaking her skirt from yesterday in the laundry room sink."

"It's silk. You shouldn't get it wet."

"Yes, well, I figure if I got the whole thing wet we wouldn't have to worry about a water stain. And that's so much better than a bloodstain."

Too tired to continue the conversation, Maisy pulled out a chair next to her mother and kissed her cheek before sitting down. She took a long sip of her coffee, staring at the jar of Grandpa's tupelo honey that had sat in the middle of the kitchen table ever since she could remember, then stood abruptly. "I forgot to check my phone. The hospital might have called."

"Don't bother," Georgia said. "They already did, on the house phone. He's stable but they want to keep him a little longer. I made an appointment for us to talk with his doctor at eleven."

Maisy gripped the handle of her mug until her knuckles whitened.

"Or I could go myself, if you have other things you need to do. We also need to find someone to help us with moving the hives. Grandpa will be so disappointed if he doesn't get his tupelo honey—"

"Stop it," Maisy said, hearing the words before she'd even convinced herself to say them.

Georgia turned off the burner and lifted the pan from the stove top, what looked like genuine surprise crossing her face.

Maisy slammed the coffee mug down on the table, causing coffee to splash over the top. She was aware of Birdie putting down her fork. "Stop acting as if you care, as if we've saved a spot and waited for you to come back and resume your place. It doesn't work that way. It was never meant to work that way."

"It's been a long time, Maisy."

Maisy placed her palms flat on the wood table, glad for the cool feel of it. "This isn't some game where you're allowed to change the rules midway just because you're losing."

Georgia slammed the pan down on the counter. "This was never about winning or losing. And I didn't want to come back—ever. But it's been a decade! When this opportunity came up I said no at first. I knew you wouldn't be happy to see me. I knew that I promised I wouldn't come back. Then I told myself I was doing it for work, for James, really. But I think in the back of my mind I knew it was time. Regardless of what other people in town might think or say, my own sister can't still hate me. I just needed to find out for myself."

Maisy had a sudden memory of Georgia teaching her how to

drive in their grandfather's old Buick, and how Maisy had been too scared to press the accelerator until Georgia promised her that she wouldn't let her get hurt. And she'd believed her. Believed her enough that she'd stomped her foot hard on the accelerator, jumping the car forward, and would have hit the magnolia in the front yard if Georgia hadn't yanked the steering wheel.

"I don't hate you," Maisy said quietly. "I've wanted to, but I can't. It's just easier not to hate you when you're four hundred miles away."

Birdie seemed to be watching Georgia, her gaze focused. Georgia approached and took their mother's plate. "Would you like some coffee?"

She didn't say anything, but she turned her head toward the counter where the coffeemaker sat. There was something not right about that one movement, something that made Maisy glance at Birdie, wondering whether she'd missed something.

Maisy watched as Georgia poured a mug of coffee for their mother, remembering the two spoonfuls of sugar and dollop of milk even after all this time. And it annoyed Maisy even more, as if Georgia had remembered on purpose because she assumed that Maisy would expect her to forget.

"When are you leaving?" Maisy demanded, wanting to get the conversation under control again. It was what she did best. Georgia was good at mixing things up and making a mess, and Maisy was good at cleaning it all up and fixing things. It was the way it had always been. "I'm assuming your plans have changed now because of Grandpa." Maisy walked toward the pantry to pull out a box of cereal regardless of how enticing the smell of eggs and pancakes was. She could make her own breakfast and take care of her family. She'd been doing it for years.

Georgia placed the mug of coffee in front of Birdie. Without meeting Maisy's eyes, she said, "With Grandpa's stroke, it would seem that our visit has become open-ended."

"Doesn't James need to get back to New York? You can't just drag him down here and leave him stranded."

Georgia's spine stiffened as she pulled her shoulders back, a sure sign that her sister was preparing for a fight, and Maisy was glad for it. Georgia had come back to Apalach like a sunbather dipping into the warm waters of the gulf, carefree and unconcerned. Somebody had to remind her why she hadn't been back for so long.

"I didn't and I'm not," Georgia said offhandedly, but with clipped words. "I offered to drive him to the airport so he could fly back to New York, but he told me he was fine here for as long as I need to stay. My boss said just about the same thing. I'm worried about Grandpa. I want to make sure he's okay and help with whatever needs to happen next. And that will give me more time to do what I came here for, too. Maybe even have time to talk with you. It's not my goal to inconvenience you, and I'd like to think that talking with you wouldn't fit into that category."

Maisy was shaking her head before Georgia had even finished speaking. "Inconvenience me?" She thought she heard a knock on the front door, but she was too focused on the conversation to go check. "That's like calling a category-five hurricane an inconvenience. I honestly thought you'd show up under the cover of darkness and slip out the same way. Because that's what I would have done if I were you. But I keep forgetting that you're nothing like me."

Georgia's lips had become as pale as her skin. Maisy was vaguely aware of Birdie sliding back her chair and walking from the room. "Well, thank goodness for that," Georgia shouted. "Because we all can't be doormats."

Maisy slammed her mug into the sink, hearing the gratifying sound of it cracking against the porcelain and satisfied to see Georgia flinch. "Well, somebody had to stick around to fix your mistakes and clean up your mess."

Georgia took a step toward her, her balled fists pressed against her heart as if to protect it. "That was your choice! You chose, and I went along with it because I thought it would make you happy."

Maisy clutched her head, wondering whether it was possible to have one's head actually burst, then remembered something else Georgia had said. "Why on earth would James want to stick around here? That makes no sense. How much have you told him?"

"You mean my version or yours?" Georgia's cheeks were flushed, her nostrils flaring.

"The real version," Maisy shouted, glad Becky was with Lyle, and not a witness. Maisy never raised her voice, either in the classroom or at home. She'd learned that from Birdie. Ladies didn't make a commotion. But she was lost somewhere between anger and heartbreak, and desperate to leave things unsaid. Except it was far too late for that. Ten years too late.

"The real version?" Georgia spat back. "Would that be actual events or the way you want to remember them?"

"The version that includes you being so busy being the town slut that you let something horrible happen to an innocent child!" Maisy screamed, the ugly words staining the air between them.

They both became aware of movement in the doorway and turned in tandem to see James standing there, holding an armful of china catalogs. "Your mother let me in." He held up the catalogs as if in explanation. "I walked to your aunt Marlene's and she told me you were here. I brought these over thinking that if we had time, we could get started. . . ." His voice faded as if the echo of Maisy's last words were still ricocheting against the kitchen walls like bullets, leaving burning black holes in everything they touched.

He set the catalogs on the kitchen counter, then retreated, pausing for a moment. "In answer to your first question, Maisy, I'm here because I've recently lost my wife, and Georgia was kind enough to let me come along on her mission to identify my grandmother's china because I needed a distraction." His gaze flickered momentarily to Georgia before returning to Maisy. "As for your second question, I knew nothing about her family or why she'd been gone so long." He paused. "But I guess I do now."

With a brief nod in their direction, he left the room. They listened as his footsteps moved down the back hallway to the foyer, followed by the sound of the front door opening and then closing with a solid snap.

Neither one of them moved for a long moment, until Georgia walked over to the counter and picked up the catalogs. With her chin held high she spoke through bloodless lips. "I'm going to the hospital now so I can meet with Grandpa's doctors. You can be there or not; I really don't care. Then I'm calling his beekeeping friend Florence Love to ask her to come over and give me some pointers on what I need to do until Grandpa is back on his feet again to take care of the hives on his own, and ask her about moving the hives to the swamp.

"But I'm not leaving town until Grandpa is better and things are settled, so you'd better get used to having me around for a while." She left the kitchen, her heels pounding into the wood floors like a punishment.

Maisy's mouth opened and closed several times as she thought of the thousands of things she wanted to say to her sister. Instead, her gaze strayed to the dirty pan and cold pancakes on the kitchen counter. "You left a mess in the kitchen!" she shouted after Georgia, the words all too familiar.

Georgia answered with the slamming of the front door.

chapter 11

*To remove honey from the hives, the bees must first be pacified by
smoke from a bee smoker. The smoke triggers a feeding instinct (an
attempt to save the resources of the hive from a possible fire), making
them less aggressive. In addition, the smoke obscures the pheromones
the bees use to communicate with one another, leaving the hive
vulnerable to anyone wanting to take their honey.*

—NED BLOODWORTH'S BEEKEEPER'S JOURNAL

Georgia

Outside to take advantage of a temporary lull in the rain, listening
to the buzzing of the bees, I stood in my grandfather's apiary and
turned my face up toward the wan sunshine. The constant hum was the
sound track of my childhood, the taste of honey its sweetener, and for a
long while the perfect substitution for my mother's presence.

Maisy was different. Her need for Birdie's acceptance was like the
black bear reaching into a hive to steal honey, impervious to the myr-
iad stings on her paw. There was a good reason for this. Maisy was
only five when our mother went away for the first time. Grandma and
Grandpa said she needed a place to rest, and to talk to special doctors
so she'd feel well again. Except she never really got well. Every time
she went away she came back brighter and shinier, like a ballerina in

a jewelry box spinning and smiling and sparkling. And just as plastic. By the third or fourth time she went away and came back, Maisy finally understood that it was as good as it was going to get. But that didn't keep her from reaching into the hive.

It was why Maisy hated bees. Grandpa and I knew you had to be calm around the bees, that they know how you're feeling before you do. If you're agitated or angry, they're going to get agitated and angry, too, and that usually means you're going to get stung. Not that I'd ever tell Birdie, but I always hummed one of her favorite show tunes, making me think that at some point in my babyhood she must have rocked me to sleep singing it.

But when Maisy found out that Birdie had left without saying good-bye that first time, she went screaming into the apiary, looking for her and whipping up the bees. She was stung so many times that her airway began to close. She was bigger than me, but I hardly noticed as I hoisted her up on my back and carried her all the way to the house so I could call an ambulance.

Aunt Marlene said Grandpa should burn the hives, but I begged him not to. The bees were only protecting what was theirs, giving their lives in pursuit of the safety of the hive and their queen. I argued that they were a good example of the way things ought to be, something Maisy and I wouldn't be exposed to without the bees. I suppose Aunt Marlene and Grandpa agreed because the bees stayed, but Maisy was forbidden to go anywhere near them and had to carry an EpiPen all the time. And she hated the bees after that. I wanted to tell her that she should hate Birdie instead, and that hating the bees for stinging was like hating the clouds for raining. But I didn't. Probably because I hadn't yet found a way to hate Birdie, either.

A soft brush of wings touched the air around me as the bees examined me. I stayed still, softly humming "Over the Rainbow." I heard footsteps approaching and turned my head. It was James, his face devoid of fear or apprehension, and I was glad. The bees always knew if you were afraid.

"Stop, but don't stand in front of the entrance—that makes them angry," I said quietly. "Let them know you're not a threat."

He did as I asked, and I found that I couldn't meet his gaze. I turned back to the nearest bee box, the blue paint faded and peeling in the sun. "Hum something softly," I said.

He was silent for a moment, and I imagined him deep in thought, and then he began humming something that seemed vaguely familiar. When I recognized the song "Popular" from the musical *Wicked*, I smiled in surprise, before remembering he grew up in New York City and had four sisters, and going to musicals might be something he did often.

I met his eyes for a moment, then immediately turned away, remembering the scene from the kitchen that morning and what he'd overheard. "I'm glad you're wearing light colors. Most novices make the mistake of wearing something dark, making them appear as bears to the bees. Very few make the same mistake twice."

He paused his humming and I could imagine him smiling. "Why are the hives painted in different colors?"

Doing my best to imitate Mrs. Shepherd, my kindergarten teacher, using a calm and reassuring voice that I was sure lulled bees as much as five-year-olds, I said, "Maisy and I painted them one spring before Grandpa moved the bees to the deep swamps near Wewahitchka, so he could tell which ones were his."

I looked at him just as he opened his mouth to speak, and I quickly began to babble, if only to keep him from asking me any questions about what he'd overheard. "He brings them to a spot so deep in the swamp that the only way to get there is by hauling the hives onto a raft. There's been a lot of rain this year, so some of the lower places where the hives usually go might be flooded. They might have to find another spot."

"I was about to ask if I could go, too, but I'm not so sure I want to go out to a flooded swamp. I'd probably see more wildlife up close than I'm comfortable with."

"Probably. Unless you've spent a lot of time with panthers and alligators. And water moccasins. Makes for good security if you're trying to get around the revenue man. Back in the day they say boot-leggers used to put their stills out in the swamps near the makeshift apiaries and use beekeeping as a cover for their illegal operations."

I felt him watching me with those clear blue eyes, but I couldn't meet his gaze, reliving the profound embarrassment of the morning every time I looked at him. Which was why I was telling him more about bees and tupelo honey procurement than he'd ever wanted to know.

He continued to hum softly as I spoke. "I've only gone once, and remember the mosquitoes the most. Unfortunately, that's where the white tupelo blooms, between the middle of April and early May, but it's the only way to make tupelo honey. Grandpa's is a smaller opera-tion, mostly for his own personal use and to sell a few jars at some of the downtown stores."

His humming paused again. "Sounds like a lot of trouble to get just a little honey."

"It is. But it's the purest kind of honey, and worth the effort. It doesn't granulate, so it keeps for a long time—some say as long as twenty years—and is more readily tolerated by diabetics than any other kind of honey. Grandpa has been taking his hives there every spring since before I was born." I barely paused for a breath, trying to fill up any empty space where he could ask any questions. "His daddy was in the lumber business but sold it when Grandpa was a boy and took up beekeeping as a hobby. He even sent Grandpa all over the world to study different kinds of beekeeping."

James stopped humming, and when I looked up I realized that he was standing next to me now, his eyes focused on the hive, seemingly unconcerned with the bees zigging and zagging around us. "What's going to happen this year?"

I turned away again and began walking slowly down the row of bee boxes. "I spoke with a beekeeper friend of Grandpa's this morn-ing, and she said she'll bring his hives along when she takes hers. Although she's afraid that if the rain keeps up, the bees won't leave the hives. Could be a wasted effort, but we've got to try."

He touched my arm, and I knew he wanted me to look at him, but instead I began to babble again. "When the white tupelo is at its fullest bloom, the bees work extra hard, as if they know their time is limited. The life span of the worker bees during that period can be as short as twenty-one days. They wear out their wings and die."

I looked at his hand on my arm and we were both silent, listening to the incessant buzz of the hives. One alighted on his sleeve and he didn't flinch, moving only after the bee flew away. "If you get stung, lick it," I said. "Bees have over two hundred pheromones they use to communicate with each other, and they leave some on your skin when they sting to alert the other bees that there's danger."

James finally spoke while I drew breath. "I'm sorry I walked away so abruptly this morning. I—" He stopped as if suddenly deciding to tell me something else. "I thought you might want some privacy."

He dropped his gaze, and I began to walk back toward the house, sensing a change in the atmosphere, a growing agitation that vibrated from me like a taut wire that had been pulled too far.

I heard his footsteps behind me. "You can't ignore me forever, you know."

I stopped, then whirled around to face him, hearing a loud buzzing near my left ear. "Aren't you going to ask me if it's true?"

His eyes were troubled, as if he'd been having the same internal argument for a while, and I found myself holding my breath. "No." He paused again, and I was sure this time that he was definitely arguing with himself, as if it were important that he knew the truth, just as much as he knew he shouldn't.

He met my eyes again. "I'd much rather know why you collect antique keys and locks. That's a lot more relevant to me than something that did or didn't happen a long time ago."

I was so surprised by his response that I wasn't aware at first of the sharp sting on my arm, staring dumbly at the carcass of my attacker as it tumbled to the ground. I remembered my grandfather telling me to always remove the stinger as quickly as possible, because it will continue to pump venom into the skin for as long as ten minutes. But all I could do was stare at the small pink welt and feel sorry for the dead bee.

"Aren't you going to lick it?"

I shook my head, almost enjoying the pain as just punishment. "Let's go look at china catalogs. And while you're doing that, I'll make some phone calls to the Limoges museums and other collectors I know—including the one you found on the Internet. Unless you're ready to leave now. I imagine you've had enough drama, and I'm happy to continue here on my own."

My arm throbbed but I ignored it, knowing the pain would eventually fade. It always did.

"You know why I'm here, and I'm prepared to stay for the duration. I'm the stranger on a plane, remember? It's not my place to pass judgment."

I studied him in the bright sunshine, noticing how the light turned his hair different shades of gold and reflected off the tips of his unshaven cheeks and jaw, and I wondered where he'd been when he'd received the news that his wife had been killed; if they'd kissed good-bye that morning and said, "I love you," or if they'd argued. And I realized that my little dramas were tiny blips in the grand scheme of things.

"I search for padlocks because I believe everything has a key. Every question, every relationship. Everything has a lock and a matching key. That's why, when I find a padlock and a key that fits, I put them in a place of honor in that vitrine you saw in my apartment. I feel like I've finally found an answer to what had once been an unanswerable question."

He smiled and I saw again how beautiful he was. "I was right. That's a lot more relevant. And very telling."

I turned back toward the house. "Come on then. Let's go look at those catalogs."

He followed me inside while the pain in my arm continued to throb, a reminder of what Maisy had said, and how pride and resentment could poison a relationship between sisters as surely as bee venom could stop a person from breathing.

〜✦〜

I awoke to the sound of breaking china, unaware whether it was real or part of my dreams that flittered through my head like a bee, never settling for long. Sitting up abruptly, I was aware of a blanket that I'd last seen on the back of the couch sliding off my shoulders as I blinked my eyes and tried to remember where I was. My lap was covered with books—I was pretty sure they were china catalogs—and I was still fully dressed. I widened my eyes, taking in the moonlit room, the old familiar couch and chairs, the rectangles on the wall that held school photos of Maisy and me.

Catalogs slid to the floor as I stood, then stumbled toward the light switch that I'd been pretty sure I'd left on when I sat down to go through one more pass of the catalogs after dropping James off at his hotel. A cool breeze blew in through the window screen, bringing with it the scent of the bay. I pressed my face against the screen, trying to remember what it was that had awakened me, and wondering whether the bees could smell the pittosporum and roses my grandmother had planted for them. Grandpa had once told me that bees had a sophisticated olfactory system in their antennae instead of noses. I'd been fascinated at how bees navigated without noses, and wondered if, like humans, they just used their consciences to find their way home.

I heard the sound again, that sharp, screeching, shattering noise that at work always put my teeth on edge, because it usually signified that something with meaning and value had just been rendered worthless on both accounts. Realizing it hadn't been a dream, I quickly made my way toward the dining room.

Maisy sat on the floor next to the china cabinet, a small pile of broken dishes pushed against the wall. Her hair was pulled back in a high ponytail, and she wore her nighttime uniform of T-shirt and boxers, and she was suddenly my little sister again, my shadow, and the one person I loved most in the world. I took a step forward, realizing how much I'd missed her, and how until this moment I'd been unaware of how much I needed her to look at me the way she once had, back when I was the only one who could make things all right instead of turning everything upside down.

She glanced up without surprise, then continued sorting through a stack of plates on her lap. "Don't worry about the broken ones—it's just my cheap wedding china."

I winced inwardly but didn't respond. That was the thing about sisters: We always knew where to point the arrow. "What are you doing?"

She reached into the open cabinet door and pulled out another stack of plates. "We were looking for the soup cup the first time I searched through here, so now I'm looking for anything I can find in that bee pattern. Because the sooner we find something, the sooner you can leave."

I bit my lip, knowing it was the only way I was going to keep myself from letting things escalate again. "All right," I said, sitting next to her without asking permission. "Then I guess I'd better help." Leaning forward, I opened up another cabinet door. "I can't imagine I'll get any more sleep with you crashing around in here."

I peered into the dark recess, noticing that there was very little in the way of cups or plates or even serving pieces in this section, but it was more of a repository for the things Birdie and our grandfather didn't have a place for. "We should probably look again in Birdie's closet, since that's where I remember seeing the soup cup."

She didn't even look up from her sorting pile. "I'll try to get to it tomorrow when she's awake. I didn't think the middle of the night would be a good time to disturb her."

I returned to the open cabinet. Liberally scattered within the stacks of old bills, birthday cards, theater programs, and receipts were photographs of random vintages. Knowing these would probably be another minefield for Maisy and me, I quietly made a stack as I discovered each one, planning to go through them later.

We pretended to be absorbed in what we were doing, that we were each alone in the room, although I found myself stealing glances at Maisy, noticing the subtle changes that happen during absences. Her hair was just as dark, her eyes the same pale gray—two things she'd received from her father, and which I'd coveted since I was old enough to notice that she had something I didn't. But she seemed stronger somehow, as if she'd been forced to develop muscles to confront life. I thought about what Aunt Marlene had said: how I was smarter than Birdie because I knew when to bend in the wind. I thought maybe Maisy had simply learned how to be tougher so she could face the wind head-on.

She didn't look at me, but I felt her awareness like a ladyfish senses the shadow of a heron on the water's surface. Even as a girl, Maisy was much better at pretending than I was. Most likely because I'd been subjected to Birdie's mood swings four years longer than my sister, so I'd already been exhausted by my efforts to capture Birdie's attention and had simply succumbed to the need to scream and cry and generally misbehave. I remembered our grandmother remarking on how calm and sweet Maisy was, how content to stare out from her bassinet at the world. I threw a fit when I heard that, too. Because they should have known that Maisy was content because I was there to make her happy, to give her attention so she wouldn't miss it.

A color photograph slid off a stack of yellowed linen napkins. It showed Maisy and me, about six and ten years old, sitting astride purple Nessie at Marlene's Marvelous Marbles before the statue had been moved to Marlene's front yard, me with bloodied knees and Maisy with a worried look on her face. She was up there only because I'd put her there and then made Aunt Marlene take the photo to prove to the bullies in her class that she wasn't a baby. I remembered that she fell off right after the photo was taken. I was about to show the photograph to Maisy but stopped, a sudden thought occurring to me.

"Did Aunt Marlene call? I don't want her to be worried that I'm not there."

"No, she didn't. She's used to you not coming home at night, I guess."

She went back to her sorting without glancing at me to see whether her arrow had hit the target. I watched her for a moment, something the girl I'd been would have said waiting on my tongue, but I held back, the memory of the blanket falling from my shoulders coming back to me, a nudge as to who had placed it there. The years between us were like rocks from an avalanche, heavy and forbidding and seemingly impenetrable. But my name would always be the first word my sister had uttered.

I began shifting through a stack of napkins, some of them paper, a few of them cotton, but a good number of them fine lace and linen. There'd been a time when my mother had liked to entertain, enjoyed setting the table with her mother's mismatched china and silver and crystal, liked to play hostess to friends and neighbors. Maisy and I would watch from between the spindles of the stairway, hearing brief snatches of conversation, noticing how our mother was the most beautiful woman in the room. I remembered thinking that she always had a look of desperation about her, that she was playing some part in a play and was afraid of being unmasked. Maisy said she looked that way because it must be hard to be that beautiful, to never want to appear to be less than perfect. I wanted to tell her that she was wrong, because Maisy was just as beautiful and still could act normal. I didn't tell her because Maisy wouldn't have believed me.

I slid out a crocheted place mat—one of my short-lived hobbies, which had lasted just long enough to make a lone place mat—and an old dark brown folder came out with it. It felt soft under my fingers, like book pages left outside in the humidity, and had something written in faded ink on the front. I squinted, barely making out my grandfather's name, *Ned Campbell Bloodworth*. A string wrapped around a small cardboard circle on the front snapped as I began to unravel it, allowing me to lift up the flap and peer inside.

"What is it?"

I hid my smile, not wanting to acknowledge that my sister had been watching me as closely as I'd been watching her. I looked at the small pile of papers, trying to register what I was looking at. "Seems to be Grandpa's military records from World War Two." I slid the top page over to her. "This is his honorable discharge in 1945."

I flipped through the remaining pages, a couple of typed letters on official-looking letterhead. A stiff manila card was wedged near the bottom, and I pulled it out. "And here's his medical record." I glanced at it briefly, noting that his height—six foot four—and the color of his eyes—light blue—were still the same, although his shoulders had rounded over the years. His hair had been brown, though, a surprise to me, since I'd only ever remembered it being gray.

She held the paper in her hand carefully. "I forget sometimes that he was a veteran. It all seems so long ago. I just . . ." She paused. "I just don't think of him as a ninety-four-year-old man. That he won't be here forever."

I wanted to say, "Me, too," but I'd lost that right. I'd left him behind along with everything else. She handed the card back to me and I returned it to the folder.

I began flipping through the remaining napkins and place mats, searching between them to see whether anything might be hiding. "Maybe we'll find Birdie's birth certificate, so we'll know how old she really is."

Maisy tried to suppress a giggle. It had been our quest as girls to guess Birdie's real age, since our direct questions received only a scolding about how impolite it was to ask a lady about her age. Despite our constant nagging to divulge Birdie's secret, Grandpa would tell us only that she was born during the war. That narrowed it down somewhat, but never quite satisfied our search for the truth. It was one of a thousand little things that Maisy and I had shared, each connection like the seemingly indestructible sand fortresses we'd build on the beach, each wave a tiny hurt that eroded it bit by bit.

She placed a broken honey jar near me and I noticed the smattering of freckles on her forearm. As children, Birdie had kept us out of the sun, saying it was bad for the skin and we'd end up looking like Aunt Marlene. I wasn't convinced that was a bad thing, but following Birdie's rules was always a lot easier than breaking them.

"You don't wear long sleeves all the time and even in the summer?" I asked half joking.

Half of her mouth turned up. "No. I haven't done that for years. But I still wear a hat when I'm outdoors. I guess we should both thank Birdie for saving our skin."

"Remember that time I deliberately got the worst sunburn of my life just to make her mad?"

Maisy laughed out loud. "Just to get out of a beauty pageant. You cried all night because it hurt so bad."

I smiled, remembering. "And you stayed in my room and put aloe lotion on my back, even though Birdie told you not to because it served me right."

Our eyes met and our smiles faded, almost as if our cheeks couldn't withstand the burden of the years between.

"I guess I should be glad she never thought I was pretty enough to enter any of those beauty competitions." Maisy turned away, then stood to gain access to the deep drawers at the top of the chest.

I fingered the crocheted place mat on my lap, the mention of Birdie reminding me of something I'd been meaning to ask. "Has Becky told you that she has conversations with Birdie?"

Maisy looked annoyed. "Of course not. Birdie hasn't uttered a word in years. Just hums or sings those silly show tunes." She frowned. "Why?"

"Because at the hospital, Becky said Birdie had told her something."

"Told her what?" I had Maisy's full attention now.

I hesitated for a moment, not sure whether I should tell her. I took a deep breath. "That Birdie wanted me to stay. And that she needed my help."

Maisy shook her head. "Becky has a vivid imagination—she's definitely Birdie's granddaughter. But that's it. She would have told me if Birdie had said something to her. She's probably just looking for reasons to get you to stay." She avoided my eyes and began restacking teacups.

I resumed emptying the cabinet I'd started with, finding more photos to add to the stack, and four mismatched salad plates from various patterns. I had inherited our grandmother's love for garage sales and junk stores, so the mass quantities of random items didn't surprise me, and certainly explained why there would be just an odd piece from the bee-pattern china.

I was vaguely aware that Maisy had stilled, but I didn't look up at her until I heard a choking noise in the back of her throat. I scrambled to my feet. "Are you all right?" I was about to pat her on her back when I saw the small lace baby's bonnet in her hand, the pink ribbon threaded through the brim and meant to fasten under a tiny chin, as bright as it had been the day I'd purchased it.

"Oh, Maisy," I whispered. "I'm sorry. I'm so, so sorry." As if those words could ever atone for a single act. As if "I'm sorry" could be more than a Band-Aid on a widening crack in a dam. As if those two words could bridge the chasm between sisters.

Maisy stared at the bonnet without saying anything, her quiet sobs worse than any screaming grief. But she'd already done that.

I stepped toward her, wanting to hug her and help her hurts go away, just as I'd done when we were little. But she moved away from me, swatting at me with the bonnet, letting it fall to the ground as if it didn't mean anything. She shook her head, her face contorted with pain, the pride and resentment that we'd honed to shiny perfection looming between us.

"Go away, Georgia. Just go away. We don't need you here. I can handle all this on my own, just like I've been doing."

I lifted my arms as if to encompass her marriage, Birdie, our grandfather, as if that one gesture could really include all that clearly wasn't all right. "Maisy, look around you. Please—let me help you."

"You of all people should know better than to ask me that. No, thank you." She brushed by me and ran up the stairs.

"Maisy, please stop." *We used to be allies.* With a sick feeling I went to follow her, and even made it to the top of the stairs before stopping. Birdie was silhouetted in the light from her open doorway, her head turned in the direction of Maisy's door that had just been slammed shut.

"Birdie?"

She turned her head, and for a moment I knew she was seeing me, *really* seeing me. I took a step toward her to determine whether it was only a trick of the light.

She backed away into her room and slowly shut the door, leaving me in the darkened hallway. I stood there listening to her humming, something low and toneless, as the house settled itself in its spot alongside the bay. I tried to tell myself that I'd imagined what I'd seen, that it had been an illusion. But as I turned and made my way down the stairs, I couldn't completely dismiss the thought that when Birdie had turned to me, her expression had reminded me of Maisy's as she'd held the baby's bonnet. I was heartened somewhat by the knowledge that Birdie was still capable of emotion.

There was something else, too, though—something I couldn't

quite identify. I walked slowly, placing both feet on the same step before moving on to the next. I paused on the bottom stair, my hand on the newel post as my fingernail worried the nick in the wood on the edge.

Lost. Yes, that was it. Birdie had looked lost, confused. Not the blank, absent stare I was used to, but an active grieving for something she couldn't find. But why? I stood in the dark, smelling the salt air of the bay, and decided that the list was far too long for me to examine right then.

I gathered up the photographs, then let myself out the back door. I had planned to go directly to my car, but new light was beginning to tingle the bottom edge of the sky, pulling me forward to the dock that had been my refuge for most of my childhood—and the scene of the infamous retaliatory sunbathing. Its sun-bleached boards led out into the water, like a finger pointing to my destination on the map.

A brown heron sluiced through the cascading colors of the clouds, and it seemed as if an old friend were welcoming me home. I stared at the brightening light until my eyes watered, thinking of Maisy's grief and Birdie's loss, of promises made and promises kept, all of it amplified by the passage of years in the same way a storm begins with a single drop of rain.

I didn't want to stay any more than Maisy wanted me to. I wanted to go back to New Orleans and lose myself in the objects of dead people and forget who I was. Who I'd been. But I couldn't. Not yet. I told myself it was because of Grandpa and Birdie that I needed to stay. Yet a part of me knew that it was because Maisy wanted me to leave as if nothing had changed—as if nothing were actually *capable* of changing—that made me dig in my heels. There was Becky, too, of course. I'd learned nothing in my thirty-five years if I'd thought I could just come back for a short while and then leave, as if I could shuck a bucketful of oysters without getting calluses.

I turned my back on the approaching light and headed to my car, my thoughts battling between wondering how long I could stay, and how soon I could leave.

chapter 12

The bee's brain is oval in shape and only about the size of a sesame seed, yet the bee has remarkable capacities for learning and remembering things. It is able to make complex calculations on distance traveled and to recall where it's going and where it's already been.

—NED BLOODWORTH'S BEEKEEPER'S JOURNAL

Birdie

Since Daddy broke that teacup and saucer, there's more light flooding through the darkness inside me, forcing me to see and to hear. To *remember*. It's like the sound of shattering china broke something loose in me, too. There's a part of me that's glad, but there's the other part of me, just as big, that wants to retreat into the darkness again, to step in front of the curtain and resume my role. It's safer there. Because sometimes when I think of myself stepping off the stage, I have the strange urge to scream and scream and scream. There's something there that scares me. Something I don't want to see.

While I was lying in bed trying to sleep, I heard Maisy and Georgia shouting, and I was back to the time before, before my final breaking point, to the time when they were teenagers and hated each other with the same ferocity with which they loved each other. My mama hadn't been able to give me siblings, so I had no reference, but I'd always thought their fighting was my fault, that it was because I was a bad mother. All I'd ever wanted to be was a good mother. The best mother. But I always managed to fail more than I succeeded. I tried to console myself that everything I'd done had been done out of love, but watching the wreckage of my daughters' lives was like facing Saint Peter at the gates of heaven and being held accountable for all my sins.

I opened my door, needing to find Becky. It had been her cries as a baby that first allowed the light to flicker inside my mind. I'd been the one to hear her first nighttime sobs before her parents knew she was awake. I'd picked her up and her cries stopped, and she looked at me with eyes that were just like mine. Even then Becky had worn a serious expression, as if she could see into my head and it all made sense to her. As if she shared my memories of a long-ago afternoon with the smell of bread and sun and honey and all that happened afterward.

Maybe she did. Maybe it was possible to inherit traits that went beyond the color of eyes or the ability to sing in perfect pitch. I knew then that we had a special connection, that we could communicate without the need for words, and that I had found an ally.

She seemed to fear the night, as if she, too, felt herself pursued by something she couldn't see or hear. As if whatever it was waited in the corners of her room, waiting until night fell to pounce. As Becky grew older, her newfound voice grounded me to this world I wanted to flit away from. She babbled nonsensical vowels and consonants that I would string together in a lullaby until she would fall asleep again. I'd hear Maisy tell people that Becky had slept through the night since birth, and that always made me smile to myself at our little secret.

When Becky graduated from her crib and into a real bed, she'd often not wait for me to come to her, but would crawl into my bed so we could lie awake together and wait for the darkest part of the night to pass before she returned to her own bed. Those visits didn't happen much anymore, her need for sleep surpassing my need to be consoled.

At least until the day of Georgia's phone call. Like a small shift in the wind thousands of miles away that signals the start of hurricane season, that one ring of the telephone shifted the air around us. Lifted the antennae of the bees in unseen static. Maisy practically shimmered with it, and Daddy's shoulders softened as if someone had just lifted off a backpack full of rocks. I looked at him, *really* looked at him, and saw us both as we truly were: two old people carrying secrets, like a bee carries pollen back to the hive to become honey.

My Georgia was coming home. Maisy would have her ally back, even though I knew she didn't think of it that way. And the light flickered in my head, the sense that we were near the end suffocating me. I'd wake from a fitful sleep feeling that I was supposed to *do* something. That I needed to find something.

But when I opened the door to my room looking for Becky, I saw Georgia standing at the top of the stairs, the sound of Maisy's slamming door reverberating like a shout. And I saw my daughter clearly, the beautiful, damaged woman I'd created. The years away had been good for her. She had a confidence and fierce independence that were uniquely hers but would have been lost if she'd remained, and I was glad for the turmoil of that last year here. Her eyes met mine and I knew she wanted to speak to me, would expect an answer. I would have, too, but I had a flash of memory of Georgia in my closet, pulling something out. Showing it to me.

I closed my door, wanting the dark to swallow me again. Instead I watched as dawn bled through the closed curtains, a yellow finger of light pointing across the room. I approached my closet, pulled open the door, and smelled the scent of Chanel No. 5 that saturated all my clothing. I liked that, liked how everyone could recognize me by that scent. That anybody standing in my closet would know that all these beautiful clothes and shoes belonged to me. Or the me I wanted them to know.

I shut my eyes, remembering that day again: a younger Georgia looking at me with guilty eyes, knowing she'd been caught sneaking clothes from my closet. She held something in her hands, something that made the curtain in the back of my mind quiver, allowing sporadic spears of light to pierce the dark. I'd felt sick to my stomach, and I'd had to look away. I wasn't strong enough to see it, to face what it meant. And I still wasn't. Because I remembered being sent away right afterward and I couldn't survive that again. I needed to be here, with Maisy and Georgia. I'd need their help when I was ready. But not yet.

I knelt on the floor at the back of the large walk-in closet, staring at the pile of discarded shoes and handbags, belts and scarves and the accoutrements of a life that I didn't remember living. A life that always seemed to have belonged to someone else. I began to pull things out of the pile: a shoe, a vintage Keds women's sneaker, a pair of yellow patent-leather sandals, a leather purse with fringe. A ruffled half slip. I reached past an old suitcase, then slid out a wide black leather belt. A boot. When I reached my hand in again I touched the soft leather of an old suede purse, vaguely remembering hiding it a long time ago, knowing no one would look inside it if it was ever found. Pressing my palm flat I felt something hard against the suede, felt the rounded shape of the object inside. Carefully I slid the purse out from its hiding place and held it in my lap. My eyes fluttered shut, trying to block out the flickering light.

A ringing began in my ears, until I realized it wasn't ringing. It was the remembered sound of buzzing bees, of the female workers falling to the ground and writhing in their death throes of twitches and the small, ineffective flap of gossamer wings.

My hand trembled as I held the purse and the hard object inside of it, recalling the broken teacup and saucer, and bloodstains on a pink skirt. They were connected somehow, and in my fragmented mind I knew how. But I kept the answer in the dark corners, and all I knew was that I couldn't let it escape.

I crossed the room to my large chest of drawers and opened the wide bottom drawer, empty candy wrappers littering the top like bread crumbs. I pushed them aside, then lifted the old christening gown that both my daughters had worn, and placed the purse beneath it in the back corner of the drawer before sliding it closed.

I thought I heard the sound of a door downstairs closing, and I peered out the turret window toward the bay. Georgia walked down the dock with her shoulders back, her face turned toward the sun as she stopped at the end and watched as a large brown bird flew past, searching for its breakfast beneath the water.

She was so achingly beautiful. I'd been mistaken in believing that because she looked like me she would *be* like me. But the harder I tried to force her into a mold, the harder she fought. I was proud of her for that, for all the pushing against me. It had made her stronger. I wondered when she'd realize that.

Georgia turned around and headed back down the dock, her face troubled. As a baby she'd had that expression, as if even then she'd known that what she wanted was in direct opposition to what I did.

Good. I needed her to be strong. The light in my head was fanning over larger spaces, showing me the parts I'd kept hidden. I was torn between suffocating and taking deep gulps of air. I knew it wouldn't be long now, but Georgia was home. I just hoped she'd find her peace with Maisy, because they would need each other. The oncoming wave would swallow all of us, and only the strong would find their footing in the shifting sand.

I crawled back into bed and let the darkness settle over me again, praying that it would stay with me so that I wouldn't remember what I'd just done. Memories pressed against me, trying to nudge away the black. Memories of something else I'd seen in the closet that was still there, waiting to be discovered. Something that reminded me of a long-forgotten person. Of a smile. A song. I closed my eyes to get them to stop, a name I'd not uttered in years slipping from my lips.

chapter 13

"He is not worthy of the honey-comb,
That shuns the hives because the bees have stings."
William Shakespeare

—NED BLOODWORTH'S BEEKEEPER'S JOURNAL

Maisy

After a few pointless hours of trying to sleep while the morning light prodded at her eyelids, Maisy finally climbed from her bed and made her way downstairs. She paused on the threshold of the dining room, relieved to find Georgia gone. She was about to turn toward the kitchen to start the coffee when she spotted the bonnet on the ground where she'd let it fall, and suddenly the memories were there, pointed and sharp, as if there had not been years between to buffer the pain.

There are things a mother always remembers. The smell of a small, downy-covered head. The feel of skin so soft it doesn't seem real. The cry of your baby that you can recognize out of a nursery of screaming infants. Those things remain tethered to the heart long after the child is gone.

Becky wanted a sister so badly, almost as much as Maisy wanted to give her one. She'd told her daughter about Lilyanna, gone two years before Becky, who was born when Maisy was still in college, came into the world. Maisy and Lyle married young, but Maisy hadn't wanted to wait to start having children, and after two miscarriages she'd become pregnant with Lilyanna.

Becky had listened with her serious face, and then, after a brief moment, had asked whether that was all the babies Maisy was ever going to have. Maisy had lied, saying she wasn't sure, unable to tell Becky that the doctors had told Maisy she was through having babies.

The grief and blame over Lilyanna had wedged itself into her marriage, a small windshield chip that could become a wide crack with any stress. It had taken years for the crack to become a break, but by then it was too late to repair it.

Maisy picked up the bonnet and carefully folded it before tucking it way back in the china cabinet. She hadn't even made it out of the dining room when a knock sounded on the front door. She wasn't wearing makeup and still had on the boxers and T-shirt she'd slept in. She winced, thinking it might be Lyle bringing Becky back, then remembered it was Saturday and Becky would still be in bed.

Maisy threw open the door, then winced again as she saw James on the front porch. The man was entirely too good-looking, and she belatedly thought of the tube of lipstick Birdie always kept in the hall drawer.

Trying to shield herself with the door, she smiled up at him. "Good morning. If you're looking for Georgia, I'm afraid she's not here, although I guess she'll be back, because she left all of her china books."

He smiled and she saw something in his eyes she must have missed before. It wasn't a darkness, but more of an absence of light. She knew it well, saw it when she looked at Lyle and Birdie. At her own reflection. It was the look of a person who'd survived a catastrophe but was too shell-shocked to know for sure.

She opened the door wider. "You're welcome to come in and go through those catalogs while you're waiting."

"Are you sure you don't mind? I can come back."

"Please—come in. I'll even help you."

He raised his eyebrows, but she turned away to close the door.

"I've dumped most of the china books on the dining room table, although I think Georgia probably left some on the couch in the living room. Feel free to grab them and add them to the pile. I haven't had a chance to make coffee yet, but it's all there in the kitchen if you'd like to help yourself. I'm going to run upstairs and change."

When she returned, she found James standing at the dining room window, looking out at the water and the morning sun skipping beams across the surface. A cormorant stood sentry at the end of the dock, unmoving as it searched for its prey beneath the water. There'd been a time when Maisy would have grabbed her camera and photographed the bird and anything else she'd found beautiful. But that had been before the exhaustion of motherhood and work and nursing old hurts had taken hold so that all of those things she'd once fostered had tumbled out of her and rolled out of sight.

"It's beautiful here," he said, and Maisy could tell he wasn't saying it just because this was her home. "There's something about the water. . . ." His words faded away, and she wondered whether she'd imagined the catch in his voice.

"Do you get to the beach often? I know you live in the city."

He turned to her and she saw his sad eyes again, and it was her turn to watch the cormorant. "My wife's family has a house on the Massachusetts shore, and my wife and I would go there as often as work would let us. I sometimes wish we'd made it more of a priority." He shrugged. "The thing with water . . ." He paused again, and she felt him move his head so that they were both focused on the serene water of the bay. "Kate—my wife—used to say that we're all drawn to water because that's where we come from, in our mother's womb. The soft, rocking movement brings us back to when we were unconditionally loved and protected. I'm not sure I agree with her."

"Why not?"

"I imagine my sisters would laugh at my attempt at being philosophical, but I think it's because I know you're a teacher that makes me want to give you the right answer." He took a deep breath. "I've always thought my attraction to water was because it offers an unending source of renewal. It's there with each wave—with each tide. Always wiping the shore clean of all imperfections in time for the next tide."

Maisy faced him again, wanting to ask him what he felt he needed to be cleansed of, but she held back. There was a sorrow in him she was not prepared for, knowing she held enough burdens in her own boat and that one more would sink her.

Instead he spoke. "Any news about your grandfather?"

"I spoke with his doctor earlier, and I'm planning on visiting with him this afternoon. The stroke has impaired his ability to speak and walk. As soon as his doctors have him stabilized they're going to start with his rehab while he's still in the hospital. He'll need a lot of rehab, and they said it could be months or even a year until he's back to normal. But they do expect he'll be able to come home early next week. We'll convert his study into a bedroom for him, bring him to his rehab appointments, and then just hope for the best."

"How's Becky?"

Maisy looked up at James and saw the real concern in his eyes. Nobody had thought to ask her that, and it warmed her to him. "I'm worried about her. She's taking it hard—like she's already lost him. She's very sensitive—empathetic, actually. I think that could be my mother's influence—all that drama is bound to affect a child somehow."

"I don't think that's a bad thing. My oldest sister is like that. It took me years to realize that she sees more than most people. I just wish I'd paid attention."

His tone had almost sounded like a warning. Maisy turned away from the window. "Let me call Aunt Marlene's and see if I can get hold of Georgia and tell her you're waiting." She patted her jeans, looking for her cell phone, realizing she must have left it upstairs.

James was looking at her with narrowed eyes. "Why doesn't Georgia carry a cell phone? You said that I should ask you sometime."

Maisy paused, debating.

"Do you want to tell him or should I?"

They both looked up in surprise as Georgia strode into the room, then slammed down another stack of books on the table before staring back at her sister expectantly.

Without waiting for an answer, Georgia said, "I hate phones of any kind—because they're intrusions into my life, annoying interruptions while I'm doing something I'd rather be doing than talking on the phone. When I lived here I wasn't really good about phoning in to let Grandpa know where I was—mostly because it was usually where I wasn't supposed to be or with someone I shouldn't have been with. I guess that reluctance to pick up the phone, and probably not a little bit of guilt, has carried over into my adult life. I have to use a phone for work, but I do so only reluctantly."

James's face was without expression as he regarded Georgia. "When I was a teenager I used to throw eggs out of our fourth-story window to splatter pedestrians. I got away with it for a long time, until someone called the police, and I cowered under my bed while my older sister answered the door and calmly told them that she was alone and that she'd keep an eye out. I had to make her bed and do her math homework for a month so she wouldn't tell our father."

Maisy crossed her arms over her chest. "I think Georgia's story is worse."

James settled himself into one of the dining room chairs. "I wasn't telling you that story to determine who was a more horrible teenager. I was telling you so that you'd know I understand siblings. There's nobody you can love and hate so much all at the same time."

Maisy met Georgia's gaze and her cheeks warmed; she felt as if she'd just been caught bullying her sister on the playground. She busied herself by removing the candlesticks and fruit bowl from the center of the table and shoving the books toward the middle to make them reachable from all chairs. She sat down across from James and looked at her sister expectantly. "So, let's get on with this. The sooner we start, the sooner we'll be done."

Without a word, Georgia sat down at the head of the table

between James and Maisy and slid a book in front of each of them. Then she placed the broken saucer in front of her. She'd used duct tape to temporarily keep the pieces together, and Maisy gave an involuntary wince, remembering when it had broken, remembering how the sound of anything breaking had upset Georgia even as a child. It had seemed, even then, that Georgia blamed herself for things beyond her control that would make a teacup slide off a saucer, or a door slam against a wall. Or a father putting a gun to his head because he couldn't live without her mother.

Maisy looked down at the book that had been placed in front of her, trying to push away those unwelcome thoughts or anything that would make her soften toward Georgia, would make her forget Georgia taking the blame for one final transgression. Maisy read the title of the book out loud. "*Two Hundred Patterns of Haviland China, Book III*, by Arlene Schleiger. Sounds fascinating."

"It is, actually," Georgia said, somehow managing not to sound too pompous. "James has already heard all this, so bear with me," she said, nodding at James. "The Havilands were Americans who built china factories in the Limoges area of France because of the fine white kaolin clay, which was used to make brilliant, durable white porcelain, and the family became hugely successful. They even designed a custom pattern for Lincoln's White House. Haviland Limoges is still pretty popular today, and appears on lots of bridal registries."

She smiled with enthusiasm, and Maisy could picture her in front of a group of collectors or investors listening with rapt attention. She felt an unexpected rush of pride, almost as if she were proud of *herself*. Just like it had once been when every hurt, every joy, had been felt equally. Each poison-tipped arrow killing a part of each of them.

Georgia continued. "It's fascinating because most consumers associate Haviland Limoges with being a French thing, and it's not. It really got interesting as the success of the company grew in the eighteen hundreds and prompted other family members to open up factories in direct competition. Gives a whole new meaning to 'sibling rivalry,' doesn't it?"

Maisy sighed. "There are a lot of books here, and I have to be back at work on Monday. Can you just tell us what we should be looking for?"

"Yes, of course." Georgia cleared her throat. "Yesterday I had James looking for the actual pattern in these catalogs, and I'm going to have him continue doing that. But you're going to search in a different place. I'm pretty sure I've identified the blank—that's the shape of the plates. I believe it's blank eleven produced by Haviland and Co. in the second half of the eighteen hundreds. Once we're one hundred percent sure that's it, we'll know the approximate time period, which narrows down the number of patterns we have to search through."

"Thank heavens for small mercies," Maisy said under her breath. She looked up to find both Georgia and James staring at her, making her feel small and petty. Which she knew she was being at the moment. There was just something in Georgia's competence and expertise that bothered Maisy. As if Georgia should have spent the past ten years wearing a horsehair shirt and shaving her head instead of finding herself in a career to which she was not only well suited, but in which she was also admired and respected. She heard her old teenage whine of *It's not fair!* echoing in her head, and she cringed involuntarily.

"Sorry. It's just that I need to pick up Becky from her tennis lesson at eleven, and then we're going to go see Grandpa."

"Can I pick her up?" Georgia asked, her words spoken quickly, as if her heart had told her to speak them before her mind could stop her.

"No." Maisy met her sister's eyes, as if to ask, *Remember?* "That's not a good idea." She felt James glancing between her and Georgia as if he could possibly make sense of it.

"Fine." Georgia reached over and flipped open the cover of the book in front of Maisy. "This is volume three—I've already gone through the first two. You want to focus on the blanks—show me any that you think match the saucer shape—since there's always a chance I'm wrong and we'll have to look at patterns in another blank. We'll be focusing on the shape first, but if you happen to see any patterns with bees at all, let me know. They're very rare for twentieth-century

Limoges porcelain, so that would be ideal if we spotted the pattern. Just know that won't necessarily be the china we're looking for, since the same patterns were used on different blanks. And with gold rims or without."

Maisy examined the black-and-white page of half-moon sketches of plates in front of her. "So I just need to go through each page and see if I recognize the shape from the saucer. Or bees. That's easy enough. I should be able to get through all of these little books in plenty of time to get Becky."

"You think so?" Georgia asked in the same petulant tone of voice Maisy had used as she opened up the thick, hardbound book she'd set in front of James and opened it to a premarked page before giving him his instructions.

Maisy caught James's expression. He was smiling, *definitely* smiling. Irritated, she asked, "Do you find something funny?"

He didn't even bother to hide his smile. "Not funny. More reassuring, I guess." His phone buzzed and he quieted it without even looking. "I feel like I'm at home when I listen to the two of you. Except my sisters are a little bit louder."

"Stick around long enough and I bet you'd change your mind about that."

His expression sobered. "Good. I've learned that you shouldn't hold back what you really want to say. You might not get a second chance."

Both she and Georgia were saved from responding by a shout from Birdie upstairs. Maisy was halfway out of her chair when Georgia touched her shoulder. "Let me go. She's my mother, too."

Maisy wanted to argue, but could feel only relief. And also a sense of justice—at least while Georgia was home she could pay her dues.

"All right. She's probably just had a nightmare—she has one at least once a week. Just hold her hand. I think she's replaying some theatrical production she was once a part of—never changes. It's always some dramatic farewell scene where she's being forced to leave against her will. She'll eventually fall asleep, but you might convince her to come down and eat instead. She hasn't had breakfast."

Georgia nodded, then headed up the stairs.

Maisy and James studied the pages in front of them, the sound of Birdie's shouts and moans a distracting backdrop. "She wasn't always like this," Maisy said, needing to offer an explanation. Something about his warm eyes and his recent loss made him an easy target for unsolicited confessions. Like the statues of saints she'd seen in Italy on her honeymoon, their stone faces eroded by centuries of weather and unanswerable prayers.

"When did she change?" he asked.

Maisy thought for a moment, the sketches of dishes swimming in front of her eyes. "Birdie has always been . . . different. Not like our friends' mothers, anyway. Georgia used to say she fell into motherhood like some people slip off a curb and into a mud puddle—except she couldn't figure out how she got there or how to get it off of her."

She paused, wondering if he would stop her. "Aunt Marlene said Birdie as a girl was hard to get to know because it was like she was always pretending to be somebody else. Like she was acting in a play. It was just accepted that Birdie was different, which was why Grandma sent her to a performing arts school in Jacksonville—where different was probably a good thing."

Maisy raised her hand to her mouth to chew on a fingernail, but withdrew it as soon as she realized what she was trying to do. "I don't know if Georgia's told you, but Birdie's spent time in and out of mental institutions for brief periods of her life. I think the first time was right after she started dating Georgia's daddy. Marlene said she wasn't sure what instigated such a drastic measure, but said it had been a long time coming."

"And the last time?"

Maisy met his eyes. "The summer Georgia left. A lot was going on then, and sometimes I wonder if, had I been paying attention, I would have known when she'd reached her breaking point. But . . ." She stopped, not wanting to share any more, but needing to say it out loud. It had been so long that she'd begun to imagine that it had never happened.

"I'd just lost a child, you see. A little girl. And my marriage . . .

well, you can imagine how that might have affected a couple. Georgia was doing absolutely nothing productive with her life, working in a bar downtown. And then Birdie decided that the house needed redecorating because some big Hollywood people were supposedly coming to film a movie here, and she thought one of the stars or director would want to stay in our house."

He didn't flinch or roll his eyes or return his gaze to the catalog, and Maisy took it as a sign that she should continue. "She met with a decorator who came from Tallahassee, who told Birdie that before spending money on new furniture and accessories, she should go through all the closets and attic to see if there were any antique pieces they could feature in the redo. She only made it halfway through the attic. Grandpa found her in a catatonic state on the attic floor. Georgia and I took care of her for a few months until Grandpa decided she needed to go away again to get help. Birdie hasn't spoken a word since—just sings."

"So she doesn't speak to anybody?"

"Becky seems to think Birdie talks to her, but that's just wishful thinking. In the beginning it was like Birdie had forgotten how to speak English, but then she started to sing, which was a huge relief. So we know she's in there somewhere, and can understand us. She just chooses not to communicate with us."

He didn't say anything for a long moment. "That's why you and Georgia were so close. Because of Birdie. Nobody else could understand what it was like being her daughter."

"Why would you think we were close? We're certainly not now."

"Because no one can hurt us as much as those we love the most."

Maisy opened her mouth to tell him that she hated her sister, but her lips were unable to form the words.

"Maisy? Can you come up here, please?" Georgia's voice came from upstairs, seemingly calm, but Maisy recognized a note of panic.

Maisy stood, holding her palm out to James to discourage him from coming with her. "I'm sure it's fine. Just stay here and we'll be back soon." She ran up the rest of the stairs and straight into Birdie's bedroom. She almost had to double-check that she'd entered the right room. Instead of the usually neat and orderly space, clothes, shoes, and accessories were strewn haphazardly all over the floor and unmade bed, as if someone had left a window open in a strong wind.

"Georgia?"

"We're in the closet."

Maisy followed her sister's voice toward the open closet doors, where more clothing items were stacked in uneven piles. It almost seemed that whoever had made the mess had started off with a plan, and had begun emptying the closet item by item until rationality had disappeared and a frantic search had taken over.

Birdie, still in her nightgown, knelt by the corner of the closet swaying back and forth, her mouth open in silent agony. Georgia knelt next to her, her hand on Birdie's arm. She didn't seem panicked or confused about her role, and Maisy felt an odd jab of anger mixed with admiration.

"She was here when I found her," Georgia said. "I think this is what's got her upset."

She reached behind her and pulled out an old leather suitcase, something a person would expect to see in a vintage shop. "It was open, but empty. It's pretty dusty, so I think it's been here for a while. I think I even remember seeing it in here before, tucked in the corner. And the soup cup isn't here anymore, either. I looked."

"I know," Maisy said, irritated. "I told you we already looked in here. We even opened the suitcase. Although we definitely closed it and put it back in the corner when we were done." Maisy sat back on her heels and looked closely at their mother, wishing that Becky really could communicate with her grandmother. A light, almost airless sound came from Birdie's lips as a vaguely familiar tune filled the air.

"What is that?" Georgia asked.

Maisy closed her eyes and listened. "It's a children's song—the alphabet song. But it's a little different, like she's thinking of different words and changing the tune to make them fit."

"Should we call her doctor?"

Maisy shook her head. "She's been like this before. Usually she goes to sleep, and when she wakes up she's forgotten all about it. I'll call her doctor if she doesn't." She stood. "Come on; help me get her back into bed."

They took her gently by her elbows, the strange, familiar-yet-not song teasing her ears. Like a docile child, Birdie allowed them to tuck her under the covers.

"Do you have something to give her? Something to calm her?"

"Of course," Maisy said, her irritation returning. "We have a drawer full of prescription meds, but she refuses to take them."

Birdie curled up on her side, her eyes finally closing as the last notes of the melody faded.

They watched her for a moment and then Georgia spoke. "Have you ever heard the name Adeline before?"

"No, why?"

"I think she said it. When we were in the closet."

"She spoke to you?"

"Not exactly," Georgia said, her eyebrows knitted. "It was more like a moan, but the name seemed so clear." She looked Maisy in the eye. "What are we going to do, Maisy?"

Maisy met her sister's gaze and raised her chin. "What we've been doing. We'll continue as we have been, and you'll go back to New Orleans and your work. There's no reason things have to change."

"There's something we're missing, something important. I think it's something about that suitcase."

Maisy shook her head. "It's all about something in the past that we can't change. All we can do is move forward. She's made her choices."

Birdie's breathing held the smooth rhythm of sleep. Georgia stepped closer and hissed in Maisy's ear, "But what if whatever it was that made her this way wasn't her choice? She's our mother, Maisy. For better or worse. If there's some key to unlocking what's wrong with her, shouldn't we do our best to find it? We used to be a team, remember?"

Maisy turned and headed out of the room, shaking her head. She heard Georgia following her and then the soft snap as she closed Birdie's bedroom door. "I already agreed to help you with finding James's china and searching for any matching pieces we might have here. But never make the mistake of thinking of us as a team. You gave up that right a long time ago." She took a step, then paused. "And don't ever ask me if you can pick up Becky or spend time alone with her. The answer will always be no, and you know why."

She headed down the stairs and back to the dining room, still hearing in her head the tune her mother had been humming. It wasn't the alphabet song, not exactly. But she knew she'd heard the version her mother had hummed somewhere before, a long time ago. The answer would come to her eventually. It always did.

She smiled at James as she resumed her seat and bent over the book in front of her, even more determined than before to identify the pattern so everything could return to normal. But as she stared at the pages she kept hearing Birdie's tune playing over and over in her head, except now she imagined it was accompanied by the droning of bees.

chapter 14

*"The bee is more honored than other animals, not because she labors,
but because she labors for others."*
Saint John Chrysostom

—NED BLOODWORTH'S BEEKEEPER'S JOURNAL

Georgia

I leaned my head against the rocking chair on the back porch and held
my breath as I began to count the birds I could spot flitting over the
calm waters of the bay or lingering closer to the shore. It was another
silly game from my childhood, one in which I wouldn't allow myself to
catch another breath until I'd reached the count of ten. I'd often wondered why I'd felt the need to create these little personal entertainments,
or why I continued to do them. Maybe I'd never quite grown out of the
childish need to create order and routine in a scattered, unorganized life.

"What are you doing?" James asked.

I uncrossed my legs and placed my feet flat on the ground, stopping the chair. I realized my cheeks were puffed out and that I'd been
holding my breath for so long I was getting light-headed.

My cheeks flushed. "Just thinking to myself."

He regarded me calmly, his eyes never wavering, but I saw the corner of his mouth tilt up; he was probably too tired to laugh out loud.

We'd been poring over the catalogs and the Internet—thanks to his laptop—for the past week, and I'd made dozens of phone calls to my contacts in the country and all over the world. Nobody had seen a pattern like ours, or anything vaguely similar. I'd been given more leads on where I should look or what it could be, but I was beginning to feel a lot like Alice chasing the elusive rabbit down a hole that apparently had no bottom.

The sound of an approaching motorcycle slowing and then stopping had me on my feet and walking down the porch steps by the time Aunt Marlene appeared from around the corner of the house.

"You come in so late and leave so early that I figured if I wanted to spend any time with you, I'd better come find you here." Her hair was windblown from riding without a helmet, and she wore boots with her shorts instead of flip-flops, in deference to her mode of transportation. "I figured I'd see you at home, but you leave before the sun comes up and come back long after the dogs and me are snoring. Best way to visit was to come over here and risk running into Birdie."

James stood as Marlene approached. "It's good to see you again, Ms. Chambers."

Marlene glanced at me and raised her eyebrows as if to say, *Now, that's a gentleman*, then turned back to James. "Please sit down. And it's Marlene. Nobody's called me anything else for such a long time that I don't think I even know who Ms. Chambers is anymore."

He indicated his chair for her to sit, but she waved her hand, then perched herself on the top step. "How's your granddaddy?"

"He's getting better, and he won't need surgery. The doctors say it could have been much worse—we're so thankful that Lyle was close by to get him to the hospital as fast as he did. He still can't talk or walk very well, but rehab will help."

With help from Lyle and James, we'd moved Grandpa into the newly set-up bedroom in his study downstairs surrounded by my grandmother's watercolors. It was almost as if the painted flowers and honeybees had brought his beloved apiary inside, the silent bees keeping vigil.

"How's his mind?" she asked bluntly.

"It's still hard to tell, because he's not speaking yet, but the doctors say his brain function is good. We're taking him to a rehab center several times a week, and then working with him at home. I think he's frustrated by the lack of communication—I feel like he wants to ask me something. But he can't write yet, either—his right side is the one affected by the stroke.

"We know depression can set in, so we make sure someone's with him all the time. Birdie keeps him company a lot, but it's my job to get him up and to walk him around the living room a few times a day while Maisy is at work."

Marlene nodded. "I'm sure Maisy's happy to have the help."

I coughed and James looked away.

Taking a hint and changing the subject, Marlene said, "I saw Florence Love yesterday, and she said she'll be here tonight right before dark to close up the hives so she can pick them up first thing in the morning and take them to the swamp. That's real nice of her."

I nodded. "I'd love to help, but I don't think she'll want my interference. It's been so long that I barely remember all that's involved. I do remember that the most important thing is to make sure the queen stays with the brood frame on the bottom and isn't somehow left behind."

James leaned forward, seeming to be genuinely interested. "So the queen calls the shots."

I smiled, remembering having the same discussion with my grandfather. "It's a chicken-and-the-egg sort of thing. The queen can't survive without her worker bees to feed her and to take care of all the baby bees and the hive. But the worker bees can't survive without her eggs, either. They each have their purpose, their own reasons for being. They know their roles and behave accordingly. Otherwise the order of things would be in total chaos and the entire hive would die."

A corner of his mouth lifted. "So it's a matriarchal society. That means the worker bees probably ask for directions when they're lost and that's how they all find their way back to the hive at night."

I grinned. "Yes and yes. They do a sort of dance to tell the other worker bees where good sources of food can be found, and the girl bees do all the work around the hive. The male drone's job is solely to mate with the queen—which she does with several at a time."

"Lucky them." James was grinning now, too.

"Not really. The drone's penis breaks during intercourse and he drops dead."

"But what a way to go," Marlene interjected with a smirk.

James let out a genuine laugh, and I realized that he didn't laugh often. I wondered whether it had been different before his wife's death.

"Will Florence let us help if we promise not to get in the way?" he asked.

It was my turn to raise eyebrows. "Are you interested in becoming a beekeeper? The world needs more, you know. Bees are dying off, and if Grandpa and Florence had their way, there would be a law making it illegal not to have a hive in your backyard."

"Who knows? I'm pretty much open for suggestions right now. And I kind of like bees."

"I'm sure Florence will let you watch, but I think she'd prefer to do it on her own—she has a system. Besides, you don't have to, you know. I don't think it's in your job description. You've already been such a help with Grandpa."

He shrugged. "I don't mind. I'm actually enjoying myself. I never imagined I'd ever be in a place like Apalachicola." His phone buzzed and he turned if off without even glancing at it. "And learning about the sex lives of bees, among other things."

Marlene gave me a knowing smile and I immediately sent her a sharp shake of the head. *No. Don't even go there.*

I recalled something I'd been meaning to ask her. "Have you ever known somebody named Adeline?"

Her brows knitted together as she thought for a moment. Shaking her head, she said, "No, I don't think so. Not in this town, anyway, and I pretty much know everybody who's lived here for the last sixty years or so. Why?"

"I thought Birdie said the name when she was having one of her spells. I'm curious who it could be."

Marlene looked up at me with sympathetic eyes. "It's probably a character she once played, that's all." As if to change the subject, she twisted around to face James. "Has Georgie taken you to Up the Creek Raw Bar for the best oysters in the world? Or to the Old Time Soda Fountain for a chocolate soda?"

James sat back in his chair. "Not yet—we've been pretty busy. Although I did buy a beautiful painting of the river at the Robert Lindsley Gallery on E Street. I thought that would make a nice memento of my visit. But I should eat some oysters while I'm here. Apalachicola is the oyster capital of the world, right?"

I nudged his foot with mine, knowing he'd read that on the welcome sign as we'd driven into town. Marlene threw her head back and laughed, her smoker's voice like sandpaper against stone.

"You got that right. Most of the restaurants around here brag that their oysters were in the bay yesterday and on your table today. Don't get any fresher than that." She jerked her chin in my direction. "Georgia's daddy—my brother—was an oysterman, just like our daddy and granddaddy. Had his own skiff handmade right here in Apalach from marine plywood—lasted for three generations and would have lasted longer." She was silent for a moment watching a pair of oystercatchers swooping and hollering in flight as they searched for dinner. "Mama sold it after he died—couldn't stand the sight of it."

Marlene leaned against the porch railing. "Did Georgia tell you she's named after her daddy? His name was George. George the third, to be exact. We called him Trey when he was younger—that means three in French, in case you didn't know, but with an 's' at the end instead of a 'y'—because there were already too many Georges in the family and it got confusing. But when our granddaddy died, he wanted to be called George to honor him, so we did."

James began to tentatively rock back and forth in his chair, as if he were unfamiliar with the movement or even sitting still for long periods of time. His phone lay quiet on the floor beside him, and I wondered whether he'd turned it off. "And then he had a daughter, so he figured he should pass on the name to her."

Marlene barked out a laugh. "Nope. It was Birdie's idea. She said it was because it was a family name, but I always thought that she gave it to Georgia because it was the only part of her husband she was willing to share."

"Aunt Marlene, don't . . ." I began. I glanced at James and his eyes were calm, as if to remind me that he was just a stranger on a plane.

"Sorry, sweetie. You know I have a lot of grievances against your mama, and sometimes things just pop out of my mouth like a bullfrog's tongue snatching a fly. I have to remind myself that she has reasons for being the way she is. And I get that; I do. But it's hard to forgive a mother who doesn't cherish her daughters the way they deserve to be."

She wasn't saying anything that I hadn't thought myself over the years. I just didn't like them being said out loud, even with Maisy. Birdie was still our mother, the soft-skinned, perfumed presence in our childhoods, the warm fingers on our temples as we drifted to sleep. The remembered tunes sung softly in the dark. It was as if as children we had known Birdie's indifference hadn't been intentional any more than you can blame a bee for stinging in self-defense. Maybe even then we recognized that she was as lost as we were, trying to navigate an unfamiliar world. To us, Birdie was a ghost we could feel but not see, an unexplained force in our lives we'd stumble into head-on, the resulting bruise the only evidence she'd been there at all.

I took a deep breath. "Daddy died when I was three. I hardly remember him—except when I'm walking along the marina and the scent of fish is so strong there. But I do remember that Birdie wouldn't let him near her after he'd been out on the boat, but he'd swing me up in his arms and hug me, because I didn't mind. Even today I can't be offended by the smell of fish."

James rested his elbows on the armrests of his chair, steepling his fingers, a slight grin lighting his face. "I've walked around town and been down to the marina several times. I think it's a gift if you can find the scent in the air there a pleasant one."

Marlene threw her head back again and cackled while I smiled at James in appreciation. Maybe it was being raised with so many sisters that had taught him the perfect timing of when to lighten the mood by saying the right thing.

"There's that," Marlene said. "Birdie loved George something fierce, I will give her that. And he loved her back. It was a wild kind of love, though. You know how they say there's a thin line between love and hate? I think they crossed it too many times. It seemed to me that they each desperately needed something from the other that neither was prepared to give. It was hard to watch." She paused, looking out over the bay, seemingly unaware of the screaming gulls overhead. "I've never seen two people more bent on self-destruction than they were. Poor George. I don't think he ever recovered from watching our daddy drown. Their boat got stuck in a storm they never should have been out in. I think George always blamed himself, because he was the one who said they should stay out a little longer before they headed home. Always looking for the next big catch. I guess that can be a heavy burden to carry."

We sat in silence as James continued to rock. I was about to suggest getting a few beers, but Marlene spoke again.

"But, Birdie." Marlene shrugged. "I gave up trying to figure her out. Her mama sent her to that performing arts school, so we didn't see much of her except summertime. I remember the first time I saw her and I knew there was something not right about her, like half of her was missing, and the other half was doing something much more interesting. Poor George. He was so smitten you could have punched him in the stomach and he wouldn't have noticed."

A door slammed somewhere inside the house and I realized it was time for Maisy and Becky to get home from school. Marlene straightened her shoulders just as I was doing the same thing, and I wondered whether Maisy had that effect on everybody. "It's kind of funny," Marlene said. "This talk about china. It reminds me of something George once told me."

"Really?" I asked. "What did he say?"

"That when they got married Birdie refused to pick out china—said she hated it and would rather eat off of paper plates. I said it was probably on account of your grandma being such a junker—she was never one to turn away from a garage sale or Dumpster—and her owning about a thousand different plates in all kinds of patterns. When I said that he got a funny look on his face and told me that wasn't it, but he wouldn't tell me what it was. So as a wedding present I bought them some cheap no-brand white china on sale at Penneys and that's what they ate off of their whole married lives."

I remembered seeing some of it in the china cabinet as Maisy and I sorted through it, easily placing it in the discard pile. I wondered now whether I should pull a piece or two out just to save, or see if Birdie wanted to keep it. I doubted it. As with most of her marriage, there wasn't a lot she'd hung on to.

Before I could ask her more, the back door flew open and Becky ran out onto the porch full of youth and energy and shining blond hair. I didn't look to see whether everybody else was holding their breath, too, watching this magnificent creature.

Her tennis racket clanked to the ground as she reached for my arm. I watched as she focused on getting her breath under control, to school her tongue and command the words to leave her mouth without stuttering. I'd begun to smile to encourage her, but it slipped as I had a premonition of what she was about to ask.

"Come on, Aunt Georgia. Let's go swimming! My friend Brittany has a pool and she said we could go over this afternoon."

I was shaking my head before I even realized why. "I don't have a bathing suit."

"I don't remember that ever stopping you before."

We all turned around to find Maisy in the open doorway, her arms crossed over her chest like an avenging angel. The shrieks of the seagulls and the quiet chirping of crickets were the only sounds for a long, excruciating moment. I tried to remember that I was ten years older now and no longer prone to hurt feelings or direct emotional jabs. But the thing with siblings was that no matter how old we got, our relationship remained tied to the twin beds of a shared childhood bedroom and the after-dark confidences and morning taunts.

"I guess I could borrow one of your suits, but it would be way too big." I wanted to call the words back as soon as they were out of my mouth, but, as with most good intentions, it was too late.

Silently Becky dropped my hand and moved to Maisy's side like a pawn on a chessboard protecting her queen.

Maisy put an arm around her daughter and they looked at me with accusing eyes, which only added to my shame and embarrassment.

James stood and stretched, then smiled at the grim faces around him as if he had somehow missed the last exchange. "I was hoping somebody might mention a swim. I didn't bring a swimsuit, either, but there are some great shops downtown where I'm sure I can find something. I'll bring Georgia along with me so she can shop for one, too."

Becky looked shyly up at him, her cheeks pink. "Y-you can swim? I thought you lived in the city."

I saw the sadness seep into his eyes again, like moss on a still pond. "I can swim. But I'll wear water wings if that'll make you feel better."

Becky laughed out loud, and there seemed to be a collective sigh of relief. It was then that I decided to stop regretting my decision to bring James Graf on this trip. I could only hope that he was thinking the same thing.

We heard a car door slam, and after a moment we all turned toward the corner of the house to see Florence Love, the beekeeper, walking toward us. She waved. "I knew I'd find y'all back here on such a pretty day. Why aren't y'all swimming?"

Before we could start that conversation again, I hastily stood and made introductions. James grinned as he took in Florence's swinging silver earrings in the shape of bees and her T-shirt graphic of a bee with "Show me the honey" written on the front. Her shiny dark brown hair, cut short and wavy, poked out from under a wide-brimmed straw hat, and her eyes were the same pale blue as my grandfather's. I knew she was around Marlene's age, but she looked about twenty years younger, most likely due to the hats she never stepped outside without. She certainly hadn't aged a day since I'd last seen her.

"I brought my screen wire to close up the hives, and also a catch hive for any stragglers who come back after I've sealed their home. But thought I'd like to speak with Ned first, if he's up to it. I know he can't talk, but I'm pretty good at talking for both of us."

"I just checked on him," said Maisy. "He's awake and sitting up in the bed watching reruns of *The Andy Griffith Show*. I know he'd love to see you."

Florence flashed a warm smile with bright white, even teeth, then held up an amber-colored jar. "I brought some of my tupelo honey from last year as a surprise. He said he'd been out of his own for a couple of months, and this should make him feel much better. Just needs a hot biscuit to put it on."

"I can take care of that," I said, feeling Maisy's eyes boring into me as if she'd cornered the market on making our grandmother's buttermilk biscuits. I hadn't made them for years, but I was pretty sure the recipe was engraved somewhere in my brain.

We left James, Becky, and Marlene outside chatting about lawn art while Maisy, Florence, and I went inside. We filed into the study, now made much smaller with the hospital bed and nightstand squeezed in between piles of books and the large desk that wouldn't fit anywhere else in the house. My grandmother's watercolors on the wall shimmered in the early-evening light that leaked through the windows, a large honeybee caught in flight circling a sunflower that appeared three-dimensional. I imagined I could almost hear the bee's buzz.

Grandpa was sitting up in bed, Birdie beside him, the TV loud and jarring. Maisy found the remote control and muted it while I turned toward the figure in the bed. He was still gaunt, his face as gray as his hair, his pale eyes holding a new wariness I didn't remember seeing before.

Birdie looked up at us when we entered, her gaze resting on me. She held something in her hands, and when I glanced down I saw it was a broken shard from the teacup that I'd left on the dining room table along with the Limoges catalogs and duct-taped saucer. I remembered the deep cut and the blood spots on her skirt, and I wanted to take it away from her. But she seemed to be aware of it in her hands, holding it delicately between her forefinger and thumb as if she knew it could hurt her.

I kissed my grandfather on his cheek and sat down gingerly on the side of the bed. "How are you doing? It's good to see you sitting up."

He smiled, his lips quickly falling, as if the effort had been too much for him. He looked up, his eyes brightening at the sight of Florence. He'd been her mentor when she'd first started keeping bees and they had become good friends. Her children, now all grown, called him Grandpa.

Since Birdie was on the other side of the bed, Florence stayed at the foot, beaming down at him. "Well, you gave us a fright, Ned. If you needed a vacation you could have just said something instead of going through all this trouble."

A rough chuckle grumbled in his throat as he nodded.

"I've come to seal up your hives tonight—I'm waiting until it's almost dark to make sure all the bees are in there. And I've brought sugar water for your bees, since I'll be taking their honey frames out before I move 'em—don't want anything mixing with our pure tupelo honey, do we?"

Grandpa shook his head slowly.

"I'll leave the party girls in the last two boxes," she said, referring to the two aggressive hives that sat in the back of the apiary. Grandpa had learned early on that each hive had a different temperament, and it served every beekeeper well to figure that out.

He nodded somberly.

"It's been raining so much, we're thinking we'll have a smaller harvest than usual. I'll probably only take about four of your hives. And we're going to have to drag the rafts to higher ground, too—everything else is flooded. You remember where old Mr. King's still is? Nobody has used that part of the swamp for their hives since the end of Prohibition because it's a little far from the tupelo trees, but I don't think we have much of a choice at this point."

We were all looking at Florence so that at first we didn't notice that something was wrong. It wasn't until Birdie shouted that we turned around to find Grandpa desperately trying to get out of bed, his face completely bloodless, his mouth open as if he wanted to shout or tell us something.

I reached for the phone to call 911 while Birdie, without being asked, placed both hands on his shoulders and pressed him against his pillow. As the phone rang, I turned to my sister. "Maisy, call Lyle and bring him here. We might need him again."

She ran from the room to get her phone as I spoke to the operator. It was only after I'd hung up that I noticed Birdie was holding Grandpa's hand, the broken saucer clutched between them, and that she'd begun to hum, calming him down.

Maisy rushed back into the room and our eyes met without acrimony. "He'll be fine," I said, although I wasn't sure at all. I just wanted her to believe it. "He's calmer now."

She nodded, then shifted her attention to Birdie and their clasped hands as Birdie continued to hum. Maisy turned to me, her eyes narrowed. "That song. It's that song again. What *is* it?"

It was the same song Birdie had hummed as Maisy and I had put her to bed the previous night, the notes vaguely familiar.

The paramedics and Lyle arrived at the same time. It was agreed that Grandpa should go back to the hospital for observation. We stood by the ambulance while they loaded him in, Maisy and I planning on following in my car. He seemed to be looking for someone, and when he caught sight of Florence he began to thrash his arms.

"It'll be all right, Ned. I promise to take good care of your bees."

The EMTs slid him inside the ambulance, his expression alarming not because of the bloodless pallor of his skin, but because of the look in his eyes that held not fear or regret, but seemed more like resignation. His gaze met mine right before the paramedics closed the door, his mouth forming a single word. I stood staring at the departing ambulance for a long moment until I realized the word had been "no."

chapter 15

*If the bees catch you while harvesting their honey, your first instinct
will be to run. Don't. They can fly much faster than you can run
and it will only make them angrier. And then you'll never get what
you were after in the first place. Besides, what are a few stings when
the prize is so dear?*

—NED BLOODWORTH'S BEEKEEPER'S JOURNAL

Maisy

O n her short drive home from work across the Gorrie Bridge,
which crossed the bay between Apalachicola and Eastpoint,
Maisy was reminded once again why she'd never moved away despite
all the reasons she should have. Even now, she still loved the water and
tin roofs, the sun-faded paint on doors, the wet air and the sweet smell
of salt that permeated her car when it was cool enough to lower the
windows and switch off the A/C.

She loved the way people in Apalach talked, too, their words as
slow and thick as poured honey. Growing up, she hadn't realized that
everybody didn't talk that way, but her years at the University of Florida in Gainesville had taught her that the dialect was different along the
panhandle. And that she loved it best. It was as if the briny water filled
her veins, the white snowlike sand settling in her heart like ballast.

But what she loved most about this place was the light. The way everything glowed white and bright and blue. Apalachicola Bay shimmered with it, blessing everything around it like a benediction.

Even after all that had happened, her little town tucked under the protective arms of the ancient oak trees was still the place she dreamed of at night. Maybe that was what had hurt the most when Georgia left. It had seemed like the worst kind of betrayal, turning her back on all that Maisy cherished the most. She tried not to think how she'd been the one to tell Georgia to leave. Some part of her must have wanted her sister to fight back, to beg for forgiveness and do her penance where Maisy could witness it. She should have known that Georgia, even when beaten, was too strong willed for that. It was what she hated most about her sister. And it was what she loved the most, too.

Because Brittany Banyon's mother was bringing the girls home from school, she found herself driving a different way than usual, and it was only when she'd paused outside the cemetery's gate that she realized where she'd been headed. Pulling up onto the grass, she put the car in park, waiting almost an entire minute before turning off the ignition.

A small white dog without a collar trotted across the street and then headed down alongside the cemetery fence. She'd been stopped many times by visitors asking her whether she knew where a particular stray dog belonged. It took some convincing, but she always managed to reassure them that Apalachicola was a dog-friendly town and didn't worry too much about leashes or collars. It was another thing she liked about her hometown. It was the kind of place where all living creatures always seemed to find their way home.

She opened her door and stepped out of the car, not really sure what she was doing. She stared past the rusted ornamental fencing, beautiful in its ruin. The old cemetery was almost like a synopsis of hundreds of years of the town's history. Nestled under the stately oaks and their floating manes of moss lay the town's founders as well as Confederate soldiers, and victims of yellow fever and shipwrecks. And in a small patch at the rear of the cemetery, beneath a slender cabbage palm, her eighteen-month-old daughter, Lilyanna Joy.

Maisy came to the cemetery on her daughter's birthday and at Christmas, but never any other time. The grief had become like an untreatable infection, festering beneath a bandage. Visiting Lilyanna's grave always teased at the dressing, threatening to lift it and expose the ugly wound beneath.

Letting her feet lead her, she crossed over the sparse grass and dried leaves, feeling cool in the cocoon of the matronly trees, their branches outstretched like angels' wings. The cemetery was empty except for the ancient tombstones of marble and stone, some of the carved words completely faded. She stopped in front of a small granite angel, the only words carved in the base her child's name and birth and death dates. Georgia had thought there should be an inscription, but at the time Maisy had believed there were no words that could adequately express her grief. Her opinion had never changed.

She stared at the dates, mentally calculating how old she'd be—eleven—and what she'd look like. Lilyanna had been dark haired and gray eyed like her mother, a miniature, improved model. Although Maisy loved Becky with all her heart, there was something about a child who looked like you. Like the world had given you another chance to be the best version of yourself.

The crunching of dried leaves startled her, making her turn around. Lyle was walking toward her, his pace tentative. He stopped about five feet in front of her, his eyes avoiding the small angel crouched at their feet.

"I saw your car," he said.

"I haven't been here since Christmas." Not that he'd asked for an explanation. Not that she owed him one.

"I have," he said quietly. "When it's slow and I'm passing by, I like to stop and check in on her. Make sure nobody's left a beer bottle or something." He paused. "I miss her, too."

She looked away, remembering them as teenagers and how they'd figured that the cemetery was a good place to go at night, out of sight of prying eyes. He'd never told her that he visited the grave on a regular basis. Or that he missed Lilyanna. Maybe that was one of the things that had gone wrong in their marriage—their inability to talk about subjects that were so raw. But something warm and sweet coursed through her veins as she thought about him here in the cemetery, watching out for their lost little girl.

"How's your grandpa?" he asked.

She swallowed, glad for the topic shift. "He's better—it wasn't another stroke, thank goodness. They kept him overnight, but he's home now."

Lyle looked surprised. "You didn't call me to help."

"We didn't need you. Between Georgia, me, and James, we were able to get him resettled."

He looked hurt, and she wondered if it was because he'd missed an opportunity to see Georgia. A hot, burning feeling coated her throat and made her feel like a stupid teenager again.

"How's it going? With Georgia home, I mean."

If he hadn't been blocking her way, she would have walked past him without a word. But she was trapped. "Fine, I guess. Why don't you ask her yourself?"

"Because she doesn't have a cell phone."

Maisy could tell that he regretted saying it as soon as the words came out of his mouth, realizing he'd just admitted that he'd wanted to call Georgia. "She's staying with Aunt Marlene. You'd have all the privacy in the world if you visited with her there."

"Can we not have this conversation here, please? Can't we be civil?"

Maisy crossed her arms over her chest. "Fine. The weather's nice today, isn't it?" *And I love the way your brown eyes turn hazel in the shade of the oaks. And the sound of your voice and how you visit our baby here in the cemetery.* She looked away, embarrassed at the direction of her thoughts.

"I stayed for Becky's tennis lesson on Saturday. She's getting pretty good."

A reluctant smile crept onto her face. "Yeah, she is, isn't she? I love the way it gives her confidence—it's like she forgets that she stutters. I think it's really helped." She paused. "I was wondering if we should splurge on private instruction for her. I wouldn't suggest it, except she's really good at it and she loves it, too. Much more than basketball even."

"I think that's a great idea," Lyle said. "We should be able to swing it financially."

She set her mouth, wondering whether he was still considering their financial status to be a mutual one. "Everybody says that Sally Williamson is the best tennis coach. I'll call her to see if she has any openings and how much it will cost. I'll let you know the particulars."

"Good," he said, his eyes probing hers and making her shift her feet.

"I need to get back," Maisy said around a frog in her throat. "I found something yesterday that might be a clue to determining the origins of the china pattern and I need to tell Georgia."

"Yesterday? And you haven't told her yet?"

Maisy allowed a small smile. "No. It's not often that I'm in a position to know something that Georgia doesn't." She stepped toward him to leave, expecting him to step back. But he didn't.

"I still love you, Maisy."

She looked down at the ground, the sandy soil poking up from the grass that managed to grow despite the stingy oak trees above that blocked much of the sunlight. "Please, Lyle. Don't."

"Why do you find it so hard to believe that you are worthy of being loved? Why do you always search for excuses and reasons to push those of us who love you away?"

She put her hand on his chest, wanting to move him out of her way so she could flee. She shouldn't have. He grasped her hand and held it against him and she could feel the thudding of his heart beneath her palm. "Let me go."

"You so easily believe the worst of the people who love you best. Because that's what you do in a misguided attempt to prove to the world that you're unlovable. Your childhood is over, Maisy. It's time to grow up."

She shoved hard, making him stumble backward and giving her enough room to get by. After a few steps she faced him, her hands balled into fists. "You *always* take her side. Always. I can't fight that anymore. I *won't*."

His eyes hardened and his lips pressed together in a firm line. But he didn't say anything, which said everything she needed to know. Turning away, she made her way out of the cemetery, carefully stepping over old graves that she could barely see through a haze of tears.

Maisy opened the front door to the scent of baking biscuits. It took her a moment to realize that she should be annoyed that someone else was in her kitchen. Anyone would have bothered her, but to have Georgia in there, messing everything up, was the worst possible scenario.

She dropped her satchel full of papers to be graded along with her purse at the foot of the stairs, then marched into the kitchen to let Georgia know that she shouldn't be there. She paused on the threshold, her words held back. James and Birdie sat at the table in front of china plates Maisy vaguely remembered from their china-cabinet scavenging. Florence's tupelo honey jar sat open near James's plate. A porcelain vase full of fresh foxgloves and yellow dandelions stared at her accusingly, as if wondering why they'd never graced the table before when they'd been waiting right outside the kitchen door.

Becky stood by the sink with a bunch of spider lilies in her hand, cutting the stems with red-handled scissors that had long disappeared into the back of a kitchen drawer, Georgia next to her at the ancient harvest gold–colored oven.

James stood as she entered the room and smiled warmly, but it dialed down her annoyance by only a single degree. Maisy faced Becky. "I don't think Grandma would like you cutting down all of her flowers," Maisy said, still feeling the tugging emotions from her conversation with Lyle, and hating the resulting petulance in her voice. If Becky had spoken that way to *her*, she would have asked for an apology.

Becky tucked her chin, making Maisy feel even worse. "A-Aunt Georgia asked me to. She t-told me how to do it so that I d-didn't take too many from the same spot. I arranged the ones on the t-table myself. Aunt Georgia said I have a g-good eye."

Maisy looked again at the table arrangement, at the perfect symmetry of the flowers and the way the colors played against one another. "They're beautiful," she said softly, looking at her daughter. Becky's cheeks flushed with pleasure, making Maisy wonder when the last time was that she'd complimented her instead of telling her what to do or scolding her for something she hadn't done.

She walked over to the table and kissed Birdie on the cheek before sliding a tube of lipstick from the pocket of her skirt. "I bought this for you today. It's a new color for spring and I thought you might like it."

Birdie blinked at the gold tube but showed no other reaction. One day Maisy would stop making peace offerings. Would stop wishing her mother would look up and thank her.

"Did you have a good day?" Maisy asked, giving Birdie one more chance.

"I'm not so sure," said Georgia, bending down to open the oven door and take out a baking sheet full of fluffy golden biscuits. "She's been singing 'What I Did for Love' from *A Chorus Line* all day. She stopped when she heard you come through the door."

Maisy looked at her sister in surprise, their eyes meeting in mutual understanding. That song had meant Birdie was in an unsettled mood, because she'd sing or hum it over and over until they'd be forced to stuff cotton in their ears. It was the only warning they'd have before she slid books off a bookshelf onto the floor or yanked draperies from a window.

Maisy turned her head as she heard the telltale buzzing around her ear. She jerked back and retreated to the doorjamb and the fly-swatter. She grabbed it and held it aloft. "Is that a bee?"

"Yes, Mama," Becky said. "D-don't kill it—you know it's b-bad luck to kill a b-bee."

Maisy hesitated, trying not to think of all the bees she'd swatted at in her past. Georgia walked to the kitchen door and opened it wide, then picked up a newspaper from the counter before approaching the insect as it perched on the back of an empty chair.

"Come on, little bee," Georgia said calmly. "Thanks for coming to visit, but it's time for you to go now." The bee almost seemed to be listening to her as it sat unmoving on the chair. Georgia opened up the paper to create a kind of barrier, and took a step toward the small insect. "Come on now. There's the door, and right outside are all your sisters." With a gentle flick of the paper, she brushed against the chair, shoving the bee toward the door. It buzzed out as if that had been its intention all along, and Georgia slowly shut the door.

"Why is killing a bee bad luck?" James asked.

"A bee in the house means there's going to be a visitor," Becky said with reverence, her stutter gone as she spoke with confidence about a subject she loved. "But if you kill it, the visitor will bring you bad luck." She looked pointedly at Maisy, reminding her mother about the bee she'd killed the day Georgia had called to say she was coming home.

Georgia placed the newspaper back on the counter and went back to the biscuits. "Well, James is already here, so I guess the bees are a little confused because of Florence taking some of the hives."

Standing by the freshly baked biscuits, Georgia pinched a corner off one of them and put it in her mouth. She chewed slowly for a moment with her eyes closed. James walked over and leaned against the counter. "Is it good?" he asked. "Because you're torturing us by making us watch."

She grinned, and it was the old grin that Maisy remembered from her childhood, the smile that always let her know that she and her sister were on the same team.

"Maisy—come here. I think something's missing."

Not sure what to expect, Maisy stepped forward and took a pinch from the same biscuit and put it in her mouth. It was light and fluffy and wonderful. Just like their grandmother used to make them. Except there was something else, too. Something different and delicious and unexpected.

"I added a pinch of cinnamon," Georgia said tentatively. "I know I could never improve on Grandma's biscuits, but I thought I could make them a little different."

She waited expectantly for Maisy to say something. Maisy swallowed, weighing her words. "I think you need more salt."

Georgia's smile dimmed. "You don't like them?"

Maisy had a flash of memory of the day Georgia carried her out of the apiary on her back, away from the angry bees that were stinging them both. "They're delicious. I like the cinnamon."

She took the basket and brought it to the table, then placed one on Birdie's plate and another on James's. "Come sit down and put some of this tupelo honey on your biscuit while it's still warm. I promise you that you've never tasted anything better."

James did as he was told, rubbing his flat stomach. "I'll make sure I run an extra mile tomorrow." He eyed the basket. "Maybe two."

Becky sat down next to him and Maisy gave her one, too, then watched as they poured honey on their biscuits. Birdie pinched off a crumb with her fingers, looking away at the offered honey. Georgia came to stand next to Maisy as they watched James take his first bite.

"Wow," he said after he swallowed. "That's pretty amazing. And you're right. I don't think I've ever tasted anything quite as good."

Georgia's cheeks pinkened, softening the haunted look that she now wore with the same dedication some people chose to wear team hats. It also made her look devastatingly beautiful, and Maisy saw with some amusement James seeming to notice it for the first time.

Maisy pulled out a chair and sat down across from Birdie. "I think I found something that could help your pattern search." She looked up to make sure she had Georgia's attention. "During lunch I sat down with a history teacher at the school, Carmen Daniels—you remember her; she graduated the same year as you. Anyway, I was telling her about trying to identify a china pattern that dated back to the late nineteenth century."

Maisy paused, noticing as Becky reached over for her third biscuit, and pretended not to see. "She said she always told her students that a good place to start was newspaper articles either about their exact subject or the same time period. The media center has access to lots of online newspaper archives all over the world going back a few hundred years, even, so I asked her to do a search."

"And?" Georgia prompted. She'd never been patient, and Maisy had to admit it was fun making her wait. It wasn't often that she had the upper hand.

Maisy took a biscuit from the basket and placed it on the plate in front of her before answering. "She found an article from 1901 from the *New York Times* about an exhibit of French china at the Metropolitan Museum of Art. There was a large section of Limoges from several of the American Haviland companies, with the focus being on the designs. And their artists." Maisy took her time spreading honey on a biscuit and then taking a bite while Georgia drummed her fingers on the table and James chuckled softly to himself.

"Mama—would you just go ahead and tell us?" Becky demanded.

"Well, there were lists of the various company artists—did you know the designs were all done by hand?"

"Maisy . . ." Georgia said her name with gritted teeth.

"And at the bottom of the list were two names of French artists who both designed patterns for Haviland and Co. in the late nineteenth century. What set these two artists apart was the fact that instead of painting the usual flowers or leaves or any of the other popular motifs of the day, these two chose to paint icons from the natural world. Like birds, ladybugs, butterflies." She lifted her gaze to James, and then to her sister.

"And bees," she and Georgia said in unison.

Maisy grinned. "There was actually a photo of a plate with a bee pattern on it, but it didn't appear to be ours. The photos aren't great."

"Did you make a copy?" Georgia asked, leaning over the table like a policeman during an interrogation.

"Of course. I'm a teacher. I live to make copies of interesting articles. I made three—one for each of us. They're in my bag."

Georgia straightened as if aware that she'd been hovering. And then, very slowly, she smiled. "Nice work, Maisy. This could be the break we need."

James stood and shook her hand. "Very good work. I think you might have saved my eyesight."

The sound of something being slid with force across the wood surface of the table made them turn their heads just in time to see the flower vase, honey, and basket of biscuits crash to the floor. Becky leaped up, then ran from the room crying when she spotted her beautiful flowers splayed on the tile floor. Birdie stared at a spot in front of her, her heavy breathing from the exertion of swiping everything within her reach off the table the only indication that she was aware something had just happened.

Before any of them could react, Birdie pressed her head into her hands and began to sob, words easing out between her fingers in a half song, half moan. It was unintelligible, like the babbling gibberish of a baby, but as Maisy put her arms around her mother's shoulders and helped her stand, she thought she heard a name. *Adeline*. And when she looked up at Georgia, Maisy knew that she'd heard it, too.

Their eyes met and it was almost as if they were the young girls they'd once been, sharing secrets. And for that short moment, right before Maisy looked away, they were sisters again, allies in their unconventional lives. *Oysters from the same bed, clinging together despite the vagaries of the tides.*

Maisy began to lead their mother away. She felt a hand on her shoulder and looked up to see that Georgia had her arm around their mother, too.

"I've got her," Georgia said. "You go see about Becky."

Maisy nodded gratefully as she relinquished her hold on Birdie. She stayed where she was for a moment, watching as Georgia led their mother back to her room in the turret of the old house, the name *Adeline* slipping through her lips like a chant.

chapter 16

As queen honeybees age, their egg-laying abilities decrease. When an old queen begins to falter in performing such responsibilities, workers will induce her replacement. The aging queen is killed after the new queen emerges.

—NED BLOODWORTH'S BEEKEEPER'S JOURNAL

Birdie

It was the smell of baking that brought it all back to me. Another kitchen in another house. A thousand years ago. I saw the plates, and the faces around the table, and the wood grain of its surface, and it was all so familiar. Yet so different. The people were talking yet I couldn't translate what they were saying, alien words tumbling from their mouths without meaning. I sat mute, listening to the odd cadences of the voices, wondering where I was and what language they were speaking.

The crumbs I placed in my mouth were like dry sand because I'd expected something else, fresh bread with butter. I looked down and the floor was wrong, too.

I glanced across the table at the young girl with the beautiful blond hair and I knew her name but could not form it. And when I looked at her again it was as if I were looking past her, through unrelenting years to that elusive time when I was happy.

I saw myself with my father, outside with the bees. There was a low murmur somewhere, not the buzzing from the bees but something else. Something not right. Something that made my father hold his breath.

He dropped my hand as we reached the edge of the field where the hives stuck out from the ground like scarecrows. I'd once told my father that and he'd laughed and that had made me smile because he never seemed to laugh anymore. Like all the joy in him had been leached from his skin, absorbed into the air like the light at dusk.

He placed his broad hand on my chest, indicating that I should stay back, then walked toward the hive, its red paint faded by the sun. Hundreds of bees clustered around the bottom entrance, hanging on to one another like stunt divers, their dark buzzing bodies forming what looked like a beard on the ledge of the hive.

"They're swarming," my father said. "Stay back."

I wasn't afraid of the bees, but I did as my father told me. I was an obedient child, never one to cause trouble or make a fuss.

"Why?" I asked, mesmerized by the moving mass of insects that rippled and waved like a person crawling through a field of wheat.

"It's too crowded inside the hive." It sounded as if he were making up stories for me, the way he did at bedtime. "All the worker bees are clustered around the queen to guard her, while scouts look for another hive. A new queen will be born so the existing hive won't be without one."

I blinked up at my father. "Do they mind?"

"Mind what?" he asked, and I could tell he was only listening to me a little bit. I was getting used to it. I was very young, but he'd always paid attention to me. Always made sure he understood my childish gibberish, repeating the words to make sure he got it right. Until the knocks on the door after I was in bed at night. That was when he'd changed.

"Do the bees mind leaving their home and finding somewhere else to live?"

He looked down at me and saw me, *really* saw me, for the first time in a long while. He knelt down in front of me and took my small hands in his. "Some of them might. But the smart ones will see that this is an opportunity for them. Many of them would die if they remained, and this is a chance to survive." He looked past me to the swarming bees and he seemed suddenly sad. "It is astonishing to realize what God's creatures are willing to do to survive."

He stood and I knew he wasn't talking to me anymore.

The memory was so strong and so real that it took me a few minutes to realize where I was, in which kitchen and at what table. I think it was Maisy's voice, her teasing note that I hadn't heard for years. It tugged on me the way her small fingers had once tugged on my hem, and I was floating through time, remembering my girls as they'd been when I'd returned from the hospital that first time and had been so happy to see them.

It was the mention of the china that brought me hurtling back into real time. *The china. Adeline setting the table, carefully placing each dish onto the wood surface, then washing each piece by hand. Her long, tapered fingers as elegant as the painted design.* It made me think of her soothing voice as she sang, and the way she brushed and plaited my hair. I remembered her kindness, and how she was the only one who could comfort me when the nightmares came.

Like an unexpected wave, the memory pushed against its boundaries, a wall of water breaching the dam, a steady stream spewing from a jagged crack. The flickering light in my mind threw out a bright swath of white light, illuminating all I did not want to see. All that came after. Adeline. And the swarming bees. Always the bees. And the murmur of something else in the background. Something unholy and man-made.

I wanted it to stop, needed it to stop. I reached out my arm, desperate to grab hold of the image of Adeline, to bring the happiness back to me, and instead felt the hard wood of the table beneath my arm. Only the shocked silence of the kitchen made me aware of what I'd just done.

chapter 17

"How doth the little busy bee
Improve each shining hour,
And gather honey all the day
From every opening flower."
Isaac Watts

—NED BLOODWORTH'S BEEKEEPER'S JOURNAL

Georgia

I walked down the hall to Marlene's kitchen, trailed by the wagging tails and clicking paws of four dogs. In the nearly two weeks since I'd been home, Marlene's four-legged shadows had glommed onto me, as if they thought I was in need of companionship. Each night they followed me into my old bedroom and lined themselves up along the foot of the bed, their expressions telling me that I wouldn't be able to get them to leave.

The slow drip of rain against the metal roof at least meant that the rain that had pelted the house all night and most of the previous two days was finally slowing. I was thinking how nice it would be to work out on the dock when I reached the kitchen and stopped abruptly in the doorway. James and Becky sat at the kitchen table eating eggs and bacon, a plate of biscuits on the table between them, the ubiquitous jar of tupelo honey next to it. Marlene stood at the counter pouring three glasses of orange juice. She sent me a grin over her shoulder.

"At last, Sleeping Beauty emerges from her lair."

"Very funny," I said, glancing at the round kitchen clock over the stove. "It's nine o'clock—a very respectable time for a Saturday morning."

"Not really," groaned Becky, her usually quiet voice louder and more confident in Marlene's kitchen, as if she found strength and acceptance here just as I had all those years ago. "You know, Aunt Georgia, cell phones now have alarm clocks on them. So you'd know when to wake up. We've been waiting for forever."

I hid my smile. "Sorry—I didn't know anybody was waiting for me."

"You *said* you didn't have a bathing suit, and then James said he didn't either and you could go shopping with him." She glanced at my tie-dyed romper with the fringe hem. "I thought I could help."

"I was thinking that with all this rain we've been having I should hold off on purchasing a bathing suit. Today I planned to head over to the library to see if they were able to find anything about those artists your mother discovered. I called my contact at the Haviland archives at the University of Iowa library, but I haven't heard back from her, so I figured I'd better start looking elsewhere while I wait. And then I need to take Grandpa for a walk."

"You can do all that *after* we shop," Becky said matter-of-factly, as if everything had been decided. "And the sun is shining now." She sounded so much like Maisy—the "little general," as Grandpa had called her. I guessed she'd been the one to coordinate this morning with James, her face earnest and serious as she manipulated everyone's schedule.

I narrowed my eyes at her. "Does your mother know you're here?"

James nodded. "I called her to make sure it was all right. She said it was fine as long as Becky wasn't late for her tennis lesson. She brought her racket just in case, and we can drop her off at the courts on the old Marshall Square on Fourteenth Street by eleven."

My stomach growled as I spied the food on their plates and smelled the bacon, forgetting my next question involving why James and Becky were sitting at Marlene's table.

James stood and pulled out a chair for me. "Why don't you eat first? Becky brought these biscuits. Maisy made them. They're pretty good."

"Are they as good as mine?" I'd meant it as a joke, but I realized it hadn't sounded like one.

I slid into the offered chair as Marlene placed a full plate in front of me, along with a steaming cup of coffee. "I enjoy having all my limbs attached, so give me a moment to answer that." James sat down. "I think both are equally delicious and different."

"Good one," Becky said, offering her clenched hand for a fist bump.

I laughed, then helped myself to a biscuit. "So why are you both here?"

James placed his napkin beside his empty plate and leaned back in his chair. "Becky texted me this morning and told me that you wanted me to pick her up and bring her here so we could go shopping."

I took a sip of my coffee. "Becky, I don't think Mr. Graf appreciates . . ." I stopped, confused as to why she was studying me so intently. "What?" I asked.

"If you and Mr. Graf had a baby, I wonder what color its eyes would be. Yours are brown, but Mama's are gray, which means you're not a pure-strain brown."

I'd made the mistake of taking a sip from my coffee and started coughing.

Oblivious to my distress, Becky continued. "Blue is recessive, but if brown eyes aren't pure-strain, then it's possible to have a blue-eyed child. Mine are brown, like yours and Birdie's. Daddy has brown eyes, too, so I'm going to have to ask Mr. Ward, my science teacher." With a serious face, she added, "We're studying fruit flies in science class."

Marlene appeared at my side with the pot of coffee. She winked at me as she leaned in to top off my mug. "Remember that your mama and aunt are half sisters. Your aunt Georgia's daddy had blue eyes just like Mr. Graf—the same shade as the bay first thing in the morning. But Georgia got Birdie's coloring—for her eyes and her hair. Those are some bossy genes; that's for sure."

I focused on my food, wondering how to tell a nine-year-old it was time to stop talking.

"My wife had brown eyes," James said quietly. "Lighter than Georgia's—with a hint of green in them. I always wondered what color eyes our children would have had." A sad smile softened his face.

Becky took a sip of juice from her glass. "Mama said that your wife died. I'm really sorry. When my cat died when I was eight, Birdie said not to be sad. And when we remember them it means they're still alive."

Marlene placed a hand on Becky's shoulder. "So Birdie's talking?"

Becky looked at me with wide eyes. "P-please don't tell Mama. It makes her m-mad."

"I won't, Becky," I said gently. "But I am curious. Birdie hasn't spoken to me since before you were born, but if she's talking to you, then I'd feel better."

She looked down at her plate. "She only talks to me. Sort of."

"What do you mean, 'sort of'?" Marlene asked, sitting down in an empty chair.

Becky's small shoulders shrugged, and I had to lean closer to hear her. "She sings songs, and then I have to guess what she's saying. She moves her eyes to tell me I've guessed right. It's been our game since I was little."

"Like how the bees talk to one another to let the others know where to find food, or if there's danger. Like that?" I said.

Becky's face brightened. "*Just* like that." And then she smiled and all of those missing years suddenly became a gaping wound, an empty space I'd never found a way to fill no matter how many times I'd told myself that I had. *I missed you. I'm so glad you have a happy life with parents who adore you. I'm sorry.* All the words I wanted to say sat frozen on my lips, impotent and too many years too late.

I stood, focusing on picking up my plate and cup and bringing them to the sink. I took my time rinsing the dishes, waiting until the lump had dissolved in my throat, the bitter aftertaste I knew would follow. "I'll go get my shoes and purse," I said without looking at anyone, hoping to have remembered who I was and why I was there before I had to return.

We decided to walk to the small downtown area. The roads were black and sodden from all the rain, the trees top-heavy. Leaden skies hovered over the bay, but blue sky was making a valiant effort to show through. It wasn't too far to walk, the distance seeming much farther during the summer months, when your hair melted onto your scalp and you felt yourself walking slowly through the wall of humidity that settled on Apalachicola like a wet blanket despite the breezes that blew in across the bay. I sent a sideways look at James, who wore long pants and a button-down shirt with rolled-up sleeves.

"If you're going to stay here much longer, you're going to need some shorts and short-sleeved shirts. And probably lots of sunscreen." I took in his reddish gold hair and blue eyes. "Are you Irish or Scottish?"

"Mostly Swiss, actually. Graf is a common Swiss name. Believe it or not, I actually have some Italian and French in me, too—my grandmother's mother was French, her father an Italian. So I'm not 'pure-strain,' according to Becky," he said with a slow smile. "I do sunburn if I'm not careful, but I've got enough Italian and French in me that I've been known to actually have a tan."

We strolled in silence, watching as Becky walked with hunched shoulders ahead of us, avoiding the cracks in the sidewalks, just as I'd done as a child. We walked past the wedding-cake Victorians with crushed-oyster-shell drives that sat next to Apalachicola bungalows, and shotgun cottages with their slender columns and filigreed overhangs, most lots interspersed with tall pines and thick oaks. The architecture was as diverse as the people and history of Apalachicola, something I'd always loved about my hometown. And one of the things that made it hard to forget.

"It must have been difficult to leave," James said.

I swallowed, wondering how he could have read my mind, and quickly tried to think of a lighthearted quip. "You haven't been here in August. You might think differently."

His expression was serious, and I sobered immediately, getting ready to deflect any uncomfortable observations.

"Your roots are here—your family, the house, your history." A car sped by and James took my elbow to move me away from the road. "I remember my grandmother's stories about how they moved to Switzerland during the war. She was a teenager at the time, but she always said part of her soul had been left behind. I've wondered if you felt the same about here."

I felt the anger in me rise, tempered only by the memory of his face as he'd told me about his wife. "You could ask yourself the same question. You're here, aren't you?"

His face stilled. "But this is temporary. As diverting as it's been, it's not permanent."

I continued walking, Becky almost a block ahead of us. "Yeah. I used to think that, too."

He was silent for a moment. "Have you ever thought that you haven't looked at the situation from every perspective—this thing between you and Maisy? I know hindsight's twenty/twenty, but I can't stop thinking that if I'd only taken the time to notice things, to ask questions before Kate's death, I wouldn't have all these feelings now." He frowned, his gaze focused on the ground in front of him. "It's like living with a deep cut that you don't remember getting, and having no idea how to stop it from bleeding. I would give away everything I own for just five minutes with her again." He looked at me, his eyes dark. "If Maisy disappeared from your life tomorrow, would you regret anything?"

Something that felt a lot like panic gripped me, making it hard for me to breathe, making me want to lean over and rest my hands on my knees as if I'd just sprinted for a mile. Even when I'd lived in New Orleans all those years, I always knew that Maisy was here. That if I wanted to I could call her, or come visit. If I could just push back my pride for five minutes and pick up the phone. That the option might be removed permanently shattered something inside of me. I felt bared, exposed. Resentful. Yet when I looked into his clear eyes, I felt the unmistakable nudge of thankfulness.

"I'm too afraid, I think."

"Afraid?"

I stopped walking to think for a moment, to make sure I understood what, exactly, I was afraid of. "I'm afraid that she won't meet me halfway. That she'll turn around and walk away and everything will be as it's been." I swallowed. "Because then I'll have lost all hope. At least this way I still have hope."

"But what if she doesn't walk away?"

I opened my mouth to answer, then closed it when I realized I had nothing to say. I began walking toward Becky, who'd stopped and was staring back at us with her hands on her hips, looking startlingly like Maisy.

"If we don't hurry, I might not get to see Paco."

I stopped in front of her. "Paco? Is that your boyfriend?"

She screwed up her face as if she'd just eaten something bitter. "No. Paco is a cute little dog who lives at the art gallery on the corner of E and Market. Mr. Lindsley always lets me pet him."

I hid my smile. "We can always come back," I said.

We walked half a block before James spoke again. "My wife was an architect. Her specialty was contemporary spaces, with lots of chrome and glass. She designed several boutique art galleries in the city, and was quite well-known. I never really appreciated her love for sharp angles and hard surfaces, but I was proud of all of her accomplishments. I should have made sure she knew that. I told her many times, but I don't think she really ever believed me. I just wish I'd tried harder."

I didn't have to ask why he was telling me. He played the role of referee well, and I knew that with each morsel about my life that I threw at him, he'd reciprocate. I hadn't known James Graf for a long time, but I'd learned that he was kind and sincere, and didn't hide his hurts so much as disguise them as opportunities for courage.

We caught up to Becky again, who was frowning at us. "We won't have any time to do anything if you keep moving like turtles."

I looked at my watch and realized we'd been walking for only ten minutes. "We have plenty of time. I thought I'd take Mr. Graf to see the John Gorrie tomb and monument."

Becky rolled her eyes, and it was a relief to know that she could act like a normal girl who didn't have a disconnected grandmother and parents who didn't live together anymore. "Do we have to?"

"Yeah. We kind of do. The world should know about John Gorrie. Personally, I think he should be sainted."

"That's for sure," Becky said as we caught up to her and continued down Avenue F toward Sixth Street and took a right. "We studied him in science."

"Who is this Gorrie person?" James asked with a hint of amusement.

Becky looked like she might burst, so I said, "Why don't you tell him?"

She took a calming breath to slow her words before speaking. "He was the inventor of the first ice machine and mechanical refrigeration—which led to modern air-conditioning. My teacher said we probably wouldn't have any big cities in the South if it weren't for John Gorrie and air-conditioning. And I told her that I'd rather live in Florida in one-thousand-degree heat than freeze to death anywhere else."

I had once said the same thing, and wondered whether Maisy had liked it enough to repeat it in Becky's hearing.

"That's a pretty serious statement," James said.

"Because it's true." Becky looked at me for backup, and I nodded in agreement.

We approached the only traffic circle in Apalachicola, with two Civil War cannons planted in the middle of the green space, the Gorrie museum, library, and Trinity church rounding out the tourist attractions surrounding the circle. We stood in front of the large cement urn lifted to its lofty position by an elaborate base and four white steps.

"His final resting place, I assume," James asked.

I nodded. "He used to be buried in Lafayette Park before they moved all the bodies to make it into a park."

Becky squinted. "You mean I used to play in a cemetery?"

"I think she said they moved the bodies," James said with a straight face. "But I guess it's always possible that they could have forgotten one or two."

An exaggerated shudder went through her small body. "If you had a phone, Aunt Georgia, you could take a selfie here."

I stared at her blankly, trying to communicate my complete disdain for people who relentlessly took pictures of themselves with their phones.

"You know. A picture of yourself with the monument in the background."

"I know what it is," I said. "But why would I want to do that?"

"So you can put it on your Facebook page or Instagram or tweet it."

It was my turn to roll my eyes. "Do you really think somebody without a cell phone has anything to do with social media?"

She scrunched up her nose. "I guess not." I leaned closer so I could hear her. I'd found that if you showed her that you wanted to hear what she had to say, and didn't make her speak too loudly, she didn't stutter. She continued. "Mama said you weren't on Facebook because it's a place for people who want to keep in touch. And who don't want old embarrassing photos showing up." She squinted up at me. "My friend Brittany was really embarrassed when her mama put a photo of her in the bathtub when she was a baby and tagged her."

The rumbling sound of a car motor approached, distracting me from the heat rising to my cheeks and the two sets of eyes watching me with anticipation. The Charlie Daniels Band shouted from rolled-down windows as the vehicle approached, and for that brief moment before I knew for sure, I said a brief prayer that it wasn't who I thought it was.

But when I turned around and saw the red Camaro, the paint now faded to a dusky pink, I was once again reminded that God had stopped answering my prayers a long time ago. The car rumbled to a stop, its engine vibrating.

"Georgia Chambers—is that really you? I was a block away and I caught sight of that hair of yours." A tanned arm with a tattooed sleeve from wrist to shoulder rested on the door. "Wasn't until I got nearer and saw your backside that I knew it could be no other. Come over here, girl, and give me a hello kiss." The man grinned, white teeth behind sun-darkened skin and black stubble. "For old times' sake."

I knew I had to say something; I just couldn't think of anything I could say in front of Becky. Or James. "Bobby Stoyber," I finally managed, the name as heavy as a cannonball.

He tilted his head. "Is that all you got for me, sweetheart?"

In my peripheral vision I saw James move and assumed he was walking away. I felt a tug of heartsickness, but was too horrified by the situation to think why.

And then James was standing by the driver's side and offering his hand to shake. "James Graf. A business associate of Georgia's. Nice to meet you."

Bobby stared at the proffered hand for a moment before taking it, a grin leaching across his face like spilled oil. "Yeah. Likewise. A 'business associate,' you say? Is that what she's calling her boyfriends these days?"

An odd expression crossed James's face, something a complete stranger might actually take as a smile. But I'd seen enough of his genuine smiles to know this wasn't one, and that Bobby should actually be a little afraid.

James leaned into the open window, his large hands braced on the door. "I'm sure you've known Miss Chambers longer than I have, Bobby, but that doesn't mean you need to disrespect her. Especially in front of her young niece. You've said your hello; now I think it's time you move on."

"Who's going to make me?"

James stood to his full height and looked calmly down at Bobby. "I have a black belt in karate, and I could sterilize you before you even knew I moved."

A car with an underutilized muffler chortled slowly down Avenue D toward the circle and the Camaro. Bobby glanced at it as he shifted his car into gear. "Whatever." He pointed his chin at me. "Call me. So we can catch up."

I managed to find my voice again. "Yes. I'm sure I've got your number on my cell."

He pulled away without a backward glance, and I stayed where I was, afraid to look at either Becky or James. It seemed that the satellite that was my past had finished circling me and decided it was time to crash into the middle of my present.

I felt Becky's slight presence at my side. "I d-don't like him."

I put my arm around her, angry that Bobby had brought out Becky's stutter on what had promised to be a stress-free outing.

"Me, neither," James said, moving to stand on my other side. "I almost wish he'd stepped out of his car."

I forced myself to meet his eyes. "Thank you."

"No need." He smiled softly. "It's amazing how some people never change. And how some people do."

I was embarrassed again, remembering how Maisy had once said the same thing to my departing back. "How do you know I've changed?"

He looked a little sheepish. "Mr. Mandeville. He told me to keep you at arm's length. That you were a virtual nun and I needed to behave like a gentleman."

I closed my eyes so I could at least pretend that the ground beneath me was swallowing me up. "I need a beer."

"It's not even t-ten o'clock," Becky said softly, her voice pained.

James jerked his head in the direction of downtown. "Come on. Let's do our shopping and then we'll stop for lunch and we'll both have a beer—after we make sure Becky gets to her tennis lesson."

I paused, wanting nothing more than to head back to the house and close the door behind me. "Sure," I said instead, and we began walking toward Market Street.

A buzzing sounded from James's pocket, but he ignored it, shortening his long strides to match ours. "Aren't you going to answer that?" I asked after it had buzzed five times.

He hesitated before responding. "I wasn't planning to. It's probably just one of my sisters again, asking me when I'm coming home.

I've already told them the answer, so I don't understand why they keep bothering me."

The buzzing stopped, and we hadn't walked three paces before a text message pinged. Reluctantly he pulled his phone from his back pocket and looked at it. He stopped short, his eyes on his phone. "Well," he said. "It's from Maisy."

I looked at him expectantly. "Is it my grandfather?"

He shook his head. "No. Your friend at the Haviland archives has been trying to reach you." He met my gaze. "She says she thinks she's found your artist."

I'd sent her the two names Maisy had given me from the *New York Times* article. "That's terrific news. I can't wait to find out what she has to say." I'd already turned around to go back when James put his hand on my arm.

"But first we're going to go downtown, to go shopping and to be seen, and to visit with people you haven't seen in a while. Then we'll go home and you can call her back."

I bristled, torn between thankfulness, embarrassment, and anger. As if he'd heard my unspoken question, he said, "Because you and I aren't that different."

The expression on his face made the back of my eyeballs prickle. It reminded me of Maisy, standing in a windblown cemetery, her eyes reflecting the new empty space in her heart. It gave me the courage to nod and to keep walking in the direction of downtown.

chapter 18

"That which is not good for the beehive cannot be good for the bees."
Marcus Aurelius

—NED BLOODWORTH'S BEEKEEPER'S JOURNAL

Maisy

Becky sat at the foot of Grandpa's bed, her thin legs pulled up in front of her, arms hugging them close. She gnawed on the fingernails of the closest hand, but Maisy didn't tell her to stop. Becky had been agitated ever since the shopping trip with Georgia and James, but had made it clear that she didn't want to talk about it.

Birdie sat in the chair by the bed, and before Maisy had walked in she felt sure she'd heard a murmur of sound, like voices from a TV talk show. But Grandpa was asleep and the television off. Birdie, dressed in an elegant knit wrap dress and high-heeled pumps, cradled the broken saucer in her hands, but it lay inert like a sleeping baby while her attention rested on her father.

Maisy recalled Georgia's question about whether Birdie talked to Becky. *Of course she doesn't.* She'd been angry when she'd answered, mostly because she didn't really know. Despite all logic, Becky and Birdie had been inseparable since Becky's birth, as if they had their own special language that excluded everyone else. Including Maisy.

Mostly, though, she was angry because if Birdie could communicate, it should be with *her*. Maisy was the one who took care of her mother, who was there every day seeing to her needs. Who bought her lipstick. If Birdie had something to say, she should say it to Maisy. Then maybe Maisy could unravel the secret that was her mother, peeling back the layers of years that would allow her to peer into her mother's past and perhaps find understanding. And clarity. To maybe even ease the hurt and anger and sense of abandonment that followed Maisy like a recurring nightmare.

When Maisy had taught eighth-grade science, in one of the textbooks she'd come across a fish that willingly starved itself to avoid conflict. Because it didn't compete for the food source, the alpha fish would let it be instead of tearing it to shreds. Maisy had identified with that fish, its name long forgotten. She knew what it was like to try to fade into the background to avoid getting hurt. But that never stopped her from trying to eat.

She placed her hand on Becky's shoulder. "Did he do his exercises?"

Becky nodded, her finger in her mouth as she nibbled on the nail.

"The doctors say he's getting better, so please don't worry, all right, sweetheart?"

"He's w-worried about s-something."

Maisy looked down at her daughter. "Did he say something to you?"

Becky glanced over at Birdie for a moment before returning her gaze to her shredded nails. She shook her head. "I c-can just tell. He w-wants his bees b-back."

"His bees? The ones Florence brought to the swamp? How do you know that?"

Keeping her gaze focused on her hands, she shrugged.

Maisy felt a flush of anger. Once again she was on the periphery of the inner circle, excluded like an aging queen bee.

Birdie stood and began to study her mother's painting of the honeybee in midair, a corner of the hive visible in the background. Soft brushes of paint outlined the bee's flight pattern, a seemingly aimless path. Georgia had once told her that bees never did anything haphazardly, that even random movements followed precise calculations. Maisy would never admit it, but this fact had always fascinated her, had even made her imagine the lives of those who lived in the house on the bay as ever-widening circles, their patterns of flight always leading them back here. It was how she'd known that Georgia would never be gone for long.

Maisy spoke to the back of Birdie's head. "Do you need anything, Birdie?"

Her mother turned to her and Maisy noticed she was wearing the new lipstick she'd given her. But there was something about her eyes that really caught Maisy's attention. They were brighter, *focused*. As if she were actually seeing Maisy. As if she might actually answer.

"Well, if you need me I'll be in the dining room with Mr. Graf and Aunt Georgia."

No one looked up as Maisy left the room and headed across the foyer.

James sat at one end of the dining room table with his laptop, while Georgia sat on the opposite end with several of her thick volumes spread out on the table in front of her. The list with the two artists' names Maisy had provided for them sat next to Georgia, with annotations added next to each name, the second name now circled in red and the other crossed out, thanks to the new information from the Haviland archives. Maisy recognized the round, looped handwriting, remembered it from sneaking peeks at her sister's diary when they were younger. The only thing it had in common with her own was its messiness and near illegibility to anybody unfamiliar with it. Becky's handwriting was the same way. It had never ceased to amaze Maisy that their grandmother had been such a talented artist, yet neither her daughter nor granddaughters could write even their names with any sort of artistry, much less draw with anything more than stick figures.

"Find anything yet?" Maisy asked.

James looked over the top of his laptop. "Nothing new. Georgia's contact at the museum looked at the two names you gave them and knew immediately which one of them might have painted the bee pattern. Emile Duval designed patterns for Haviland and Co. in the late eighteen hundreds, as well as having been privately commissioned to design exclusive patterns for wealthy customers. The other name on the list designed only for the commercial market, and his designs are well-known."

Georgia slid back her chair. "So the private market is the angle I'm pursuing now, since I think I've looked at every single Limoges pattern ever designed for commercial use over the last one hundred and fifty years and have not seen anything that looks remotely like the one we're looking for. Nor have any of the experts I've contacted and sent a photo of the pattern to. I'm going to assume for now that it was a custom pattern, designed specifically for a single client, by Emile. The good news is that a commissioned pattern will be a lot more valuable. I could be wrong, but I'd rather prove myself wrong than continue to search for a needle in a haystack. At least this gives me a direction, and I might be pointed on the right path during my search."

"How long will that take?" Maisy asked.

She felt their eyes on her.

"I mean, it could go on forever," Maisy continued. "And how do you know you've found the right guy? I'd feel better spending time looking for information about Emile if we had more reasons to pinpoint him other than that he painted for the right company at the right time and was known for painting insects."

Georgia's demeanor was of calm certainty, and Maisy found it annoying. "My source told me that Emile's father was a beekeeper near Limoges and his designs were almost exclusively of bees. Since we've found nothing else, I think it's a strong enough lead that we should pursue it until we either hit pay dirt or move on."

Georgia stood and reached for a stack of old and yellowed papers, then walked around the table and handed the stack to Maisy. "While we're searching for the pattern and its artist, maybe you can do this."

Maisy looked down at the pile Georgia had given her, recognizing its contents as what they'd pulled from their grandmother's china cabinet. "Do what?" she said stiffly.

"Go through these and look for the name Adeline. Read any names on the backs of any of the photographs. The name means something to Birdie."

Maisy looked into her sister's eyes, her refusal stranded somewhere in her throat. It had always been hard to tell Georgia no. Especially for a younger sister who'd only ever wanted to be included. "Why?"

Georgia's nostrils flared and Maisy felt a brief moment of satisfaction.

"Because if you don't then I will, and that will delay my departure that much longer."

Maisy swallowed. "Fine, then." She took the stack and slapped it down on the table before sitting. She looked up to find James eyeing her with amusement.

His phone buzzed on the table and he glanced down at it before reaching over and ending the call, then returned to his laptop. The phone buzzed again but he didn't even look at it this time.

"You can take that, James," Georgia said. "You won't be bothering us."

Without taking his eyes from his laptop, he said, "But it will be bothering me. It's my oldest sister, Caroline. Again. She thinks that if she doesn't hear from me every day, then something's wrong. I texted her yesterday, and I probably will today as well. If only to keep her from tracking me down and showing up on your doorstep."

He looked up for a moment, and his expression implied that he wasn't completely joking.

As if an explanation was required, he said, "Our mother died when I was a freshman in high school, and ever since, Caroline thinks she should act as a surrogate mother. I keep telling her that I don't need one, but she doesn't listen. The other three are pretty hands-on, too."

"Sounds just like a sister," Maisy said under her breath, then returned to the stack in front of her. She began by sorting them by type—receipts, photos, newspapers, other. The tendency to organize had started long before she became a teacher. She remembered as a child organizing her Barbie shoes by color and her stuffed animals alphabetically by type. She wasn't even aware of it until she noticed Georgia counting things, and holding her breath, and setting clocks fifteen minutes ahead. It was as if they both realized they existed in constant chaos, their mother at its center, creating a need for some kind of order. And for a long time they'd held hands, grounding themselves to an unstable world until even that connection had been pulled apart.

They worked in silence for almost an hour before Becky joined them at the table. "I'm bored."

Without thinking twice, Maisy slid a folder off the top of the stack and pushed it across the table. Becky had said the two words she usually remembered not to say in front of her mother. "Good. Because there's plenty of work to go around. I'd like you to go through every single page—front and back—including photos—and look for the name Adeline. All right?"

Becky sighed as if she'd just been asked to haul rocks up a mountain. Barefoot. And on an empty stomach. She dutifully opened the folder and picked up the first paper on top of the pile. After another heavy sigh, she bent over the papers and began to read.

They worked in silence for a while, until Georgia got up and turned on the antiquated console stereo in the adjacent living room. Maisy hadn't checked recently, but she was pretty sure her mother's collection of movie sound tracks in the eight-track format were still stored in the bottom. When they were children, Birdie always had music playing in the house, and she sang along to the lyrics and sometimes danced with Maisy and Georgia.

But that had been before Maisy recognized the disappointment in her mother's eyes, before she and Georgia understood that whatever life existed inside their mother's head would always be better than what stood right in front of her.

The overture to *Jesus Christ Superstar* spilled out into the quiet house as Georgia returned. "It's low enough that it shouldn't wake Grandpa." She tapped James's shoulder as she passed behind him. "I tried to look for some jazz, but it's all show tunes."

"That's all right. I like show tunes." Except the expression on his face said otherwise.

Georgia must have noticed it, too. "If you don't like this one, I can change it."

He shook his head. "No, that's all right. It's just that . . . well, this was one of my wife's favorites. One of her most-loved wedding gifts was the double album in vinyl. From my best man." He smiled like a man who'd just been slapped. Hard.

Georgia started to walk back to the living room. "Let me change it. . . ."

"No. Leave it. Please," he added hastily. "It's better to rip off the Band-Aid in one swipe than lift it little by little, right?" He looked at Maisy, his gaze finally resting on Georgia. "I was always the kind of person who would leave a Band-Aid on a cut until it disintegrated. I'm squeamish that way, I guess. But Kate always reminded me that we can't expect a wound to heal unless it's exposed to air."

Georgia pulled back her shoulders. "But if you keep it covered long enough, you forget about it."

"Do you, though?" James asked, the words devoid of confrontation, as if he wanted Georgia to examine them on her own time.

"Who's this?" Becky slid a photo toward Maisy, ending the conversation. Becky had a knack for interrupting at the right time, as if in her nine years she'd already learned that there were some things adults didn't want to talk about.

Maisy studied the color photo of a shirtless, tanned man sitting at the edge of the dock behind this house, a fishing rod held in his hand. He was hatless, his dark, glossy hair glistening in the bright sunshine, and he grinned behind dark aviator sunglasses as he looked over his shoulder at the photographer.

"That's my father—your grandfather Chris. You've never met him. He and Birdie were married for about three months. The only thing that survived that marriage was me." Her smile faltered, quickly skittering across her face. "He lives in Arizona now with his second wife and family. I had to find that out on my own—Birdie never talked about him. I've never met him, either."

Georgia's eyes softened as she regarded Maisy. If anybody could commiserate with what it was like to be a victim of one of Birdie's whims, it was Georgia.

Becky was regarding her with the same dark eyes. "Then why'd she marry him?"

Maisy shrugged. "Sometimes people think that good enough is a fair substitution for what they really want." She avoided looking at Georgia, feeling her sister's eyes boring into her.

"What's mumps?" Becky asked.

With relief, Maisy refocused her attention on her daughter, who was staring down at one of the papers in the folder. Maisy moved to stand behind her, and saw that she was looking at her grandfather's WWII medical card. The word "mumps" had been scrawled in typical doctor fashion in a box on the bottom right corner of the form under the typewritten words "Childhood Illnesses," and right next to the words "chicken pox."

"It's a disease that we don't see too much of anymore because of vaccinations. You and I both have been vaccinated against it. I don't know too much about it other than that it was pretty prevalent among children before the vaccine. I don't think it was like influenza that would kill large numbers, but I think the symptoms were nasty enough that nobody wanted to get it."

"Mumps?" James asked, looking up from his computer.

Maisy nodded. "Yes. Apparently my grandfather had it as a child. Didn't prevent him from active duty during World War Two, but they did note it on his medical record."

James looked thoughtful. "Interesting. My great-uncle had it, too, when he was a little boy. I only know about it because there's an old photo of him with his neck swollen like a balloon that my younger sisters and I used to find hilarious. Uncle Joe would be about your grandfather's age, so I'm guessing the vaccine didn't come along until after they were into adulthood."

The music stopped abruptly, a victim of worn-out technology, and

Georgia seemed so wrapped up in the book she was examining that she didn't seem to notice. As if to fill the void, Becky began humming. It took Maisy a few moments to realize that she was humming Birdie's tune, the one that Maisy found so familiar yet so annoyingly vague.

"What song is that?" she asked Becky. "It sounds like the alphabet song, but it's not, is it?"

Becky didn't even glance up as she reached for a small stack of photographs and began flipping them over for names. "I don't know— I learned it in kindergarten. From a show called *Songs from Around the World* or something like that. I got to sing all by myself."

Maisy sat back, relieved. She remembered now how Becky had rehearsed the song over and over again until they all knew it backward and forward, and how Birdie had sought Becky out to sing it, just like a proud grandmother who actually cared. It certainly explained how they all knew it.

"Do you remember the name of it?" she asked.

Becky's brow furrowed as she thought. "It wasn't English. Mrs. Miller said we had to pucker our lips to say some of the words right."

"French, maybe?" Maisy asked.

"Yeah—I think that's it." Becky flashed one of her beautiful smiles, one that was unaffected and guileless and had become much too rare. The phone rang and Maisy stood to answer it in the kitchen. She glanced at the caller ID and saw it was Florence Love, the beekeeper.

"Hi, Maisy." The connection wasn't good, but Maisy could tell that Florence's voice didn't sound normal. "I need to speak with your grandpa, and it's kind of urgent. I know it's hard for him to talk, but I've got something to tell him that he'll need to hear."

"Sure, let me walk back to his bedroom and see if he's awake." Maisy gently pushed open the door and found Grandpa sitting up in bed, staring at one of the watercolors of flying bees. The television was off and Birdie's chair was empty.

"Grandpa? It's Florence on the phone. She says she needs to tell you something. I'll stay here to answer for you if you need me."

She placed the phone carefully in his left hand, and he almost seemed to shrink at the touch, a mollusk disappearing into its shell at the first sign of danger. She could hear Florence speaking, not what she was saying, but Maisy saw her grandfather's face, and a tremor of dread began at the base of her skull.

The phone fell from his hands, and when she bent to pick it up, the dull thud of the dial tone reached her ears. She tried to meet his eyes, but he glanced away. She started to ask him what Florence wanted to tell him, but was distracted by the crunch of tires on the front drive. Looking through the curved front window, she spotted Lyle's cruiser coming to a stop.

She dropped the phone and ran to the front door, pulling it open before Lyle had the chance to knock. He looked at her with surprise. "Hi, Maisy. This isn't a social call."

His gaze moved behind her and she stiffened, knowing Georgia was there. Looking back at Maisy, he said, "I need to talk to your grandfather."

Georgia stepped forward. "He's not really up to it, Lyle. Can you talk to us instead?"

Maisy bristled at the word "us." "What's this about, Lyle?"

"A pickup truck your grandpa reported stolen back in 1953. Looks like we've found it. But I need to talk to him in private."

A rush of movement from behind them made Maisy turn around to see Birdie attempting to run up the stairs so fast that she caught the heel of her shoe in the skirt of her dress and stumbled twice before racing up the rest of the steps. A door slammed upstairs, the old house shocked with the sound. And then, almost imperceptibly, came a small mewling sound that erupted into a keening moan.

chapter 19

Changing queens will alter the personality and behavior of bee colonies. This fact can be used to control certain behaviors of a hive, such as aggressiveness and industriousness.

—NED BLOODWORTH'S BEEKEEPER'S JOURNAL

Birdie

addy's truck. I could suddenly see things with startling clarity, like the moment the moon's shadow slips off the face of the sun after an eclipse. My eyes stung with the brightness of it, yet I couldn't close them, afraid that I would stop seeing. Afraid, too, that I wouldn't.

I imagined I smelled the newness of it, felt the hot dashboard that burned my palms. Saw the indentation in the driver's seat where my daddy sat inside the powder blue cab. He said he'd bought a blue truck because it matched the color of my mama's eyes.

There was something else about Daddy's truck I remembered, a dark, curled-up memory stuck inside my brain like gravel in the bottom of a shoe. I felt it scraping with every step, but I couldn't dislodge it. I turned my head, hoping to see the memory, to face it. But each time I tried, it sidestepped out of my field of vision, a fleeting ghost.

I ran up the stairs as fast as my knees would allow me, tripping and stumbling, following the ghost. A part of me wanted to remain downstairs in the hallway, staring at Lyle, and sing so loudly that I could no longer hear the recriminating voices in my head. To disappear back into the person they all thought I was. But I couldn't. Not now. Georgia had come back, turning the key on a giant clock that ran in reverse, and all I could hear was the slow unraveling of hours.

I ran into the closet, eager to search while my eyes were opened and I could *see*. I tore clothes from hangers and threw handbags and shoes out of the closet and onto the floor, crawling on my hands and knees.

It's not here. A stray thought teased at my brain, but I couldn't get it to stay long enough to make sense. I ran back into my bedroom and ripped the sheets from my bed, then crawled underneath it, no longer sure what I was doing. The darkness dipped over my vision, threatening to obscure my newfound clarity. I tried to focus on Georgia, and Maisy. And Becky. I needed to do this for them. To save them. To save us all.

From what? I sat in the middle of my bedroom floor as the light began to fade in my mind, a total eclipse. I threw my head back in frustration and began to cry.

~~~

"Birdie?"

I blinked up into familiar eyes. *George?* No. George was dead.

"It's Marlene, sugar. Georgia came and got me because she didn't know what else to do. She said you might want to see another familiar face."

I closed my eyes, wanting to see George's face again, to remember how things had been before. *Before what? Something to do with the truck.*

I was sitting in the middle of the front seat of another truck—the one Daddy bought to replace the blue one—with George as Daddy drove us to the high school dance. I'd been home for Easter break from my school in Jacksonville. Mama said she sent me away to get a better education, but we both knew it was to keep me away from George. We were both sixteen, and even back then we'd had a hold on each other that was good and awful all at the same time. We shared each other's dreams, and fears. And secrets. The darkest kind, which could drown a person if she had to bear it alone. I sat in my tiers of pink lace with the hyacinth corsage wrapped around my wrist like a shackle. George's bow tie matched my dress, and we both pretended not to notice that my gown was as out of place in the sea of soft chiffon as George was in a tuxedo and bow tie. But as with most of our relationship, we didn't much care what other people thought.

A roughened hand moved the hair off of my forehead. "What were you looking for, Birdie?"

I shook my head, wanting her to go away, to stop interrupting my memories. They were all I had left of George.

"Mama?"

It was Georgia, and she must have been scared, because she hadn't called me Mama since she was a teenager. I kept my eyes closed but opened my hand and felt her smooth, slender fingers close around mine.

"I want to help you. If you can tell me what you're looking for, I can help you find it." She leaned in closer and I could feel her warm breath on my cheek.

The suitcase. It had meant something to me, a memory like the smell of lavender from my mother's drawer sachets that always reminded me of her.

I turned my head, but kept my hand in Georgia's, not wanting her to leave, but not understanding what she wanted me to answer. I closed my eyes tighter, seeing George's face, his pale blue eyes and his lips always carrying a smile. We were standing at the marina looking out over the river, at the uninterrupted miles of water and light. *I'll love you as long as the stars light the sky.* Then I'd said, *And I'll love you until the last one burns out.*

I let go of my daughter's hand, reaching for my beloved, knowing that if I tried hard enough I could touch him. But my hands reached only empty space.

"Sugar, let us help you," Marlene's voice rasped in my ear. Then closer, quieter, so no one else could hear, she whispered, "Is this about the beekeeper, Birdie?"

The light flickered in my head again, the projector slowing down. I fought hard to hold on to George's image, to smell the salty sweat of him. And I did. He was in Daddy's old blue truck and he was looking at me from the passenger seat, Daddy behind the wheel. He wasn't smiling. Something was wrong. I tried to squint to see what was making me so upset. I called his name, but George didn't seem to hear me. They drove away, the fumes from the exhaust choking me. But I could see his face as he passed me, and it made my heart hurt to see that he was crying.

"I've told you—she can't be helped. Don't you think I've tried everything at least twice? That I've taken her to every doctor I could find who might be able to diagnose her and make this better?"

It was my sweet Maisy, my daughter who'd managed to become the mother I'd always tried to be. She had no idea, since Maisy never trusted anybody who gave her a compliment. I'd taught her this in my misguided attempt to show her that she was different from Georgia, that she had her own beauty and gifts. But she only ever heard the "different" part, and nothing that came afterward. Maybe it's those who have to fight so hard to be noticed who become the best people. And that was why I always wore the lipsticks she bought me. Not because I wanted or needed any, but because I wanted her to know that I'd noticed.

The side of the bed moved as someone sat down. I smelled dog and fresh air and that horrible Charlie perfume that Marlene had always worn. There was something comforting in it, something familiar that reminded me that not everybody deserted you. We'd never been friends, but when you'd known somebody long enough, they found a way to grow around you like a vine until you couldn't remember life without them. Marlene and I had nothing in common except that she'd been George's sister, and she loved my Georgia more than I knew how to love someone.

"That doesn't mean we should give up trying, Maisy. There's something new here. She might get worse if we can't figure it out." Marlene shifted, a waft of stale Charlie moving over me. "Did you tell her they found the truck in the swamp?"

"It's really not the time, Marlene . . ." Maisy began.

"She's right." It was Georgia, coming to Maisy's defense just like she'd done when they were children, and a jolt of warmth shot through the icy stillness in my veins.

"What's this?" Marlene leaned forward and slid something off the nightstand. "It looks like a piece of broken china."

Broken china. Those two words, in Marlene's voice. A memory. *I'm getting you cheap china for your wedding, because George says you hate good porcelain.*

"It's the broken saucer from James's grandmother's set. That's the pattern we're trying to find." Georgia's voice seemed to be coming from very far away. "I'm wondering . . ."

I saw it then, the piece of china in my closet, Georgia holding it up to me. *There,* I thought. I'd put my finger to my lips and she'd put it back and she'd never asked for it again. Like pressing on a bruise, I let my mind travel back to that moment. *There,* I thought again, the thick rush of fear pulsing through me. *That's it.*

I thought I could smell the exhaust from the old truck, the acrid scent teasing my nostrils, the grit of the driveway pelting my face as George and my daddy pulled away from me, George's hand clenched into a fist where it rested on the doorframe. Tears rolled down my cheeks and I knew my mama stood somewhere behind me, and she was crying, too. I watched the truck until it was only a small speck of blue, leaving behind a bewildering sense of finality. I wanted to run after them, but something held me back. Something I didn't want to remember.

Opening my eyes, I sought out Georgia's. Maybe she remembered, would know. Would understand what it was my flickering mind wouldn't let me see. But she turned her back on me to speak with Maisy, saying something about getting me a glass of warm milk so I could rest. I closed my eyes again, letting the darkness take over.

chapter 20

*"I dreamt—marvelous error!— / that I had a beehive / here inside
my heart.
And the golden bees / were making white combs / and sweet honey /
from my old failures."*
Antonio Machado

—NED BLOODWORTH'S BEEKEEPER'S JOURNAL

Georgia

Bees buzzed and flitted around my head. I counted each one as I'd
done as a child, lulling me into a sweet space where I couldn't see
my mother's tortured face or hear my sister's bitter and accusatory
words. Or remember the person I had once been, and who I was afraid
still lurked inside of me.

Without my grandfather and the hives that had been moved to
the swamp, the apiary seemed more than just diminished, like a child
labeled with a failure to thrive. I couldn't help but think this change
was irreversible, somehow permanent. A turn of the tide that could
not be pulled back.

At the base of the bee box in front of me, a bee—larger than
most—lingered on the platform in front of the exit. Making sure it

was clear my intent wasn't to block the bees from entering or leaving the hive, I leaned in from the side and scooped up the bee, cupping it inside my closed palms.

"Won't it sting you?"

I hadn't heard James approach, but I'd sensed his presence. There was something about the apiary that had always heightened all of my senses. Maybe because it was the only place I'd known as a child where Maisy wouldn't follow me or interrupt.

"It's a male—a drone. They don't have stingers." I stepped back from the hive so that I stood next to him. "My grandfather showed me this when I was a little girl—they just buzz in your hands like a little rattle. But they can't hurt you."

I touched my closed hands to his and, without being asked, he cupped his hands. Careful not to hurt the bee, I transferred the drone to James. He smiled broadly. "Neat. But how can you make sure you're not picking up one with a stinger?"

"Well, you can usually *see* the stinger, but if you're that close, it's probably too late anyway. The drones are bigger—not as big as the queen, but bigger than the worker bees."

"So they're strong enough for the fatal aerial love dance with the queen if they're chosen."

"Exactly. You're a good student."

His smile dimmed as he opened up his hands and let the bee fly away. "If only people were that easy to figure out."

I lifted my brows, waiting for him to say more, but he didn't.

"Did you need to ask me something?" It had been a day since they'd found my grandfather's truck and Birdie had had her episode. Birdie hadn't left her room since, and my grandfather's agitation and Lyle's inability to tell us anything more had kept Maisy and me on edge.

Even though James now wore a short-sleeved golf shirt and cotton twill shorts, he didn't look like a native. I'm not sure whether James Graf would look like a native in his hometown, either. There was an aloofness about him, almost a carelessness, that spoke of someone not quite aware of the world around him or other people's reaction to his presence. It was strangely appealing, the foreignness of him, the otherworldliness. If I'd been up to the challenge, I would have tried to unravel him, to understand what motivated him. There was more there than the loss of his wife. There was a depth to his despair that only similar dark souls could recognize.

"Not really. I needed a break from the Internet. I've been searching for anything I can find about Emile Duval. I did find out where he apprenticed to another porcelain painter—in a small town in Provence called Monieux. It would make sense that if he was commissioned by a private client, they had probably seen his work and most likely lived in the same area. It's a stretch, but a place to start. I figure after lunch I'm going to start doing an online search for wealthy families from near Monieux who lived there during the late eighteen hundreds—people who could afford to commission a set of one-of-a-kind china."

I grinned up at him. "If I'm not careful, you're going to be after my job. That's pretty much along the same lines as I was thinking. And if we can identify the artist, that would be very good news for you, as that will certainly affect the value in a positive way."

He didn't smile back. "Actually, I did want to talk with you about something else. . . ."

"Yes?" I swallowed back the lump that had lodged itself in my throat at the thought that he was about to tell me that it was time for him to go back to New York. He needed to go back to his life, and the online research he was doing here could certainly be done anywhere. Yet in the short time since I'd known him, I'd come to rely on his calm, solid presence. It was as unfamiliar to me as snow, yet comforting in the way a person gravitates toward a favorite sweater. The thought of him leaving now made me feel somehow bereft.

"It's Lyle."

I felt a huge relief, until I realized what he'd said. "What do you mean?"

James shrugged. "When I was standing in the foyer wondering if

I should run upstairs after you and Maisy or join Lyle, I overheard one of his questions he directed at your grandfather. He wanted to know if your grandfather remembered if there was anything important he'd left in the truck when it was stolen. Your grandfather didn't respond—and I imagine Lyle didn't expect him to—which made me wonder why Lyle would think it important enough to come ask."

"Or why Lyle would want to keep that private. He's referring to a truck that was stolen sixty-two years ago."

"That made me curious, too, and because I have a lot of time on my hands I started sticking my thoughts where they don't belong." He squinted at me in the bright sunshine. "There's definitely more to this story, and I'm guessing that Lyle didn't say anything because he's trying to protect Maisy. He still loves her, doesn't he?"

I nodded. "He always has." I watched as a bee circled us before heading for the hive.

"Does that bother you?"

I met his gaze with surprise. "No. Of course not. Lyle and I were very close—best friends, really. It didn't occur to me until it was too late that Maisy might not have appreciated it. But they do love each other, regardless of what's going on in their marriage right now, and they've raised a wonderful daughter together. Maisy has . . . trust issues. I hope they can find their way back to each other."

Sweat dripped between my breasts under my vintage orange nylon shirt. I pulled it away from my chest, feeling overheated and embarrassed under his scrutiny. I'd never cared what people thought about me, most likely because Birdie had cared too much. But I realized with some surprise that James's opinion mattered to me, no matter how much I wished it didn't.

I began to walk back to the house. "I'm going downtown to do some antiquing—see if I can find something unexpected."

"Maybe a new lock or key?"

I shielded the sun from my eyes with my hand as I looked back at him. "Maybe. I always like to think in possibilities."

He smiled softly. "That's a good perspective to have." He looked back at the hives for a moment before turning back to me. "If it's all right, I'll come with you. I need a break from my laptop and Limoges artists and towns with French names. I'll treat you to lunch."

"You need a break from all of us, I should think. I'm Birdie's daughter and it's still hard for me, even though I should be used to the craziness. I can't imagine what this has all been like for you."

His eyes darkened. "It's nothing that I'm not familiar with. I understand fragile minds."

Yes, I thought. *Yes, you do.* I would have known this about him even if he hadn't told me. It was in the creases on the sides of his mouth, and the hollowness behind his smile. It was in his sensitivity, his ability to know the right thing to say and do. *Yes,* I thought again. *You understand a fragile mind.*

I slid my moist palms down the sides of my maxiskirt, feeling suddenly out of breath. "Sure. I'd like the company." I began walking again, but stopped when I realized he hadn't moved.

"My wife had an affair. I found out when I went through her text messages after she died."

I didn't look at him. Words filled my head and were quickly dismissed as an adequate response. *I'm sorry. That's awful.* There was nothing I could say that would make it better for him. I'd known loss and betrayal, but this grief was his own, a shirt made just for him. There was no room for empty words that did nothing to cushion or erase.

I'd been so young when my father died, but old enough to know that death meant he was never coming back. Aunt Marlene had looked at me with my father's eyes and then scooped me up in her arms and hugged me for as long as I needed it without saying anything. Even without words, I'd known that she understood my grief, but that she wasn't going to pretend she could make it better. All she could do was let me know I wasn't alone.

Before I could think twice I turned and walked toward him, and then, standing on my tiptoes, I put my arms around him and placed my head against his chest. I heard his quick intake of air, his startled surprise that made his heart thump next to my ear. And then I felt him relax, his bones softening into mine, his chin resting on the top of my head. "Thank you," he said as his arms came around me.

I hugged him a little tighter, knowing that for perhaps the first time in my life I had done something right and good.

The back door banged shut, jerking us apart as Becky ran across the yard toward us. "Mrs. Love is here to see Grandpa, but Mama took him to the hospital for his physical therapy, so she wants to see you."

Not really sure why I was feeling embarrassed or guilty, I avoided looking at James as I walked toward the door. His long strides meant he beat me to it and held the door open for Becky and me, the latter rolling her eyes to let us know that she'd seen us hugging.

Florence stood awkwardly in the foyer, looking out of place indoors and away from the sunshine and her bees. She wore her ubiquitous bee earrings, and although she was smiling, her eyes were worried. She greeted us both, and after she declined my offer of something to drink, we headed out to the back porch to catch the late-afternoon breeze that blew in from the bay.

After we seated ourselves in rocking chairs, James spoke first. "I can't thank you enough for the tupelo honey. I understand now why honey is called the 'nectar of the gods.'"

He grinned as Florence's cheeks turned a bright pink. "You're more than welcome. So glad you enjoyed it. You might want to make it last. Doesn't look like it's going to be a good harvest this year. This dang rain—it's only good if you're a duck."

She smiled a little at her own joke before her face turned serious. "I need to speak with your grandpa. I know he can't communicate so good right now, but I just wanted to let him know what I saw, so that he's not blindsided by the police. Although I'm assuming they've been here already?"

I nodded. "Lyle stopped by and told us they'd found Grandpa's truck, but would only speak with Grandpa, so we're not sure what was discussed, and neither of them has told Maisy and me anything."

Florence nodded. "It's just, well, as his friend I wanted to make sure he knew."

"Knew what?" I asked, gooseflesh pricking at the back of my neck.

She pursed her lips together. "I'm only telling you because you're his granddaughter and you love him. And he's been a good friend to me."

I didn't say anything, waited for her to continue.

"It was me and my guys who found the truck. I made the men stay back, because I'm smaller than they are, just in case I needed somebody to rescue me, but I went up close to look inside." She swallowed. "There was . . ." She paused, shook her head as if trying to unravel something twisted tightly inside. "A person." She stopped, perspiration beading her upper lip.

"A person?" I asked.

"What . . . what was left of one. A skeleton. Still wearing clothes. I thought it was a real live person at first, because of the clothes."

For a moment it felt as if I were swimming in the ocean and I'd just reached a cold spot. I took a deep breath to reassure myself that I could. "Could you see anything else—if it was male or female?"

Florence looked away toward the water for a moment, her hands gripped together in her lap. "Definitely a man. Wearing overalls and a cap."

"Oh." Somehow it wasn't what I'd expected to hear.

"I stuck around after the police got there—my uncle and my brother were both police chiefs, so I know lots of the officers, and they're kinda used to seeing me around places most girls shy away from. Anyway, this probably shouldn't be repeated, since it's an open investigation, but they're saying that it's probably the person who stole the truck and that he got lost in the swamp trying to get away. But you know how rumors and conjectures get started." She gave us a tight smile. "I just wanted y'all to know before the stories reached you."

She stood as if to leave, but hesitated.

We stood, too, and after a moment she said, "There's something else. I wanted to ask your granddaddy if he remembered a man who showed up in town right before his truck was stolen. I was just a little girl, but I remember it because my daddy had a story about it that he used to like to tell me. He was selling honey at the farmer's market and a man approached him, said he was looking for your granddaddy. Daddy had never seen the man before—and you know how it is here. Everybody knows everybody. Anyway, the stranger knew your grand-daddy by name—said they'd met before the war."

"And this was the same week the truck was stolen?"

"Yes. And I know it because it was the week of my fifth birthday. The man gave Daddy a jar of honey—his own he'd harvested from wherever he was from—I can't remember if Daddy never told me or if I've just forgotten it, but he said the man had an accent, so probably not from around here. Mama made me buttermilk pancakes for breakfast on my birthday, and I put that honey on them. It was some of the best-tasting honey I've ever had—not including tupelo, of course." She licked her lips as she thought for a moment, as if she were tasting the honey again. "I remember it tasted like lavender."

She smiled at us again, sliding her palms against her shorts as if mentally clearing her to-do list. "I should be going. Please tell your granddaddy that I was here asking after him."

"I will. Thank you for coming, Florence."

She headed toward the steps but paused at the top. "I almost forgot. And this is definitely something you shouldn't repeat. But . . . I was still there when they opened up the truck and could see what they pulled out. They found two jars of honey in a knapsack inside. It didn't have a label, but it's too dark to be tupelo honey—although if it's been there for over sixty years, who knows what color it used to be? But that's what made me remember the stranger—the honey." With a final wave, she stepped off the porch and onto the walkway toward the front drive, her bee earrings swaying.

I sat down in a rocking chair, breathing deeply of the salt air and the green scent of sun-baked needlegrass, but could see only an old pickup truck drowning in swamp water, and a faceless man holding a jar of lavender honey.

chapter 21

"He who wants to lick honey must not shy away from the bees."
Scottish proverb

—NED BLOODWORTH'S BEEKEEPER'S JOURNAL

Maisy

Maisy was pushing her buggy through the produce aisle at the Piggly Wiggly, heading toward the checkout, when she heard her name called. She turned to find Caty Greene, the librarian at the municipal library, walking quickly toward her. Miss Caty, as everyone called her, was a transplant from somewhere up north, but she'd been in Apalach for so long that Maisy no longer remembered from where. She had quickly assimilated into her new home, her fast-paced gait the only giveaway that she wasn't native.

Miss Caty was reaching into her oversize satchel as she approached. She wore dangling oyster-shell earrings and a matching necklace on a blue silk cord—both of her own design. Maisy had several pieces of her own that she'd purchased over the years at Caty's stand at the weekly farmer's market.

"Your house was my next errand, so I'm glad I ran into you. Saved me a trip." She smiled as she pulled out a thick stack of white paper, rubber-banded both ways to keep any errant pages from slipping out.

She smiled as she waited for Maisy to take the stack. "It's about the china your sister is looking for. She stopped by a few days ago asking me if I had access to various databases." Miss Caty looked at the ceiling as if asking for divine guidance. "I'm a librarian. Of course I can access pretty much any obscure information one might need."

"Of course," Maisy said, taking the stack with both hands, noticing tiny cursive handwriting photocopied onto the first page. "What is this?"

"Georgia gave me the name Château de Beaulieu, an estate she found in her research near Monieux, France, and asked me to see if I could find any sort of paper trail—business transactions, marriages, legal proceedings, that sort of thing—from the second half of the nineteenth century that made mention of it."

Maisy's eyes widened. Georgia hadn't mentioned this angle to her. Her first impulse was to feel slighted, the old feeling of being left out a familiar one. But it was quickly replaced with an odd pride in her sister. It was a unique track to the answer to the question of the china's provenance, one that would never have occurred to Maisy.

"And you found something," Maisy said, eyeing the thick stack.

Miss Caty nodded sagely. "I would say so. There's a small museum in Monieux that has done an excellent job of digitizing all of the old records from the town's archives that have survived both world wars and a terrible fire in the early thirties. It only took a few clicks before I was directed to their database, and then shortly after that I turned up what looks like an estate manager's account books listing all expenditures at Beaulieu starting from around 1855 through 1939."

Maisy carefully set the stack in the top of her buggy. "Thank you, Caty. I know Georgia will appreciate it."

"No problem. It's what I do." She smiled. "And tell Becky that I've just received those biographies of female tennis players that she asked for. Come by anytime—you know where to find me."

They said good-bye, and then Maisy headed for the checkout.

The smell from the store's smokehouse drifted across the parking lot as Maisy loaded her grocery bags into the trunk of her car. She looked up in surprise as someone grabbed hold of one of the bags in her hand. It was Lyle, wearing jeans and a T-shirt, and looking so much like the boy she'd known in high school that her heart did the old familiar flip.

"Let me help you," he said, lifting the bag from her hands and neatly placing it into the trunk.

"That's the milk. Make sure it's not on its side."

"It's not," he said without looking.

They continued loading the car without speaking. When they were finished, Maisy fished in her purse for the keys while Lyle returned the buggy to the corral. She slid behind the steering wheel and turned on the A/C, letting the cold air blast her in the face. She'd need cooling off even if it weren't almost summer.

He reappeared at her open door. "I'm guessing you've heard."

Maisy nodded, unable to meet his eyes. Because every time she did, she thought of him in the cemetery telling her that he visited Lilyanna Joy there often. And that he still loved Maisy.

"Yes. From Florence via Georgia. She was there, so we got a first-hand account before any embellishments were added." Maisy grabbed hold of her old anger so she could look into his face. And immediately regretted it.

"I'm sorry that the story about your granddaddy's truck got leaked before I could get a better handle on it. I wanted more time to gather the facts. It's an ugly story, and I was trying to shield you and Becky. I should have known better."

"I don't need you to shield me, Lyle. And I can take care of Becky." She lowered the window, then shut the car door, needing the separation from him. "Granddaddy isn't doing too well. Will you need him for your investigation?"

"Actually, I'm officially off the case. On account of Ned being my wife's grandfather. If they need a statement, they'll send somebody else. But unofficially I did pull the original police report, and it looks like your basic car theft. In his original statement, Ned said he left the truck in the driveway overnight and in the morning it was gone. He got the insurance check and bought a new truck. Looks like a closed case to me. If the poor guy who stole it got stuck in the swamp, then I guess justice was more than served. Won't know a lot until the coroner determines the cause of death, and that could take weeks—if at all. The truck's been in the swamp for over sixty years, so there's a lot of deterioration of evidence. I'll keep you posted."

"Thank you." Maisy turned the key in the ignition.

"One more thing," he said, placing his hand on the door as if to prevent her from closing the window. "I was wondering if you'd like to go to the Tupelo Honey Festival in Wewahitchka on May sixteenth. Becky asked me to take her, but I thought it would be fun if we went as a family. Just like old times."

She was already shaking her head before he finished speaking. "I don't know, Lyle. She works with her new tennis coach on weekends now. . . ."

"The coach is flexible on time and date if we need to move it. Or we can go after her session on Saturday. She's doing so well in school, and working hard on her tennis. I think she'd appreciate us both being there. We're still a family, you know."

A memory of the last festival she'd been to turned the blood in her veins icy cold. It had been the Seafood Festival, but it didn't matter. The association poisoned all festivals for her. She opened her mouth to speak, unable to stop the words even if she'd wanted to. "Should I ask Georgia if she'd like to go?"

She watched as anger flashed over Lyle's face. He leaned down toward her, his face only inches away. Narrowing his eyes, he said, "Only if you'd like her to join us. I'm just inviting you."

He straightened, then slid out the pair of Ray-Bans he'd left tucked into the neck of his T-shirt and placed them on his face. "Just let me know," he said as he tapped the flats of his hands on her door and walked back to his truck. Maisy watched just for a moment, then slowly slid her window up and drove away, careful not to look into her rearview mirror, afraid that she'd see him watching her. And just as afraid that he wasn't.

The house was quiet when Maisy returned home. As she unloaded the groceries and put them away, she was surprised to find the dinner dishes loaded into the dishwasher and the pots and pans already scrubbed and drying in the dish drain. She smiled to herself, knowing Becky had done it without being asked, and wondered whether it was to sweeten Maisy up to get her to say yes about going to the festival with Lyle.

Or maybe she'd done it because even though she was teetering on the threshold of tweendom and was adept at getting on Maisy's last nerve, she was still a good kid who loved her mama. Maisy folded up the grocery bags and stuck them in the pantry, then went to find her daughter to thank her.

The door to her grandfather's room was slightly ajar as she passed it, the sound of a woman's voice coming through the opening so quietly Maisy thought she must be imagining it. Tapping lightly, she pushed it open to reveal her grandfather sitting up in bed, Birdie in the chair next to him. She held the broken saucer, and was leaning forward as if she'd just whispered something in his ear.

Neither one looked up as she entered, but Birdie sat back in her chair, looking down at the saucer cupped in one hand, the other placed loosely on top as if to hide it from view.

"Hi, Grandpa," Maisy said as she entered, then stood next to Birdie. "Is everything all right?" She found herself half expecting Birdie to look up and say something, the words Maisy imagined hearing floating somewhere right outside her grasp. Her heart beat with a panicked thrum. What if Becky wasn't lying about Birdie talking?

Birdie stood and Maisy held her breath, waiting. But Birdie just leaned over and kissed her father's forehead, then walked toward the door, pausing briefly before leaving the room. Maisy clenched her teeth, focusing on the sense of panic, trying to identify its source, then realizing with some surprise that it wasn't the thought that Becky hadn't been lying to her, but the fact that Birdie might have something to say.

"Do you need anything?" she asked her grandfather.

He slowly turned his eyes toward the water glass on the nightstand. Carefully she picked it up and helped him take a few sips before he turned his head away.

"Would you like me to turn on the television?"

He shook his head, his gaze focused past her shoulders toward the window.

"Would you like to go outside? I bet your bees miss you."

He turned just his eyes toward her, the way a small child did when he knew he'd done something wrong. He grunted something that sounded like the word "no."

She watched him for a moment. "I'll take you for a walk down to the dock tomorrow morning when it's a little cooler, all right?"

He didn't respond, his gaze focused on the window again.

Maisy checked the chart to see whether he'd been given his nighttime medications, including the antidepressant his doctor had prescribed. She saw Georgia's initials next to the checkmarks. She made a mental note to talk to his doctor about upping the dose.

He turned his head away from the window, an indication that he was ready to go to sleep.

She helped him move down in the bed, then fluffed the pillows behind his head before kissing his cheek.

"Good night, Grandpa," she said as she stood, but his eyes were already closed. Maisy carefully took off his glasses and placed them on his bedside table, noticing his beekeeper's journal flipped open and upside down, like a bird stalled in flight. It was the notebook he carried with him every day as he went into his apiary, and where he jotted his thoughts and observations. He'd never allowed her to read it, although from time to time he'd share a favorite quote or proverb he'd discovered.

She glanced at him to make sure he was sound asleep—his ability to fall asleep quickly a side effect of his mediation—and after a brief moment of hesitation picked it up, feeling like a child left unsupervised around a cookie jar. There were too many questions and not enough answers, and it wasn't her nature to wait until problems resolved themselves. The cover of the journal was old and soft from age and use. He didn't write in it every day, but he'd told her he'd been writing his observances in the same journal since he'd started beekeeping with his father in his late teens.

She opened it to the first entry, the pen strokes on the page faded to a pale blue. The date at the top read, *April 10, 1954.* She paused at the date, a thought jabbing at the back of her head. After a quick calculation, she looked down at the date again. In 1954 her grandfather would have been thirty-three. Glancing up at the full bookshelves against the wall that had remained despite the room's conversion to a bedroom, she scanned the spines, looking for another journal, one that might have been started when he'd been a teenager.

Not seeing one, she returned to the journal and read the entry.

There are no secrets to bee behavior that cannot be explained by science. The jobs of each bee are preordained at birth: the worker, the drone, the queen. And yet some bees will find themselves far from the hive, wayward wanderers, almost as if their predestination had been to wander far from home and forget they were meant to be just a bee.

Maisy opened the journal to the last entry, noting that it had been written two days before his stroke. *The bees have returned to their hives for the evening, where they will not sleep but continue in their duties for the good of the hive. Yet there's a low hum, not restful or peaceful but agitated. It's as if they, too, sense the ripples in the atmosphere around us. Can predict the approaching change that I've sensed in my old bones since I learned my granddaughter is returning home. I will observe them closely, hoping that they will tell me what I need to do now.*

She read the last entry twice, then replaced the journal where she'd found it. She stood by the bed and watched her grandfather for a long moment, wondering what it was he needed to know.

After she arranged the bedclothes up around his shoulders, she left the room, pausing just for a moment in the foyer, the evasive words she'd imagined hearing suddenly as clear to her as if they'd been shouted. *Tell me.*

She turned around for a moment to stare at the closed door, those two words reverberating in her head. Surely she'd imagined it. The stress of the last weeks and her lack of sleep were affecting her.

She climbed the stairs slowly, dreading her empty bed and the quiet of her room because there was no one there to talk through the day with. She still slept on one side of the bed, being careful not to feel the cold absence, the missing indentation on his pillow. Her bedroom had become a mausoleum, a solemn memorial of a marriage that had passed.

Birdie's bedroom door was closed, but there were soft voices coming from Becky's room. As Maisy neared, she recognized Georgia's voice. She sucked in her breath, suddenly angry. Becky was supposed to be doing her homework, and it was typical of Georgia to assume that she could come and interrupt Becky anytime she wanted.

Becky's voice was low. "Mama won't let Birdie do my hair. She says as long as it's clean and cut nicely and I wear it out of my face, then I shouldn't think twice about it."

Maisy stopped outside the room and looked inside. Becky sat cross-legged on the bed, while Georgia sat on her knees behind her, French-braiding her hair, their backs to the door.

"Well, she's right," Georgia said.

Maisy's anger jammed in her throat.

Georgia continued. "You're too young to be worrying about your hair. You should use your brain cells for school and tennis."

Becky groaned. "I figured you'd take her side."

"Why's that?"

"Because you're sisters. That's what you're supposed to do."

There was a long pause. "You're right. That's what we're supposed to do."

"Why is Mama so mad at you?"

Georgia's fingers stalled on the yellow strands. "It's an involved and complicated story, sweetie. Maybe when you're older we can have a long talk."

Becky let out an exaggerated sigh. "That's what Mama says, too. Can't you at least give me a hint?"

Maisy pressed her lips together, holding back the hot words that threatened to spill out of her mouth.

"Let's just say that your mama and I didn't have the kind of childhood you have. We were raised mostly by Grandpa after Grandma died, and he loved us, but we were two little girls and he didn't have too much experience with being a single dad. That just wasn't something men of his generation ever expected to do."

"What about Birdie? She's your mama."

"Theoretically. But I don't think motherhood was anything she ever planned on. She married for love the first time and for security the second time, and us girls were just sort of collateral damage."

"Did you ever want to be a mother?"

Maisy squeezed her eyes shut, picturing Georgia's face at the hospital the day Becky had been born, the smell of blood and longing and retribution forever linked in Maisy's mind. She remembered, too, the way her heart expanded when she'd held Becky for the first time.

"Not really. At least when I was younger. Not sure how I feel about it now, either."

Becky twisted her head to look at her aunt, the strands of hair slipping from Georgia's fingers. "What does collateral damage mean?"

"It means that your mama and I had to stick together, because we were being brought up by two people who were raising us by default. Not like you, Becky. You have a mama and daddy who love you very much, and are doing their best to raise you right. If your mama is grumpy or telling you to do things, be grateful. That means she cares and that she loves you. It will make a big difference in your life when you get older." Georgia's elegant fingers threaded through Becky's hair again, returning to where she'd left off.

"But she's grumpy all the time, and she never wants to listen to what I have to s-say."

It was the first time Becky had stuttered in the whole conversation with Georgia, and it made Maisy feel hollowed-out, knowing it had been the mention of her that had started it.

"Your mama has a lot going on in her life right now, so be kind to her. If I thought for one minute, or one second, that she wasn't the best mother in the world, I would have moved back here years ago to keep an eye on you. From the first moment I saw her holding you, I knew that you could search the world over and never find someone who could love you more."

Georgia's voice cracked, and Maisy wondered whether Becky had heard it, too, had recognized the sound of a broken heart.

The quietly sung words from "Send in the Clowns" from behind Birdie's closed door punctuated the silence. Becky's voice sounded strained. "She's singing it for me."

"What do you mean?"

Becky shrugged. "She always sings it after one of her 'episodes'— that's what Mama calls them. It's like she wants me to know she's all right, that her thoughts are in the right place again."

Maisy could almost hear Georgia's thoughts running through her head, mirroring her own. "The right place?"

"Uh-huh. It's like when you're playing tag and you're on base. She's on base right now, where she's pretending she's in a play and nobody can catch her or take her away."

"She told you this?" Georgia continued threading the blond strands in and out of the long braid, slowing slightly as she reached the bottom.

"Sort of." There was a long pause, and Maisy imagined Georgia keeping silent on purpose, waiting until Becky was ready to tell her more. But Becky didn't saying anything else.

Georgia sat back on her heels. "Did you know you're missing a big chunk of your hair?" She held up a small quadrant of hair toward the back of Becky's head. "Looks like it's been cut clean." Using a hair tie, Georgia quickly wrapped up the bottom of the braid, the shorter strands lying conspicuously untethered on the side of Becky's face. "Did you cut it?"

Becky shook her head. "No." She began gnawing on her thumbnail, obscuring her voice.

Georgia waited for a moment for Becky to elaborate. When she didn't, she asked, "Then who did?"

Becky tilted her head down so she was staring at her crossed legs, her thumbnail lodged between her teeth. "P-promise you won't be mad?"

"Not if you tell me the truth."

"It was Madison Bennett. She sits behind me in math."

Maisy drew in a breath. Why hadn't Becky told her?

"Why would she do such a thing?"

Becky was silent.

"I won't be mad, remember? Just tell me the truth."

The singing stopped, as if even Birdie were waiting for an answer. "Your friend Bobby that we saw the other day? Madison is his niece. He said something not very nice about you, and she was telling people at school. So I told her to shut up."

Maisy pressed herself against the wall so she wouldn't be tempted to rush into the bedroom and give her daughter a high five. Not just because it wouldn't be the right thing for a mother to encourage her child to tell another child to shut up, but because she wouldn't want Georgia to see her praising Becky for sticking up for her aunt. Her second instinct was to call the school's principal and ask for a meeting. It was too late, of course, but Maisy made a mental note to do it first thing in the morning, and that made her feel slightly better.

"Do you want to tell me what she said?"

Becky shook her head.

"That's all right. Is Madison a friend of yours?"

"She's one of the popular girls. They have a special table in the lunchroom, and you have to be invited to sit with them."

"And you haven't been?"

The French braid flopped as Becky shook her head again. "I don't want to. I sit at the jockettes' table."

"Jockettes?"

"Those are the girls who play sports. But we let other people sit with us if they want."

"That's nice—to have a group of people you're comfortable with, and still welcome others. It's a good way to be."

"Did you have a group you hung out with when you were in school?"

The boys, Maisy thought. *Always the boys.*

"Not really. I wasn't into music and ran on the track team—much to Birdie's disappointment. But I loved art, so I hung out with a bunch of the other kids who were into art. I especially liked to paint, although I was terrible at it. That's probably what got me interested in antiques and old china. Well, that and my grandmother's love of collecting it."

"Did you have a best friend?"

Maisy listened as the bedsprings creaked, and when she stole a glance into the bedroom, Georgia stood next to the bed, her profile outlined by the beside lamp, looking somehow small and lost and alone. "Not really. I didn't need one."

"Why?"

"Because I had a sister. And that's all I needed."

Maisy turned from the doorway and tiptoed down the hallway to her own bedroom, carefully closing it without a sound. She stood with her back pressed against the door for a long time, watching the light fade from the sky as a night crier began its endless calling from its perch in a tall cypress, searching for something in the vast darkness it couldn't seem to find no matter how long it cried.

chapter 22

"Life is the flower for which love is the honey."
Victor Hugo

—NED BLOODWORTH'S BEEKEEPER'S JOURNAL

Georgia

James and I sat in the shade of the giant magnolia tree near the apiary, he with his laptop and I with the thick folder filled with photocopies from the Beaulieu estate ledger. The handwriting was tiny, old-fashioned, and, to make it even more difficult for me, in French. Happily, I needed to know only the words Limoges and Emile Duval. Not that I expected a nineteenth-century estate manager to make it convenient for an American in the twenty-first century to decipher his work, but I'd hoped that the tedium of the last weeks had bought me at least one convenience. But life, I'd learned, rarely made sense, was fair, or cared about what was convenient or easy.

James closed his laptop with an annoyed expression, then put it on the ground. "I just lost the Wi-Fi connection again—I guess I'm too far from the router. I wish I'd brought my personal Wi-Fi hotspot, but I wasn't really thinking ahead when I decided to take the trip down south."

I shook the pages in my hands. "See? Modern technology is vastly overrated. I'm not having a problem accessing my data."

He snorted. "But by the way you're squinting, I'm guessing you're having trouble reading it. If it were online you could make the font bigger. And let's not forget that the only reason you're looking at it here in your backyard in Apalachicola, Florida, is because somebody in France decided to make it available online."

Feeling a lot like Becky, I rolled my eyes. "I'm not a Luddite— really. I think a lot of modern technology is great, especially for research. I just don't think there's a need to be in touch twenty-four/ seven. When do people have time to think if they're being constantly barraged by bings and texts and alerts? I've just opted out of all that."

James leaned back, crossing his legs at the ankles. He was barefoot—that was a first—and I tried very hard not to stare. It was really unfair that a man should have such nicely formed legs and feet. I wondered whether his sisters were built the same way, or if they resented his good fortune.

His eyes narrowed, a darker blue in the shade. "So it has nothing to do with cutting yourself off from a past you want nothing to do with?"

I wasn't angry at him because he'd spoken the truth. I was angry at myself for being so transparent to him. "I already told you why I choose not to have a cell phone."

"Yes, but I'm assuming your reasons don't really apply anymore."

His phone buzzed three times, then stopped, and then after only a brief pause it began again.

"Case in point," I said, pretending he hadn't spoken. "You're obviously annoyed that somebody is trying to reach you, but you're too addicted to your phone to turn it off or just leave it at your hotel. So you end up torturing not only yourself, but those nearby."

He reached into his pocket and held out his phone. "I didn't answer because I knew it was my oldest sister calling yet again. I've spoken to her several times since I've been here and have exchanged numerous texts and see no need to beat a dead horse. I'm hoping she'll come to realize that and stop—although it's not in her nature to leave things alone where I'm concerned."

For some reason I felt the need to leap to the defense of a woman

I'd never met. "She's just being an older sister. She obviously cares about you."

He leaned forward, his eyes probing. "And Maisy always did what you wanted her to do because she appreciated your caring?"

I swiveled to face him, the papers slipping from my lap. "You have no idea—"

The screen door slammed shut and we both turned to find Becky standing on the back steps. She was still in her school clothes, and I looked at my watch in surprise, having no idea it had gotten so late. My stomach growled as I realized I hadn't eaten lunch.

"There's somebody at the front door. For Mr. Graf. She says she's his sister."

I felt James stiffen beside me, his eyes searching the apiary as if it offered an escape route. "Speak of the devil," he said, as if our conversation had somehow conjured her. But it was apparent from his face that this wasn't completely unexpected.

I bent to gather up the pages and stick them in the folder. "Speaking from experience, the first few minutes are pretty hard, when you try to remember why you haven't spoken for so long. And then it gets harder from there as you both try to get past that thing between you before you realize that it's not going anywhere."

"Thanks for the help," he said, his long legs striding toward the house. He held open the door for Becky and me, and we followed him into the cool air-conditioning.

Maisy and the visitor were sitting on our grandmother's prized antique sofas, found at an estate sale in DeFuniak Springs. I'd spotted them first, their horsehair upholstery splitting at the seams, a foul odor of cat pee and something else I didn't want to identify. But even as a young girl I'd recognized good lines and strong bones, and timeless style and craftsmanship. My grandmother had stopped at the estate sale to find a large gilded mirror to hang in the stairwell, and had instead come back with the two couches. My grandfather had simply smiled indulgently. Grandma had the couches professionally cleaned and reupholstered in an elegant pale gold brocade and had always called them Georgia's sofas.

The woman sitting opposite Maisy now seemed to belong in that room of beautiful furniture. Tall, slender, and elegant, she looked just like her brother, with the same graceful lines and bone structure. She had her brother's golden red hair, and her eyes were the same dark shade of blue, but they were different from his. It took me a moment to realize that they were missing the haunted look that pooled behind his eyes like empty spaces.

She had smooth, pale skin that had obviously been sheltered from the sun for most of her life. She stood as we entered and smiled at James, fine lines appearing around her eyes.

He didn't step forward. "Hello, Caroline."

Caroline. His oldest sister, who must be in her mid-forties, since I knew James was about my age, in his mid-thirties. The sister whose calls he'd been ignoring.

"What are you doing here? And how did you find me?"

She took a step forward with outstretched arms. "Aren't I allowed to see my baby brother? Besides, you needed to know what happens when you don't answer your phone. I worry."

James took a step toward her and met her halfway before embracing her. Even though she was tall and wore heels, she just reached his jaw. When she pulled back, her eyes were damp. "Believe it or not, it wasn't that hard to find you. It's a small town."

He digested that for a moment before speaking again. "I'm assuming you've already met Maisy. This is her sister, Georgia Chambers," he said, indicating me. "She's the china expert I told you about who's doing a good job of chasing down Grandmother's china."

She extended a slender-fingered hand, but her grasp was surprisingly strong, her gaze probing. "It's a pleasure to meet you." Her gaze slid down my outfit and I braced myself. She wore an exquisite emerald green silk blouse that set off her hair, tucked neatly into a white linen skirt that hadn't dared to wrinkle. Understated. Elegant. Expensive. "Is that vintage Pucci?"

I looked at her with surprise. "Yes, actually. It is. How did you know that?"

"My youngest sister, Elizabeth, and I owned a vintage dress shop in the Village for a while—until she got pregnant with her third and couldn't do it anymore. But I adore vintage clothing. You really have a good eye—that color is striking on you."

"Thank you," I said, sending James a wary glance. "He didn't mention your store to me, which you'd think would be a given, considering."

Caroline actually rolled her eyes, which made me laugh, and I decided right then that I liked James's sister. "He's got that male gene; what can I say?"

Looking seriously annoyed, James said, "If you're done, maybe you'd like to tell me how long you plan to stay and if you need me to arrange for your flight back home."

Ignoring him, she directed her attention at me. "I'm actually starving. May I take you and your sister and niece to a late lunch or early dinner? James can come, too, if he promises to stop scowling at me."

"That's very kind of you," Maisy said, "but I need to stay here. My mother and grandfather haven't been well, and I'd feel better if someone were here." Almost reluctantly, she added, "Georgia's been with them all day while I've been at work, so it's my turn."

I sent her a look of appreciation, but she was staring at Becky's upturned and hopeful face. "And you've got homework and a science test tomorrow."

"Thank you," I said to Caroline. "James and I were so busy working that we sort of forgot to eat. I'm famished." I looked at James, expecting him to say something similar, but he just scowled at his sister. I was once again reminded of how little time it took for a sibling to return us to our childhood and the squabbles in the backseat of the family sedan.

Caroline picked up a black quilted Chanel bag—definitely vintage—from the sofa and slid the gold chain over her shoulder. "Great. It's all settled. Are you coming, James? Because you know if you don't, you will be the lead topic of conversation."

Without a word, he headed toward the front door while I grabbed my purse. As he closed the door behind us, he said, "I suggest we take the car. Caroline isn't used to the heat and would probably melt."

Ignoring him, Caroline tucked her arm into mine, her fingers clutching a little too tightly, belying her light banter. "I can't wait to get to know you better. I already think we have lots in common."

I felt James's eyes boring into our backs as we headed to my car.

We spent the entire drive listening as Caroline gushed over how great my car was. She knew a lot more about cars than James did and actually knew how to drive, and even admitted to owning a minivan to shuttle carpools involving her four children under twelve in her Connecticut suburb.

James didn't say a word until I'd snagged a curbside parking spot on Commerce right in front of the Owl Café. He opened my door while I was still hunting for my purse, and I watched as Caroline waited for him to open hers. I remembered what he'd told me about her protecting him after he'd been caught tossing eggs from their apartment window when they were kids. It seemed sisters were the same everywhere, a best friend and a best enemy all rolled up into a single person who would always know you better than you knew yourself. Which told me, too, that there was a very good reason Caroline had come all the way to Apalachicola, and there was more to it than just checking in. I rubbed my arms where her fingers had clenched my arm, convincing me that I was right.

Caroline stood on the wide sidewalk looking down Avenue D toward Riverfront Park and the Apalachicola River in the near distance, the historic brick two-story mercantile buildings with overhangs sheltering the sidewalk like old ladies with parasols. "This is really stunning. Not to sound snobby, but I've always thought that to be a real city there needed to be skyscrapers and lots of neon lights. I've been here all of an hour and I can already see how misguided I've been. Looks like people down here have been keeping this place a secret."

"It is called 'the Forgotten Coast' for a reason," I said. "Unfortunately, developers have set their sights on this part of the gulf, and I don't think they'll be happy until there are condos lining the shoreline here and on St. George Island across the bay."

She sent me a wide smile that looked just like her brother's. "I *knew* we had a lot in common. I'm a card-carrying member of the National Trust. I've got a real soft spot for preserving our collective history."

I could almost sense James groaning behind me. Ignoring him, I said, "If we have time, I'll take you to Riverfront Park, where you can see where the old steamboats used to line the docks."

"I'll look forward to it." She tucked her arm into mine again, her grip not as desperate this time, and I led them to the door of the restaurant that had just opened for the four-o'clock dinner crowd.

The Owl Café was a childhood memory of after-church brunches with our grandparents and Birdie. The food had always been good, which was why I'd suggested it—that and the image of my grandparents and their friends making me hope for an older crowd. Or at least people who wouldn't remember me from high school.

James finally broke his brooding silence as we waited for our table. "So, really, how did you find me?" he asked Caroline.

"After I failed to get hold of you, I called the Big Easy Auction Gallery and spoke with Mr. Mandeville. He said Georgia didn't have a cell number where she could be reached, but he did say you'd driven here together from New Orleans and that Apalachicola was small enough so that it wouldn't be too hard to find you.

"I didn't believe him, of course, until he told me there was technically only one full stoplight in the entire town. So I flew into Panama City, rented a car at the airport, and drove straight here. I passed an interesting establishment with a lot of lawn ornamentation for sale and asked the woman there if she knew where to find you and a Georgia Chambers. She was very helpful, although she seemed mostly interested in selling me a mermaid for my front yard at home."

I choked back a laugh. "I'm assuming she told you that she's my aunt Marlene. And be thankful that her Loch Ness Monster is at her house instead of the business. It would probably be in your backseat right now."

A smiling waitress whom I was thankful I didn't recognize appeared and picked up three menus from the hostess stand. "Would you like to sit outside?"

I was about to say yes when I saw the look of concern on Caroline's face. Turning back to the waitress, I said, "Inside is fine. It's pretty humid today."

The waitress smiled indulgently. "It's only eighty-five percent—not bad, considering it's early May."

I saw Caroline's eyes widen briefly before following the waitress to our table. We opened our menus and I was happy to find several of my old favorites. "I highly recommend the crab dip for starters, and then the fried-oyster salad. All the seafood here is locally sourced, so it's really fresh."

James continued to glower as Caroline squinted at her menu. "Are fried oysters anything like oysters Rockefeller?" She looked up at me expectantly.

"Well, they both have oysters in them, but these are battered and deep fried and you will think you've died and gone to heaven when you eat one. Especially if you dip it in the homemade creamy horseradish dressing."

James thrummed his fingers on his closed menu, waiting for us to finish. "How long are you planning on staying, Caroline?"

Her eyes appeared wide and innocent. "My original intention was just to have a quick visit with you and then be off, but this is such a charming town, and Georgia and I seem to have so much in common that I was thinking of staying a few days. Take a little vacation. Henry needs to learn how hard it is to run the household and schedules of four children, so this will be good for both of us."

A tic appeared in his jaw. "Where are you staying?"

"I'm at the Consulate in a suite overlooking the river. They mentioned a young man who looked like me was staying there, too."

James gave his sister a hard stare, and he reminded me so much of Maisy when she was angry with me that I almost laughed. We were saved by the appearance of the waitress to take our orders.

We all sipped from our ice waters, Caroline and I making small talk while James sat in stony silence. Either Caroline was used to this facet of James's personality and didn't comment on it, or maybe I was unnerved because of how different it was from the thoughtful and mature man I thought I'd grown to know and like.

The food arrived and the conversation switched to their grandmother's china. "How close are you to finding a value for the Limoges?" Caroline asked.

"Closer," I said, "but it's proven to be a lot harder than I thought it would be. It appears it may have been a custom design created by a French artist named Emile Duval in the latter half of the nineteenth century.

"What's skewing my whole thought process is that I believe I saw a piece from the same set here in my mother's house—years ago. Unfortunately, we're still looking for it. Common sense tells me that if it's the same pattern, it couldn't be a custom design. Because that would be a million-to-one chance that they're pieces from the same set. But until I can put eyes on it, I can't say for sure."

Caroline nodded thoughtfully. "So what's the next step?"

"I have a contact at the largest Limoges porcelain museum in France who's checking the old records to see if there is a paper trail with Emile's name that might lead us to the client. We're also going in the opposite direction, checking an account ledger from an estate in Emile's hometown, hoping to see a payment made either to him directly or to the Haviland Company."

Caroline sliced into a fried oyster with a fork and knife. "Isn't just knowing that it's a Limoges pattern from the late nineteenth century enough to give a value?"

"Certainly. I could rattle off something today. But that might mean a lowball estimate. If it is a custom design, and the client was somebody prominent, or a historical figure, the actual value would be much higher. I'm running out of trails to follow, and if I get to the end and still don't have more information, I think we can assume it wasn't custom but a limited-run pattern and leave it at that. Then I'll be able to prepare a value estimation based on that assumption."

I glanced over at James. "Your brother has been a huge help—sifting through the Internet for hours as well as poring over volumes of china catalogs. He could probably describe dozens of Limoges patterns in his sleep."

A corner of his mouth softened in an attempt not to smile. He quickly picked up a pita point and dragged it through the crab dip. I put an oyster in my mouth and chewed thoughtfully. "Did your grandmother ever tell you anything about the china? James said all he remembered was that she was proud of it, but never used it. But since you're older, I was hoping you might recall something she might have said about it."

Caroline delicately wiped the corners of her mouth with her napkin. "I do remember her being upset by a couple of missing pieces. She left a space for them in her china cabinet, as if she expected that one day they would be back. One of them was a large piece—its space was front and center."

"Had it been broken?" I asked.

"I don't know. You'd think if it had, she would have just closed up the ranks so nobody would notice it missing."

I looked down at my empty plate, fleetingly wondering whether I should be embarrassed for eating so much food. "Do you remember which pieces?"

Pale gold eyebrows drew together. "No—but I could ask Elizabeth to go look. She still lives in the city and can go over to Grandmother's house in Long Island. Why?"

"It's a long shot, but the piece I found here was a soup cup—with finger loops on two sides. Just out of curiosity, it would be interesting to know if that's one of the missing items. Even if the patterns aren't identical, if we find it, it could be a nice fill-in for your grandmother's set."

Caroline shook her head slowly. "I really have no idea if that's one of the missing pieces. I'll ask Elizabeth to check and to take a photo of one of our soup cups and text it to you so you can see if it's the same one."

James pushed away his plate. "Have her send it to me—Georgia doesn't have a cell phone." He held up his hand as she opened her mouth to speak. "I promise I won't delete it without looking at it first."

Caroline grimaced. "How reassuring to know that our brother treasures every word from us."

"Maybe if my sisters had something new and interesting to say, I might be tempted to listen."

To ease the tension that seemed to bristle in the air between them like static electricity, I turned to Caroline. "Where was your grandmother from? James thought she'd brought the china to the United States when she moved here after World War Two."

"That's the assumption, anyway. It's a long story. I don't know how much James has told you, but they came from Switzerland. But my grandmother was half French and half Italian. She moved to Switzerland during the war and met our grandfather, a Swiss national, and they emigrated to the United States soon after the war ended, along with her entire family that included seven children, and an entire set of china. It was a sweet love story—remember, James?"

He barely nodded.

Caroline continued. "They were dirt-poor, and all of them living in a single-bedroom apartment in Brooklyn." She was silent for a moment. "My great-grandmother got sick and some of the younger children had to go live with other families because they couldn't afford to take care of them. Our grandmother worked in a jewelry store in Manhattan as a salesgirl, and they needed her paycheck to pay for her mother's medical care and living expenses."

"And yet she didn't think to sell the Limoges?" I asked.

"No." Caroline shook her head. "My great-grandmother made her swear not to sell a single piece of it, no matter how bad things became. To my knowledge, none of it was ever sold."

Her gaze met her brother's. "Our family managed to not only survive, but thrive despite the hardships. My grandfather put himself through college and got a job on Wall Street in the mailroom of a brokerage firm and worked his way up while feeding his wife's siblings." She reached across the table and placed her hand on James's.

"We come from a line of strong, resilient people, don't we?" It almost seemed as if she'd forgotten I was listening.

The waitress appeared with the check, and James took it and stuck his AmEx on top of it before abruptly sliding his chair back, the legs scraping noisily across the wood floor. "Excuse me, ladies. I'm going to the men's room. I'll meet you outside."

I started to slide my own chair back, but Caroline's solid grip on my arm stopped me.

"Please excuse my audacity—I know we've just met. But how is he? How is he really?"

Her desperate look told me that my first instinct that she was here for another reason than just to check in was right.

"He seems fine. He doesn't seem depressed or anything, if that's what you mean. He's interested in researching the china, seems to be enjoying meeting my family and interacting with new people." I paused for a moment, feeling unfaithful to James. "He told me about his wife."

"About her dying? Did he mention anything else?"

I nodded. "He told me that she was having an affair, and he didn't know about it until after her death."

Caroline closed her eyes for a moment. "Did he tell you with whom?"

I shook my head.

She studied me for a long time, considering her words and whether she would say anything at all. Finally, she said, "I'm only telling you this because James has already trusted you with more about him than he allows most people to know. I think he considers you to be a friend, and that's something that doesn't come easily to him these days." She took a deep breath. "Kate was having an affair with James's best friend—the best man at their wedding. And it had apparently been going on since the three of them were at Wharton together. Before they were married."

I pressed my fingers over my mouth.

She leaned closer to me. "He had a nervous breakdown. We . . . we were afraid that he'd hurt himself, so we checked him into a facility with doctors who could help him, because he kept telling us that he wanted to die."

I understand fragile minds. Now I understood what James had meant. Understood those empty spaces behind his eyes. And why he'd said we had a lot in common. As if brokenness were a private club.

"That's why I'm here. To really make sure he's all right." She reached for my hand just as she'd done to James. "Is he?"

"He seems to be. But I'm glad you told me so that I know. And I'll let you know if I think anything's changed. But I really think he's okay."

She gave me a tentative smile. "Thank you. I can't tell you how much better I feel knowing that you're here with him."

I pulled away, looking down at my hands. "You don't know me. You might not be confiding in me if you did."

"I know you more than you think I do. James told you that he needed a distraction because of his wife's death and you let him come here without question." She looked away for a moment, as if considering whether she should share another confidence. "He told me that you collect antique locks and keys because you believe everything has an answer. He needs someone right now who really believes that."

She straightened suddenly, then pulled back her chair. It wasn't until I felt someone helping to pull out my own chair that I realized James had returned.

Pleading a headache and a need to get home, I left James and Caroline to walk the short block to their hotel, Caroline promising to pick up her rental car at the house the next day. After only a moment's hesitation I put the top down on my car and drove across the Gorrie Bridge to Eastpoint and then over another bridge to St. George Island. I needed to feel the wind in my hair and the sun on my face, and to try not to think about fragile minds, or how the heart needed more than the slip of years to mend its brokenness.

chapter 23

In cooler weather, the bees remain in the beehive but don't hibernate.
The queen doesn't lay eggs but stays in a bee cluster surrounded by
her worker bees. They flap their wings nonstop, keeping the
temperature in the beehive around ninety-one degrees until warmer
weather arrives.

—NED BLOODWORTH'S BEEKEEPER'S JOURNAL

Maisy

Maisy sat on a stool at the counter of the Old Time Soda Fountain next to Becky, looking up at the menu tacked above the scalloped green-and-white awning on the wall in front of them. "I want an ice-cream sundae," Becky said after about five minutes of deliberation.

Maisy smiled at the young ponytailed girl behind the counter. "Make it two, please. One scoop chocolate and one scoop vanilla, extra chocolate sauce, and just a pinch of sprinkles." Despite a difference in opinion about many things, Maisy and Becky were always in agreement about their ice cream. "And two Cokes, please."

She was rewarded with a rare grin from her daughter. Although she was exhausted from a week at work and wanted nothing more than to return to her bed after taking Becky to an early Saturday-morning tennis clinic and spending the rest of the morning running errands, they'd ended up at the Soda Fountain. It was something the three of them had done before Lyle had moved out, which meant Maisy had avoided it for months. But when Becky had asked to go, she hadn't been able to say no.

When the sundaes arrived, Maisy stuck her spoon into the dome of whipped cream on top and automatically handed the cherry over to Becky. Even though she loved them as much as her daughter did, it had been something her grandfather had done for her and Georgia when they were girls, always asking for two cherries on his sundae so he could share with his girls. If only Maisy could enjoy her treat without hearing Birdie's voice in her head reminding her how many calories were in each bite.

"Where's Aunt Georgia?" Becky said with her mouth full.

Maisy sent her "the look" and Becky immediately closed her mouth.

"I texted James that we were here, so hopefully he got the message and told Georgia. But they were touring the Orman House, so they might not make it in time."

Maisy tried to ignore the look of disappointment on Becky's face. What was it with near strangers in their lives whose absence only served to make them more mythical? Maisy was the one who'd been there through colic, and nightmares, and first-day-of-school jitters. And two emergency-room visits, with a broken arm and a concussion. Yet Georgia wore the halo, the breastplate of steel earned through annual birthday cards and Christmas gifts.

The door opened behind them, bringing a slap of heat against their backs. Maisy and Becky were too immersed in their ice cream to turn around until they heard the two young voices behind them.

"L-look, Em-mily. It's B-Becky S-Sawyers."

Becky stiffened beside her as Maisy turned around to see who'd spoken, too surprised by the blatant *meanness* of the voice to find her anger. She recognized Madison Bennett as one of Becky's best friends from kindergarten through fourth grade who no longer came by the house or called. She was also the girl in Becky's math class who'd cut a chunk of Becky's hair. When Maisy had asked Becky about it, she'd pleaded with Maisy not to make a big deal of it. Reluctantly Maisy had agreed, but still had a meeting with the principal and Becky's teacher to keep an eye out and to defuse any future bullying by Miss Bennett and her crew.

The girl practically attached to Madison's hip was Emily Nichols—another one of Becky's former best friends—whose most distinguished accomplishment was being Madison's current best friend.

Maisy swiveled completely in her seat to face them, and when the girls recognized Maisy, their eyes quickly darted away. She looked behind the girls and saw Madison's uncle, Bobby, staring at her with a grin twisting his lips. Her stomach lurched every time she saw Bobby, even after all this time. She'd always imagined that with Georgia gone she could forget. But that was the thing with memories, those little blades that cut you when you least expected it. Even the smell of barbecue or the sound of a baby's laughter could make her double over. Still.

"Well, it's Miz Sawyers. We were just talking about you and your sister who used to live here, weren't we, girls?"

The girls gave noncommittal nods. "Hello, Ms. Sawyers," they said in unison before pretending to study the menu.

Ignoring Bobby, Maisy slid from her stool, prepared to teach the girls something about manners, since Bobby seemed oblivious. Becky's hand reached out and grabbed her arm. In an urgent whisper, she said, "P-please don't, M-Mama. You'll only m-make it w-worse."

Maisy froze, blinking at her daughter without seeing her, feeling the impotent rage she'd felt only once before. All she could see was her younger self standing in Birdie's empty bedroom as Georgia told her that Birdie had gone away and left them behind. She hadn't believed her and had run into the apiary, looking for her mother, succeeding only in getting stung over and over.

Maisy tried to tell herself that she was an adult, that she knew what she needed to say and do. And then the door opened again and she heard Georgia's voice as she entered with James and his sister Caroline.

"Great—so glad y'all are still here," Georgia said as she approached Becky for a hug. "Do they still make the chocolate sodas?"

Becky only shrugged, the words apparently sticking to her tongue. Georgia leaned in closer. "Are you okay?"

When Becky didn't answer, Georgia looked up at Maisy, who indicated the group behind her. She turned slowly, the stiffness in her shoulders indicating to Maisy that she'd seen Bobby and the girls.

"Lookin' good, Georgie," Bobby said as he let his eyes wander over Georgia, taking in her undoubtedly vintage Lilly Pulitzer mini-dress and her exposed legs.

"Hello, Bobby," she said. Her eyes moved to the girls standing next to them. "One of these girls must be your niece, Madison."

He reached a beefy arm around the girl. "This is her. Gets her good looks from my side of the family," he said with a loud laugh that sounded more like a bark. He jerked his chin at Becky. "Your niece is just as pretty as her aunt, too. Just as long as she doesn't open her mouth to talk, right?"

The girls pretended to try to hide their giggles, but Becky's restraining hand held Maisy back.

With a frozen calmness that alarmed even Maisy, Georgia turned to the waitress at the register. "We'll have three chocolate sodas, please. With straws and spoons."

Caroline and James smiled tentatively at Maisy, as if they realized that they had somehow walked in on the middle of a gunfight.

"I think you must have lost my number, because my phone ain't been ringin'," Bobby said.

Georgia took her time fishing in her purse to retrieve her wallet and then to count out the right amount of bills and change. "No, I didn't lose it," she said as she handed over the money to the cashier. "I was just waiting for hell to freeze over."

His face sobered quickly. "That's not a very nice thing to say, Georgie. I think we can both remember a time when you were a lot sweeter to me. Surely one bad memory can't erase all the good ones, huh?"

For a moment Maisy thought she was going to throw up. *One bad memory.* Had he really just said that?

James's eyes narrowed, assessing the situation, but he didn't say anything, as if even he realized that Georgia had everything under control.

While they waited for their fountain drinks, Georgia kept the icy smile on her face. She put her arm around Becky's shoulders and squeezed. When the waitress had finished making the chocolate sodas, she placed them on the bar, and then, with a wink at Becky, put a spoonful of cherries on top of her half-eaten sundae.

"Th-thanks," she said, her smile foundering when she realized the word had skidded off her tongue.

The two girls began giggling, not even trying to hide it, while Bobby stared at Georgia.

With her frozen smile, she approached Madison and put an arm around her. Emily wisely shrank back. In a voice loud enough for Maisy and Becky to hear, she said, "I sure hope you're getting good grades, Maddie. Because you'll need a good job to pay for all the plastic surgery you're going to need when you're older so you don't end up looking like your uncle Bobby." She smiled over at Becky. "Not everybody can be as lucky as Becky to get brains, beauty, *and* talent."

"Now, see here, Georgie . . ." Bobby took a step near Georgia.

Georgia picked up the plastic cups and handed one to James and one to Caroline, then took one herself. After a long pull from her straw, she addressed Bobby. "Nobody calls me Georgie anymore, Bobby," she said, emphasizing the last syllable. "Because I'm not nineteen years old. I'd like to think I've matured enough to use my full name." Facing Maisy, she said, "When you're done, come on outside with us. I need some fresh air, and I want to show Becky the most amazing tennis outfit I bought for her. It will show off her wonderful arm muscles and make her opponents tremble."

Becky was staring down into her melted sundae, the extra cherries bobbing in the runny ice cream, a trail of red running into the vanilla. Her cheeks were ruddy, like they usually got when she was in the middle of a match. She was looking at the sundae with such intensity that Maisy was sure that Becky wanted to dissolve into the ice cream, too, to disappear and pretend she'd never been there at all.

Maisy recognized it because she knew what it was like to pretend to be invisible, to wait it out while Georgia fought her battles for her. *Because we're a team. Because Birdie is our mother and none of this would happen if we had a normal mother. We don't, but we'll always have each other.*

Maisy turned to Georgia to make her stop, but she was already crossing the black-and-white tiled floor toward the door, her cheeks ruddy like Becky's. Caroline's hand clutched James's arm, as if to stop him from interfering. His rigid face and clenched jaw made him seem even more like a Viking warrior, and in any other circumstance Maisy might have laughed. Might even have pointed it out to Georgia, because still, after all these years, that was usually the first person she thought of to share something funny or interesting.

Before Georgia reached the door, it opened and Lyle stood there in his uniform, a surprised look on his face when he spotted Georgia. "What a nice surprise . . ." he began, before his gaze traveled behind her to Bobby and the two girls, and then to Maisy and his daughter, who looked like she wanted to melt alongside the vanilla and chocolate puddles in her dish.

An ugly glint appeared in Bobby's eyes. "Well, look who's here. You back to start another catfight? Or maybe that one never ended."

Maisy had her hand on Lyle's chest before he could step forward. After a warning glance at him not to move, she faced Bobby, and in her sternest teacher voice, using her index finger to emphasize each word, she said, "Not one more word from you. Do you understand? Or I will be happy to tell everybody why your mama won't speak to you anymore. Just because I don't gossip doesn't mean that I don't know things." She smiled at the two girls as if to reassure them that she was still nice Ms. Sawyers, a classmate's mother. Turning back to Bobby, she said, "People who live in glass houses shouldn't throw stones. If you don't understand what that means, ask Becky to explain it to you."

Then she slid a few bills across the counter to pay their tab, grabbed Becky's hand, and led all six of them out of the store. They stood facing one another out on the sidewalk, blinking in the bright sunlight.

"Daddy!" Becky ran to her father and buried her face in his chest as if she could burrow there until spring. One arm went around her back while his other hand cradled her blond head, and Maisy was reminded of when Becky was a baby, and how carefully Lyle had held her, as if she were the most precious thing in the world.

Caroline's hand was tucked into the crook of James's arm while she lifted her straw to her mouth and took a long sip. "Well, this certainly is delicious."

Maisy and Georgia looked at each other and slapped hands to their mouths to hide the insidious laughter that was creeping up their throats. Only the very well-bred would come up with something so innocuous to say after such a scene, and only Maisy and Georgia would find it hilarious.

"I'm sorry," Maisy said to Caroline and James. "For all of this. I'm sure you didn't expect front-row seats to a soap opera."

"Please don't apologize," Caroline said. "We're no strangers to drama, are we, James?"

James didn't seem to hear her, his gaze focused on Lyle and Becky.

"Are we, James?" Caroline repeated.

"Um, no," he said, apparently guessing at an answer. "Have you met Lyle Sawyers? Lyle, this is my sister, Caroline Harrison. Caroline, this is Maisy's husband."

Maisy opened her mouth to correct him, to let Caroline know that Lyle was still her husband only because she hadn't filed the divorce papers yet. But they'd been filled out and were waiting in the top drawer of her desk, where they'd been for three months.

Lyle reached his hand around Becky and shook Caroline's. "It's nice to meet you."

Becky lifted her head from her daddy's chest and looked at Georgia. "Did you really get me a new tennis outfit?"

Georgia cleared her throat. "No, but I've been meaning to. I just . . . Well, those girls needed to know that you're a great tennis player and that you've got fans." She looked nervously at the door behind them, as if expecting Bobby to come out any minute. "Why don't we take these back to the house? We've got plenty of rocking chairs and porch steps for everybody."

"I'm on duty, so I'll take a rain check, but thank you," Lyle said, and Maisy looked away so she wouldn't see the smile he gave Georgia. "It's nice to meet you." He nodded toward Caroline. He kissed Becky on the top of her head and gently pulled her away. "I'll call you later, gator."

Only Lyle was allowed to be corny with her anymore. The corner of Becky's mouth tilted up. "After a while, crocodile."

"Now we're talkin'," he said as they shared a fist bump. He said good-bye to the rest of them and headed back to his patrol car, Maisy missing his kiss on her own forehead more than she'd ever admit.

"Thank you." Georgia's voice was close to Maisy's ear.

"For what?"

"For what you said in there."

Maisy shrugged, uncomfortable. "I learned from the best. And I should be thanking you for sticking up for Becky." The words were stiff, but needed to be said. She only wanted to add, *I should have done it. You've just always been faster.*

"Can I ride back in Aunt Georgia's car?" Becky asked.

Maisy ignored the feeling of swallowed splinters in her throat. "Sure, sweetie. I'll see you back at the house."

"I'll come with you, if that's all right," Caroline said. "As long as I'm allowed to drink this in your car."

"Of course." Maisy smiled.

They'd gone only a few feet down the sidewalk when Caroline's phone beeped. They paused a moment for her to look at the screen before her head popped up, an excited expression on her face. "Georgia? Come look at this. I just got a text from my sister Elizabeth. She said one of the missing pieces is a soup cup. She sent a picture, too. Is this the one you saw in your house?"

Georgia moved next to Caroline, a full head shorter even with two-inch wedge sandals, and peered at the phone. "Oh," she said, stepping back, her lips pale.

"Is it the same?" Caroline asked.

Georgia nodded, then lifted her eyes to meet Maisy's.

"What does this mean?" Maisy asked.

Her voice seemed to lack the air needed to force the words out. "It could be that it wasn't a custom set, and Grandma found a few pieces at a yard sale somewhere."

"Or," James said, "they're both from the same set, and at least a piece of it somehow ended up in Apalachicola."

Georgia continued to look at Maisy, as if the answer lay somewhere between them, somewhere in the knowledge that Georgia had once seen the piece of china in their mother's room and Birdie had told her to keep it a secret.

Maisy sucked in a breath of air, trying to eradicate the feeling that she was drowning, latching onto Georgia's smile like a life preserver.

"Without knowing more about the pattern, I can't explain it," Georgia said, her voice sounding unnatural. "All we need to do is find that piece if it's still in the house, and hope it's a different pattern."

"Why would we hope it's different?" Caroline asked.

"Because if it's from the same pattern, then we'll have to figure out how it got here. And I . . ." She swallowed, her eyes meeting Maisy's. "I don't have a clue where to even start." She paused. "Or what it could mean."

chapter 24

Once the space for eggs becomes limited, the queen bee starts to lay drone eggs followed by young queen bee candidates. After laying eggs for the next generation, the old queen leaves her beehive with half of her children. The new queen bee then goes out for a mating flight and returns to the beehive to lay eggs, which is the most important function of her entire life.

—NED BLOODWORTH'S BEEKEEPER'S JOURNAL

Birdie

*S*kid. *Scut. Drag.* I tried to focus on my crayon dragging color against a black-and-white page, if only to erase the sounds from the attic above. Each movement seemed to flash a light, illuminating a corner too briefly for it to register. I pressed the crayon down harder, wondering when I could stop. When I could stand to turn on the light myself and begin to speak.

My knees cramped from being stuck beneath the small child's table in Becky's room for too long. We were coloring even though we were both too old for coloring books. One of the dozens of therapists I'd seen had suggested to Maisy that it might be a good artistic outlet for me, and she'd bought me a stack of what she called "adult coloring books" and a boxed set of one hundred and fifty-two crayons in more colors than I knew existed.

In many ways she was right: It kept me from pulling out my hair or shredding my clothes with scissors. Or staring into a murky past that seemed to have no beginning or end. Becky seemed to enjoy it, too. It calmed her, helped her smooth her words as she talked to me.

I tried to adjust my legs under the pink table, a piece of furniture that was more suited to a three-year-old than a nine-year-old. Maisy and Becky must have noticed, too, but neither had done anything about it. It was almost as if they were trying to hold on to Becky's childhood with both hands, afraid to let go and have her spin off into an uncertain future. I wondered sometimes whether I had passed this on to both of them, the fear of the unnamed and unknown. A fear of not remembering your own past.

The sliding and scuffing noise returned above our heads. Maisy and Georgia were up in the attic now, carefully examining everything. When they'd returned to the house, Georgia had been excited about a picture on a phone, and they'd rushed upstairs to the attic, Maisy complaining the whole time that she'd already looked there. But first Georgia had shown the picture to me, and I could almost hear the sound of the projector starting in my head, a bright beam of light showing me a piece of china hidden in the back of my closet. It wasn't there anymore. I knew that much. It was somewhere else, and I was glad I didn't remember where. I'd stared at the phone screen and had kept my expression blank.

"Birdie?"

I looked at Becky when I realized she'd said my name several times.

"You're coloring out of the lines."

The page I'd been working on was an intricate drawing of an anonymous field in summer, with various insects and birds filling the air, and a row of cypress trees on the edge of the page. I had chosen a purple crayon, Vivid Violet, because it reminded me of something pleasant, but I'd been busy scribbling over the field without thought to the individual plants or leaves or feather or wing. It was as if wiry purple tumbleweeds had rolled onto the field, collecting everything in their tangled mess.

Scratch. The noise of something large being slid across the attic floor sat me up straight, turning my insides to melted wax. I smelled the wax, felt the heat go out from a lit candle, felt myself immersed in darkness again. I heard a small snap and I latched onto the sound, opening my palm to see I'd broken the crayon.

They won't find it. The thought wafted through my fractured mind like smoke, teasing me with a gossamer memory. *What? What won't they find?* My mind darted away from the question, unwilling to hear the answer. *Something important. Something that could break a heart.*

I remembered back to the summer the movie people came to Apalach, how the scouts had visited the house three times, saying it would be perfect for the director or even one of the main stars to stay in during the duration of the filmmaking. Except it would need updating, with new furniture and curtains. They liked my grandmother's paintings, and said they could stay, but we'd probably need to move the beehives for the duration. Daddy hadn't been happy about it, but he'd never been able to tell me no. Maybe he should have, just that once.

Scratch. The sound came again from another corner of the attic. *They'll find it.* My thoughts skittered away again before I could ask, *Find what?*

A tap sounded on the partly opened door, and I let the broken crayon drop to the floor.

"May I come in?" my sister-in-law, with her leathery skin and rough voice, called from the doorway.

"Hi, Aunt Marlene," Becky said with her beautiful smile. "We're just coloring."

"Hello, sweetie." Marlene entered the room, the smells of dog and motorcycle gas preceding her.

"Hello to you, too, Birdie." She stood over the table and looked down at the books. "Nice job, Becky. Not sure about yours, Birdie. I think you're supposed to stay within the lines."

I responded by turning my face and pretending I hadn't heard. "She knows," Becky said. "I told her."

Marlene edged backward and sat on the edge of the bed. "Where is everybody? Nobody answered the door, but I saw Georgia's car."

"They're up in the attic looking for s-something." Becky's stutter meant she'd sensed my apprehension, her awareness like that of a bee's antennae in charge of all movement and behavior.

Marlene smoothed her sun-spotted hands on the soft pink bedspread. "What are they looking for?"

The light began to fade in my mind, the flickering projector grinding to a stop. But I forced my eyes to see myself ten years ago, rushing up the attic stairs to see what antiques the designer might think could add an air of sophistication to the house, to make my house fit for a Hollywood actor.

I remembered passing Maisy on the stairs and shouting at her to go put on some lipstick and do something with her hair, and she'd started to cry. I didn't have time to tell her that I thought she was beautiful the way she was, but that Hollywood had different standards. She was pregnant again, too soon after losing Lilyanna. It was her fourth pregnancy, her first since Lilyanna, but I could tell already by how her face seemed hollowed out, her eyes sunken in their sockets, that this one wouldn't last, either. But I pretended I didn't see her pain, too afraid that if it got too close to me, I'd be lost again. I wished I could go back to that day and make myself stop on those stairs with Maisy, to tell her what I really saw when I looked at her. To stop myself from going up to the attic. But I can't. Life cannot be lived in reverse, no matter how much we wish it could.

And then I remembered Georgia stopping me in the hallway outside her room, angry at me for making Maisy cry, and I was near tears for disappointing Georgia once again. *Mama, I'm in trouble.* I shook my head at her, told her that I didn't have time. I was too busy with my new distraction, anything to avoid remembering a past that got farther and farther away with each new project and halfhearted dream of being more than ordinary.

The wave of heat that hit me as soon as I opened the attic door almost made me retreat. The single dormer window shot sporadic beams of light through the dust-encrusted shutters, guiding me across the attic floor. Holding my breath, I threw open the shutters and after several attempts was able to lift the window sash, allowing in warm, fresh air. I gulped it in, then fanned my hands, hoping to clear out the mustiness of the unused attic.

I'd been creating a pile of useful things by the top of the steps, including some of my mama's estate-sale finds of miscellaneous china vases and silver pillboxes, when I spotted what looked like an old cedar chest against the wall. It had once been at the foot of my parents' bed, but had been moved up here after Mama died. Hoping it contained some of her artwork, I carefully raised the lid and peered inside. For a moment it seemed as if I were staring into a time tunnel, colors and faces and places swirling in front of me, peering around the dark curtain into my past.

Blood rushed through my head, the bright white pain sending me stumbling backward, as everything I'd forgotten filled every fold in my brain, the knowledge a sharpened blade cutting deep. The only way I knew to make it stop was to close my eyes and make myself forget again, make myself forget the very words that could be used to share a story that should never be told.

"I actually came by to ask Birdie something."

Marlene's voice pulled me back to the pink table and the coloring book and the mackerel skies outside Becky's window. They showed a storm was coming and there would be no shelter from it.

Marlene came and sat down next to me on the floor, her skinny dark legs crisscrossed like a child's. She looked up at me with George's eyes and I wondered if she did that on purpose, if she knew that every time I looked into her eyes my heart broke a little more.

"Ever since they found your daddy's truck in the swamp, something's been bugging me."

The silver-skinned clouds with their pink and orange tint slid by in the sky outside. *Mackerel sky, mackerel sky, never long wet, never long dry.* The song came to me from deep in my memory, a memory of standing on the dock looking out across the bay toward the rippling sky that looked so much like the side of a fish, my hand tucked inside my father's.

"Something my brother, George, said to me before he shipped off to Vietnam."

The projector in my head flared to life, illuminating everything, leaving nothing in the dark corners. I closed my eyes, wanting to shield them from the truth, but the light came from inside my head so that nothing was hidden.

"He said that you knew who'd stolen your daddy's truck. And if they ever found it, they should ask you about it."

I stared at her, but it was George's face I saw, his angry eyes as I told him I didn't know if I could wait for him to come back from Vietnam. He was twenty-five—too old, I told him—having a bad feeling about him leaving. As if I knew that we shouldn't be separated. That being left alone with a secret we shared would be like digging a moat without a bridge to cross it. But he left anyway, saying he had to. That maybe a bullet to the head would fix what was broken in him. I understood what he meant more than he probably thought I would. I've never been able to make those I love stay with me.

I tried to find a song that would drown out the memories, to sing it loudly so Marlene would back away, would stop asking her questions. But I could only sit and look at her and see her brother, remember his leaving me and me pretending that I could be strong one more time.

chapter 25

"The busy bee has no time for sorrow."
William Blake

—NED BLOODWORTH'S BEEKEEPER'S JOURNAL

Georgia

I sat on Marlene's front steps and tilted back my beer bottle, letting the cold liquid slip down my throat. Marlene sat beside me, surrounded by her panting dogs, and in my own exhaustion I couldn't help but wonder why they were so tired.

The night air lay heavy and still, the sweat that coated my skin unable to evaporate. As soon as we'd finished searching every last nook and cranny in my grandfather's attic, I'd volunteered to look through Marlene's, just in case the soup cup had ended up there. After my grandmother had died, Grandpa in his grief had decided it would be easier to get over his sadness if he packed up everything that reminded him of her. I had saved some of Grandma's garage-sale finds before they could be hauled away and carted them over to Marlene's attic, where they still languished.

Among the few things that had escaped exile were a few of Grandma's paintings, because, he'd said, neither Birdie, Maisy, nor I was a skilled enough artist to make replacements. Only the fact that he was right took the sting from his words.

"You looked in all the drawers in the house?" Marlene asked.

"Almost. I mean, there's the bedroom furniture we haven't gone through, but it wouldn't make sense for it to be there. And Maisy said she and Grandpa already looked. I'll look just because you mentioned it, but I'm not holding out any hopes."

I drained the beer and had just set it on the step beside me when Marlene handed me another. "You deserve it, and you're not driving anywhere. You must be plum tuckered out, not to mention disappointed."

I took the bottle without argument and popped off the cap. "Why am I even here? I should have known that finding that soup cup after all these years would be impossible. It's been too long. It was probably a flea-market find, and Birdie kept it as a memento of her mother. I always assumed she wanted me to keep it a secret to hide it from Grandpa. He throws away everything."

"You're probably right," Marlene said, taking a swig from her own beer.

"It's just . . ." I slapped at a mosquito on my exposed abdomen. I'd changed into cutoff jeans shorts and a vintage patchwork halter top when I'd headed up to Marlene's un-air-conditioned attic. It was nothing I'd ever wear in public, but I felt safe donning it for attic scouring. I continued. "It's just that when James first showed me his teacup and saucer, I was pretty sure it was the same pattern. I just need to *see* it. I pride myself on being very accurate in my estimates, and I don't want to be wrong if the answer is *this* close," I said, holding up my thumb and index finger less than an inch apart.

I stretched my legs out in front of me, leaning my elbows on the step behind me. "Otherwise, why am I here?"

"Do you want me to answer that?"

I took a sip from my bottle. "Not really."

"Well, whether or not you find this piece of china, or if they find out who the man in your granddaddy's truck is, you can't leave until you've taken care of some unfinished business."

"Sure I can."

"But you won't. You're like your daddy with that streak of stubbornness as wide as the river. You've been looking for a reason to come down here where it didn't look like you were standing with your hat in your hand. And now you're here. What are you going to do next?"

I pulled up my knees and rested my chin on their rounded tops, searching for words, the beer making it difficult to catch my thoughts before they floated away. I looked up at the dusk sky and the pale outlines of clouds, but could only see fragments of broken china. "Nothing has changed. Not between Maisy and me, or with Birdie. I've tried; I really have. But I can't make people change. And I miss my job, and my house. My antique things."

"You're right about one thing, darlin'. You can't make other people change." She sent me a knowing glance, but I returned my gaze to the sky above again, and the moving bits of china that seemed to be searching for a place to fit like some giant jigsaw.

I took a deep breath, smelling the beer when I exhaled. "I told myself before I came over today that if I didn't find that soup cup, it was the universe telling me it's time to pack up my marbles and go home."

"What about Becky?"

The hurt was there, even cushioned by the alcohol. "What about her?"

Marlene was silent for a moment. "I saw Becky when I stopped by the house. She reminds me so much of you when you were her age—same gnawed fingernails and all. She seems to be carrying a world of troubles on her little shoulders, though. You sure can't keep things from those young ones. They might not know what it is, but they know when things aren't right. It comes out when she talks, too."

Marlene put her hand on my shoulder and began collecting our empty bottles from the steps. "I hate to think of her going into her teenage years like that. Kids aren't too nice about anybody different."

And I should know. I stared into the neck of my bottle, remembering a childhood of playground taunts about my mother, who thought she was more than ordinary and walked around town with fake-fur stoles and high heels, looking as out of place in Apalachicola as a polar bear. My biggest mistake had been in trying to defend her, at least until I realized the futility of it and developed my own dubious methods of separating myself from her.

"Maisy is doing a great job with Becky and wouldn't welcome my interference anyway. Whatever relationship Maisy and I had is too broken. I can't fix it."

"Not unless you're both willing to give up a little of your pride and resentment." She raised her eyebrows before tilting the remainder of her beer into her mouth. "If you want things to change, you have to stop waiting for someone else to make the first move."

I blamed the alcohol for my inability to argue with her, to let her know that I was fine with my life. That existing alone and without connections except to antiques and old china made life easier. And the past was an easy place to hide, an easy way to keep my eyes focused behind me instead of into a future I was afraid would look too much like my past.

Softly, Marlene said, "You need to give up something old if you want to gain something new."

I thought of Maisy and me as we'd once been, the bruises of nine years of separation a riptide in my mind. I felt strangely close to tears trying to imagine Maisy out of my life again. "But what if I ruin everything?"

"What if you don't?"

I twisted my neck to look up at my aunt. "You're supposed to tell me that I've given it my best shot and it's time to go home."

"Darlin', I'm not going to tell you to do anything—only you can decide what you're going to do next. I just don't think leaving right now is the answer. But this thing with your granddaddy and Birdie has got me worried. I'm thinking that you and Maisy are going to need each other. You're a lot stronger together than you are apart."

I held the cold bottle against my neck, and saw Maisy's face as I'd seen it in the crowd at the Seafood Festival ten long years ago. Being there when I was supposed to be traveling the country with my latest boyfriend and his band would have been shocking enough. If only that had been the worst of it.

"We were. But that was a long time ago."

The sound of an approaching car caught our attention as we watched the beam of two headlights turning into the drive, illuminating the slopes and curves of Nessie's serpentine cement back. I stood, too, wondering who would be stopping by at this time, then relaxed when I recognized Lyle's cruiser.

I remembered what I was wearing and turned to Marlene in panic. "I've got to go change."

She waved her hand at me. "You look fine, and Lyle's not interested anyway." She winked, then turned to go inside.

"You're leaving us alone?"

"Sugar, you and I both know I don't have cause to worry."

"It's not you I'm worried about. What if somebody else drives by and sees us? It'll get back to Maisy before sunrise."

Marlene seemed to consider for a moment before putting down the beer bottles and reclaiming her seat on the top step.

Lyle parked the car on the white oyster-shell parking area in front of the house. He left his hat in the car but carried something I couldn't identify in the dim porch light.

"Hey, Miss Marlene. Hey, Georgia." His eyes didn't even register my outfit, and I found myself wishing that Maisy were there to see for herself.

"Can I interest you in some garden statuary, Officer?" Marlene asked with a smile, but Lyle and I both knew she was only partly joking.

"No, ma'am. I actually came to see Georgia. I went to the house to see Maisy first, but she was tutoring a student. Your grandfather was sleeping, or at least he was pretending to, so I figured I'd come find you."

The weight of the humid air pressed down on my skin, burning me, making me want to dive into the bay and swim as far away as possible. Birdie had once told me that she woke up each morning like that, feeling pursued, hunted. That all she wanted was to disappear into her empty spaces. I'd never really understood her until now, looking into Lyle's eyes, and knowing that whatever he was about to tell me would make any sudden departures from Apalachicola much more complicated than gassing up my car and loading the trunk.

"What is it?" I asked.

"Just remember that if anybody asks, I wasn't here. I can't be, since I'm not working this case anymore. This is just a social call, all right?"

I nodded slowly. "Sure, Lyle. Whatever you say."

He held up the objects in his hand, and they looked like two clear Ziploc bags with something no bigger than a wallet inside each. "Can we go in the kitchen?" he asked. "We'll need better light."

Marlene stood and held open the door for us, and we filed in behind her, the dogs yapping at her heels. "I'll go get out of your way and take the dogs. If you want anything to drink, help yourselves. There's sweet tea in the fridge."

We thanked her and sat down, and I watched as Lyle placed the bags on the table.

An old book and faded postcard, each partially blackened and spotted with mold, stared out at me from their plastic prisons. The postcard was closest to me, and I could barely make out that there was faded handwriting scrawled across the back.

"It's not that I don't trust any of the other guys on the force to do a good job, but I figure knowing Ned as well as I do might be an advantage. And if I discover anything, I'll pass it on so that it doesn't come from me."

Lyle flipped the postcard bag over to reveal the picture on the front. Half of it showed a beautiful white-sand beach and aqua waters; the other half showed the old Gorrie Bridge, the through-truss swing bridge that had been replaced in 1988. In what had once been bright red letters splashed across the right-hand corner were the words, "Welcome to Florida!"

"Where did these come from?" I asked, although part of me thought I already knew.

"In your granddaddy's truck." He cleared his throat. "Inside a jacket pocket the, uh, occupant was wearing. The postcard was stuck inside the book, which is how it survived pretty much intact."

I picked up the book. Its beige cloth cover was spotted with mold, and it felt soft under my fingers, like a knit sweater. I sounded out the title in my head, my tongue slipping over the unfamiliar words. *Voyage au bout de la nuit.* "Have you looked inside it?"

He nodded. "A name was handwritten on the inside of the front cover that is faded but legible, and managed to avoid the mildew that ate up most of the bottom half. The first initial is 'G,' and the last name is Mouton. Could be our truck thief, or not. The copyright is 1939. I asked Miss Caty at the library about it and she looked it up— second edition. She also told me the translation of the title is *Journey to the End of the Night*." He drummed his fingers on the table. "As you can probably guess, it's all in French. Can't read a word of it."

Our eyes met in mutual understanding. "As far as I know, my grandpa doesn't speak a word of French, either. So if that book was found in his truck, my guess is that it belonged to the man found inside."

"That's what I thought." He leaned forward and tapped his index finger on the postcard. "This one baffles me completely."

I picked it up again, trying to make out any of the writing. The sender's name was completely obliterated, as were any dates or post-mark. But the front photo was definitely Apalachicola, and pre-1988, when the current bridge was built.

"It looks like the address is almost legible," I said. "Has anybody examined it more closely?"

"Yeah, we did." He fumbled in his breast pocket. "I wrote it down here—someplace in France. Maybe your grandpa has heard of it—I figure he can nod or shake his head, right? And if he hasn't, maybe you or Maisy remembered him mentioning it." He placed a small piece of paper on the table and slid it toward me.

I glanced down at the words scrawled in Lyle's familiar hand-writing. *Château de Beaulieu, France.* I felt suddenly light-headed.

Lyle continued. "I looked it up and it's located near Monieux, in southern France. If you Google it, there's a picture. Mostly ruins now, but apparently it wasn't what we consider an estate or castle—more like a large farmhouse with lots of land. Ever heard of it?"

The alcohol in my system seemed to dissolve immediately, leaving me with startling clarity. I nodded. "I've heard of both. But not from my grandfather."

He looked at me expectantly, and for a moment I didn't know what to say, as if I'd already discounted what I was thinking as being as close to unlikely as to be impossible.

"The artist we believe painted the china pattern we're looking for, Emile Duval, lived in Monieux while an apprentice—which led us to a nearby estate owned by the Beaulieu family. It's a leap, but we've found a business ledger from the Beaulieu estate that I have been going through in the hopes of finding a payment to Haviland Limoges or, if we're really lucky, the artist's name to show that he was paid by the estate for the china design." I spread my hand over the postcard, the red lettering peering out between my fingers. "What an odd coincidence to see this town's name twice in as many weeks, when I'd never heard it before in my entire life."

"It would be," Lyle said, unblinking. "Which is why I think it isn't."

"Isn't what?"

"Isn't a coincidence." He sat back in his chair, the fingers of both hands now drumming on the table. "Let me know if you find anything in the ledger book. I'm not sure what it will mean if you do, but we've got to start somewhere. Ricky Cook is the officer assigned to the case, but he's pretty overwhelmed with both his daughters getting married this month, so I've offered to help him out with some of the footwork—unofficially, of course. He's going to try to stop by sometime tomorrow to talk with your grandpa—as much as he can communicate, anyway."

He pulled his chair to stand up and I stood, too. "Florence Love said she remembered her daddy talking to a stranger in town the week the truck was stolen. Definitely a foreigner, because he spoke with an accent—what kind we'll never know, because Florence's daddy died a long time ago. But the stranger said he was a beekeeper, and had brought some of his own honey from home."

"Honey?"

I nodded. "The man gave some to her father and Florence said it tasted like lavender. Since she mentioned that a knapsack with several jars of honey was found in the truck, I thought you might find it relevant."

He pulled a notepad out of his pocket and jotted something down. "I'll pass this on to Ricky." His pen hesitated over the paper for a moment. "Seems like an odd thing to travel with. The book makes sense—and even the postcard if he was using that for a bookmark. But honey?"

"When Grandpa used to travel to visit friends, he'd always bring a jar of honey as a hostess gift. So if our man was a beekeeper, carrying honey in a knapsack would make sense."

Lyle jotted something else in his notepad and stuck it back in his shirt pocket before picking up the two plastic bags. "I should get going. Let me know if you find out anything and I'll do the same."

He turned the doorknob but didn't open the door. "How much longer do you think you'll stay?"

"Not too much longer, I expect. I think Maisy's looking forward to seeing my back."

"If that were true, she would have packed your bag and put it in your car already." His smile softened. "She's scared, you know."

I sucked in a breath. "She's got nothing to be afraid of from me. You and I both know that."

"Yeah, well, she doesn't. She needs to be reminded."

"That's the whole point, Lyle. She should know who I am without my having to remind her."

He smiled sadly. "So you're just going to fly away again, your conscience clear because you think you tried?"

"Don't put this all on me, Lyle. I came down here, didn't I?"

"You had a client, Georgia, and another reason for coming. That's like saying you threw your line into the water without a hook and you're disappointed you didn't catch any fish." He shook his head, ending the conversation. "Before you tell me to mind my own business, forget that I said anything. But it's been good having you back. Just . . ." He pulled open the door and stepped out onto the steps. "Just don't leave too soon. In ten more years Becky will be in college."

"Good night, Lyle," I said, hearing the frost in my voice.

"G'night, Georgie." He paused on the top step, then turned around briefly, giving me the once-over with his eyes. "Nice outfit, by the way. I bet James would love to see you in it."

He jumped off the steps and was climbing into his cruiser before I could think of an appropriate response. He started the engine; then with a wave he pulled away, the tires crunching on broken shells.

I went back inside and turned off the porch light before heading back to my room, my thoughts full of honey, and French books, and a small town in the south of France. And when I finally drifted off to sleep, I dreamed of bees flying over fields of lavender, their movements erratic and random, as if they no longer knew the way home. Then, one by one, they slowly fell to earth.

chapter 26

"When you shoot an arrow of truth, dip its point in honey."
Arab proverb

—NED BLOODWORTH'S BEEKEEPER'S JOURNAL

Maisy

M aisy stared into her grandfather's makeshift bedroom with a start. The blinds were open, the empty bed was made, his walker—the new piece of equipment they equally hated and pretended to be temporary—missing.

The smell of coffee and baking biscuits wafted out from the kitchen, teasing her nose and clenching her stomach as she guessed who might be in there baking. Digging in her heels with each step, she hurried to the kitchen, stopping abruptly in the doorway.

Georgia was taking another batch of biscuits from the oven as Becky, already dressed for school in a navy knit polo and pressed khakis, was reaching across the table to pour honey on Grandpa's biscuit. His ham had been cut into bite-size pieces, a dirty knife on the edge of Becky's plate identifying the person responsible. Becky's favorite juice glass, the one with Elsa from *Frozen*, was filled with orange juice and sitting next to Grandpa's plate.

Maisy's jaw unclenched as she studied her daughter's face. Becky's lower lip was clasped between her teeth as she carefully poured the honey, then used a napkin to wipe off the top so nothing clogged or dripped. When had her little girl learned to be conscious of others' needs? To know that honey congealed and clogged the tiny hole at the top of a squeeze bottle unless somebody thought to keep it clean? She felt close to tears as she watched Becky take her seat, then wait a moment to make sure Grandpa was all set before placing her napkin in her lap and picking up her fork.

"Good morning, Mama," Becky said as Maisy walked into the kitchen, her glossy blond hair pulled back in a high ponytail, emphasizing the elfin look of her face.

"You've done a great job," Georgia whispered in Maisy's ear before handing her the coffee mug with the big "M" on the side, a conspicuous crack showing evidence of glue. "Drink this first. And then you're allowed to talk." She moved to the table and pulled out a chair and motioned for Maisy to sit.

Maisy gave her grandfather a good-morning kiss on the cheek before sitting down in the proffered chair. Then Georgia grabbed a plate, placed two biscuits and a slice of ham on it, and silently put it in front of Maisy.

"Do you want gravy or honey?" Georgia asked, placing a gravy boat in the center of the table next to the honey. "No need to say anything—here's one of each."

Maisy took two long gulps of coffee, not caring whether she scalded her tongue. She needed the fortification more than she needed to feel her tongue. "Why are you here so early?" she asked, reluctantly taking a pinch from one fluffy biscuit.

"I thought I'd spend more time with Grandpa. I need to get back to New Orleans soon and I realized we hadn't spent much time together."

Maisy took her time with her next sip of coffee, needing to stare into the dark brown depths and hide her eyes. She *wanted* Georgia to leave. They'd survived nearly ten years apart; surely that meant they could survive another ninety. That had been the mutual agreement, something they both thought would make them equally happy. So why then did she feel so *bereft* imagining Georgia gone again?

The doorbell rang and Becky slid back her chair. "That's Brittany Banyon. Her daddy's walking us to school this morning so you don't have to, Mama."

Maisy had to think for a moment through her complicated car-pool schedule made necessary by two working parents. She didn't have to be in that morning until later, and was relieved to be off duty. "Whose idea was that?"

Becky hurriedly placed her dishes in the dishwasher before swiping her face on a napkin. "Mr. Banyon's."

Maisy casually eyed her sister. "Wasn't Danny Banyon a friend of yours, Georgia? Why don't you go say hi while Becky runs upstairs to brush her teeth?"

Georgia's face paled, the only color her dark brown eyes and two bright splotches of pink on her cheeks. "Sure," she said, lifting her chin in a move that would have made Birdie proud. And managed to fill Maisy with shame.

Grandpa reached out his hand and grabbed Georgia's wrist as she walked past. He grunted something unintelligible, but his intention was clear.

Without looking at either one of them, Maisy stood. "Go on, Becky. Run upstairs and brush your teeth. I'll let them know you're on your way." Without waiting to see whether Becky would do what she was told, Maisy went to the front door.

Before she could turn the knob, Georgia caught up to her and grabbed it out of her hand and pulled it open, not even pausing to catch her breath before speaking to the two figures standing on the other side. "Hello, Danny. It's so good to see you again. Becky's brushing her teeth, so she'll just be a few moments." She smiled at the pale little girl standing at his elbow. "And this must be Brittany. Becky has told me so much about you. You're best friends, right?"

The little girl nodded shyly as Maisy studied Danny. He was staring at Georgia openly, an odd glint in his eyes hinting at their previous relationship—if it could be called that, and the oddest feeling of needing to wipe the smirk off his face rose up in Maisy. But before she could say anything, Georgia reached her hand out to him to shake. "It's been a while. Good to see you again."

Danny looked at her hand with an expression that said he thought she was joking, but when she didn't remove it, he took it. "Good to see you, too."

"And this is your little girl—she looks just like you." Georgia turned to Brittany. "Do you have any brothers or sisters?"

She nodded vigorously. "I have a little brother who's six and another sister who's three. And my mommy's going to have another one around Thanksgiving. I hope it's a girl, because I don't want another brother."

Georgia grinned. "So you think sisters are easier?"

"Yes, ma'am."

"Just wait a few years," Maisy said quietly.

Ignoring her, Georgia said, "Congratulations, Danny. I'd heard you married Susan Zinn. I always thought you made a cute couple."

He grinned, exposing white teeth and a single dimple on his left cheek that used to make the girls have thoughts that would shock their parents. Even being four years younger, Maisy hadn't been immune. "Thank you. What about you? Husband or kids?"

The pause was almost imperceptible, but Maisy noticed it. "No," Georgia answered. "I don't think I'm cut out for domestic bliss. I guess you could say I'm married to my work."

He nodded thoughtfully. "I've spoken with your grandfather a few times about your job. He's real proud of you. Like I try to teach my children, do whatever makes you happy."

Georgia smiled as if in agreement, but the light had left her eyes.

Becky bounded down the stairs, grabbing her backpack from the hall table as she headed for the door. She stopped for a moment and took a deep breath, an exercise her speech pathologist had suggested and that seemed to work in most situations. Then Becky hugged Georgia and almost as an afterthought threw her arms around Maisy and gave her a loud kiss on the cheek.

Maisy and Georgia stood together watching them walk away, unsaid words darting between them like angry bees. Maisy turned to go inside and Georgia followed her, closing the door softly behind them. Maisy headed back toward the kitchen to clear the dishes, but Georgia's voice called her back.

"Maisy?"

Something that felt like hope bloomed somewhere in her, surprising her with its suddenness and intensity. As if she'd been waiting for something for so long that she'd forgotten why.

She turned around. "Yes?"

"I've been meaning to ask. When Becky was going through all of Granddaddy's papers, did she find any mention of the name Adeline?"

Disappointment thickened her throat. She shook her head, forced herself to swallow. "No. She didn't have time to go through them all, but I finished looking through them and didn't see anything. Why?"

"When I arrived this morning, I went upstairs to ask Birdie what she wanted for breakfast. She was still asleep, but seemed to be having a nightmare. She wasn't talking—but singing that name over and over. To the tune of that French song."

Maisy frowned. "We should ask Grandpa."

A sound made them both turn toward the back hallway leading from the kitchen, where their grandfather stood leaning heavily on his walker. He grunted, the word "what" buried in the sound.

"About someone named Adeline," Georgia said. "Birdie's sung it several times, like she's calling for her. Like it was someone she once knew and not part of a song lyric."

Grandpa stared back at them, unblinking behind his smudged eyeglasses. Finally he shook his head.

"Can I get you some water?" Maisy asked, already halfway to the kitchen.

Ignoring her, he began to clump his walker into the kitchen and toward the back door, the most direct route to his remaining hives.

Georgia looked past Grandpa's shoulders toward Maisy and raised her eyebrows, communicating in the way that sisters did where no words were required. There were so many things they needed to talk about with him, and this was as good a time as any.

"You want to go see your bees? Let me grab a glass of water for you and help you down the steps."

Leaving the dirty dishes in the kitchen, they managed to get their grandfather and his walker down to the backyard and settled in a chair under the large magnolia tree. His chair faced his beloved apiary, his eyebrows knitted as he looked at the two remaining bee boxes.

Maisy pulled her chair close to his. "Florence stopped by yesterday while you were at therapy. She said she might stop by again today, but to let you know that she'll probably be bringing the hives back early. She said the tupelo harvest was just pitiful this year, and she doesn't want to starve the bees. She'll extract the honey for you, but she says not to expect more than two or three jars."

He didn't seem to hear her, his focus on the hives and the movement of the bees around the entrances. The fingers of his left hand plucked at his pants in agitation, and he seemed like an insect under glass, under scrutiny and unable to escape.

Even though his doctors had told her that his brain function was normal, he wasn't the same man she remembered. The doctors had told them that after the trauma of the stroke and with the medications, their grandfather might have a few memory and behavioral issues that should improve with his recovery. She studied him for a moment, at his kind, intelligent eyes, his thinning gray hair, his arms that had never seemed frail, and couldn't imagine her grandfather being less than he'd always been to her.

She shifted her gaze to Georgia, and recognized in her sister's eyes that she was thinking the same thought.

He continued to stare at the hives, as if he could see the hundreds of small, buzzing bodies huddled inside, their wings fluttering at two hundred and thirty beats per second. It suddenly occurred to Maisy why he and Georgia were so attached to the bees, why the insects were admired and even loved. Because they were easily *understood*. Bees existed for a purpose, and behaved the way they were supposed to, their reactions to adverse situations predictable. In a chaotic world, it almost seemed natural that Georgia and Grandpa would gravitate to a smaller world in which things made sense.

Maybe that was why Maisy hated the bees. Because life should make sense on its own. It was people like Birdie who sent people searching for meaning and understanding in the world of insects. For the first time Maisy felt sorry for Georgia, for being the oldest child whose job had been to explain a confusing world to a younger sister who didn't understand or like honeybees.

"Good morning." They looked up to see Lyle emerging from around the front of the house, waving with one hand and with a small plastic-wrapped package held in his other. Maisy assumed it was the postcard and old book Georgia had phoned her about the previous evening.

Maisy pressed the heel of her palm against her chest to stop the wild thudding, then immediately dropped it when she realized what she was doing. Lyle smiled politely at Grandpa and Georgia before resting his gaze on Maisy. "I've always loved you in that color."

She looked down at the pale green blouse she'd pulled from her closet that morning, knowing how Lyle liked it on her but wearing it anyway.

"I've always told her that green is her best color," Georgia said, making Maisy wage an internal battle between resentment and gratitude.

"Hello, Ned." Lyle pulled up a metal lawn chair to sit next to Grandpa. "Glad to see you up and about."

Grandpa's face remained blank as he studied Lyle, as if trying to remember who he was.

"Ricky's tied up right now but asked me to ask you a few questions about your truck. Unofficially, of course, just in case anybody asks. He thought that because you knew me you might be more comfortable answering questions. Are you feeling up to it?"

A gurgling sound came from Grandpa's throat, his hand moving faster, plucking at the fabric of his jeans.

Georgia took Grandpa's hand, stilling it. The right hand lay useless and palm up on his other leg. "He can nod or shake his head, and he's been working on his words. Can you handle a few questions, Grandpa?"

His eyes turned to Georgia. He didn't show any indication that he'd heard her, or that he understood, and his face was devoid of all emotion except what Maisy could only describe as fear. She half stood, wanting to tell Lyle to stop, that something wasn't right. But Georgia caught her eye and shook her head. Georgia had always been better at facing unpleasant things head-on, dealing with the emotional fallout later. Maybe it was because she was the older sister. Or maybe it was just her being Georgia.

Lyle continued. "Finding your truck sure has brought up a lot of questions. This might sound a little off-the-wall, but I have to ask. Have you ever been to France, Ned? Maybe during the war?"

Grandpa took a moment to respond, finally shaking his head.

"He fought in the Pacific, Lyle. Fighting the Japanese. I really don't think he's up to—"

"Do you speak any French?" Lyle pressed, and Maisy could see why he and Georgia got along so well. They were relentless, unconcerned for the feelings of others.

Grandpa blinked several times, as if he didn't understand the question. He grunted, then shook his head. Maisy handed him the glass of water she'd brought from the kitchen. He took long, deep gulps while they waited, seeming reluctant to stop drinking.

Lyle leaned back in his chair as if he were just having a relaxing conversation, but Maisy could see his shoulders were tensed, his heels bouncing up and down with nervous energy. "Well, as luck would have it, I'm staying with my parents right now." He shot a look at

Maisy, and she had to remind herself why she was so angry, why she'd chosen to push him away.

Lyle continued. "Remember your old pal Gene Sawyers? He's my granddaddy. I hear y'all were good friends back in high school—both played on the football team. Said you both signed up together in 1942, right after Pearl Harbor."

Grandpa nodded slowly, his eyes focused on the flat horizon behind the hives. Two gulls barked at the cumulus clouds that hovered over them, promising fair weather. His hand tightened on the chair arm, brown sunspots highlighted against white skin.

"Says he hasn't seen much of you lately, since he can't drive anymore. Anyway, he moved in with my parents a couple of years ago—after my grandma died. He sleeps as little as I do, so we were chatting late last night out on the front porch, having a beer. He's lived here his whole life and remembers everything—every hurricane, every red tide. Every Seafood Festival queen and king, even." He gave a small chuckle, but his eyes remained serious.

"He remembers your daddy—had some great stories about the timber business and how your daddy was successful because of his honesty and charity. That says a lot about a man, and he says you do your daddy credit. He also remembers how your daddy sent you on a European tour for your high school graduation. He remembers it because he and most of your schoolmates were either working on the boats or shucking oysters, and they made fun of you because you defended your trip by saying you were going to work."

Grandpa's jaw worked, his mouth opening and closing, broken words tumbling out of his mouth sounding like they'd been poured over gravel.

Maisy handed him the glass of water again.

"What were you doing?" Lyle's voice was friendly, but his heels continued to bounce up and down.

"I can answer that," Maisy surprised herself by saying. She remembered the late nights she sat with their grandfather in the darkened living room, waiting for Georgia to come home. She'd kept him company, listening to his stories, trying to distract them both from the ugly truth of where Georgia was and what she was doing.

She patted her grandfather's arm. "Let me know if I get it wrong." Facing Lyle, she said, "His daddy wanted him to study different ways of making honey and compare varieties, see which ones would make sense to try here. He'd sold his lumber business and wanted to do something else. Never got beyond a hobby for him, though. Lost interest when Grandpa's brother didn't come home from the war. But at the time he thought it would be a great education for Grandpa. I don't remember every country he visited, but I do know he went to Spain and Italy. I'm not sure about France."

She felt Georgia's eyes on her, but didn't turn her head.

Lyle placed the plastic bags on a rusted metal table between his chair and Grandpa's, and waited for the old man to notice. Grandpa stared straight ahead toward the hives but, after a few moments, reluctantly looked down at the table.

"Have you ever seen either one of these before?" Lyle asked.

Grandpa's face showed no recognition, but the blue veins on his hand stood out through the thin veil of skin. His fingers tightened almost imperceptibly on the arm of the chair, slowly choking it.

"The postcard was sent from Apalach. All we know about the book is that it most likely belonged to a G. Mouton, and the postcard was sent to Château de Beaulieu near Monieux, France. Maybe you came across it in your travels?"

Grandpa continued to look at the postcard, as if willing it to be something else. Slowly he lifted his thin shoulders in a silent shrug.

Maisy frowned at Lyle. "He visited dozens of towns throughout Europe—more than seventy years ago. Surely you don't expect him to remember which ones."

"What about this?" Lyle slid the novel closer to Grandpa. "Ever seen this before?"

Grandpa jerked his head left and right in an emphatic no, then glanced at the book again, as if he weren't completely sure of his answer.

"We were hoping you'd be able to tell us more, and maybe lead us to the identity of the man we found in your truck with these items. They found a few jars of really old honey, too. We're having it analyzed. I was hoping you'd know the man. Apparently, at about the time your truck was stolen, a man saying he was a beekeeper showed up in town asking where to find you."

Maisy handed her grandfather the glass of water again, and waited until he drained it, small drops dribbling down his gray-stubbled chin. "I think I can answer that, too," Maisy said. "Grandpa was the president of the Florida Beekeepers Association for a long time—even when Georgia and I were little. He always had people coming to see him to ask about bees and honey."

"I figured that's what it had to be." Lyle slapped his hands on his thighs and stood. "I was just hoping you could shed a little more light on all this. If you think of anything, Maisy knows how to reach me. Or just call the station and ask for Ricky."

Lyle picked up the bags and then paused. "Oh, I almost forgot. Ricky wanted me to tell you that we got the coroner's preliminary report. The body has been there for a long time, so we've lost a lot of evidence, but from what they can tell there are no obvious signs of foul play—meaning no bullet wounds or broken bones or that kind of thing. Not that there wasn't foul play, just that there's no evidence of it. But there was evidence of severe malnutrition."

"That's not very conclusive," Georgia said, sounding irritated. It was as if she wanted a clean answer, a period at the end of the sentence. A clean slate she could leave behind. It was almost as if she'd already packed her bags.

"No, it's not," Lyle said. "But considering he's been there for over sixty years, it's something."

"So he could have died from natural causes, but we'll never know."

"Probably not."

Lyle paused a moment, looking everywhere except at Maisy before forcing his gaze to meet hers. "Any more thoughts on coming to the honey festival with Becky and me?"

Maisy made a point of not looking at Georgia. "I already told you no."

His old smile twitched at the corner of his lips. "But you know I've always had a problem accepting no for an answer. Call me when you change your mind."

He said good-bye and left, and it took all of Maisy's willpower not to watch him walk away. Instead she turned toward her grandfather, who watched as a honeybee landed on his sleeve. He sat absolutely still as the bee explored the mesh of his shirt and then flew away, its wings fluttering at a furious pace, as if it needed to be somewhere else.

For a moment his eyes met hers, and she saw the tears in them, threatening to spill over. Before she could ask him why, he looked away, brushing off their assistance as he lumbered his way toward the house.

Maisy and her sister watched his slow progression. When Maisy turned to look at Georgia, her own confusion was mirrored in her sister's eyes.

"What was that about?" Georgia asked, annoyance creeping into her voice. Not at their grandfather, but at her inability to snap all the puzzle pieces in place.

"I don't know," Maisy said.

Their grandfather stopped at the base of the back porch steps and Georgia began walking toward him to help.

Maisy stayed where she was, deep in thought. Could it be just confusion caused from his stroke and medication, and that was why he couldn't remember those parts of his past? Or maybe, like a jigsaw puzzle, there were still too many pieces missing, and he was too afraid to imagine it all together and see the whole picture?

A bee droned near her and she started to walk quickly back to the house, not fast enough to make the bee chase her, always mindful of the things in this world that had a nasty habit of biting you when your back was turned.

chapter 27

Bees see colors in the ultraviolet range that humans cannot. Some flowers have colored maps like little runways to show the bees where to land. Humans are blind to these special markings, but the bees see them.

—NED BLOODWORTH'S BEEKEEPER'S JOURNAL

Georgia

I sucked in a deep breath as my sneakers pounded down Water Street along the river, the bent arthritic arms of a docked shrimp boat almost prehistoric against the orange sunrise. I heard James's running feet next to me, keeping pace, but I didn't look at him, preferring to be in my own thoughts.

As we approached the Grady Market I allowed myself to slow down, gulping in the warm air already thick with humidity despite the early hour. With my hands on my hips I forced myself to keep moving at a brisk walk, my lungs protesting.

James thudded to a stop next to me, breathing heavily, his skin coated with a thick sheen of sweat that did nothing to lessen his attractiveness. He grinned at me and I had to force myself not to look away. "It's like running through water," he managed to say through gasping breaths.

"I told you that you should find an indoor treadmill. We locals have gills, so it doesn't bother us as much."

He laughed, exposing those perfect teeth. I wondered whether he had any idea of his appeal. "I've been running four miles every day since I arrived. I thought I'd get used to it by now. Guess it takes longer to grow gills."

"As I said"—I panted, leaning on a bench, trying to force more air into my lungs—"you have to be born with them."

His phone beeped and I gave him my "I told you so" look that I'd given him when he'd strapped it to his arm at the beginning of our run. I didn't listen to music when I ran, finding the exercise a good way to untangle my mental threads. The only time I did listen to music was when my past wanted to push beyond the locked door where I liked to keep it.

"It's Caroline. She wants us to stop by after our run. Says she has something new to share." He looked up. "She's already waiting for us."

After the conversation the previous day with Lyle and our grandfather, I was no longer sure that I wanted to dig any deeper into the mystery of the stolen truck or the origins of the Limoges pattern. Whatever the answer, it had been hidden for so long and so well that there had to be a reason. I already had enough complications in my life.

"I'm glowing pretty profusely, and really need a shower before I see anyone."

"Glowing?"

"Yeah," I said, brushing back sweaty hair that had escaped my ponytail. "I keep forgetting you're not from here. In the South, horses sweat, men perspire, but women glow."

He threw back his head and laughed. "Well, you're certainly glowing. Like a lighthouse beam."

"Gee, thanks." I frowned. "Can you tell her I'll be there in an hour?"

"You're fine," he said, pulling on my elbow and crossing Water Street. "Although you might be cooler if you wore something more appropriate for warmer weather."

I looked down at my capri running pants and long-sleeved sweat-wicking athletic top. It wasn't what I usually wore when I ran in New

Orleans. I'd just felt the need to cover myself up when I ran through the familiar streets of my hometown. "It's all I brought with me," I said, avoiding his eyes.

"For a quick cooldown we could go run down your dock and take a dip in the bay," he suggested.

"And there you'd be wrong. It's only early May, but the water temperature is probably in the eighties. It never really gets cooler than sixty even in January."

"No kidding. Sounds like a nice place to be in January."

"It is," I said. "But we'd like to keep that to ourselves. Meaning if you tell anybody and tourists start flocking down here to make this like Panama City, I'll have to kill you." I flinched, remembering what Caroline had said about his state of mind after his wife's death. He didn't appear to notice.

"Sounds like you still think of this place as home."

I stopped in the middle of the sidewalk, considering my answer. "Regardless of how far you go, home will always be the place you started. There's really no way to change that, no matter how much we wish we could."

His eyes were warm with understanding as we resumed walking. "My grandparents' house on Long Island was beautiful, every detail and piece of furniture carefully selected. But when my grandmother talked of her home, she was referring to the farmhouse where she was born. I don't even think they had running water."

"In Italy?" I asked, wanting to form a picture of this woman in my head.

He shook his head. "No. My great-grandmother was French, but she married an Italian and lived on a farm in the south of France, where they raised my grandmother and her many siblings. It was crowded, but she says there was lots of love. She said the hardships meant they just loved harder. It made them stronger."

"That's probably why she loved her French china. Because it reminded her of home."

"Probably," he said, although his brows knitted as if he was contemplating an internal question.

"What is it?" I asked.

"After going though all those catalogs and researching so much about china, it just occurred to me that Haviland Limoges has never been a 'workingman's' china, right? In other words, it wasn't something you would see on a farmer's table."

"No, generally you wouldn't. It's always been considered fine china, and always marketed to the well-heeled."

Our gazes met. "So where did it come from?" James asked. "And why did they never sell any of it when they were so destitute after moving to New York?"

His phone beeped again and he looked down at it. "Caroline says she's waiting in the garden at the back of the hotel."

We passed the front of the old mercantile building with the French flag dangling over the entrance to the former French Consulate—now converted to a hotel on the second floor and the Grady Market on the first—and headed around the block to the back of the building. The garden was a beautiful oasis in the middle of downtown, a lush greenscape of flowering bushes, potted flowers, various benches, and strategically placed oak barrels—harking back to the building's origins as a shipping-supply company and hardware store—all connected with brick walkways.

Caroline sat in the shade on one of the benches, a stack of papers and a thick catalog next to her. She was tapping something on her iPad, but looked up with a smile as we approached.

"Before you say a word, you must tell me what that beautiful fragrance is."

I'd smelled it too as we'd passed the plantings in the middle of the garden, and I'd recognized it immediately as something my grandmother had cultivated in the backyard, equally pleasing to bees as to humans—my grandfather's only input into my grandmother's garden.

It reminded me of my conversation with James, and one more

thing I needed to tell him about what home meant. How sometimes it took only a whiff of one of my grandmother's flowers and I would be back in Apalachicola again, holding Maisy's hand and telling her the bees wouldn't hurt her as long as I was there.

"It's pittosporum," I said. "I'm surprised there are still a few blooms left—it usually blooms in late spring for only a couple of weeks. Definitely subtropical, though, in case you were thinking of planting it in your garden in Connecticut."

"You're a gardener?" Caroline asked.

I shook my head. "No. My grandmother was, though. I always imagined I'd be one, but my job keeps me pretty busy."

"I imagine it does. I love to garden. Not because I'm good at it—I'm not—but because it gets me out of the house and allows me to let my thoughts wander. That's not always a good thing, is it, James?"

"No. Because when you start letting your thoughts wander they always land on me. Maybe you should start collecting antique china instead."

I lifted a foot behind me to stretch my quads. "You're up early, Caroline. I'd hoped to squeeze in a shower before our meeting."

"Four kids in six years means I've forgotten how to sleep. So I might as well be up and productive."

James used the bottom of his shirt to wipe the sweat from his forehead, revealing more than I needed to see. "You can go for a run with me tomorrow morning at six."

Caroline grimaced as if her brother had just suggested she eat sawdust. "No, thank you. I'll wait until I get back home to my Pilates trainer. We do that inside in the air-conditioning."

She looked past James to me, peering at me from above her Chanel sunglasses. "You look more like a cheerleader than a runner."

Knowing she had meant it as a compliment, I grimaced. "My mother wanted me to be a cheerleader, so I tried out for track instead."

Caroline laughed. "I certainly understand that. We should write a book on oldest daughters and their mothers." She shrugged. "I swore my whole life that I wasn't going to be a lawyer like my mother. I don't know who was more surprised when I decided to go to law school, her or me. But enough of that." She patted the seat on the bench next to her. "I've got so much to show you. I must say, if this is the sort of detective work you get to do in your job every day, I definitely chose the wrong profession."

"It's not all that glamorous, believe me. I'm basically a glorified Dumpster diver." Ignoring the seat next to her in deference to my dripping face and hair, I perched myself on the armrest on the opposite end of the bench.

"Thank you for the collector's encyclopedia for Haviland and Co. Limoges. I found what I was looking for, but I was hoping you'd let me borrow it for a few days, because I'd like to read the rest of it. The history of the company is really interesting."

"That's fine," I said. "You can even take it back home with you if you're not done with it when you leave. I've got more editions of it back at my office."

"And I'm sure you need to be getting home, Caro," James said, giving his sister a hard stare.

"I'm enjoying myself too much right now to want to leave. I haven't spent this much time with James in years. The history of this place is truly remarkable. Did you know that this little town has tons of historic homes and buildings, and even a few on the National Register?"

I smiled. "I don't think it's possible to grow up in a place like this and not love history or old things. It's probably why I moved to New Orleans—same kind of vibe."

James cleared his throat. "If you don't mind, Caroline, some of us are melting and would like to take a shower, so if you could go ahead and share what you've learned?"

Pointedly ignoring him, Caroline said, "Be glad you never had a brother. All right, then, where were we?" She touched her iPad screen to wake it up. "Elizabeth went to Grandmother's house yesterday and took more pictures. I told her the first photo of the soup cup wasn't clear, and that we needed a photo of the bottom, too. She also did an exact inventory and shared that with me. Because of the helpful encyclopedia that Georgia gave me, I made a list of serveware Haviland Limoges of the late nineteenth century made in blank number eleven. Not exacting, as I'm sure you can guess, but I wanted to give Elizabeth some kind of guideline in determining what was missing. Did you know there was such a thing as a covered muffin server? The dome is higher than a pancake server."

Caroline tapped in her password, then opened her photo album on the iPad. "But first, here's a better picture of the soup cup. Now that you can see it better, is it the same?"

She handed the iPad to me and I took it, then stared at the clear picture of the soup cup, the bright pattern, the bees in flight connected by swirling dips of green paint. Clear enough to bring back the day in my mother's closet when I'd thought it was a small thing to keep a secret, a rare moment of sharing something with Birdie, the only thing worth remembering the fleeting sense of being cherished.

"Going on memory, I'd say it's definitely the same one," I said, sliding onto the bench next to Caroline, who seemed oblivious to how I must look or smell. I held the iPad away from me, as if the photo might change. "Did she take a picture of the bottom?"

"Yes. Just swipe for the next photo. There are more pictures of the other pieces as well as the mark on the bottoms."

I stared at her for a moment. James came to my rescue by reaching over and showing me how to use my index finger to swipe across the screen to bring up the following photo. The next one was clearer, showing small yet familiar letters. On one line was "H&Co," underneath that the capital letter "L," and then beneath both, in a curve that looked like a smile, the word "France."

"Is that the marking you were looking for?"

I nodded. "It's the Haviland blank mark used from 1888 until 1896. At least, I think that's right—I'll have to look it up to be sure, but I'm around this stuff so much it's practically engraved in my mind. And it's the same mark on the teacup and saucer, verifying that at least those pieces are part of the same set. I don't always like to assume that, but now I know they are."

"Does that tell you anything?" Caroline asked.

"Confirms more than tells me anything new. We were pretty sure we knew the blank, and this marking tells us that we're right, because it's in the correct time period. It narrows down where I need to look in the ledger for the Beaulieu estate, as well. I've got about one hundred years of entries and I'm in the eighteen seventies now, but I'm going to jump ahead and start with 1888."

"Could your soup cup be part of my grandmother's china?" James asked.

"I can't rule it out," I said quietly, as I slowly flipped through more photos—dinner plates, salad plates, a sugar bowl with a lid. A honeybee sat on top, suspended in porcelain.

"Maybe this will help," Caroline said as she slid out a piece of paper she'd stuck between the pages of the Haviland & Co. catalog. "It's the list of missing pieces Elizabeth sent to me."

I hesitated just for a moment before taking the paper from her. It was from a lined piece of notebook paper, the spiral edge shredded from being ripped out. "It appears that my grandmother's set contained only the basics—twelve eight-piece place settings with a few serving dishes, such as the cream and sugar and a couple of covered vegetable dishes."

I looked down at the paper, easily reading Caroline's handwriting, which was as neat and precise as she was. *Missing items: teacup and saucer (James), soup cup, and large piece—unknown.*

"That's all?" I asked.

Caroline nodded. "Elizabeth and Lauren—another sister—have gone through every single piece of china, crystal, and silver and itemized it all. There are twelve of all the dinner, salad, bread-and-butter, and dessert plates, yet only eleven of the teacups and saucers, of course." She glanced at James, and I blushed, realizing he must have taken the blame for their destruction.

She continued. "There are eleven soup cups and twelve saucers, so it's a logical assumption that a soup cup is missing. As for the large object, all we know is that there was always a hole in the middle front of the china display in the cabinet. Both Elizabeth and I remember our grandmother saying she was saving the spot. We both assumed she was waiting to either buy the piece or be given it as a gift. Elizabeth used the list I sent her of pieces made in blank number eleven to see what might have been the right size, but that's pure conjecture. Elizabeth thinks it could be a covered cake plate, or a coffeepot. Possibly even a teapot." She shook her head. "I just wish we'd thought to ask while she was still alive. Although, to be honest, I never liked the pattern very much. I'm afraid of bees."

My mind was so busy whirring in circles that I didn't think to start my lecture I usually gave about why people shouldn't be afraid of bees. I lowered the iPad, needing to get away from the bright colors and intricate design. It was so unique, so special. So *personal*. So unlike any china pattern I'd ever come across.

"I think we have more questions than answers now, but I'm fairly confident that this was a custom design. Otherwise we would have run across it by now, or at least one of my contacts in the field would have seen it at some point. Even a limited-run pattern would be listed *somewhere*. It may have been created for somebody who had a last name that had something to do with honeybees or even flowers."

"Or it could have been commissioned by somebody who just liked bees," James said. "It would be helpful to find the soup cup, to verify that it came from the same set. It's such a long shot that I just can't believe it without seeing it and knowing for sure. But we've looked everywhere in the house—the attic, the closets, the dining room, and kitchen cabinets. I'm thinking we need to assume it's gone."

A stirring that felt a lot like panic flitted through my chest. It was time for both of us to go back to our lives, and I was unsure whose departure bothered me the most.

I placed the iPad on the bench, remembering something Aunt Marlene had said. "I asked Maisy to go through all the bedroom furniture upstairs, but she hasn't said anything, so she either forgot or she didn't find anything. I'll follow up with her, and then I'm going to finish searching through the old accounting ledgers today even if it blinds me. I hope I find something, because if I don't, I haven't a clue as to where to look next." I stood, my feet heavy.

Caroline stood, too, and surprised me by taking my hands. "You'll think of something. You strike me as somebody who's not only smart and resilient, but also knows a bit about reinvention." She kept her eyes on mine, but I was pretty sure she wasn't just talking to me. "We all need to learn to be more like that, or just hang around people who are for long enough so it rubs off on us."

I gently pulled away, uncomfortable. I was the one who ran away, because it was the easiest way out. I was about to tell her that she didn't know me, but I stopped, recalling already telling her that, and how she'd responded. *He told me that you collect antique locks and keys because you believe everything has an answer. He needs someone right now who really believes that.* Except I wasn't so sure I did anymore.

I stepped back and smiled, eager to change the subject. "I'll see you for lunch?"

"Absolutely. Do you have something in mind?"

"Have you ever shucked a raw oyster?"

Her mouth twisted as she pretended to think. "Not that I recall." She turned to look behind me. "James, have you?"

"Once, but not in the oyster capital of the world. I have a feeling that we're going to be taught by a pro."

"I've done my fair share of shucking, but I'd never call myself a pro. How about I meet you both at Boss Oyster at noon? It's right across the street. I'll finish going through the ledgers by then and will hopefully have something to share."

James's phone buzzed but he didn't make a move to answer it.

Caroline gave him the same look I'd seen Maisy give Becky when she left her tennis racket in the middle of the floor. "Aren't you going to check to see who it is? You know it's not me, so it's safe to answer."

"Yeah, well, there are three more where you came from."

Caroline's back straightened. "I told them not to call you while I was here. That I would let them know how you were doing. Maybe it's Dad."

James sent her a withering glare as he began to remove his phone from his arm case. "He knows better." He glanced down at his phone, his face paling under the pink tint from his exertion. He touched the screen with his thumb and the phone stopped buzzing.

"Who was it?" Caroline asked.

His eyes darkened as he regarded his sister. I stepped back, but she remained where she was, almost as if she knew his answer before he said it. "Brian."

She nodded. "You can't avoid him forever, James."

He stepped away. "I'll see you both at lunch," he said before jogging out of the garden, the sound of his steps gaining momentum as they pounded down the street, as if he planned to run for as long as it took to forget.

"His best friend," Caroline explained, as if I hadn't already guessed. "It's been two years." She said it with resignation, as if she'd been fighting the battle herself. As if betrayal and hurt had an expiration date.

"Don't you think some things are unforgivable?" I wasn't sure why I'd asked that of her, because I'd never asked anybody before. Because I was sure I already knew the answer.

She studied me for a long moment. "It's not really about forgiveness, is it? It's about power. When you let your hurt from the past control you, you are tied to it forever. You will never change your life until you learn to let go of the things that once hurt you."

My anger came to me with an unexpected intensity, the kind of rage that once made me curse and throw things. Or head to the nearest bar and drink until I didn't feel anything. To welcome the attention of any man who was willing to give it. "You have no idea. . . ."

She held up her hand. "Yes, I do. My first husband died during the nine-eleven attacks. He was having a business breakfast in Windows on the World. I was thirty years old and thought that I'd figured out what life was supposed to be, and then everything changed. I was so angry for a long time. Angry at my husband for going to that stupid meeting. Angry at the people who were responsible. Angry at the survivors. I couldn't see through all of that anger.

"My family made me go to a grief therapy group, and I met a man there whose wife had died of cancer. She'd been in remission for five years when they married, and then it came back. They were only married for three years, but all he could talk about was how grateful he was for those three short years. I told him he was an idiot. He just smiled at me and said he'd been called worse things and then asked me out for coffee."

"Did you go?"

"Yes, I went. And I married him a year later."

I raised my eyebrows. "So you're not angry anymore?"

"Only at myself. For wasting so much time looking back and wishing the past had a fork in the road where I could choose an alternate ending."

"Why are you telling me this?" I held my breath, waiting for her to answer.

"I guess because I need practice. I want to help James, to share what I've learned, but every time I try to sit down and have a serious talk, he runs off."

I saw her now not as just an elegant middle-aged mother of four, but as an older sister. Whose love and concern over her sibling didn't need to be explained to me. "It's not that easy, is it? Sometimes I think the hardest thing to do is just wait until we figure things out on our own."

"Very true. But we both know that life is a limited resource. There are no guarantees that there will be enough time to tell our loved ones what we want them to hear."

I realized I'd been clenching my teeth, as if I'd been called into the principal's office for writing on the wall. After consciously relaxing my jaw, I asked, "What is it you want James to know?"

She stared at me evenly. "That we need to ask for forgiveness even when we believe we've done nothing wrong." She paused, as if wondering whether she should continue. "And to forgive ourselves. That's usually the hardest kind of forgiveness."

I crossed my arms over my chest and stared at her, feeling absurdly like Becky. "I thought when we first met that you were an easy person to like. Now I'm not so sure."

She smiled James's smile and I thawed slightly. "I get that a lot. It's always hard to hear something that goes against the grain of everything we've always thought was true." She began gathering up her iPad, papers, and purse. "I hope we can be friends. I think we have a lot in common."

She smiled her good-bye, then walked out of the garden.

I was torn between running after her and asking her to explain how I was supposed to move forward after nearly ten years of running in place, and making my way home to finish going through the ledger. Each held such potential for disappointment that I stood still, my feet leaden as I smelled the last lingering pittosporum blooms, reminding me of a complicated childhood that refused to let me go.

chapter 28

*It is a common misconception that bees won't sting at night. But, like
all creatures when backed into a corner, a bee will sting whenever it
feels threatened.*

—NED BLOODWORTH'S BEEKEEPER'S JOURNAL

Birdie

I stood at the edge of the bay, the warm water lapping at the hem of
my nightgown, the needlerush bared to the rising sun by the low
tide. George had known so much about the tides and the weather, had
taught me how a fisherman had to show respect to both or pay the
consequences. *When the wind shifts against the sun, trust it not, for back it
will run.* I closed my eyes, feeling him near, imagining the morning
breeze as his breath on my neck.

My memories were pinned butterflies beneath glass, their wings
fluttering, eager to escape. I needed to let them go, to set everything
free. I wanted to speak again without being afraid that my words
would become pointed projectiles. Maybe it was too late for Maisy
and Georgia, but not for Becky. She needed to know the truth so she
would understand what invisible fist grabbed at her throat and stuttered her words. She needed to know that none of it was her fault.

Shadowy silhouettes of boats dotted the horizon, making me squint so I could pretend, just for a little while, that one of the boats was the one George called *Birdie*, and that he would be coming home to me.

The water reflected the crimson sky, and I thought how appropriate that was, that it must mean that George was nearby in the briny smell of the water, the cries of the shorebirds. I could never separate those from my memories of him. Or the dark splash of red that made the water look as if it were bleeding. George and I had met during the summer of the longest red tide to date at that time, in 1953 when we were both thirteen. The red bloom poisoned the gulf, destroying the shellfish industry for nearly two years, and grounding the shrimp and oyster boats. It was the red tide that brought George into my life. He would have been out on the boat with his daddy and granddaddy harvesting oysters instead of loitering at the marina with the rest of the town staring at the bloated carcasses of dead fish and birds floating against the red stain of the water.

George's mama always said that should have been a warning to us both, that nothing good ever comes from a red tide, but we never much cared about what other people said. Maybe we should have. Maybe Daddy and I should have listened to my mama when she said we should move inland, that the spray from the red surf was poisoning the air. My mama's parents lived in Gainesville and would have welcomed us, just as they had when I was a baby. We'd lived there until I was eight and we moved to Apalach and the house on the bay with the beautiful turret.

But I would not be separated from George for the little time outside of school that I had to be with him. I have since learned that people rarely do what they should when every thought and action is filtered through their hearts.

I took a step forward, barely aware of my saturated nightgown wrapping around my legs, straining my ears to hear George between the laps against the dock posts. *If red the sun begin his race, be sure the rain will fall apace.* How easy it would be to keep walking, to let the wet arms of the bay pull me under until the sun was only a distant blur. To be reunited with George.

Being with him was the only thing I'd ever really wanted. I'd once believed that a shared secret would bind two people together. But that's the thing about secrets. They're like little worms that burrow under the skin, growing and growing, eating at your flesh, wanting to get out. The longer you keep them, the more they destroy, until nothing is left of you except skin and bone.

"B-Birdie?"

I turned around, startled for a moment into believing that time had run in reverse and Georgia was there, giving me another chance. But I'd heard the stutter, recognized that Georgia had never been hesitant to speak or act.

Becky clutched her large stuffed rabbit, a gift from Georgia when Becky was born. It had always surprised me that Maisy had allowed it to become Becky's favorite.

One of its ears was missing—in Maisy's mending box, presumably—its white fur long since grayed by overuse and excessive washing. It had a zippered abdomen for storing pajamas, but Becky had always used it for her personal collections throughout her life's stages: pacifiers, socks, hair bows, seashells. It used to go everywhere with her, but now Rabbit stayed in Becky's room, still loved but not something she wanted to advertise.

"Why are you in the w-water?"

I quickly waded back to the solid shore, ashamed that I had scared her. I smoothed her golden hair from her face and kissed her forehead. She sat in one of the Adirondack chairs while I squeezed the moisture from my nightgown, already missing the water. I sat down in the chair next to hers and smiled with encouragement. She smiled back and sat up, perching herself on the edge of the seat just like I'd shown her, and she began to sing.

We'd started this ritual right after Georgia had returned, when I'd noticed Becky's stuttering had become worse, as if all the tensions in the house had bound her words together. Two days after Georgia's arrival, I'd had another sleepless night. The rising red of the sun teased at my eyelids, reminding me of George and the water, and like a magnet I'd headed out to the dock. Becky had awakened and followed me, her tension and mixed emotions as thick as the air around us.

She'd loved to sing as a child, but was shy about other people hearing. Maisy had a beautiful voice, unlike Georgia, whose voice warbled into three different keys within the confines of a single stanza. Maisy's voice had been clear and strong, but she was shy about it, too, afraid it meant people might look at her. I'd been so focused on Georgia, trying to get her to enter beauty pageants and take acting classes, that I hadn't noticed how badly Maisy wanted to sing, or how unprepared I was to encourage her. My intentions had been good. All I wanted was for them to be more than ordinary, to give them the confidence needed to live the kind of lives where they were always moving forward instead of looking backward.

I'd failed, as I had with most things. With Becky I saw a chance for redemption, a chance for her to discover her own talents, while I pretended that a small bucket was all that was needed to bail out a boat full of regret.

At first I just encouraged her to sing with me, and then I began to share sheet music with her, singing along with her before backing out to let her hear her own voice, amazed at her range and pitch. Mostly I was surprised at how she never stuttered when she sang, her voice confident and flawless. We kept this our secret, knowing that Maisy would discourage it because it reminded her of me, and of the frivolity of beauty pageants and drama school and all the things she thought were the cause of our private disasters and personal disappointments.

Becky began singing "Oh, What a Beautiful Morning," but I didn't join in, letting her know that she didn't need me. Purple half-moons under her eyes marred her skin, and I knew we couldn't continue our early-morning sessions. Perhaps we didn't need to. Maybe, just this once, I'd taught something worth knowing.

Becky finished and sat back in her chair, a smile on her tired face. A fish nearby flung itself out of the water for a brief moment, in search of an airborne insect breakfast, then disappeared under the surface.

"I wish I didn't have to go to school today," Becky whispered.

I reached out and placed my hand on top of hers and squeezed. I'd never been taught that the small gestures matter most. Or that words weren't always necessary. Becky had shown me both.

Slowly she slid from her chair, her oversize T-shirt coming nearly to her ankles. It was an old shirt of Lyle's and read, "He was a bold man that first ate an oyster." It was a Jonathan Swift quote that Lyle said often, and the shirt had made the perfect gift once from Maisy.

"I wish we could all be happy. We were all happy before, weren't we?"

I smiled at her, wanting her to be reassured even though I was no longer sure I knew the answer. How far did I have to go back before I reached the truth?

An image of Adeline brushed my consciousness, a flutter of a butterfly's wing, a memory from long before the scent of briny water became a part of me. Adeline and I, on a bench at the heavy wood kitchen table while she braided my hair. The table set with ten plates for dinner, the smell of roasting chicken and potatoes thickening the air. I turned my head, sure I could catch a glimpse of her, to tell her I still thought about her. That I always thought I'd see her again.

"Weren't we?" Becky's face wore an expression that was too much like Georgia's when she used to challenge me. "Mama says you don't talk because you're punishing her for not being the daughter you wanted. I heard her say that to Grandpa once. But that's not true, is it?"

I slowly shook my head, seeing Maisy the way she'd been the day she was born, dark haired and light eyed and looking nothing like me. And remembering how Maisy had spent most of her youth trying to rectify that small slip of fate.

Becky tilted her head back so that the pink tinge of the brightening sky reflected off the smooth curve of her jaw, and in that moment I saw Adeline again. She was pressing something cold and hard into my hand and telling me never to forget, and then she showed me a picture on cardboard. *It will be all right.* She put her larger hand over mine and released it, then wiggled her fingers like a blooming sunflower. I had imitated her, an old ritual we'd learned from someone else, someone whose face I couldn't remember.

Her tears were wet against my skin as others pulled my hands from hers, their accents foreign to me. I dragged my heels across the tiled floor, but I didn't cry out. I'd been through this before and knew that nobody cared enough to listen. I think that was when I first learned that words meant nothing.

"I need to get back in bed before Mama gets up." Becky ducked her head, looking like a small child again, and my heart ached. "Don't be mad, but I found something in your room."

The whir of a small motor drifted with the tide toward shore, giving me a moment to process her words. "A couple of weeks ago I was looking for the chocolate you hide in your drawer." She placed Rabbit on her chair and unzipped the abdomen. "I think Aunt Georgia is looking for this. I didn't want to get in trouble for snooping through your drawers if I told Mama, and I didn't want you to get mad at me for taking it. So I hid it in Rabbit."

Her small hands held the object toward me, but all I could do was stare. It was a piece of china, a shallow bowl with a finger hole on each side, its delicate shape and bright colors so familiar, the pattern of bees flitting around the curved white porcelain so real that I imagined I knew their names. *Marie, Lucille, Lisette, Jean.* I could almost hear my own childlike voice singing them in a lilting tune.

I took the bowl, cupping it in my hands, the white roundness of it reminding me of a skull. The wings of memory beat inside my brain, making my head hurt. I closed my eyes, suddenly smelling the poisonous fumes of the red tide, the air thick with the miasma of rotting fish and dead vegetation.

I stared at the bowl. There was something missing. Or maybe not . . . missing. Maybe . . . I turned it over in my hand, my fingers expecting to feel something different, a lid perhaps? A spout?

And then there was the smell again, making me look into the water to make sure it wasn't crimson. Something about this bowl reminded me of the red tide, but . . .

The sun rose higher in the sky, spilling orange and yellow light onto the boards of the dock, illuminating the cracks and the water that undulated beneath, reminding me of another dock, at George's house at Cat Point. I blinked in surprise at the memory of my first kiss, of the warm water sluicing beneath our feet, his lips soft and unpracticed on mine, and how I'd thought I'd rather die a thousand times than never to have him kiss me again.

But the cup in my hand was something else, another memory from George's dock. George's mama calling from the house that there was a man there looking for me saying he knew my daddy.

We'd stood, George's sun-browned hand clasping my pale white one, waiting for the man to approach. He wore dungarees and a long-sleeved work shirt, his face lined and worn. But I could tell, even at thirteen, that he wasn't as old as he seemed, that it wasn't the sun or the water that had added years to him in the same way barnacles on dock pilings showed the passage of time. He was small and wiry, and thin, achingly thin, his clothes hanging from him like loose skin. But not thin like so many of the oystermen who worked the boats. They had firm, knotty muscles that bulged from their arms and shoulders. This man seemed to be flesh held together by loose bones, his nose bent in the middle as if once severely broken and not set properly, his smile revealing three missing teeth. He carried a small knapsack on one scrawny shoulder, making him lean slightly to the side, as if he toted a great weight.

But there'd been something in his smile, something familiar about his eyes that didn't make me shy away from him, no matter how hard George tugged on my hand and told me to stay back.

The man wasn't tall, but I was small for my age, and he knelt down on one knee so he could meet my eyes. "You are Ned Blood-worth's daughter, yes?"

I couldn't answer at first. His voice had brought with it a memory of warm bread and sun-baked hay. I wanted to ask if I knew him, but I was positive that I didn't. I would have remembered meeting him before. It was his accent, I thought. I didn't know what it was, but he wasn't from around here.

His gaze took in my hair and face the way Mama studied flowers and bees before painting them, as if she were trying to picture the universe from their eyes instead of the other way around.

"The man at the market said Ned is collecting his hives from the swamp, yes? But that I might find you here."

His words seemed out of order, his pronunciation odd, but I wasn't afraid. He set down his knapsack and dug through it, holding out a jar of honey for a moment to search the bottom before replacing it. He placed on the dock an object wrapped inside a lump of shirts, the waves from a passing boat moving us up and down, and the man grabbed the lump, afraid it would fall. I wanted to tell the man that he shouldn't worry, that George could get it because he swam like a fish on account of him being raised more on the water than on solid ground. But I didn't, because the man was crying.

I wanted to hug him, even knew that the man wouldn't have found it odd, but George held me back, and we both watched as the man slowly unwrapped the shirts, revealing a small china bowl with elegant loops on each side, like a giant teacup with two handles.

"You recognize it?" he asked.

I was already shaking my head before I noticed the bees. He placed the bowl in my hands so I could see every detail of the flying insects— the movement of their wings, the small fuzz on their black-and-yellow bodies—could almost believe I knew their names. Without thinking, I began humming a tune I didn't remember, the words unknown.

"You remember," the man said gently, the tears coming down his face freely, and George pulled on my arm as his mother called from the house to come inside, saying a storm was brewing. But the sky was bright blue, the wind blowing in the west.

"Yes," I said, but then shook my head. "Not the bowl. The bees. I remember the bees."

His eyes widened, his head nodding rapidly, Mrs. Chambers's voice more insistent that we come inside *now*. "You remember another piece in the same design, yes?"

George pulled me away, and we were running down the dock,

and there were tears streaming down my face, too. "Yes," I said, trying so hard to remember what he wanted me to, knowing somehow that it was important.

I looked back at the man as we ran. He was standing now and smiling back at us. Mrs. Chambers slammed the door behind us and latched it, then picked up the phone to call the police. It was only then that I realized I still held the china cup.

Now, staring down at the piece of china in my hands, I knew what it was that the man had wanted me to remember. And the pins holding down the butterflies finally sprang loose.

chapter 29

*Piping is a high-pitched buzzing sound made by honeybees. Piping
usually occurs directly prior to swarming, but can also occur during
the disturbance of a hive. Some beekeepers think that the queen starts
first. Others say that the piping begins with a small group of forager
bees that primes the workers for swarming. It's a good idea to stay
away, as the bees are prepared to defend the hive and their queen,
even if your intentions are not to harm.*

—NED BLOODWORTH'S BEEKEEPER'S JOURNAL

Maisy

Maisy sat with Becky in the Lafayette Park gazebo having an
early Saturday-morning sketching session. Maisy's grandmother had been such a wonderful artist, yet neither she nor Georgia
could draw more than stick figures. Becky was only marginally better
but at least seemed to enjoy the process. Maisy wanted to encourage
it, and any other interest Becky expressed either proficiency or passion
for. As long as it wasn't acting or music.

White folding chairs filled the gazebo, either from a party the
night before or for a wedding that evening. It was still early enough
that she and Becky had the space to themselves, accompanied by only
a small yoga class on the nearby grass and the occasional runner or dog

walker. A portable volleyball net had been set up, drooping with moisture into a smile. Fat raindrops still clung to the grass and trees, remnants of the previous night's storm, which had brought with it slightly lower temperatures and a cooling breeze.

"There's another one," Becky called out, pointing at an orange-beaked royal tern flying over the pier and silhouetted by the morning sun.

"See if you can sketch its head from memory," Maisy suggested, wondering how anyone could ever capture the delicate markings of its wings, the fierce look in its eyes inside its black-capped head, the desperate wag of the tail of the fish caught in its beak.

Maisy remembered their grandfather bringing her and Georgia to see the terns nesting on the causeway that once linked the old bridges to St. George. What seemed like thousands and thousands of birds—royal terns, gull-billed terns, Caspian terns—were packed tightly together on the narrow strip of sand, the sound of all the cawing and squawking like bickering among neighbors, the sound almost overwhelming.

But what Maisy remembered most was what Grandpa had said when Georgia asked him why they were so crowded together when there were so many other places they could go and nest. He'd replied that it was because when they stuck together, they were better able to ward off predators, like gulls and egrets and other dangers. His eyes had settled on them as if he understood what their own predators looked like, and how Maisy and Georgia had each other.

Maisy thought he'd worn the same look the afternoon Lyle had come by to show him the French novel and the postcard. She'd been too afraid to ask whether Georgia had seen it, too—afraid not that her sister would say yes, but that Georgia might also recognize the invisible thundercloud that seemed to hover over them, waiting for the lightning to strike and the rain to begin to pour.

"I w-want to go to the Tupelo Honey Festival."

Becky had spoken so quietly that Maisy wasn't sure she'd said anything at all.

"What, sweetie?"

"I w-want to go to Wewa with you and Daddy for the honey festival next weekend."

"Oh, sweetie. I don't think I can. They're bringing back Grandpa's hives from the swamp tomorrow and we'll be so busy extracting honey. . . ."

Maisy stopped at the expression in Becky's eyes. Her daughter was nine but not stupid. It had been a long time since Maisy had been able to evade the truth just because of her daughter's age.

"You're allergic to bees, Mama. I've never even seen you outside when they extract the honey. Besides, I heard Aunt Georgia say that Ms. Love said there was hardly any tupelo honey this year, and that she would take care of the extraction this year to help out Grandpa."

Trying to defend herself, she said, "But with Grandpa being ill, I figure they'll probably need help. . . ."

Becky raised her eyebrows, an indication that Maisy should stop. With a sigh, Maisy said, "I don't know how I feel about spending a day with your daddy, that's all. Everything's so confusing, and I just need to be away from him to sort through my thoughts."

Becky took a deep breath, slowing her words. "I can't draw, but you still make me do it because you say practice makes perfect. Seems like being married is the same thing." Becky squinted up at her. "Do you still like Daddy?"

"Of course I do. He's a good person, and a great daddy to you."

"But do you *love* him?"

Maisy frowned, wondering whether all only children were this precocious. Realizing it was pointless to lie, she said, "Yes."

"Daddy still loves you, too."

"How do you know that?"

"He says so all the time."

A brown pelican glided low over the marsh grass before settling on the pier's handrail as Maisy's heart seemed suspended, too, waiting to land.

She heard someone call her name, and they both looked over at the curb, where Georgia's car, top rolled down, was parking. James's sister sat in the passenger seat beside Georgia, and as soon as the car stopped, James was exiting the backseat to open up the front doors.

Maisy stood to greet the newcomers.

Caroline, looking cool and crisp in a linen skirt and blouse, kissed Maisy on the cheek. "The weather was so beautiful this morning that we decided to take a drive around the historic district, and Georgia saw your car."

Georgia's eyes were wide. "We stopped by the house first, because I think I found something in the estate ledgers and I wanted to share it with you."

"You could have just called me," Maisy said, trying to remain aloof but unable to completely curb her excitement. She watched with some satisfaction as Georgia's face fell.

"I don't have your cell number. This town is only three miles wide, Maisy. It's not like you'd be hard to find without a phone."

She has a point, Maisy thought as they all climbed up onto the gazebo and settled into the vacant chairs. Georgia reached into her leather-fringed handbag and pulled out a photocopied page of what looked like minuscule writing in a foreign language.

"This is a page from the records of the Beaulieu estate that we talked about. I didn't find Emile's name, but I did find this."

She handed Maisy the page, a single line item highlighted in yellow. She could make out the words *Haviland* and *Limoges* on the far left of the line, and a date—*19 Juin 1893*. There were two lines of words in what appeared to be French, and then on the far right a number that started with a nine but which had been rendered illegible by either water or a tear in the original page.

"Do you know what it says?" Maisy asked.

Caroline leaned forward. "I'm fluent, although I must say it's almost impossible to read. But I could translate enough to know that it says a twelve-piece place setting of china with a custom design." She pointed to a word, *abeille*. "That's the word for honeybee. I think that means we're on the right track." She grinned widely.

"Good job," Maisy said, smiling at her sister for a moment before remembering she shouldn't. "So where do you go from here?"

Georgia glanced at James. "I'm not sure. I think I have enough information to give a fairly accurate estimation of the china now. I'll need to refer to my records of previous valuations that I keep in my office in New Orleans, but I think my detective work here is done."

Maisy wondered whether she'd imagined the slight hitch in Georgia's voice.

"Is it?" James asked casually. "What about a possible connection to your grandfather? The postcard found in your grandfather's truck was from Apalachicola to Château de Beaulieu—that's definitely more than a coincidence. And what about the people who commissioned the china? If we find out more about the original owners, we might find out how our grandmother came to be in possession of it. And how a piece of it may have found its way to your grandfather's house."

Caroline looked at her brother with sympathetic eyes, as a mother looked at a child who begged to be allowed to stay up a little while longer.

"That's true," Georgia said, studiously avoiding looking at any of them, keeping her gaze focused on two men and a young boy carrying their fishing rods down the pier. "But that won't affect the valuation, which is what you hired me for. If you decide to pursue the rest of the story, that's up to you. Mr. Mandeville called me yesterday saying that I have a backlog of valuations on my desk, along with a few estate sales he'd like me to attend, and that I'd probably done everything I could here. I need to get back."

She finally looked at Maisy. "And Grandpa is doing much better. I think it's time to go."

"No, not yet!" Becky threw her arms around Georgia, burying her face in her side. "You've hardly been here at all."

Georgia dipped her head, hiding her eyes. "I know, Becky. It hasn't been nearly long enough." She didn't make any promises to come back. She couldn't, Maisy knew. But they'd been sisters for more than three decades, strangers for only one. Maisy suddenly imagined all those years thrown on a scale, one side touching the ground, the other floating weightless. But then she saw Becky hugging Georgia, and all the pain and fear pulled at her like a riptide, drowning those years as if they weighed nothing at all.

Caroline's eyes widened as she looked past Maisy's shoulder to the street. "Looks like your friend is here, Georgia."

They all turned to see Bobby Stoyber wearing a tank top, shorts, and flip-flops approaching with two friends, all carrying fishing gear. His niece, Madison, and her friend Emily tagged along behind them, Madison holding a primary-colored beach ball, not looking pleased to be up at that hour on a Saturday morning.

Maisy stiffened, wondering how she'd managed to run into Bobby twice in the same month when she'd spent almost an entire decade avoiding him altogether. Bobby held a beer, despite the early hour, and grinned at Georgia when he spotted her. "You gotta stop following me, or people gonna talk." He winked and took a swig from his bottle. He indicated his friends with his beer. "You remember Rich Kobylt and Scottie Ward, don'tcha? Hey, I think she dated all three of us, right, boys?" The two other men at least had the decency to look embarrassed.

Ten years, Maisy thought. Ten years was a long time to be the same person you'd been, seeing the world just as you had in your twenties. Her grandmother had always said that life wasn't about standing still—that was how barnacles happened. Maisy found herself regarding Bobby and his friends with disdain. Until she realized she had more in common with them than she'd imagined.

Bobby jerked his head in the girls' direction. "Sister got me babysitting this weekend and said I can't leave 'em alone. But the fish are bitin' and they wait for no one." He screwed up his lips to one side as he regarded Becky. "Why don't you girls make nice? Let me have a good report for your mama."

Becky tensed beside Maisy as the girls stopped by the gazebo steps. Madison rolled her eyes before she spoke. "Wanna play some volleyball?"

Before Becky could answer, Maisy said, "She has a tennis lesson at eleven."

Becky looked up at her with a betrayed look. "But it's only eight thirty."

Maisy realized her mistake. She'd tried to give her daughter a way out of a potentially bad situation. But Becky was a lot stronger than most people realized, including herself.

Maisy forced a smile. "All right. Just don't wear yourself out."

Becky sent her an embarrassed look as she walked past Georgia, receiving a reassuring squeeze on her shoulder from her aunt, and all of Maisy's insecurities returned.

"Me and Emily against you," Madison shouted as she ran toward the other side of the net.

Maisy held back the teacher in her to correct the girl's grammar, but only because Becky was present.

"But that's not f-fair," Becky said matter-of-factly, and without any kind of a whine in her tone.

Emily snickered.

"Hey, Georgia," Bobby said. "I remember you playing volleyball on St. George when we were in high school, 'member?" We'd have those summer parties at night with a bonfire. 'Member that, boys? 'Cept I don't think you can play without your top on here or somebody's gonna get arrested."

Regardless of the lost years between them, Maisy's first response was to grasp Georgia's hand and squeeze. *We're a team.* It was almost as if Georgia had spoken those words aloud, reminding them both.

Georgia's face had turned a bright pink, starting at her ears, and she seemed to be fumbling for words. Before she could get them out, Caroline slipped off her Tory Burch flats and began walking down the gazebo steps. "I'll play. I'm taller, but not at all athletic, so that should even the playing field."

Becky smiled appreciatively, then grinned that grin that would probably stop the world in a few years.

"So, Maisy," James said, turning to her. "You mentioned you knew the reason Bobby's mother wasn't speaking with him anymore. I'm dying to know."

Bobby glared at him. "Look, I don't mean no harm. Me and my buds are just here to do a little fishin'." He drained his bottle, then headed toward the pier, his friends following. He turned back to tell Madison not to go where he couldn't see her, then continued on without another word.

They turned their chairs to watch the volleyball game. James leaned over to Maisy and whispered, "So why doesn't she speak to him?"

Maisy shrugged. "I have no idea. I just figured it had to be something bad, because he's always been such a mama's boy and she won't have anything to do with him now."

Georgia laughed, making Maisy grin.

"I could guess, but I won't. There are some visual images that are best left unseen," Georgia said. She pointed toward the water. "They've done a great job restoring the pier."

"Yeah," Maisy said. "I forget that you haven't been back since then."

"Since when?" James asked.

"Since the 2005 hurricane season. Dennis in July and Katrina in August. Apalach didn't get anywhere near the damage of the Louisiana and Mississippi coasts, but we took a punch. Pier was completely destroyed—took them three years to rebuild it. Georgia left in the fall after Katrina."

Maisy's gaze met Georgia's, and it was like when they were children sharing a room, each knowing what the other was thinking. And Maisy wondered whether Georgia thought about those ten years as a time of simple absence or of rebuilding, of just growing older or growing wiser. Of considering that acceptance and understanding might be an adequate substitute for forgiveness.

"Ouch!"

They looked over at the volleyball court, where Becky was rubbing her nose, the ball rolling away behind her. "You did that on p-purpose."

Madison and Emily shared a smirk, but didn't say anything, most likely on account of Caroline's presence. Caroline retrieved the ball and prepared to serve it. "New rule," she announced. "If a person is hit above the neck with the ball, the opposing team loses a point." Without waiting for comments, she served the ball directly into the net.

James's phone buzzed and he looked at the screen, frowning. "Excuse me—it's my sister Lauren," he explained. "She lives in Westchester near our great-uncle Joe and keeps an eye on him and our great-aunt Joyce. Seems Aunt Joyce has been calling nine-one-one on a nightly basis, asking for the police to arrest the teenagers having a party in the backyard." He tapped a reply, then returned the phone to his pocket.

"I'd probably call the police, too," Maisy said.

"Which you once did." Georgia sent her a sidelong glance.

"Because it was a school night and I had an exam the next day and Grandpa wasn't there to make the call." She paused. "Somebody had to play the mother."

Georgia drew up her knees and wrapped her arms around them. "Yeah," she said quietly. "Somebody did."

Maisy felt a stab of guilt, remembering the summer nights lit by lightning strikes, shaking with thunder, and Georgia crawling into Maisy's bed to hold her hand not because she was scared, but because she knew Maisy was. And Maisy was too proud to admit it. She cleared her throat. "I think we took turns."

Georgia didn't look at her, but the side of her face creased in a soft smile.

James kept his face neutral, as if determined not to take sides. "Yes, well, in this case there's no actual party—it's all a figment of my aunt's imagination. I think it's time we look at full-time care for them. They're in their nineties, and my uncle is getting too frail to take care of Aunt Joyce."

"They don't have children nearby who can help?" Maisy asked.

James shook his head. "They never had any." He thought for a moment. "I mentioned Uncle Joe to you before—we were talking about mumps, and how as kids my sisters and I used to laugh at the photo of him in the hospital with his neck so swollen it was bigger than his head. Yes, I know, that's rude—but we were kids. Anyway, it was the mumps that made him sterile. They didn't know it until after they got married and tried unsuccessfully to have kids. Not that either one of them would have ever married anyone else. They were pretty much made for each other."

There were loud shouts from the volleyball court and Georgia sat up, as if trying to determine whether she might be needed as referee.

But there was something James had said that caught Maisy's attention. "I'm sorry, did you say it was the mumps that made him sterile?"

"Yes. And most of the male patients affected didn't know until they tried to have children."

"Not all of them, though, right?" Georgia asked. The hairs on Maisy's arms stood at attention.

"I'm trying to remember what my mom told me—something about how it only affects postpubescent boys and young men who develop a secondary infection in their 'man-parts,' which is how she referred to testicles."

"Wasn't there something about mumps on Grandpa's World War Two enlistment exam?" Maisy looked at Georgia for corroboration.

But Georgia was already halfway out of her chair by the time Maisy heard Becky shout, "I got it!"

The earth's rotation seemed to slow, the waves thick as honey, the birds calling without sound. The only thing that moved at normal speed was the bright plastic ball, rolling over the grass toward the street, a blur of orange, yellow, and green, bouncing as it hit a tree root protruding from the ground. And Becky's small figure racing behind it, oblivious to the ancient Suburban rambling toward them on Avenue B.

Georgia was already running before Maisy was out of her chair, her feet stumbling, moving in a dream-run where each step was anchored to a sticky ground.

"Stop!" Maisy screamed, the voice coming from somewhere deep inside her, from someone else. From the Maisy of more than a decade before, when all her emotions were fueled by anger, a rage with Georgia at its center. And suddenly it was another beautiful summer day, people chatting, children playing. The splash of water, a baby crying, a man laughing, and the inexplicable absence of Lilyanna's babbling.

"Stop!" she screamed again, running toward Becky and the ball, reaching out to grab the back of Georgia's shirt, blinded by panic and terror and the memory of a single moment when time had melted and the sun dimmed. *Like now.*

Maisy stumbled, skidding onto her knees just as Georgia reached the edge of the road at the same time as Becky, hooking her around the waist with her arms, pulling them both down on the grass while the sound of squealing brakes seemed to go on and on and on. The ball bounced twice, coming to a stop in the grass across the street.

Sound came back first. The sound of her heavy breathing, the tires of the truck rolling over crushed gravel, a gull screaming in the sky above them. The anger came next. But then, Maisy realized as she stumbled to a stand and began running toward Becky and Georgia, it had never really left.

They were standing on the edge of the road hugging and crying, Georgia saying over and over, "It's all right. It's all right." Except it wasn't. It never could be. "Get away from her," Maisy screamed, yanking on Georgia's arm.

"Mama—I'm okay." It was Becky, stepping away from Maisy.

"I know, I know," Maisy said, putting her arms around Becky, trying to move her away from Georgia.

"I wasn't looking," Becky sobbed. "And Aunt Georgia . . ."

"Sshhhh," Maisy said, shaking her head so violently the earth began to spin.

Georgia put a hand on her arm. "Maisy, it's okay. Becky's okay."

"No, she's not," Maisy shouted, no longer recognizing her voice, or recognizing the gazebo or the people standing around her, seeing instead red, white, and blue balloons and fluttering American flags on sticks in the ground, and a small baby pool, the still figure facedown in the middle of it, the yellow bow at the back of the little bathing suit bobbing up and down.

"You were supposed to be watching her," Maisy said, her voice hoarse, as if she'd been screaming for days. Maybe she had.

"We were all watching her," Georgia said softly, as if she'd also been transported back in time to a summer celebration, and it was the Georgia from ten years ago, wearing a tiny pink bikini, her eyes blurry from too many beers and who knew what else, her fuchsia lipstick smeared, a small bruised pucker on her neck.

"You were too busy doing God knows what with Bobby behind the house. You *were not* watching her," Maisy hissed.

"Neither were you!" Georgia shot back, regret haunting her eyes before the last word had been uttered.

For a moment Maisy couldn't breathe. She closed her eyes, seeing Lilyanna at the blue plastic picnic table with three other children, eating a hot dog that Maisy had carefully cut into tiny bites so her daughter couldn't choke. Lyle was flipping burgers on the grill and Maisy had gone inside to the bathroom. She was gone for less than ten minutes. *Ten minutes.* She *had* told Georgia before she'd left. She knew she had, even if she didn't really remember.

"I'm sorry, Maisy. I'm so sorry. I didn't mean that."

Maisy looked at Georgia, seeing her older sister, the one person she had once loved most in the world, and for a moment her grief was as strong as an actual loss, a permanent absence. Maybe it was the passage of years, or growing older, but for the first time Maisy felt her own guilt, her own complicity in their disintegrated relationship. But that was Georgia's fault, too. She'd always been the one to accept blame on Maisy's behalf, to take the punishment, to assign responsibility. It was a pattern as permanent and as reliable as the tides.

Maisy took Becky by the shoulders and led her away from the silent group of people and back toward their house, feeling as if her feet were walking on shifting sand, where nothing was ever going to be the same.

chapter 30

"From the same flower the bee extracts honey and the wasp gall."
Italian proverb

—NED BLOODWORTH'S BEEKEEPER'S JOURNAL

Georgia

My bare shoulders pressed against the roughened wood boards of the dock as I stared at the dimming sky above Apalachicola Bay. I'd been there since about three o'clock, waiting to talk with Maisy about what had happened that morning. Before that, I'd hung around Aunt Marlene's house phone waiting for Maisy to call first.

I tried to justify my inability to pick up the phone by telling myself that I had already said I was sorry. *To ask for forgiveness even when we feel we haven't done anything wrong.* Caroline had said that to me that morning in the garden, but I thought we'd been talking about James.

Finally Marlene had pushed me out of the house, telling me that if I wasn't going to call Maisy, then I needed to go see her face-to-face. I'd taken my time walking the short blocks and then had stood on the front porch for longer than I cared to admit before finally heading toward the dock. I hadn't yet decided whether I was waiting to find the courage to face Maisy, or if I was waiting for her to notice me and come outside.

I heard footsteps behind me, too heavy to be Maisy's or Becky's. I knew it was James before he sat down next to me and pulled off his shoes, setting them neatly on the edge. "Hope you don't mind. Marlene told me I might find you here."

I closed my eyes for a moment, taking a deep breath and smelling the salty scent of the water that always reminded me of home. "It's my favorite place on earth." I sat up, bracing myself on my hands, and watched the amber light of sunset skip over the shallow waves for a moment. "When we were small, Maisy and I believed there wasn't a problem that we couldn't solve by lying on our backs here on this dock and staring up at the night sky."

"I can understand that." He smiled, showing me a hidden dimple. "Has your family always lived by the water?"

"As far back as anybody has ever bothered to look, they've lived right here on the bay. I guess it's in our blood to read the sky for weather and navigation." Hollowness expanded in my chest, the same feeling I used to get after I'd moved to New Orleans and thought about home. "I just don't think I'm a good enough translator, because I've never been able to figure out which way I should go."

He followed my gaze, toward the stripes of orange and yellow in the sky that seemed to thin as if inhaled by the universe as we watched them, the wide sky sealing us in under a dome of night. "What's that?" he asked, pointing toward a white orb glowing close to the moon.

"That's Venus. It's the closest planet to Earth."

He continued to study the sky. "Living in the city doesn't give a person a lot of opportunities for observing the moon and stars. It's like a whole new world out there. And all we have to do is tilt our heads back to see it." We were silent for a moment, listening to the gentle swish of water pushing at the dock. "Why is it so bright? It looks like a giant star."

"Because its thick clouds reflect most of the sunlight that reaches it. Grandpa used to call the moon and Venus Georgia and Maisy. Because you rarely saw one without the other."

I waited for him to comment, but he didn't. I liked that about him, I decided, his innate understanding of when something needed to be said and when it was better not to say anything at all.

He pulled out his phone. "Have you seen Becky's Instagram photos?"

Maisy had recently given Becky her first cell phone, but so far I'd seen her use it only to take pictures. "What do you think?"

"Oh, right." He moved closer to me so that his hip brushed mine. "You should take a look." He held out his phone for me to see. "She took all of these. I think she has a really good eye—especially considering how young she is."

After he showed me how to flip through the pictures, he placed the phone in my hands. The photos were artfully filtered and cropped and were mostly scenes around Apalach—oyster shells being used as ground cover in street medians, skiffs heading into the bay early in the morning, nesting terns under the bridge. But there were photos of people, too, some of Lyle and her friend, Brittany, but mostly of Maisy and me.

"She's very observant," James said softly.

He showed me how to spread my fingers on the screen to make a photo bigger. It was the first in a series of four showing my sister and me at the dining room table, looking at Limoges catalogs. In the first one I was pointing at something on a page and talking. Maisy stood behind me, but instead of following my finger she was looking at me, her expression not one I could easily identify. Something between loss and regret, maybe. Or it could have been resentment that I was there at all, sitting in a dining room she'd called her own for nearly a decade.

The next two showed us both listening to something James was saying, each of us taking turns to steal a look at the other instead of at him. It was as illuminating as it was startling, and I wondered if Maisy had seen them.

Finally I paused on the last one, a photo Becky had changed from color to black-and-white. She had used a filter that looked like moon glow, our faces having an almost angelic aura. We were both looking at Becky as she'd snapped the photo, our eyes focused on her. We wore identical smiles—more grimace than smile—and staring at us side by side I could see, for the first time, our similarities: the small, elfin chins, the wide, almond-shaped eyes that almost seemed the same color in black and white. The high cheekbones and delicate shell-shaped ears that looked just like Becky's. It was how I always pictured Maisy when I'd thought of her during my long absence, her beautiful face that I never thought looked like mine, and those eyes that missed nothing.

"You look like sisters."

"Yeah. We do." I flipped through the photos again, examining each more closely. "I've been wondering why Maisy thought it was okay to give a cell phone to a nine-year-old," I said, all the negative emotions inspired by the morning's events suddenly gone, as if someone had shifted my viewfinder so that everything was now in focus. "But I wouldn't think of asking Maisy. She'd think I was being critical."

"I did ask. She said Becky really was the only child in fourth grade without one, and it made her a target. So Maisy got one for her—albeit with restrictions. She felt like a neglectful mother, but she couldn't stand to have Becky picked on for something Maisy could actually control."

I watched as the stars seemed to brighten against the darkening sky, anticipating the coming night. "I would have done the same thing," I said with certainty. I handed the phone back to him and lay back on the dock, not surprised when he followed me, his shoulder touching mine.

"You'd make a good mother."

I tensed beside him, but he continued as if he hadn't noticed.

"Probably for the same reason that Maisy is. I've found that we either emulate our parents and turn out exactly like them, or we do the exact opposite so that we won't. Sometimes all we need to do to forgive our parents is to understand their own childhoods."

"Birdie never talked about her childhood. What we do know, we heard from Grandma. I do know that Grandma wanted more children, but they couldn't have them. I guess that's why Birdie was so spoiled. Doesn't really prepare a person for being a mother."

"No, but she did pass on some really good genes. I know she must be in her seventies, but she doesn't look a day over forty-five."

"It's always been a joke between Maisy and me. Birdie has never told us how old she is. We looked for her birth certificate when we went through all the papers in Grandpa's desk and in the china cabinet but didn't find anything. I know she and my daddy were in the same grade in school, which means they must have been about the same age." I was silent, doing calculations in my head. "He was born in 1940, which means he'd be seventy-five now. If she's the same age, that would mean she was about thirty-nine when I was born, and forty-four when Maisy was born. Not a popular choice back then, but certainly doable. And probably both accidental pregnancies, knowing her. Can't see her really planning on being a mother."

James didn't say anything for a while, his breathing smooth and even, as if he were waiting for me to speak. Finally he said, "It's your turn, you know."

The fists I hadn't remembered clenching softened, as if I'd been anticipating a confession, a letting go of demons. "Are you referring to the scene this morning in the park?"

He didn't say anything, but I felt his steady blue gaze on the side of my face.

I took a deep breath, wondering as I did so why I felt compelled to tell him. *Fragile minds.* The understanding of what they were like was something we shared. Something we both understood. I closed my eyes and began to speak. "Lyle and Maisy had a little girl, Lilyanna Joy. She was named after both grandmothers, but her middle name was because Maisy had already had two miscarriages and they were so thrilled when she carried another baby to full term." I opened my eyes wide to stare at the stars and the curve of the moon so I wouldn't see the still face of Lilyanna as Lyle had lifted her from the pool. "She was a sweet little girl, always so happy. And she looked just like Maisy." I smiled at the memory, hearing my sister call her daughter Mini-Me.

I turned my head away from him, letting the tears slip onto the wood planks. "She drowned in a baby pool at a Fourth of July party. Everybody was watching her, which meant that nobody really was."

"And Maisy blames you?"

I nodded, glaring at the cold face of the moon that placidly ruled the night despite all the turbulence below. "She says she asked me to watch Lilyanna while she went to the bathroom. I don't remember that. I'd had too many beers, so maybe she did, but Lilyanna drowned because nobody saw her run over to the little pool."

"So you were to blame." He didn't say it as an accusation, but almost as if he wanted to make me hear it the way somebody else would. To see the fault lines in the reasoning.

I sat up because it made it easier to breathe. "I was the older sister, the one in charge. I was the one who always took responsibility, because that was the role we both understood." I faced him, his skin blue in the moonlight. "It was how we navigated the world when we were kids."

"Because Birdie was your mother."

He made it a statement of fact, not one of condemnation or question.

"You're very observant," I said, resting my chin on my knees.

"It's a newly acquired skill." Our eyes met. "Is Lilyanna why you left?"

I wrapped my arms tighter around my bent knees, the damp evening breeze cool on my bare arms. "It's your turn now," I said.

He sat up, too, but faced me. "All right. But you'll still have to answer the question."

I met his eyes, wondered whether I had a choice. "All right."

Venus glowed even brighter, as if trying to outshine the moon, and I found myself cheering it on.

"Caroline told you about Brian?"

"Yes," I said. "And what happened afterward. She only told me because she was worried about you."

He dipped his head. "I know. And I'm glad you know." Lifting his gaze, he said, "But there's one thing she doesn't know, nor ever will."

I watched the moonlight play against the smooth planes of his face, the forgiving light an artist's brush smoothing any imperfections. Maybe that was what this was, this mutual confession. To illuminate life's potholes that couldn't hide the beauty and strength of the person beneath. Not to compare whose life had been harder, but to confirm that it could be survived.

I didn't prompt him to continue, knowing it had to be his choice.

"Kate was three months pregnant when she died. She hadn't told anyone."

When he didn't say anything else, I asked, "Was it Brian's?"

He shook his head. "No." He paused. "It wasn't mine, either. I had to go to a lot of trouble to get that information. But I was like a man possessed, desperate to find a way to hurt Brian as much as he'd hurt me."

I was silent for a moment, letting his words settle into the crevices of my brain. "Have you told anyone?"

"No—not about the pregnancy or the fact that I will never know who the father was. And I never will. She's dead and there's no changing that. I won't do that to her family or her memory." I heard him exhale deeply, as if exorcising demons. "I loved her. The good parts of her. I imagine I always will."

I turned to him with a realization. "Is that why you don't want to speak to Brian? Because you're afraid you'll tell him?"

James's eyes were like black holes in his face. "No. It's because I'm afraid that I won't." He looked away as if to hide something. But in the light of the moon I'd seen the guilt of wanting to own a piece of someone else's hurt.

I took his hand and squeezed, to let him know I understood how you can hate someone as much as you loved them. But how the love never went away.

The light from the sky had completely gone now, the sun swallowed by the waves of the bay. The words came to my mouth as if I'd always known them. *"Entre chien et loup."*

"I thought you didn't speak French."

My eyebrows knitted together. "I don't. I just recall that one thing—something Birdie used to say when Maisy and I were small."

"What does it mean?"

It took a moment to respond, to remember past all those years to when Birdie and I would sit on the dock watching the sky. "The literal translation is 'between dog and wolf.' It's used to describe when the darkness and light are equal so that you can't tell the difference between a dog and a wolf."

"Birdie taught you that?"

I nodded. "It was a long time ago. Before everything changed."

Something large splashed in the water beneath us, but neither of us flinched. It was almost as if our clasped hands meant we were protected from harm. Like when Maisy and I used to lie in my bed during thunderstorms and hold hands.

"Two thousand and five, right? The year they were going to make a movie here and Birdie was trying to fix up the house."

I nodded. "Yep. She just collapsed in the attic while looking for something, and she hasn't spoken a word since."

"Did they ever make the movie?"

I shook my head. "No. Everything was pretty torn up after the '05 hurricane season, so they moved on. Didn't really matter. Birdie was practically catatonic, and Maisy was pregnant again too soon after Lilyanna's passing. And then I left."

I felt him watching me, our hands still clasped, and I welcomed the warmth, the closeness. It reminded me again of how much I'd missed being touched, and the reasons for my abstinence.

"It's my turn now, isn't it?" I asked, wishing the breeze would steal my words.

He didn't speak, allowing me to let go of his hand and walk away without saying anything if I chose. *I'm just a stranger on a plane.* Of course he wasn't, not anymore. I didn't know what he'd become to me, but I trusted him with my need to find understanding. And maybe even compassion.

I stayed where I was, looking up at the two glowing orbs in the sky, so close but not touching, the entire night sky their domain. "I was pregnant when I left. I was twenty-five years old, living at home and working as a barmaid on the riverfront. I got pregnant as if I were some stupid clueless teenager who didn't know any better. I know that's true, because that's pretty much verbatim what Maisy said when she found out. Well, minus a few other things about my character that I don't care to repeat. She couldn't understand why I'd been allowed to get pregnant when she was the one who'd done everything right."

"I imagine that dealing with Birdie and your unexpected pregnancy was pretty hard for both of you."

I closed my eyes, tilting my face to the moon. "If only that were the worst of it."

"There are worse things?"

The day at the Seafood Festival all those years ago came to me with sudden clarity. Seeing Lyle unexpectedly, seeing my newly rounded face and immediately realizing my predicament, and then Maisy, also about four months pregnant, turning the corner to see Lyle consoling me, promising to help make everything all right. "Maisy accused Lyle of being my enabler, of encouraging my choices. Of believing I was much more interesting and exciting than she could ever be—all those things my mother's inattention had fed her for years. I know it was the hurt over my pregnancy; I do. But she didn't think to ask if I was okay. Or if I needed help. Lyle did, and that made it worse somehow."

James didn't show any surprise. "Were you?" he asked. "Okay, that is."

"No." I shook my head. "I was a mess." I closed my eyes, blocking the shining planet from view. "We always hurt the ones we love the most, don't we?"

He didn't answer, and I thought of his wife again, and his best friend, and the kind of hurt a person could drown in.

"What about you? Did you ask Maisy if she was okay?"

"No," I said quietly. "I knew better than to try, knowing I'd set myself up for more hurt. Maisy has always been very good at pushing people away. Like she doesn't believe she's worthy of love. Birdie taught us that, I think. I just took it in a far different direction than Maisy."

We were both silent for a moment, the dock rocking gently beneath us. "What happened to your baby?"

"I gave her up," I said quietly, watching as a night heron dipped slowly over the water, the moonlight tinting the top of its black crown with silver.

His hand squeezed mine, a reassuring gesture. "Is Becky your daughter?"

I wanted to tell him that it was none of his business, that part of the reason I agreed to let him come with me was because he said he wouldn't ask me any questions I didn't want to answer. But maybe he hadn't.

"Yes," I said, the word escaping into the air, no heavier than a single drop of water.

"And her father?"

"A guy named Sam whose last name I never knew." I looked down at my feet, spreading my bare toes against the pale wood of the dock, remembering Maisy and me as little girls, stealing Birdie's polish and painting our toenails on the dock. The memory made me want to cry. "I left to go on the road with a band who played at the bar where I worked, because I thought the lead guitarist looked like Jon Bon Jovi and I was looking for a way out of my life. When I told him that I was pregnant he made it clear that he wasn't interested in fatherhood, so he ditched me after a gig in Louisiana. I'd hitched a ride with another band that was perform-ing at the Seafood Festival, hoping to throw myself on my grandpa's mercy—at least until the baby was born. I didn't think much past that."

"And you ran into Maisy and Lyle."

"She was pregnant again—due about a month or so after I was—and her doctors told her that had to be her last, whether she carried to full term or not." I took a deep breath, trying to keep the emotion out of my voice so I wouldn't fall apart. "Lyle was the only one thinking straight, so he took me to Marlene's. It was her idea to move me to her friends' house in New Orleans before anybody even knew I was in town, much less pregnant. I lived there until the baby was born in March. I moved in November—just three months after Katrina. Just to give you an idea of how little thought I gave to the whole plan.

"And then fate sort of intervened. Because Maisy's was a high-risk pregnancy, she'd been seeing a specialist in Panama City. But after

Katrina, he moved temporarily to New Orleans to help out after the storm. She was in New Orleans when Becky was born. And when she miscarried." I stopped speaking for a moment, trying to find my breath. "It's funny, but even from the start I never thought of the baby as mine. I loved her, and wanted her to be healthy, but I never felt like more than a surrogate. And when Maisy lost her baby, it was like I'd been given a chance for redemption."

"Redemption?"

"For Lilyanna. I thought Maisy would forgive me if I could replace the child she lost, and we could go back to the way we'd been before."

James shook his head slowly. "I can't see Maisy just going along with it. She just seems so . . . responsible. A rule follower."

"She didn't want to. Not at first. She'd actually changed her mind and was getting ready to drive back to Florida without the baby. And then they put Becky in her arms." I finally looked up and met his eyes. "It's amazing what people will do for that one thing they want most in life."

"So you never went back home."

"Maisy told me not to go back, that she didn't want to see me again. I agreed only because it was the only way I knew Maisy would be happy—if I were gone. And I had planned to leave anyway, go someplace where nobody knew who I was. I wanted to go back to school, have a real career. Make a life for myself. So I promised I wouldn't come back. That I would never try to make Becky a part of my life." I bit my lip, remembering the first time I'd seen her small, crumpled face, and how even then I knew I could never be her mother. "I'll always be her aunt. If Maisy wants her to know the truth when she's older, that's up to her. But there's never been any doubt in my mind that I made the right decision."

"Have you ever told her that—that you don't regret your decision? That you will never change your mind?"

I shook my head. "I shouldn't have to. She's my sister."

He rubbed his thumb over my knuckles. "So that was your price for flight." He touched my chin, made me look at him. "Was it worth it?"

The price for flight. I'd never thought of it that way, of my decision having any sort of value. But of course it did. Every choice meant giving something up to gain something else.

"I don't know. I got everything I was looking for. But I no longer have a sister."

His hand left my face and I found that I missed his touch. "So Maisy knew what she wanted most in life. What about you? What was the one thing you always wanted?"

I gave him a rueful smile, thinking about what a wonderful psychiatrist he could have been. I went through a long mental list of all the occupations I used to write in my elementary school papers—veterinarian, astronaut, Olympic runner—until I settled on the one thing that had shadowed my childhood and Maisy's. "Not to be ordinary. Birdie once told Maisy and me that we never had to worry about being like her, because she'd never known the sorrow of being ordinary."

"And now?"

I shrugged. "I don't know. I miss my sister." I pulled our clasped hands apart and stood, suddenly restless. Facing the moon, I asked, "What about you? What do you want?"

I heard him stand, then felt him behind me, close enough that his breath teased my neck. "Is it my turn now?"

I smiled. "Sure."

He was silent for a moment, as if he hadn't considered it before. "I want to know my place in the world again. I want to be happy. But in my life before, Brian and Kate were part of both. I don't know if I can separate them enough to start again."

The waves swayed beneath the dock, and I moved with them, feeling as if I were part of the water, a drop easily absorbed by the whole. "Bees will fly for miles in search of pollen to bring back to the hive, but they have such great navigation systems that they never get lost. That's why folklore has it that bees are the image of the human soul—because of their natural ability to always find their way back home."

"So, according to bees, we should be able to find our way back, too, no matter how far we've traveled."

I sighed. "Yeah. Something like that. I'd really like to believe it's true."

"So you can come back here to live?"

"Not necessarily. Just back to the person I was meant to be."

He moved to face me, taking both of my hands in his. "Do you want to know what I think?" His hands tightened around mine as if he were afraid I might bolt.

"Not really."

"I can't help but think that maybe you and Maisy need to figure out what made Birdie the way she is so that you can understand that whatever happened in your childhood isn't your fault."

"Right. Like that's even possible."

His expression hinted of an apology even before he spoke. "And if you want Maisy back in your life, maybe you need to take the first step. Ask for her forgiveness. Even if you think you haven't done anything wrong."

My breaths came in hot, angry gasps. "Then maybe you should call Brian and tell him that you forgive him."

He stared at me calmly. "I guess I deserved that. And you're probably right. But it's always hard hearing it from someone else, isn't it?"

Without warning, he leaned forward and kissed me. It was soft and warm and electric, and over before I knew what was happening. He stared at me in the moonlight, waiting for me to say something.

"Why did you do that?"

"Because I wanted to."

I shook my head over and over, not really knowing why. "I think it's time you went back to New York."

Turning, I began to walk quickly down the dock toward the yard, eager to put distance between us.

"You're not ordinary," James called after me. "I don't think you could be ordinary even if you tried."

I didn't stop until I reached Marlene's house, watching as the moon's shadows crept between the statuary, still tasting James's kiss on my lips and wondering why I wanted to cry.

chapter 31

The queen bee is the only bee in the hive that does not have a barbed stinger. This means she can repeatedly sting, like a wasp.

—NED BLOODWORTH'S BEEKEEPER'S JOURNAL

Birdie

I stayed in my nightgown all day, sitting up in the turret window of my bedroom and looking out across the bay. I was aware of Maisy coming in to check on me and to offer food, and of her soft sobs from her room. Of Georgia, lying down on the dock as sunset approached. Something had happened, then. I stared off into the horizon, expecting to see heavy storm clouds. But all I saw was Venus and the moon, and the brightly colored bees flitting around a soup cup. And George. I felt him near me again, his hand in mine. Saw us fleeing from the thin man on the dock, the man who'd asked me to remember.

I held the soup cup lightly in one hand while the fingers on my other hand traced the flight patterns of the bees around the rim. It was hard to determine where the line originated or where the bees were headed, a circle with no beginning or end.

Marry me, Birdie. I'll help you forget. I turned my head, expecting to see George, to tell him now what I didn't understand then. That some things can't be forgotten. You can push them so far back inside your head that you think they're not there anymore, but they are, shimmering around the periphery.

He said that you knew who'd stolen your daddy's truck. And if they ever found it, they should ask you about it. I could smell the dog scent and her breath on my cheek as Marlene had said that. *Marlene.* I needed to go see her, to show her the soup cup. Maybe she could tell me what I was missing, what knowledge was still lodged in the forgetting part of my brain.

It had been a while since I'd been to Marlene's, but my feet seemed to know where to go, even in the dark. I walked slowly, my eyes and ears focused inward to the year of the red tide again, of the beginning of George and me. Of him kissing me, hidden beneath the magnolia tree near the apiary, and seeing the thin man approach Daddy and embrace him as if they were old friends.

Mama was in her rose garden with her sprayer, murdering weeds, as she liked to call it. It was her own chemical concoction, toxic enough that weeds would brown and shrivel within hours. She'd let me watch sometimes, as long as I never got near enough to touch the clear, odorless liquid. It took only a little drop, she said, to kill a weed or a rose, and she had to be careful not to confuse the two.

George and I watched as she approached Daddy and the man. They talked for a few moments and Mama's knees seemed to soften, and Daddy had to catch her before she fell. Daddy held her around the shoulders and led the three of them inside.

I looked at Mama's face as they passed. She didn't look like herself, but instead like a person who was thinking about a lot more things than what was right in front of her. She must have been distracted and forgotten that she carried the spray bottle, because she brought it into the kitchen.

The arguing began as soon as the door closed behind them. Not between the stranger and my parents, but between my mama and daddy. When the shouting grew louder, it was my mother's voice that was raised. It seemed as if the stranger and my father had said all they could say and Mama could not let that be. I heard my name and cringed, unused to hearing it in a raised voice. And then there was just silence.

Curious, George and I went inside. The three adults sat at the kitchen table, the man with a book in front of him, something thin sticking out of the top. The man smiled at me and I felt George pulling on my arm in warning, as if I should be afraid. I wasn't, even though Mama and Daddy were sitting as far away as possible from the stranger. I recognized the man, and not just from seeing him on George's dock.

Daddy introduced the man as Mr. Mouton, a man he'd met while on his travels to France before the war, although Daddy didn't explain why he was in Apalachicola. Mr. Mouton looked at me the whole time no matter who was talking, and I didn't find it odd because I wanted to look at him, too, and figure out why he seemed familiar. He didn't mention that he'd seen me the day before, or that he'd given me the soup cup. I didn't say anything, either, figuring he had to have a reason.

As George and I sat down at the table, Mr. Mouton pulled from the book what looked like a postcard and slid it across the table toward my daddy. It was a photo of the bridge that crossed the bay on one side and a picture of a beach on the other and had big red lettering on the top corner: "Welcome to Florida."

"You remember this, yes?" he asked my daddy. "You sent it to me after your visit. I keep for a long time, because we are friends. And then I give it to Yvette to keep it safe."

"But that was so long ago," Daddy said, using his arm to wipe his forehead. It wasn't warm inside the kitchen, but patches of sweat darkened his shirt.

"Yes," Mr. Mouton agreed. "It took me a long time to come back for it. They sent me to a camp—and I was there for two years." He paused and coughed into his hand, a deep, rattling sound of dry bones knocking together. "I would have died except I remembered what I'd left behind. What I promised to come back for." His eyes moistened and I felt mine tearing up, too, as if this stranger and I had shared more than just a few moments in each other's company.

He looked away from me, directing his words to Daddy. "Yvette died, you know. After her son-in-law found you here because of the postcard and brought you something precious. It seemed to me that you must have known, all those years ago, that this postcard would bring us together again. That it would bring me back to something I lost."

I'd never seen Daddy's back so straight, or Mama's lips so white.

"And now it's time to give it back." He smiled as he said it, but I could tell it wasn't meant to be funny.

"It's been ten years," Daddy said, his words rasping like a razor on a shaving strop. "You could not be so desperate if it took you ten years."

"Ned." Mama put a hand on his arm, her eyes sliding in my direction. George held my hand under the table and I was glad. I no longer recognized anybody sitting at my own kitchen table.

"I was starved in the camps, no food. Took many beatings. My health when they set me free—not so good."

He thumped his chest as if to prove his lack of health by the hollow sound, but he didn't need to prove anything. His pale skin and protruding cheekbones were enough. I had the oddest feeling that I should crawl into his lap and put my arms around him in an attempt to comfort.

"I stay in American hospital in Germany for almost a year because I cannot walk. My heart not so good anymore." He shrugged. "Two years later I'm strong enough and I go back home and find only burned buildings. My bees gone, the château open to the sky and home only to bats and mice. Another five years to find where Yvette and her family had gone, two years to earn money for passage to America. I promised to come back. And I did." He looked at me, his eyes soft and like there was a young man locked inside an old body, and when he looked at me it was as if he believed I held the key.

I looked at my parents, hoping for reassurance, or at least an explanation of what was going on, but their expressions were closed to me, their eyes focused on the stranger as if to try to draw his attention away from me.

"It's been ten years," Mama repeated, her voice cracking as if she was close to tears. "You can't just . . ." Her eyes slid to me. "We have a good family here, a good life. We are all very, very happy." I was surprised to see tears slipping down her face. Daddy placed his hand over hers, then dipped his head. "She doesn't remember any of it." Mama almost hissed the words.

The man's face became serious. "But children never truly forget." He turned to me and took my hand, rolling it into a ball inside his own fist. *"Souviens-toi toujours que mon coeur t'appartient et que tu seule peux le libérer."*

He smiled and I smiled back. I'd heard those words before, and even believed that I knew what they meant. He opened his fist and wiggled his fingers like petals on a sunflower. I remembered this part, remembered what I was supposed to do next. Watching my hand as if it didn't belong to me, I saw it open slowly, my fingers dancing in a smaller imitation of his.

And then my voice repeated the words I knew in my heart but not in my head. *"Souviens-toi toujours que mon coeur t'appartient et que tu seul peux le libérer."* I looked at my parents, their surprise mirrored in their faces. I knew those words, had heard them many times but couldn't remember where. I knew I'd heard this man say them before, a long time ago. But it also seemed that I'd heard them in the soft tones of a woman's voice, a woman with dark hair and soft skin.

"Adeline?" I said, the name suddenly familiar on my tongue. It was a name that brought back mixed memories—joy and sadness, homecoming and abandonment. Of a time that I always thought of as *before.* Before the darkness that fell inside my head.

Mr. Mouton looked confused for a moment and then his eyes widened in recognition and a smile traced his lips. "Yvette's oldest daughter, yes? She took care of you like a mother when Yvette became ill. Her husband brought you here."

A memory of me at the wooden table, filled with the beautiful china, and Adeline braiding my hair and singing to me. We were both crying and I couldn't remember why. And then I saw the suitcase by the door and knew that it was time to say good-bye.

I looked at my parents in confusion, but they were staring hard at the thin man, as if he carried some horrible disease. "I don't understand," I said.

Nobody responded, but George placed his hand in mine and squeezed.

"She doesn't remember," Daddy repeated, but it sounded as if he was trying to convince himself.

Mama covered her head in her hands and began to sob. Daddy patted her back, the anger in his eyes slipping into sorrow. "We thought you were dead. For five long years we tried to find you. We sent letters to every government official we thought could help. We even sent one to the president. There was no record of your death, but there was no record of you surviving, either." He was silent for a moment, the room still as a tomb, so that we heard the buzzing of a trapped bee, its body thumping against the glass window of the door.

I tried to stand, but George pulled me back into my chair. "Please," I said, looking across the table at my parents, who wouldn't meet my eyes. "Please tell me what's going on. I don't . . ."

Daddy held up his hand, silencing me. He leaned closer to Mr. Mouton. "I could not give my wife the children we wanted, but we had more than enough love to share." He settled his gaze on me for a moment. "And when our daughter arrived, we had a family to give her, and all the love we'd been storing up for all our lives. You don't have any of that—no wife or home. Bad health. It wouldn't be right, taking her from everything she knows. From her family. From her friends." He stared straight at George.

George shifted next to me, as if he was understanding something I couldn't quite grasp because I was seeing a picture in my head of bees and fields of lavender, and I was running as fast as I could through it, feeling chased but too afraid to turn around and find out by whom.

But I'd always been that way, Mama said. Ever since I was a little girl, when things upset me or something happened that I didn't understand, I'd disappear into my own imaginary world, where everything happened just as I wanted it to, and the real world would slip away like so much dust. I'd been doing that for so long that I didn't remember when I'd started. I'd stopped trying to remember, because every time I thought about it my heart hurt as if it were being stung by a hundred bees.

The man's face was still and serious as he listened to Daddy, but after waiting for a moment to make sure Daddy was finished speaking, he said, "The teapot. You still have it, yes? Adeline said she told you to keep it safe. She gave me a cup to show to my little girl, to see if she remembered, just in case there is no more teapot. That is her history. Of three generations of her family, and their position on a grand estate. That is all she needs. And a father who loves her. We will manage. It is in our blood. I have survived thus far, yes?"

"Then you won't listen to reason?" Daddy's voice was thick, as if a sock were stuck in his throat, preventing the words from coming out.

"What other reason is there besides a father who loves his daughter and has worked for ten years to keep a promise he made to her?"

I will come back for you; I promise. However long it takes. He'd said those words to me a long time ago. Or maybe I'd just made it up like so many of my stories.

Daddy's jaw quivered. George slid back his chair and stood behind me, his hands on my shoulders. He was only thirteen but already over six feet, with wide shoulders and muscled arms. It almost seemed as if he were trying to be intimidating.

"Who are you, Mr. Mouton?" My voice sounded like a small child's.

He leaned across the table and took my hands in his. "You know, don't you? You remember."

I stared into his brown eyes, seeing the lavender fields. Smelling sweet honey. *The teapot.* He'd said something about a teapot, and I knew it was something I should remember—could almost picture in my head. A pattern that matched the one on the cup he'd brought me. Something to do with bees and a suitcase. And me crying for someone not to leave me.

He must have heard my gasp of recognition, because he sat back with a satisfied smile. "She remembers. She knows who she is."

His words brought me back to the kitchen, to a familiar place and the two faces I loved most in the world. "I'm Birdie Bloodworth," I shouted, angry tears hitting my cheeks. "Who are *you*?"

George put his arm around me and pulled me to him, and I buried my face in his shoulder.

"Please," Daddy said, in a tone of voice I'd never heard him use before. "I beg of you. For my wife's sake. For our child's sake. Please reconsider."

"Reconsider what? What is right?" The man coughed, his breath wheezing through his nostrils. "All I am asking is for what is right."

"But my wife . . ." He stopped to look at Mama, but she no longer seemed to be listening. She was staring at the stranded honeybee crawling across the table, looking for a way out.

"Her daughter is everything to her. All of her hopes and dreams are in this one child. My wife and I can take care of her needs, and love her. She will want for nothing."

The man coughed again, then settled back in his chair. "And my daughter is all I have left in this world. All the love I have left. This is not easy for you or for me. But there is nothing but the truth." He doubled over in a coughing fit, the smell of wet pennies filling the air.

Mama watched him cough, saw him draw away a filthy handkerchief spotted with fresh red blood. Her shoulders slumped, like they did when her favorite cat had died, and I saw lines around her mouth and eyes that I had never seen before. They remained on her face until the day she died.

I remembered all that now. I stopped walking and looked down, realizing I'd walked several blocks from the house carrying a soup cup and wearing my nightgown. *Marlene.* Yes, I needed to see Marlene. To tell her I did remember the stranger's name. Mr. Mouton.

I blinked up at the moon, wondering whether there was more I was supposed to remember. Yes, something George had told me later. *This isn't something a person ever gets over, Birdie. But it's something we'll always share. Our secret.*

My hands trembled and I clutched the soup cup tighter, my mind threatening to spill one last secret, my heart just as determined to keep it safe.

The brief blare of a siren pulsed behind me and I turned. Lyle stepped out of his cruiser and came toward me. "Birdie? Are you all right? Maisy's been worried sick."

I hid the cup in the folds of my nightgown, not yet ready to share it with anybody. Words continued to evade me, so I began to hum a tune from long ago as I used to stare at the bees on the soup cup, the words of the song in a foreign language that I knew but didn't. *Marie, Lucille, Lisette, Jean.*

Lyle settled me into the front seat next to him, then slowly drove me home. I was so tired, as if I'd walked for miles instead of just blocks, and when I closed my eyes all I saw were bright purple fields of lavender.

chapter 32

*The Marquis de Sade said, "All, all is theft, all is unceasing and
rigorous competition in nature; the desire to make off with the
substance of others is the foremost—the most legitimate—passion
nature has bred into us and, without doubt, the most agreeable one."
But a good beekeeper never takes more honey than the bee can afford
to give, and never calls it stealing. That way the beekeeper remains
noble, while the bee feeds its hive, stingers ready if the beekeeper
becomes greedy.*

—NED BLOODWORTH'S BEEKEEPER'S JOURNAL

Maisy

Georgia arrived at the house right before Lyle pulled up in his
cruiser with Birdie. It reminded Maisy too much of the times
their mother had been sent away, how she and Georgia would sit in
the turret window of their mother's bedroom each night, waiting for
her to return. It made no sense, of course. Birdie wouldn't have arrived
by boat over the bay. Georgia had known it, but had made Maisy
believe that Birdie was just over the horizon, trying to find her way
back to them. It had taken years for Maisy to realize the lie, but back
when she was small it had allowed her to go to sleep at night.

The hem of Birdie's nightgown was brown with dirt, her small bare feet covered with dust. She was humming as she entered the foyer, her eyes startlingly clear. She held something down by her side in one hand, the object hidden by the folds of her nightgown.

"Where did you find her?" Maisy asked, checking to make sure Birdie was physically uninjured.

"About a block from Marlene's house. Any idea why she might be going there?"

"None at all. She's never wandered from the house before. I hope this isn't setting a precedent."

"We might need to take her to another doctor," Georgia said quietly.

We. There was that old word again that had nothing to do with who Maisy and Georgia were anymore.

Too tired to have this discussion, Maisy said, "It's almost ten. I'm going upstairs to draw her a bath and put her to bed. There's no reason for you to stay. Come on, Birdie." She moved to take her mother's hand, but Birdie began to walk with purposeful strides toward Ned's room.

Maisy reached the door at the same time as Georgia, right behind Birdie, who hadn't paused to knock. Ned was awake, sitting in the chair facing his apiary, where he'd been since that morning, when Florence had brought back his beloved beehives. He'd been agitated, watching as her team unloaded the hives from the truck, shouting something unintelligible if they got too close to the two hives that had remained behind.

Birdie lifted her hand and placed something in their grandfather's lap. He stared at it without recognition, his bushy eyebrows knitted together over his nose. Georgia stepped forward, then stopped, her fingers pressed against her mouth as if she were keeping a secret.

Maisy peered around her and saw the soup cup, its elegant curves and handles exactly like Georgia had described them, the brilliant colors of the bees in flight as vibrant as if they'd been painted yesterday.

"Is it the same one?" Maisy asked.

Georgia simply nodded, her fingers still pressed against her lips. Almost as an afterthought, she said, "Where did it come from?"

Maisy moved around Georgia to stand next to the chair. "Grandpa? Do you know what this is?"

He stared at it without seeming to see it, but Maisy noticed his grip on the arm of his chair, the pulsing of a muscle in his cheek. She had a quick flash of memory of the teacup and saucer as they'd exploded on the ground, and the look on Grandpa's face when he'd seen the ring of bees in flight. Which meant he recognized *something*.

"Grandpa—do you know where this came from?"

He lifted his head, his eyebrows still knitted. But there was a spark of something in his eyes that told Maisy that he *knew*.

Georgia reached down and took the cup, then very slowly turned it over in her hands to study the mark on the bottom. "It matches the soup cup in James's grandmother's set. Exactly." She took a deep breath. "It could be the missing cup."

Maisy was already entering her passcode into her phone when Georgia spoke again. "What are you doing?"

"I'm texting James. He and Caroline might want to come over and see it in person. And I'd like to see the picture from her grandmother's china myself."

"Don't. Please." Georgia reached for the phone, but Maisy held it away, just like they'd done as children playing keep-away. "It's the same," Georgia repeated. "They don't need to see it tonight anyway. You can wait until tomorrow."

"*I* can't wait," Maisy said, quickly tapping the screen on her phone. "Because if it's the same, then your job is done here." Which wasn't the complete truth. There was one thing no one had acknowledged yet—the *how*. If that set had belonged to James's family back in Switzerland before the war, then how did a single piece of it find its way to Apalachicola?

That it had been hidden for so long made it obvious to Maisy that it had been hidden for a reason. And maybe that reason was something they weren't prepared to know.

She felt a stab of remorse when she saw Georgia's face blanch.

"Please, Maisy. It can wait until tomorrow. I don't want to see James."

The look on her sister's face made Maisy want to undo the text, but a response had already been sent back. She looked down at her phone. "They're on their way over."

Birdie had begun humming to herself, the odd alphabet tune that Becky had recognized as a French children's song. Georgia bent down next to her chair, holding up the bowl but keeping it far enough away that Birdie couldn't grab it. "Where did this come from? I saw it once before, remember? In your closet. You told me to keep it a secret. Why?"

Birdie's humming became words that fit into the notes, each word enunciated and clear to make sure they were heard.

"Those are names," Maisy said. "Girl names in French," she said in surprise. "I'm pretty sure those weren't the words Becky sang."

Birdie reached for the soup cup, but Georgia clung to it, holding on with both hands as she brought it closer to Birdie, letting her touch it. With her index finger, Birdie traced each bee as she sang the names.

Maisy met Georgia's eyes over their mother's head.

"Grandpa?" Maisy tried again. "Have you seen this bowl before? Do you know where it came from?"

He looked up, tears brimming in his eyes.

"I don't like this. I don't like this at all," Maisy said, stepping back and bumping into something hard and solid. *Lyle.* She'd almost forgotten he was still there. His hands settled on her shoulders and squeezed.

Without warning, Birdie grabbed the cup from Georgia's hands, and for a moment Maisy thought she was going to fling it against the wall or smash it to the floor, because the look on Birdie's face wasn't the schooled, placid expression she wore most of the time. It was a mixture of grief and anger and even confusion, as if she didn't know where the cup had come from, either, but was pretty sure Grandpa *did*, because she pressed it into his hands, then moved his head with her fingers to make him look at her.

She stopped singing and sat perfectly still, forcing her father's attention. She opened her mouth and it seemed the entire room went silent, holding its collective breath. Grandpa's bottom jaw worked itself back and forth, trying to form words, his grunts resembling syllables and consonants, and drowning out any sound Birdie might have made.

There was a knock on the front door, and Lyle went to answer it as if he still lived there. After a moment James and Caroline appeared in Grandpa's doorway, Lyle behind them.

"Hello, Ned," James said. "Mrs. Chambers." He nodded at Maisy in greeting. "Georgia." She didn't turn around.

Grandpa didn't seem to have heard his name, his gaze never leaving Birdie's face. He seemed to be waiting for something from her. A look, or acknowledgment. A single word. And then he shook his head, and another sound came from his throat, this one sounding like *Don't*.

Maisy leaned forward and carefully took the soup cup from her grandfather's lap and held it up for Caroline and James to inspect. "Is it the same?"

Caroline flipped through her photos on her iPad until she found the right one, then turned the screen around so they could see. "What do you think?"

Georgia studied the photo while carefully avoiding James's gaze. "It looks identical. The order of the bees, the colors, the lines indicating movement. It's all the same." She reached over and slid her finger across the screen to turn to a photo illuminating the mark on the bottom of the cup. "Same markings, too." She pointed to the "H& Co.," the capital letter "L," the word "France."

Georgia faced the visitors but avoided looking at James, making Maisy wonder what had happened between them. In the past she could have guessed, but now there were parts of her sister that Maisy didn't recognize anymore. And, she realized, that wasn't such a bad thing.

"It's time for Grandpa to go to bed," Maisy said. She began guiding everyone from the room, but Birdie stayed where she was, her hands now holding both of her father's.

"I'll come back in a few minutes," Maisy said, leaving the door open a crack. She felt an odd disappointment, as if she'd been watching a movie where the screen went black before the ending. There was something important, something major they were missing.

They all stood in the foyer, looking at one another, hoping somebody had an answer. Lyle spoke first. "I need to go. I'm on duty at the Magnolia Cemetery again, deterring vandals. Call me if you find out anything."

Maisy held the door open for him. "Thank you. For finding Birdie and bringing her home. I'm sorry. . . ."

He put his hand over hers. "You don't need to apologize. I'm here to help however I can."

Maisy hesitated, not yet ready to close the door, but knowing she should.

The sound of Birdie singing came to them from Ned's room, the names in the same order, the monotony beginning to irritate Maisy. *Marie, Lucille, Lisette, Jean.*

Frowning, Caroline took the soup cup from Georgia and stared at it for a long moment before she began singing along with Birdie, her fingers moving from bee to bee with each name. She smiled slowly with recognition. "She's singing the names of the bees—they're all girls, of course. Even I know that all worker bees are female." She closed her eyes and waited for Birdie to start at the beginning again, then sang out loud with a strong soprano voice, *"Ah! Vous dirais-je, maman,"* the lyrics fitting seamlessly into the notes.

Her eyes popped open in astonishment. "I can't believe I remember them; it's been so long. But those are the original words. The verse with the names of the bees was taught to me after I'd learned how it was supposed to go." She nodded her head slowly as she thought. "Yes, that's right. Grandmother taught us both versions."

Lyle stepped back into the foyer, his eyes narrowed. "That's French, right?"

"Yes," Maisy said slowly.

"I don't understand." Georgia scrubbed both hands over her face as if to clear her thoughts. "How is it possible that my mother and

Caroline's grandmother knew the same made-up lyrics for a French nursery song? Lyrics that name the bees on an extremely rare set of china?"

Georgia turned to Caroline. "What was your grandmother's first name?"

James answered, as if he were trying to get Georgia to look at him. "It was Ida. Why?"

Georgia's gaze touched briefly on his face, avoiding his eyes. "Just grasping at straws, I guess. When Birdie sings that song, it's usually followed by calling out the name in her sleep or singing it."

"Yes, it was Ida," Caroline corroborated. "Although that might be the Americanized version of her real name. Elizabeth can look at her birth certificate and let us know—she's big into genealogy and has obtained a lot of family documents. I'll text her now. She usually doesn't go to bed until after midnight."

She was already reaching for her purse when Georgia held up her hand. "There's no rush. Her name's not going to make any difference in the valuation of the china. I already have all I need." She indicated the soup cup Caroline still held. "You can keep that if you like. It goes with the rest of your set. I'll have you mail me the photos so I can include them in the valuation for your records." She swiped her hands on the skirt of her lemon yellow A-line dress, as if all the little details floating around them like dust motes could be easily dismissed. "My job here is done."

Lyle took a step forward. "Not quite. We're still waiting on the complete report from the coroner. And your grandfather hasn't been able to answer any of our questions yet."

"I'm not stopping you from continuing the investigation," Georgia said. "I think we've reached a dead end as far as the man and the truck are concerned, but I know you need to do your job. Either way, it won't make a difference to the value I assign to the china. And I do need to get back."

Maisy wondered whether anybody else had heard the last word that Georgia had almost tagged onto the end of her sentence. *Home.*

New Orleans was where Georgia lived now, but it would never be home. Yet she'd spent all those years away because Maisy had asked her to. For the first time Maisy wondered what it would have been like if she'd been the one sent away, and all she could feel was a bruise on her heart.

She felt Lyle behind her, and the old insecurities, never buried too deep, resurfaced. She found herself saying words she hadn't planned. "You're right. I think Birdie and Grandpa will appreciate a return to normal. Let me know if you need help packing up."

Georgia did her best to mask her hurt, but Maisy saw it, felt the stab of guilt. She expected Georgia to say something back, words painted with poison and aimed in the perfect spot to do the most damage. But she didn't, making Maisy wonder whether at least one of them had actually managed to grow up.

Instead, Georgia turned toward Caroline, although it was clear she was directing her words at James. "I'm sure I'll see you before I leave, but just in case, I wanted to let you know what a pleasure it's been meeting you. I have a mailing address to send my report, so you can expect that in a few weeks."

She tilted her head in James's direction without speaking to him directly. "I'm assuming you'll be flying back to New York with your sister instead of driving to New Orleans. If we find out anything more about the history of the china, I'll let you know."

For the first time in the few short weeks she'd known him, Maisy saw raw anger on James's face. "Is that it?" he asked, taking a step toward Georgia and forcing her to meet his gaze. "Just, 'Good-bye; I'll let you know'?"

"James, this really isn't the time or place."

"What? You'll call me? You've got my number on your cell phone?"

Georgia opened her mouth to reply, but James cut her off. "Don't bother. But I did want to thank you for letting me come down here. These few weeks have been illuminating, to say the least—and not just because of the fascinating world of my grandmother's china."

Maisy flinched before the next words came out of his mouth, and saw Georgia do the same. "Mostly I want to thank you for confirming that I'm not the most emotionally crippled person I know. At least I know to ask for help."

He stepped past Lyle to get to the door. "Good night, everybody. Caroline—I'll wait for you outside." The door closed behind him with a gentle snap; he was always the gentleman.

Carefully avoiding eye contact with anyone, Georgia said, "I'm going to run a bath for Birdie." She ran up the stairs, followed a few minutes later by the sound of water running through the pipes of the old house.

"I guess I'd better go," Caroline said. She walked to Maisy and placed the soup cup in her hand. "Give this to Georgia, would you, please? I'm not quite sure whom it belongs to." Lowering her voice, she added, "And it will give James a reason to call and ask about it later."

She smiled and said her good-byes, following her brother out the door.

"You're just going to let her go?" Lyle asked softly.

Maisy lifted her chin, angry that his words echoed her own. "Georgia's old enough to make her own decisions."

His look of disappointment hurt more than any harsh words could have. He picked up his hat from the hall table and settled it on his head. "Yeah, well, and you're old enough to know better." He opened the door. "Please tell your grandfather that Ricky needs to ask him some questions as soon as he can scribble something on a page. Like where he went in France during his trip. And who he might have met. Somebody sent that postcard to an obscure estate in southern France, and there just aren't many candidates besides Ned."

"I'll be sure to let him know."

Lyle paused in the glow of the porch light, and it took everything Maisy could hold together not to ask him to stay. "Good night, Maisy."

"Good night," she said, closing the door before she changed her mind.

She moved into the house, turning off lights, leaving one on in the foyer so Georgia could let herself out. The rush of running water stopped as Maisy crossed the foyer to her grandfather's room. The distinctive sound of whispered words brushing against one another drew her up short. It had been Birdie's voice; Maisy was sure of it. And then her grandfather tried to speak, a rush of air and syllables, the words unmistakable: *I'm sorry.*

chapter 33

Queen honeybees are able to sting repeatedly, but queens rarely
venture out of hives and would be more likely to use their stingers
against rival queens.

—NED BLOODWORTH'S BEEKEEPER'S JOURNAL

Georgia

I'd left Apalachicola just as I'd done nearly a decade before, without saying good-bye and without looking back. I'd learned that from Birdie, from all the times she'd left us behind. I'd consoled us by saying she'd left to save us, because saying good-bye was the worst kind of hurt. At least this time, in my case, it was true.

Caroline had called to say that she and James had made an early flight and had left before sunup to drive back to the Panama City airport. I'd been hurt and relieved in equal measure, wondering at the hollowed-out feeling when I packed up the Limoges books, the sense of being haunted as I looked over my shoulder expecting James to be there. It unsettled me, made me cower under the minutiae of packing up.

I spent my last night at the house eating a short and silent dinner in the dining room with my grandfather, Birdie, Maisy, and Becky, the table cleared now of all my catalogs. One corner of the dining room was stacked with the now-organized papers we'd pulled from the china cabinet, the photos, the miscellanea of a family condensed into stacks of memories that would remain silent until opened. My gaze kept straying to the corner, a thought scratching at the back of my head, like the *drip-drip* from an old faucet. It would spring into my awareness after long moments of forgetting, the sound suddenly as loud as a bullet from a gun.

I kissed Grandpa and Birdie good night, but didn't tell them goodbye. That would have been like admitting defeat, to acknowledge that I'd been there and fled again without anything changing. Birdie was silent, her eyes darting from side to side as if following the thoughts inside her head, but seemed clearer than I'd seen them in years. I knew she could speak; Maisy had told me that she'd heard her whispering to Grandpa. I imagined I saw her lean forward, prepared to say something. I wanted to go to her and force her to talk to me, to explain our lives. To tell me what Grandpa was sorry for.

Sometimes all we need to do to forgive our parents is to understand their own childhoods. James was probably right. But I was an ordinary person, with ordinary reserves of strength and courage. I was pretty sure I didn't have enough of either to dig through the mountain of Birdie's past to get to my own.

Grandpa took my hands as I straightened, as if he knew I was saying good-bye. He stared at me solemnly, as if he wanted to tell me something important. I grabbed the pad of paper and pencil that he'd been working with during his PT sessions, then placed the pad in his lap and the pencil between his fingers.

I waited patiently, listening to the scratch of the pencil against paper. *Drape hives.*

I read the words out loud. "You mean drape them with black? But no beekeeper has died, Grandpa. And you're getting better. We don't need to worry about that, okay?"

He shook his head and wrote two more words. *Bad luck.*

I drew my brows together. "I'm not sure I understand. I know it's bad luck if the hives aren't draped after the death of the beekeeper. I won't forget if that's what you're worried about. But that's a long way away. You just need to focus on getting back your strength."

He opened his fingers and let the pencil fall to the floor, and Birdie sat up straight, watching him closely. As if they each expected the other to speak.

Maisy tapped on the open door before stepping inside. "That's an old wives' tale," she said dismissively. "It's time for Grandpa to go to bed."

"I was just saying good night."

He'd already begun to raise himself from his chair, resisting Maisy's offer of help.

"Good night, Maisy," I said.

Her look told me she knew I was leaving and was doing it the easy way, without saying good-bye. For a brief moment I thought she would ask me to stay, even hoped that she would. But the moment passed, the unsaid words like ghosts floating in the space between us.

If you want things to change, you have to stop waiting for someone else to make the first move. I knew Marlene was probably right, but I saw the hurts between Maisy and me as something impenetrable and insurmountable, rendering us both paralyzed.

"Becky wants you to say good night. She's out on the back porch getting eaten alive by mosquitoes, so don't keep her waiting."

I nodded, but before I left the room, Maisy called me back. "Georgia—wait."

Our eyes met, but neither one of us said anything, our words trapped behind too much stubbornness and too many years of hurt to count. I turned around and left the room without looking back.

I found Becky rocking in one of the old chairs. The moon was pregnant with light, its fullness mirrored on the rippling surface of the bay.

"Mama said I could look at the moon for a little while longer. It's so pretty tonight."

"It is," I agreed, sitting on the top step in front of her.

"When I was little, Mama told me that the whole world looked up at the same moon each night. She said that's how I could always stay close to you. I think she does the same thing."

I spoke past the lump in my throat. "Why do you think that?"

"Because sometimes when we'd come outside to see the full moon, she'd get sad."

I took a few deep breaths so I could speak. "It's time for you to go to bed. I wanted to say good night before I left." I stood and pulled her out of her chair, exaggerating the effort it took to lift her light frame. I hugged her to me, marveling at the sturdy feel of her, the smell of baby shampoo and nail polish. She was smart, and kind, and a great tennis player. And loved by two parents who had created the wonderful person she was. I hoped Maisy never told her the truth about who had given birth to her. That had been the easy part.

I kissed the top of her head. "Don't let the Madisons of the world ever make you think you're less than you are. When I first had to give talks in front of a large group of people, my boss gave me great advice. He said to imagine them naked. That way I'd have no reason to feel self-conscious."

Becky giggled. "I'll try." Her face became serious. "I think you should get a cell phone."

I frowned. "Why would I do that?"

"So I can call you whenever I want to. Or text you. Since you probably can't text, you can just send me a smiley face so that I know you're thinking about me."

"But I think about you all the time without having a cell phone."

"Except this way, I'd know."

I sighed. "I'll think about it."

"My phone number is the same as the house except it has a one at the end instead of a three."

"Easy enough to remember," I agreed.

"Please?" she said, and I knew it wasn't a casual request. I remembered how much I'd needed my aunt Marlene growing up, somebody who was related but removed enough from the complexities of my family life.

"All right," I said, not regretting it as much as I thought I would.

We walked into the house and I said good night, not waiting long enough to see her disappear into the hallway upstairs, already feeling like an outsider again as soon as I'd made it to the driveway. The next morning I awakened before the sun, loaded my packed bags into the trunk, and left a note for Marlene, avoiding her look of recrimination that would hurt more than anybody else's.

It took me a week before I found myself standing outside the brightly lit Apple Store at the Lakeside Shopping Center near New Orleans, looking through the glass trying to find an employee who looked close to my age. I didn't want to be made to feel inferior to someone half my age explaining how a phone worked.

There appeared to be no one inside over the age of twenty-five. With a deep sigh I entered the store, my eyes blinking under the glowing fluorescent lights that bounced off of silver laptop covers and walls of neon phone accessories. I was so out of my element that I nearly turned around and left. But all I had to do to keep my feet rooted to the floor was remember Becky's plea.

Three hours later I walked out with a phone as large as my head (so I could see the letters better, according to Tyler, whose sketchy attempt at beard growing just magnified his youthfulness), and with a rudimentary knowledge of what an app was and how to dial a phone number. He'd also helped me store the three phone numbers I knew: the house, Becky's, and Marlene's. And then I asked him to add Maisy's, but only because Becky had given it to me before I left. Just in case, she'd said. Tyler showed me how to add more, but I couldn't think of who I might call on a regular basis.

When I got back to the office, Mr. Mandeville was waiting for me, a look of excitement on his face. "Caroline Harrison has called for you twice. I'm hoping this means they would like us to appraise and sell some of the larger lots from her grandmother's estate. I would send you, of course, since you already have a rapport with the client."

I was unprepared for the surge of excitement that was immediately replaced with panic. How could I see James again? He'd kissed me and I'd run away, because fleeing was the only thing, besides valuing old china and furniture, that I was any good at. James had stirred up emotions that had long lain dormant, and for good reason. I was damaged beyond repair, a padlock without a key. He was healing from a reeling loss, and the last thing he needed was someone with as many scars as he had.

What's your price for flight? I could hear him asking me that now. And I had a ready answer: self-preservation in exchange for a life that was more than ordinary.

"You can use the phone in my office," Mr. Mandeville offered.

"Actually, I'll call back on my cell phone." I ignored his look of surprise. "Do you have the number?"

He handed me a small pink message form. "Let her know that we are willing to negotiate our rate if the estate is large enough."

"I'll make sure she knows," I said, hastily retreating to my office and closing the door. I looked down at the paper and painstakingly entered her name into my address book and then her phone number. After I'd saved it, I hit the call button.

"James Graf." I was unprepared to hear James's voice on the other end and considered hanging up.

"Hello?" he said, a touch of impatience in his tone.

"James, hi. It's Georgia. I thought I was returning Caroline's phone call."

He was silent, and I imagined him hanging up on me. Not that I would blame him. "Hello, Georgia. This is my cell number, actually. I know Caroline's been trying to reach you. She must have left my number for you to call back."

I blushed, realizing why she'd done that, and also embarrassed at the annoyance in his voice.

"Yes, well, if you could tell her I returned her call and to call me back on my cell."

"Your cell?"

"Yeah. I told Becky I'd get one so she could reach me. She said I could text her, too, but I'm not sure about that."

"Sounds like Becky." I heard the smile in his voice.

"Let me give you my number." I started with the area code, but he cut me off.

"No need. It's already stored on my phone and I can share it with Caroline. And I know what she wanted to tell you, if you have a minute."

I stared into my open desk drawer, the one filled with all of the loose keys I'd been collecting. "Sure."

I listened as he shuffled papers in the background. "She made me take notes so I wouldn't forget anything. And then told me I was in charge of keeping this and any new information together in one place."

Despite everything, I found myself smiling. It was something an older sister would do, something I would have done with Maisy when I was still a part of her life.

"I think she mentioned how our other sister Elizabeth is big into genealogy and had already gathered quite a few family documents. Elizabeth and Caroline pulled out all the papers this past weekend, looking for any mention of the china, remembering how our family had brought it with them when they emigrated in 1947 from Switzerland. We think they found something significant."

I looked at the surface of my desk, covered with facts and figures regarding my estimate of the custom Haviland Limoges pattern, the blank spaces where I needed to insert photos, but I hadn't yet called Caroline to request them. A chill swept over me all of a sudden as I remembered something Marlene had said to me the first time I'd left Apalachicola. *The past is never done with you, no matter how much you think you're done with it.*

"And?" I asked.

"They found the immigration papers from our family's entry into Ellis Island. Giovanni and Yvette Bosca, arriving with their seven children, including their eldest daughter and her husband—a Swiss national—and another child Yvette claimed was her deceased sister's seven-year-old daughter, Colette. Colette Mouton."

Mouton. I said the name out loud, hoping it would help me recall where I'd seen it.

"The name written in the book found in your grandfather's truck," James said.

"Oh." It was the only coherent word I could pull out of a brain that was whirring in circles, trying to settle on a moving target.

"There's more." He hesitated. "Caroline was right about our grandmother's name being the Americanized version. She was always known to us as Ida, but there's a French version of the name." He paused, waiting for me.

"And?" I asked impatiently.

"The French version is Adeline."

I sat back in my chair, staring at a brass carriage clock whose hands had stopped sometime in the last century at two forty-three. If only I could stop time now, or move back the hands to just five minutes before. I wouldn't have made this phone call. And I wouldn't know that my grandfather had been lying to all of us.

"Adeline?" I closed my eyes, hearing Birdie call out the name in her sleep, the anguish and grief in her voice.

"Yes." He hesitated again, aware of the effect his words might have on me. "Georgia, how old is Birdie?"

I shook my head, forgetting that he couldn't see me. "I told you before, we're not sure—and we've never found her birth certificate. If I had to guess, I'd say she's about seventy-five."

"Which would make her about seven years old in 1947."

"But that's . . ." I meant to say the word "impossible." Improbable, maybe, but certainly possible. I pressed the heel of my free hand against my temple, remembering something my grandmother had told me. "Birdie wasn't born in Apalachicola. Her parents lived with her grandparents in Gainesville when they were first married, and that's where Birdie was born and spent her early years. They didn't move here until after the war." I closed my eyes for a moment, trying to remember the whole story. "The house had belonged to Grandpa's brother, but he died in the war, and then after my great-grandpa died, Birdie and her family moved to Apalach." All the air seemed to leave my voice. "Nobody here in Apalach knew Birdie when she was a baby, because she didn't come to live there until she was older."

There was a slight pause. "Like when she was seven or eight years old?"

"Yes," I whispered into the phone. "Where is Colette now?"

"We don't know yet. Caroline has gone back to Elizabeth with the question, so hopefully we'll be able to find out something."

There was a long silence. Finally he said, "You know what this means, don't you?"

When I didn't say anything, he answered. "It means that you and I aren't done yet."

I knew he wasn't talking about the china, or Birdie, or last names. Hearing his voice forced me to remember why I hated good-byes. They always reminded me of what I'd left behind, and what I was fleeing—grief and condemnation all rolled into one innocuous word. A life without connections and commitments meant I never had to say it again. I reminded myself of this before I answered.

"Yes, we are. I'll take the research from here, and include any information I find in the valuation report I send to Caroline."

I waited for a moment for him to respond, then realized I was listening to dead air. When I pulled the phone away and looked at the screen, I read the words "call ended." Instead of being relieved, I felt hot and cold, making me wonder whether I'd caught a bug. But this feeling was worse than a fever. I stood abruptly, needing to move so that I didn't have time to dwell on the sudden emptiness that pressed against my chest wall like an inflated balloon.

I walked quickly to Mr. Mandeville's office, stopping outside at his secretary's desk. Jeannie Stokes looked up at me with big blue eyes, and brushed aside a thick lock of blond hair. I held up my iPhone. "Do you know how this thing works?"

Jeannie was probably a decade or so older than me, but managed the perfect eye roll. "Do alligators pee in the swamp?" She held her hand out, with its sensibly short, unpolished nails, and I gave her my phone. "What do you want me to show you?"

"I need to look up a phone number in Apalachicola, Florida. Can it do that?"

She didn't even bother with an eye roll this time. "Just give me the first and last name."

"Actually, it's for the public library. I need to speak with someone there."

It took Jeannie less than five minutes to pull up the number. She handed me the phone. "See this hyperlink in blue next to the picture of a telephone? Just click on it and it will dial the library."

I took the phone and, after a quick thanks, dialed the number. Caty Greene had said she had access to all sorts of databases and research sources. I needed to know about the name Mouton, and the connection to the Beaulieu estate in France. As I waited for someone to answer, I found myself hoping for a dead end.

chapter 34

"The three most difficult things to understand: the mind of a woman, the labor of the bees, and the ebb and flow of the tide."
Georgian proverb

—NED BLOODWORTH'S BEEKEEPER'S JOURNAL

Maisy

B irdie sat in the turret window of her bedroom as Maisy brushed her hair. Birdie had stopped singing, and hadn't spoken another word as far as she knew, the silence not as peaceful as Maisy had thought it might be during the years of constant noise. Instead the silence seemed full of anticipation and dread, like waiting for a jack-in-the-box to pop out.

The silence had started the day after Lyle had found Birdie wandering the streets carrying the Limoges soup cup. Or maybe it was the day after, when Georgia left. Maisy still had the cup. Caroline had handed it to her and asked her to give it to Georgia, and she'd forgotten. She'd moved it to her dressing table so she'd see it every day, but it was still waiting for her to pack it up and ship it to New Orleans. Maisy hadn't decided whether she'd include a note, not that it mattered. No matter how many times she walked past the piece of china, she just kept forgetting to send it.

Maisy pulled the brush through the pale strands, noticing for the first time that it had dulled somewhat, its shine diminished, as if Birdie walked in the shade now instead of the sun. Birdie's eyes, however, were bright and alert, taking in everything Maisy could see, and a lot that she could not. It was as if all the energy she'd once expended on her physical appearance had been consolidated into a single train of thought. Maisy wasn't sure how she felt about this change, unsure whether it was better than the old Birdie, who cared about which shade of lipstick, and who didn't wear her nightgown all day. It scared her a little, not knowing what was going on inside Birdie's head, what plans she was considering, and what they would look like once they emerged.

Maisy had hoped that Georgia's departure would mark a return to what they'd once considered normal. In hindsight their existence had been anything but, yet they'd ceased to realize it when stuck in its routine. Even Grandpa was changed. Ignoring the heat that had greeted the first week of June with a vengeance, he dragged his walker outside and sat in his apiary most of the day, disregarding the sun as it moved across the sky, baking everything in its path.

At his request, Maisy had placed his chair near the back row, which contained the two bee boxes that were never moved. She'd purchased a beach umbrella and set it up over his chair, realizing that somebody had to be concerned with heatstroke and sunburn. She'd made sure she had her EpiPen, especially since Grandpa had been stung twice already, the bees apparently forgetting who was in charge.

Ricky Cook from the police department had come by a few times to question Grandpa, but had left without anything new. Grandpa either didn't remember enough, or made a good enough show of confusion. Maisy found herself wishing that Georgia were still there. Together they would have talked to him, gotten answers, faced the consequences, whatever they might be. Maybe Maisy could do it on her own. Just not now, with everything else in turmoil. The truck had been waiting in the swamp for more than sixty years. It could wait a little longer.

Florence visited often, sitting next to him under her ubiquitous wide-brimmed hat, her dangling bee earrings flashing in the sun. The backyard and garden, always Grandpa's domain, had begun to grow wild. Maisy had resisted asking Lyle for help, telling herself that when she found the time, she'd take care of it. The problem was solved when Florence, on one of her visits, had brought her two sons, who'd begun raking and cutting back all the overgrowth, piling it all in a small hill next to the apiary. They promised to come back to burn it, and had even brought a large can of gasoline and set it by the mound of yard waste, as if to remind everyone that they would return.

Birdie stayed in her room most of the time, barely nibbling on the meals Maisy brought up to her. But she'd watch her father from her perch in the turret, each aware of the other. They were like satellites in the same orbit, never touching, always circling over and over, reminding Maisy of the bee pattern on the china. They all seemed to be holding their breath, the pressing heat of summer doing nothing to alleviate the tension that permeated the house. Even Becky seemed to notice it, her stuttering more pronounced now so that she barely spoke. Maisy found herself turning around during the course of her day, expecting to see Georgia. *Wanting* to see her. It was an old habit, this sharing of burdens, and one that even now she couldn't shake, no matter how much she wanted to.

A movement from the yard caught Maisy's attention as Lyle walked into the apiary. She'd wondered whether he'd been avoiding her since Georgia's departure. Not that she minded. Seeing Lyle did nothing to help Maisy return to the elusive normal, or at least to a place where she could pretend that she didn't think about him every day. Or regret her choices.

She watched as Lyle squatted by the side of Grandpa's chair, saw as he tilted his face upward to speak with the older man. She couldn't see Lyle's face but imagined it was his cop face, the one with serious eyes and straight lips. The expression that had always made her smile despite its intended effect on offenders.

"M-Mama?"

Maisy turned to see Becky hovering in the doorway. School had been out for a week, but Becky's mood remained dark. She hadn't gone to the honey festival with her father, saying she didn't want to go if the three of them weren't going together. Maisy wouldn't give in and agree to go, not because she wanted to hurt Becky, but because she wanted to save her from being hurt further with any unspoken promises about their future. It was the hardest part of being a mother, the choices one made that could never be understood in the mind and heart of a child.

"Come in. I was just brushing Birdie's hair. Your daddy's outside, if you wanted to say hi."

"I know," she said. "I saw his car."

Birdie stood, indicating that she was finished, then left the room, pausing briefly to smooth Becky's hair behind an ear. Both Maisy and Becky paused, listening to Birdie's footsteps walking down the stairs, and then heard the back door open. After a moment Maisy spotted her mother walking across the backyard toward the apiary, her white nightgown floating like a ghost over the grass.

Lyle was standing now, but Birdie didn't acknowledge his presence. When she reached Grandpa, she sat down in the grass next to him, looking up at her father as if waiting to ask him a question. Or waiting for him to speak. Lyle said something, his hands animated as if he was trying to make a point, but neither Birdie nor Grandpa showed any reaction.

Maisy reached her hand toward Becky. "Come here and sit and let me brush your hair."

It was an old ritual they'd shared since Becky's hair had been long enough to brush. Becky had found it soothing and relaxing, enough so that when she was older and she'd been upset and unable to get any words out of her mouth, Maisy's brushing had been able to relax her enough so she could speak again.

Becky frowned, but moved forward and slid into the chair. Maisy carefully unwrapped the ponytail and smoothed the hair across her daughter's shoulders.

"Is there something you'd like to talk about?" Maisy asked, slowly pulling the brush through Becky's hair.

Becky shrugged, which usually meant that the answer was yes, but she didn't know where to start. Maisy had learned in her nine years of being a mother that it was better to wait than to try to force out the words. That was usually a guarantee of silence.

She looked out the window again and saw that Lyle was gone, and Birdie's head was resting on Grandpa's knee as if she were a little girl. It struck Maisy that Birdie's behavior since Georgia had left had been almost childlike, the smooth adult sophistication of the last decades dissipating in the summer heat. She wore her hair in a plain ponytail, just like Becky, and moved with the clumsiness of a toddler unaware of the potential dangers in her environment. Like now, sitting at the back of the apiary where none of them ever dared to go. It was as if Birdie had decided to shed her identity and play another stage character. Maisy frowned at the window, sensing a change in the atmosphere that had nothing to do with the weather.

Becky's phone lit up, the lyrics of Echosmith's "Cool Kids" singing out. It surprised Maisy, who wondered when Becky had changed her ringtone from the *Frozen* theme song, "Let It Go." It seemed a small thing, yet Maisy saw it as a pulling away from her, a leap from child to girl long before Maisy was ready for it to happen.

Becky hit the "end" button and flipped the phone over so Maisy couldn't see who'd called.

"Would you like me to French-braid your hair?"

Becky shrugged.

As Maisy began separating the hair into three sections, she asked nonchalantly, "Who was that on the phone?"

A gnawed thumb tip went into Becky's mouth, and Maisy held back from telling her that fingernail biting was a bad habit, or that there didn't seem to be anything left to chew on anyway. Instead she waited for Becky to talk, slowly weaving the different sections of hair into a tight braid that started at the top of her head.

"Aunt Georgia," she finally said over her thumb.

Maisy didn't pause. "Oh. I didn't realize she had your cell number."

"I gave it to her. So she could call me on her new cell phone."

This time Maisy's hands stilled. "She has a cell phone?"

Becky nodded, pulling her hair out of Maisy's hands. "I wanted to keep in touch with her after she left." She replaced her thumb with her index finger. "I gave her your number in case she wanted to keep in touch with you, too."

"That's nice," Maisy said, although she wasn't sure how she felt about it. Georgia had always been able to reach her on the house phone, but this was more personal, a call more intentional. Maybe that was why Georgia hadn't yet called her. It was easier to leave things unsaid.

"Have you had many conversations?" Maisy asked, crossing the hair in her right hand with the two sections she held in her left.

"Yeah."

Maisy bit her lip so she wouldn't say anything, pretending to focus on what her hands were doing.

"We talk about Birdie."

"Birdie?" Maisy closed her mouth, wishing she hadn't spoken, yet not wanting to say what she thought she needed to. *Why don't you talk to me about Birdie?*

"Yeah." Becky's right hand began to scratch at a bright red mosquito bite, although without nails Maisy was unsure how effective that was. "Birdie talks to me."

She yanked on Becky's hair a little harder than she'd intended. Maisy remembered the stray words of whispered conversation outside her grandfather's door, and realized she'd probably known all along that Birdie was talking again. And how easy it was to have dismissed the thought knowing she wasn't ready to hear what Birdie had to say.

"I mean, like, really talks. It started the night after Daddy brought her home in his patrol car. She came into my room and sat on the edge of the bed and told me stuff. And it scared me, so I called Aunt Georgia."

Maisy gave up all pretense of being a casual observer and dropped the braid to move around to the front of Becky's chair. She sat on the window seat and faced her daughter. "What was so scary?"

There was no angst emanating from Becky. Just the troubled eyes of a nine-year-old child. "She was t-trying to remember something she s-saw that was important, b-but she couldn't remember what it was. She said that G-Grandpa knew, but wouldn't t-tell her."

"That doesn't sound very scary. Was there something else?"

Becky bit her lower lip. "She s-said the man in the t-truck knew, too."

Maisy went very still. "Does she know who the man in the truck is?"

Becky shrugged. "She didn't s-say. She said the s-secret is why she c-can't talk. It's how she k-keeps it a secret. And she w-wants to t-talk again. T-to everybody." Her voice had become very quiet, and Maisy had to strain to hear her.

"Is that it?"

Becky shook her head. "No." She stared intently into Maisy's eyes, looking so much like Georgia that Maisy almost looked away. "T-there was s-something in her suitcase that's n-not there anymore b-but she needs to f-find it." Tears brimmed in Becky's eyes. "I think she's going crazy."

Maisy had the oddest compulsion to laugh out loud. *That train's already left the station.* It was something Georgia had always said when they'd discussed their mother's mental state.

"And I think s-she wants m-me to help her."

All levity immediately evaporated. "Why do you say that?"

Becky blinked, the tears spilling over onto her cheeks. "B-because I'm the o-only one she can t-talk to."

Maisy stood and picked up Becky as if she were a four-year-old, then lifted her on her lap as she sat down in the chair, surprised that Becky didn't protest. Instead, she nestled her head against Maisy's chest as if she were a small child. "I'm here, sweetie. You know that. I'm always here for you to talk to."

"And Aunt G-Georgia, too?"

"Yes. And Aunt Georgia. We both love you so much, we only want the best for you. But come to me first next time, all right?"

"Because you're my mama?"

Something squeezed inside Maisy's neck, and she had to swallow twice before she could speak. "Yes. Because I'm your mama."

Becky was silent for a while. "I f-found the soup cup. It was in B-Birdie's drawer and I d-didn't want to g-get in trouble for snooping."

Maisy rested her chin on Becky's head, smelling the baby shampoo that would probably be replaced soon with something more sophisticated, and she found herself missing it already. "Why didn't you tell me?" Maisy asked, finally giving up on her resolve to be a better listener and not interfere.

"Because you were b-busy with school and G-Grandpa. And you d-didn't believe me when I t-told you Birdie talks to me."

"Becky? Are you up there?"

It was Lyle's voice, calling up from the foyer.

"We're in Birdie's room," Maisy called. Becky quickly scooted off Maisy's lap, as if she were afraid to be caught acting like a child.

Maisy stood, too, and had the absurd notion of borrowing one of Birdie's lipsticks before Lyle reached the doorway.

"Daddy!" Becky ran to her father with outstretched arms, just as she'd done ever since she could walk.

He lifted her with a bear hug and pretended to clutch his back after putting her down on the ground. "I think all that tennis has been building muscles. I felt like I was lifting a ten-foot alligator!"

Becky dimpled, her mood taking an abrupt about-face. "Really?"

Lyle put a serious expression on his face and nodded. "Really." He looked over Becky's head. "Hello, Maisy."

The blood in her veins betrayed her again by rushing to her heart and head, despite her best efforts to remain neutral in his presence. They hadn't really spoken to each other since she'd let him know that she wasn't planning on attending the honey festival. He hadn't argued with her, which somehow made her feel worse.

"Did you need something?" she asked, trying to get control of the situation.

Ignoring her cue, he took a step forward, wearing what she called his "dangerous" look. The kind of expression he used when he had ideas about how to spend an evening together with her. "Do I need a reason to visit my wife and daughter?"

Before she could point out that she wasn't really his wife anymore, he stopped her. "Save it, Maisy. I actually have news to share with you. It's about the man in the truck."

Becky's eyes were wide; she was listening to every word.

Maisy looked pointedly at their daughter. "I think this would be the perfect time to start cleaning out your closet, young lady. Stack all of your winter clothes that don't fit into a pile to get started. I'll join you in a minute." Maisy crossed her arms over her chest to show she meant business.

"But . . ."

A stern look from Lyle stopped her protest. Like a condemned prisoner being led to the gallows, Becky moved as slowly as possible, dragging her bare feet hard enough that Maisy thought she'd draw splinters from the hardwood floor.

Maisy peered out the door to make sure Becky had gone to her room, then stayed where she was in the doorway. She told herself it was to keep an eye on Becky, but realized it also gave her an easy escape if she needed it.

"So, what's the news?" she asked, keeping her voice calm. Because no matter how she tried not to, every time she saw Lyle she remembered what he'd said. *I still love you, Maisy.*

"Well, they were able to analyze the honey found in the knapsack inside the truck. It was pretty deteriorated, but they determined with some certainty traces of lavender."

"Lavender?" Maisy frowned.

"Yeah. Ricky called the current president of the Florida Beekeepers Association and asked him if he knew of any beekeepers who had bees near lavender fields in the fifties, but he wasn't much help. Maybe you can ask Ned yourself. You'd probably get more from him than Ricky or I could."

"I can try. Although Georgia seems to be a lot better at talking to him."

"Yes, well, she's not here, is she?" He moved over to Birdie's dresser and began straightening the tubes and bottles even though they didn't need to be. He always fiddled with his hands when he was working out how to say something the listener didn't want to hear, and it made Maisy nervous.

"There's another thing, too. How tall do you think your grandfather is? He's a little stooped now because of his age, but how tall do you think he was when you were a kid?"

Maisy smiled involuntarily, remembering the first time Lyle had come to the house to pick her up for a date and met Birdie and Grandpa for the first time. She'd been crazy in love with him already, and it had been so important that everybody like him. She could almost picture him now, standing in the foyer and shaking her grandfather's hand as they took each other's measure. Could see them standing side by side. "When you were sixteen, you and Grandpa were the same height."

He tilted his head and smiled, and she knew he was remembering, too. "I've been six foot three since I was fifteen." His face grew serious again. "The man in the truck was found in the driver's seat. The coroner's report says he was about five-six. But the seat was pushed back so that a much taller man could fit behind the wheel."

It felt as if strong fingers were pressed against Maisy's windpipe, making it hard to breathe. "What are you saying?"

"Nothing yet. And remember that you didn't hear anything from me. Everything so far is just pure conjecture. It's especially difficult when an exact cause of death can't be determined with just badly deteriorated skeletal remains. All we know for sure is that there doesn't seem to be any external trauma."

"So the man could have died from natural causes?"

"We can't rule that out. But there are dozens of ways for a man to die that don't leave a mark."

"So we might never know."

He looked at her with his cop eyes, and Maisy had to remind herself that they were on the same side. She was about to ask him what was supposed to happen next when her gaze fell on the closet door behind him.

"Hang on a minute. I just want to check something out before Birdie returns."

Lyle followed her into the closet, and held back a rack of clothing so she could reach into the corner and pull out the old suitcase. It was small, much smaller than the American Tourister she'd been given as a college graduation present from her grandfather and still used. Maisy carried it into the bedroom and placed it on the bed. With a questioning look from Lyle, she popped open the two clasps on the side, then pulled it open.

The inside lining was a faded yellow material that was burnished like worn silk. Maisy studied the empty compartment with disappointment.

"What did you expect to find?" Lyle asked.

"I don't know. Birdie's talking now, really talking, according to Becky, and she told Becky that there had been something in the suitcase that she needed to find."

"This suitcase?"

Maisy shrugged, reminding her of Becky. "Who knows? This is the only suitcase I could think of." She leaned over to close the lid, but Lyle put a hand on her arm. "There are side compartments. Did you check them?"

Maisy shook her head, then stood back while Lyle ran his fingers around all four sides of the case, neatly hidden in the lining so that they weren't easily seen unless you knew they were there, or you were a trained policeman. Not finding anything in the sides, he continued on to the top half, where a long elastic pouch—presumably for shoes—was hung. He put his hand inside, raising his eyebrows as his fingers touched something Maisy couldn't see.

She watched as he withdrew his hand from the suitcase, a small round wad of what looked like a faded ivory linen napkin held in his palm. He laid it on the bedspread next to the suitcase, then carefully unfolded each corner of the napkin.

"What is it?" Lyle asked as Maisy reached over and plucked the object out of the napkin.

"It's a lid. To a porcelain coffeepot. Or teapot." She traced her fingers around the china honeybee perched at the top, the familiar pattern of bees in flight chasing one another around the edge of the lid.

"It's the same as the soup cup, isn't it?" he asked.

Maisy nodded, a sick feeling growing in her stomach. "I don't understand what any of this means." She met Lyle's eyes above the lid. "And the more I learn, the less I want to know."

"You should probably tell Georgia about the truck, and the honey. And this," he said, indicating the piece of china held gingerly in her hand as if it were poison.

"Why?" It's not that she didn't know the answer. She didn't want to be the first person to call, but if Lyle said she should, then she'd have a reason.

"Because there's a dead man in your grandfather's truck, and all evidence is pointing at his having something to do with it. I think she needs to know. And somehow this china is connected. I just can't figure out how. Yet."

Maisy carefully rewrapped the lid, avoiding Lyle's eyes. "I'll text her. I guess I've grown used to doing everything on my own."

"You've always had me," he said quietly.

As if she hadn't heard him, she placed the lid in her pocket, then replaced the suitcase in the closet. "I've got to go help Becky. And then I'll send a text to Georgia."

He tipped an imaginary hat in her direction. "You know how to reach me if you need me."

She nodded, forcing herself to look out the window so she couldn't watch him leave. Glancing down at the apiary, she saw that Birdie was gone, and Grandpa had left his chair to stand closer to the last bee box on the left. He reached out his good arm and touched the bottom section, seemed to push on it as if to determine its strength and weight. Then he leaned his entire length against the side, as if trying to topple it over. She held her breath, noticing that he stood in front of the hive entrance, something he'd taught her not to do because the bees found it threatening.

He flinched and took a step back, and Maisy realized he'd been stung. She watched as he straightened, then made his slow exit from the apiary, his back to the boxes. She studied his face as he got closer to the house, trying to decipher his expression. When he was halfway to the house he stopped and looked up at the window. Maisy took an involuntary step backward, holding her breath as if she'd just been discovered doing something she shouldn't have. She closed her eyes and waited for her heartbeat to return to normal, and then just as suddenly it thrummed to life again as she realized what she'd seen on her grandfather's face. It had been grief.

chapter 35

*Bees do not see themselves as individuals. When bees run low on food,
they don't separate into groups to fight over it; nor will a group split
from the rest trying to preserve the queen. Instead they will continue to
divide the food until it is gone and together they will all die.*

—NED BLOODWORTH'S BEEKEEPER'S JOURNAL

Georgia

I sat at my desk trying to assemble the ten or so pieces of a Delft vase
to see if there was enough remaining to restore it. I knew several
professional restorers who could make it look like new and preserve
some of the value, if only I had most, if not all, of the largest pieces.

My phone rang with the generic tone that had come with it. Jeannie kept asking me to let her buy a ringtone for me and install it, but I'd
been successful so far in keeping her away from it. Her ringtone, "I'm
Too Sexy," was a testament to her taste, and if she chose something I
didn't like, I doubted I'd be able to figure out how to change it, and I'd
be too embarrassed to ask for help.

The phone was facedown so I couldn't see who was calling, but
the noise and vibration were enough to completely distract me from
what I'd been doing. Despite having an easy way to communicate
with Becky, I was already regretting getting a phone. Now that it was

generally known that I had one, people at the office had been sharing my number indiscriminately, which meant it buzzed and binged all day long. I answered most calls, but returned texts only to Becky, since I knew she wouldn't be judgmental about my lack of abbreviations and smiley faces.

I flipped it over and saw a number I didn't recognize with a 203 area code. Assuming it was another client who'd been given my number, I answered it.

"Georgia Chambers."

"Hello, Georgia. I apologize for bothering you at work, but I just couldn't wait to call you. It's Caroline. James's sister."

It took me a moment to compose myself. "Yes, of course. I recognize your voice. It's good to hear from you. How are you?"

An ear-piercing scream from a small child followed by the sharp bark of a dog sounded in the background. "Oh, the usual. I'm considering entering a convent just so I can get some peace and quiet. Except I'm assuming one has to be Catholic for that. Although it might be worth converting."

I smiled, picturing her beautiful face peering out from a nun's habit. "School starts in three months, right?"

"I've always liked people who can look far enough ahead to see a rainbow on the horizon."

I wasn't sure I agreed, but I let it pass. "Is this about your valuation? I don't know why it's taken me so long, but if you're in a hurry I will drop everything else. . . ."

"No, Georgia. Please don't worry about it. We haven't even put Grandmother's house on the market yet—there is simply so much to clean up and inventory. Just get to it when you can. Although what I'm calling about is actually related."

I held my breath. Maisy had sent me a text the week before telling me about the honey found in the truck containing lavender, and the lingering question regarding the height of the man and the position of the seat. It was the one time I was grateful for my cell phone, and how it had alleviated the need to speak with Maisy. She'd also texted me the photo of the china lid she'd found in Birdie's suitcase. I'd held on to all the information, unable to process it. Unable to figure out what I needed to do next. Because that would mean I would need to feel again, after I'd spent nearly a decade trying not to. It would also mean that Maisy and I would have to become allies again, a team. I just wasn't sure either one of us was ready for that, or if we ever would be.

"I just spoke with that wonderful librarian at the Apalachicola library."

"Miss Caty," I said. She'd been on vacation when I'd called, and I'd hung up without leaving a message, feeling relieved. And guilty. That had been more than a week before, and I'd yet to call back, each day distancing me further from a story that could only bring me back to a place to which I didn't want to return.

"She's very helpful. We have some wonderful research librarians here, but I remembered that Miss Caty was the one who unearthed the database with the account ledgers for the Beaulieu estate online, so I figured I'd call her first to see what she could come up with."

The summer storm that had been teasing the sky all day now crackled outside my window, and I imagined the dark shelf clouds hovering over the gulf like a vulture. "Come up with what?"

"I couldn't leave things the way we left them. Especially with all the loose ends about the origins of the china, and a possible connection with your family. Not to mention that James and I never had the chance to give you a proper good-bye. I really enjoyed meeting you, and I know both James and I would hate it if we didn't stay in touch. Hold on a moment."

Her voice was muffled, as if she were holding a hand over the mouthpiece. "Alex, your sister's retainer is not a hockey puck. Please go put that back in the bathroom.

"I'm so sorry, Georgia. Anyway, James mentioned that he called you to tell you about Colette Mouton, the little girl who emigrated with our grandmother's family."

I hoped my voice didn't betray the fact that my cheeks were flushing. I wondered whether he'd mentioned how the phone call hadn't ended well. *It means that you and I aren't done yet.* "She's been on vacation and I meant to call back, but I guess I got too caught up with my work here and forgot. Did she find anything interesting?"

"Yes, you could say that. Are you sitting down?"

I'd always thought that was just a figure of speech until I remembered the day she'd shown me the pictures of the china pieces in her grandmother's cabinet. "I am."

"It took some hunting, but it was worth the wait. Hang on a second while I go through my notes. James filled me in on all the loose bits of information so I could see the whole picture. I just have to write everything down so I don't forget anything." Another screech and bark, this time followed by a loud crash, punctuated her words.

"Do you need to call me back?" I suggested.

"Unless they're bleeding from the eyeballs or have contracted the bubonic plague, the children are fine. Okay, where was I?" The sound of rustling pages filled a worrying silence before she spoke again. "We saw in the ledger that the Beaulieu estate had commissioned what we think is the correct set of china in 1893. Or at least that was the best educated guess from the information we had. Is all of this right so far?"

"Pretty much." Another page rustled, and I found myself chewing on my thumbnail, something I hadn't done since I was a child, and had started just to annoy Birdie.

"So I asked Miss Caty to see if she could find out anything else in any of her online research resources about the Beaulieu estate. I can't tell you again how lucky you are to have her! She discovered that the Beaulieu family had owned that parcel of land since the sixteenth century apparently, and been good tenants. There was a small château, all ruins now, thanks to the Germans, but a profitable farm for the most part."

She paused, and I wondered whether this was the definition of a "pregnant pause," because I could feel her excitement and trepidation pulsating in the silence. "One of their major crops was lavender."

I sat up. "Lavender?"

"Yes. And there's more."

I stood, needing to walk around, to expend the energy pulsing at my temples and hold back the panic that pushed through my veins like blood. "Go on."

"She couldn't find a census, but in the same place she found that ledger with the estate's finances, she found an employee payroll list. And there, right in the middle, written very clearly and legibly, was the name Giles Mouton."

"Giles Mouton," I repeated, rolling the sound of it on my tongue, testing it to see whether it sounded familiar. "Who was he? Does it say?"

"It does." Another pregnant pause. "He was the beekeeper for the estate."

I had to lean against my desk, remind myself to breathe. "The beekeeper?"

"Yes. And when I asked Miss Caty to look a little deeper, she found that at least from the eighteen forties until the early nineteen forties, when most of the records were destroyed by fire during the war, the Mouton family were the beekeepers on the Beaulieu estate."

I focused on taking a deep breath, my shallow breathing making me light-headed. "Did she find a connection between the Moutons and the china?"

"Not that we could determine so far. But there's something else."

I found my chair again and sat. "I'm sitting down. Go ahead."

"The family—the Beaulieus—evacuated in 1943, but left their personal correspondence at the local cathedral for safekeeping, where they were hidden in a room beneath the narthex. Which was a good thing, since the château burned down in 1945.

"The documents survived and were discovered twenty years ago. The most recent—since 1900—have been saved digitally, making them accessible online. Miss Caty found a tax document from the estate from 1940, which is almost as good as a census report, since it lists the names and ages of the adults and children who lived and worked on the estate."

I had to move my phone to my other ear, afraid it would slip from my damp palm. "What did she find?"

"Two names: Giles Mouton, widower. And his infant daughter, Colette."

I frowned, remembering something she'd said earlier. "Isn't Colette supposed to be a relative? An orphan traveling with your grandmother's family?"

"That was on the emigration papers. But Elizabeth's genealogy research shows no connection. Yvette must have known Colette was an orphan and taken her with them when they went to Switzerland, and then on to America."

"But why would they have lied?" I closed my eyes, something I'd learned long ago helped me focus, something about restricting visual stimuli. Yet the bright colors of painted bees flashed against the blackness on the inside of my eyelids.

"I don't know. But there's more."

Her voice cracked on the final word and I braced myself.

"Caty tried to track Giles past 1940, but he seems to have vanished off the face of the earth sometime between then and the end of the war in 1945. I did my own research about the region during that time period—called the free zone at the time—and found that although it had been relatively unscathed when under the protection of the French Vichy government, when it fell in 1943 the Germans and Italians marched into the south of France. You can only imagine what happened then."

"No," I said softly. "I don't think I can." I rubbed my face, no closer to understanding all the connections than I'd been before I'd left Apalachicola. "So if this is the same Colette and she emigrated with your family, what happened to her after she moved to America?"

I heard the sound of paper rustling again. "Within a year of arriving, our great-grandmother got very sick—it might have been cancer; it's not clear. But our grandmother Adeline had to go to work to help support their large family, and three of the youngest children were sent to live with other families. Colette was one of them."

"And now? Where is she now?"

"Elizabeth was able to trace the other two children. She's even been in contact with their descendants. But there was no trace of Colette."

I was silent for a moment, trying to let the thoughts whirring in my brain settle into some recognizable pattern. "But how did your grandmother come to be in possession of the Beaulieu estate's china?"

There was a pause, and I pictured her delicate eyebrows knitting together as she sifted through words before choosing the correct ones. "I thought the same thing. I'm guessing they took it for safekeeping, to protect it after Giles and Colette left their home. And my next question was how your family came into possession of a single soup cup."

There was a long silence as she waited for me to speak. "And a lid."

"A lid?"

"To a coffeepot or teapot. Maisy found it in an old suitcase in my mother's closet. It was wrapped separately, perhaps to keep it from breaking or from knocking against the actual pot." My eyes drifted to the Limoges catalogs still stacked at the back of my desk. They'd sat there, untouched, since I'd returned from Apalach. "Hang on a second, and I can tell you which one."

I pulled out the one on top—the pattern identification guide that I couldn't look at without remembering James's long fingers flipping through the pages—and opened it to the section of blank identification. I quickly found blank number eleven and ran my index finger over all the different pieces and shapes until I found what I was looking for. I took the phone from my ear and, after a long moment of opening up the wrong apps, I found the photo album and the photo of the lid.

I brought the phone back to my ear. "It's the teapot lid. Definitely the teapot lid."

I imagined I heard her swallow. "The teapot would fit the space in the front of my grandmother's china cabinet." Caroline paused. "She knew about the missing pieces, might even have known where they were. That's why she expected them to be reunited one day, and why she didn't allow any of it to be sold no matter how much she needed the money."

"Or she didn't believe that it belonged to her."

The sound of breaking glass burst through the phone. "I should probably go see about that," she said, her voice still calm. "Any ideas on where to go next?"

My mind had already been traveling in that direction, each time hitting a dead end. "Not really, but I did think of something that's a bit of a long shot. I'm friends with the curator at a museum in Limoges. He wasn't able to offer any information about the china when I initially approached him, but he's very knowledgeable about the history of the area. I'll call him and see if he knows anything about the Moutons, or the Beaulieu estate. You never know."

"You're right, Georgia. You never know where life will lead you."

"True," I said, wondering at the real meaning behind her words. "I'll call you if I find anything."

"Actually, my husband has decided that we need a family vacation, so we're heading to Disney World tomorrow and will be gone a week. You have James's number, don't you?"

"Yes," I said slowly. "But I can wait until you get—"

"Good. He'll be looking forward to hearing from you." A child began to wail in the background. "I really must go." I thought she'd say good-bye, but instead she said, "Just one last thing. I was going through my desk yesterday and found my journal from that horrible period in my life after my first husband died. For some reason I thought of you when I read a particular passage." She cleared her throat. "'There are no limits to starting over. That's why the sun rises every day. Unless you're running in circles, and then the outcome never changes.'"

The story of Giles Mouton and his daughter filled my mind, taking the sting away from her words. "Why would you think of me—"

I was cut off by the wailing of a second child. "I really need to go. I'll talk with you soon."

I looked down at my screen and saw "call ended."

Rain began to splatter against my window, gently at first and then more incessantly, a child wanting attention. I thought of the young motherless Colette Mouton. She was an infant in 1940 and then disappeared along with her father sometime before 1945. Yet she reappeared in Ellis Island with the Bosca family, including Adeline— James and Caroline's grandmother.

Adeline. A name Birdie knew. Along with a song about bees. It wasn't that unusual a name that there couldn't be more than one. Except that I'd never heard it until James had brought the Limoges teacup and saucer into the house and Birdie had seen it.

I stared at the window glass, the rain blurring the view, mimicking my thoughts. When a possible answer skidded against my brain I pulled back, the implications too unbearable. I wanted to pack all the information into a little box and lock it in a bottom drawer. I wanted my life back, the one with no phone or sticky relationships. Just a box of keys with no locks.

But that had all been *before*. Before I'd gone home and seen Maisy again, and sweet Becky with her stutter and gnawed fingernails and awesome tennis skills. Her beautiful face and spirit that Maisy was working so hard to protect. And James. Before I'd met James and learned that my heart wasn't as dead as I'd wanted to believe.

There are no limits to starting over. That's why the sun rises every day. Unless you're running in circles and then the outcome never changes. I resented Caroline for sharing that with me. Not because she was overstepping—and we'd probably both agree on that—but because I suspected that she was probably right.

chapter 36

The queen bee has control over the sex of the eggs she lays. If she uses stored sperm to fertilize the egg, the larva that hatches is female. If the egg is left unfertilized, the larva that hatches is male. This means that female bees inherit genes from their mothers and their fathers, while male bees inherit only genes from their mothers.

—NED BLOODWORTH'S BEEKEEPER'S JOURNAL

Maisy

"I d-don't want to g-go," Becky said for about the tenth time since she'd awakened that morning.

Maisy kept her anger in check. Even without the balled-up clothes Becky threw into her duffel or the way she'd been clomping about her room, the stuttering would have let Maisy know how upset her daughter was. She searched for the voice of reason. "You were the one who suggested tennis camp, and your daddy and I saved up the money so we could pay for it. There are no refunds this late in the game."

Becky looked up with tear-filled eyes, her lips trembling as her teeth clenched the bottom one to try to keep it still. She didn't say anything, which was the equivalent of a dagger thrown directly at Maisy's heart.

Maisy sat down on the bed, trying for eye level. "Sweetheart, I'm sorry. It's not about the money. It's just that you begged and pleaded for so long, and now that it's happening you're doing an about-face and telling me that you don't want to go. I'm just having trouble understanding why."

Becky walked to her dresser and yanked open the drawer filled with all of her underclothes, including the new sports bras that Maisy had bought for her. She'd noticed that, like Georgia, Becky was developing early. *One more thing for the mean girls of the world to pick on.*

It wasn't fair. Becky was already so poised, so mature. So *attuned.* She understood Birdie in ways that Maisy couldn't, and displayed a compassion for both Birdie and Grandpa that was far beyond her years. Her physical appearance promised that she'd be a great beauty when she grew older, but that was only a small part of her.

Watching Becky brought to mind what Birdie had once told Maisy and Georgia about being ordinary. For a long time Maisy had agreed with her, had done her best not to stick out. She'd even tried to raise her own daughter that way. But looking now at her beautiful, talented, and smart daughter, she should have known long ago that was impossible. Just the circumstances of her birth had marked Becky as being far from ordinary, setting her course in life. She watched the angry movements of her remarkable daughter, wondering how it had taken her so long to realize how wrong Birdie had been. How wrong *she* had been. Being ordinary wasn't a sin, but neither was being extraordinary. Maybe a person needed to have enough years on her to look back on her childhood in hindsight to see things clearly. Or maybe it just took the return of a sibling to give new perspective to everything you thought you believed.

Maisy slid down the side of the bed, pulling the bedclothes with her, just as she'd told Becky a thousand times not to do. She watched as Becky threw an armful of ankle socks into the pile that was building like a pyramid in the middle of the duffel. "Sweetheart, why don't you tell me the real reason you don't want to go? I'm not unreasonable. And if I agree with your misgivings, then I won't make you go, all right?"

Becky frowned down at the contents in her bag, considering. For one brief moment, Maisy thought it had to do with her and Lyle, and that Becky might want to be around to make them spend more time together.

Maisy was embarrassed to admit, even to herself, that she might say yes. That was one thing she and Georgia had in common, the inherent stubbornness to wait for someone else to make the first move. She frowned, rolling her thoughts over her tongue as if she'd just swallowed a bitter pill. How was it possible that two grown women were still behaving the same way they had as children? It was the worst kind of cowardice.

Maisy sat up, trying to clarify her thoughts, feeling like the time she got her first pair of glasses and noticed that her favorite tree that had grown outside her bedroom window her whole life had individual leaves instead of blobs of green. Same tree, just a different perspective.

"It's because of Birdie."

Becky had spoken so softly that Maisy had to lean forward. "Because of Birdie?"

Without looking at her mother, Becky nodded.

"Has she told you that she doesn't want you to go?"

Becky finally met Maisy's eyes. "I n-need to watch out f-for her."

"But, sweetie, that's not your job. That's what I'm here for. I'll take care of Birdie while you're gone. I promise."

She shook her head, her ponytail whipping the air. "I'm the only o-one. She t-talks to me. B-because I l-listen."

Maisy reached over to tuck loose hair behind Becky's ear. "You said that before, and I listened. We have an appointment with a new doctor in Panama City next Monday. This is a new specialist who is an expert in older people."

Becky studied her with solemn eyes. "Like a p-pediatrician but for old p-people?"

Maisy resisted her urge to smile. "Exactly. Somebody who has experience with older people and can better help them. She's come highly recommended and I feel confident that things will be different."

Becky's expression didn't change. "But M-Monday's three d-days away and I leave t-tomorrow."

"I'll spend extra time with her, all right? I want you to go away to camp and have fun, and not worry about us here."

"Won't you b-be lonely without m-me?"

"I'll miss you, but I've got all of these projects that I can't get to during the school year—that stack of papers in the dining room that need to be filed, for instance. And I was thinking that maybe I could paint your room—after we talk about the color, of course. I could make new curtains, too. So, see? I'll be too busy to be lonely."

Becky still didn't seem completely convinced. "M-maybe you can help Birdie f-find her suitcase?"

Her suitcase. Maisy straightened. "Of course. Actually, I think I already found it—there's an old one in the back of her closet. There was a china lid inside I want to show her. I was going to wait and talk to the doctor first, but I don't see why I can't go ahead. Especially if it means you'll go to camp without any worries."

The pucker at the bridge of Becky's nose softened. "All right. That makes me f-feel better." She put her hands on her hips and walked to her closet, staring in at the neatly hung rows of clothes. She'd always been tidy, as if she'd needed a way to take control of the confusing world created by the adults in her life.

"Do you need me to help you pack?"

"No. I can do it myself."

Do it myself. Maisy swore those were the first words Becky had said as a baby. *And mine was Georgia.* She let her mind skip away from dangerous territory and instead focused on her daughter. "What about your toiletries?"

"I can't pack them until tomorrow, because I'll need them tonight and in the morning."

Maisy almost sighed with relief to hear that the stutter was gone. "Well, seeing as you have this all under control, I'll leave you to it, and I think I'll start with the filing in the dining room. And since this is your last day at home for the next two weeks, I thought we could all go out to dinner at Caroline's and sit outside in the gazebo and watch the river. How does that sound?"

Becky gave her mother her biggest and brightest smile, the one that always took Maisy's breath away not just for its beauty, but for its generosity. For a long time she'd thought it reminded her of Lyle and it had hurt her to see it. It still reminded her of Lyle, she decided. But not because it looked like him, but because of the way it made her feel.

"I'll take that as a yes." She kissed Becky on top of her head, then headed downstairs.

She checked on Grandpa first, not surprised to find his room empty. She looked out the kitchen window and found him at the back of the apiary again. The umbrella she'd set up only partially covered him, but at least he wore his straw hat, and the thick cloud cover obscured most of the sun. His head was bent, bobbing up and down as if he were talking with someone. Or praying.

She thought about bringing him ice water or sweet tea and was halfway to the cabinet to get a glass when she stopped. She'd left her EpiPen upstairs, and she wouldn't go to the back row of the apiary without it. Not only would she have to pass the first eight bee boxes, but the bees in the back had no compunction about stinging the man who loved them best. She didn't want to think what they'd do to her. She'd wait an hour to see whether he came in, and if not she'd bring him something to drink and urge him to come inside, where it was cooler.

From the dining room table Maisy grabbed a label maker and the box of file folders she'd purchased the day before and set them on the floor next to the tallest stack of papers and dog-eared folders. She needed only to label the folders and organize them in some functional way, since she'd already sorted through all of it, searching for the name Adeline, finishing the task Georgia had assigned to Becky.

Maisy had been annoyed at first, wondering why Georgia might think the name important enough for someone to leave a mention in the family documents. It was so like her to study a problem from every angle, to shine a light into cracks that others didn't even notice. It was annoying and refreshing, depending on whose side you were on. Georgia had been right, of course. She usually was, not that Maisy would ever admit to it out loud.

Adeline—Ida—was the name of James's grandmother, the woman who owned the china and had taught James's sister the French nursery song. There could be more than one Adeline, but there were too many coincidences to assume there wasn't a connection. There were so many questions, and not enough answers. She found herself wishing that Georgia were still there. It was a neutral enough topic that they could discuss it without acrimony. Or without rehashing the past.

It was the main reason she was thrilled that Georgia had a cell phone and was learning how to text. As long as they kept the conversation neutral, texting was the perfect way to communicate. Just yesterday she'd received a text from Georgia telling her what Caroline had discovered about the Moutons' connection to the Beaulieu estate, and Colette's emigration with their family after the war. If they'd been speaking on the phone, one of them would have been forced to ask what it all meant. And hearing Georgia's voice would only bring back that horrible scene in Lafayette Park when they'd both dared to scratch the protective surface of their hurt. It was as if they'd shared the same shoes for years, rubbed the same blister, and were both desperate to keep it from breaking.

Maisy lost all track of time as she labeled, resorted, and restacked the papers into their proper homes, her feeling of accomplishment and satisfaction far outweighing the actual task. She'd put aside the folder with the photos, knowing Lilyanna's pictures were there. She promised herself she'd look at them later, on a nice day in the bright sunshine, where it didn't hurt so much. Maybe one day she'd feel strong enough to put them in an album. Just not today.

The light had begun to fade when she reached for what she told herself would be the last folder for the day. Her back ached, and she'd promised to take everyone out to dinner. She recognized the folder that contained her grandfather's military records and quickly created a two-line label: NED CAMPBELL BLOODWORTH, MILITARY RECORDS, 1942–1945.

She pulled off the broken tie on the old folder and slid out the contents, prepared to simply place them in the new folder without going through them again. She was about to close the cover when her gaze settled on the form on top, a half-size page made with postcard material. It was his army enlistment medical exam, listing his height and weight at age twenty-one. *Six feet, three inches.* She thought about the seat in the truck, and how it was too far back for a man almost a foot shorter. Her gaze traveled to the bottom right, where an area labeled CHILDHOOD ILLNESSES filled the corner. The box next to the word "mumps" was checked.

She sat up, remembering the conversation with James about his great-uncle when they were in the gazebo, right before Becky ran into the street to get the beach ball. *Did you say it was the mumps that made him sterile?* James had said that was true only in some cases, and before they could say more, Becky had run out into the road and any implications had been pushed from her mind. Until now. Maisy looked down at the form again, at the big black "X."

She slammed the cover shut as if she'd been caught looking at something she wasn't supposed to see. But all she could hear inside her head was her grandmother telling her that she and Grandpa had wanted lots of children to fill the big old house, about how it had been a sad, empty place after the war. Grandpa's older brother had been killed in Normandy, leaving no children, and then his father had died of a broken heart. Children would have brought it back to life again, but Grandma and Grandpa had only had a single daughter. Birdie.

The back door slammed, announcing Grandpa's return to the house. Maisy slid the folder off her lap and stood, looking at it as if it were poisoned. She listened to the slow, steady approach of his walker while words whirred in her head as she tried to figure out what she needed to say. What she needed to ask.

She was saved by saying anything at all by a loud crash from upstairs. "Becky?" she shouted as she took the steps two at a time, pausing at the top of the staircase and sighing with relief when she saw her daughter in the hallway in front of her room, a questioning look on her face.

Their gazes traveled in tandem to the attic door at the end of the hall, the door ajar as light spilled down the step onto the hallway runner below. Putting her hands on Becky's narrow shoulders, Maisy said, "Stay right here, okay? I'll call for you if I need help."

Becky nodded solemnly as Maisy rushed toward the attic, calling her mother's name as she ran up the narrow, steep steps. She stopped once she reached the top, the source of the crash immediately obvious. A corner curio cabinet with wood shelves and a glass front lay toppled on its side, shards of glass glittering like diamonds in the late-afternoon rays of murky sunlight. It had once stood in front of her grandmother's cedar chest, blocking it from easy access.

Where it had been, Birdie sat in a heap, the heavy lid of the chest thrown open, exposing an empty interior. She wore a white cotton nightgown and her hair was pulled back into a ponytail that had half fallen from its elastic. Her shoulders moved, but she didn't make a sound.

"Birdie? Are you all right?" Maisy rushed to her side, squatting down next to her and running her hands over her fragile bones, checking the white cotton fabric for red stains. "Birdie?" she said again, willing her mother to look at her.

Slowly Birdie lifted her head, her eyes clear, as if a curtain that had been blocking years of darkness had been suddenly lifted, and just for a moment it looked as if she wanted to tell Maisy something. Instead, Birdie brought her hand up and then dropped something into Maisy's lap. It took a moment to realize what it was, to recognize the teapot lid that Maisy had removed from her pocket to take the photo to send to Georgia, and left on her nightstand in her room.

Then Birdie lowered her head again and began to sing the French names of the bees—*Marie, Lucille, Lisette, Jean*—in a voice so small and childlike that it made the hairs on the back of Maisy's neck stand on end.

chapter 37

*In Celtic mythology, the bee is a messenger between our world and
the next. And in ancient Egypt, pharaohs used the bee as a royal
symbol, perhaps for the same reason.*

—NED BLOODWORTH'S BEEKEEPER'S JOURNAL

Georgia

I approached the grand entrance to Audubon Park that faced St.
Charles Avenue, getting ready for my second lap around the road
that ringed the park, a tidy border to the park's golf course and small
lakes. Several of the giant live oaks had fallen in Hurricane Katrina,
but what remained offered shelter from the hot New Orleans sun and
those of us who insisted on exercising in the intense summer heat.

I'd moved to the Crescent City because of desperation, and Marlene's connections, on the heels of Katrina. After Becky was born,
Marlene had tried to talk me into moving somewhere else—out west,
or Texas, or anyplace that had the essential coastline but no memories
for me. But I'd chosen to stay in New Orleans, mostly because it fit
my mood and position in life. We'd both taken a beating, our defeat
so humiliatingly laid bare for the world to see. I liked to think that we
leaned on each other, engineering what could only be called a mirac-
ulous comeback.

It was only eight o'clock in the morning, the stifling humidity that seemed to be the Crescent City's flagship already out in full force, yet it didn't slow my steps. An involuntary smile lifted a corner of my mouth as I remembered my conversation with James about people along the Gulf Coast being born with gills so they could survive the heat and humidity.

I pushed myself harder, hoping the exertion and the sound of my own panting breaths would eradicate all thoughts. I ran past the giant urn-topped pillars at the entrance to the park, my muscles straining, my lungs burning, my sweat-soaked ponytail slapping my back. But I had learned that no matter how fast I ran, my memories always kept pace with me.

I passed a young mother pushing a double stroller, her face glistening with sweat, and two coeds with Tulane running shorts sprinted past me, making me feel ancient. I was focusing on a large white swan as it emerged from the water when I imagined I heard my name being called. I didn't wear headphones when I ran, so there was nothing wrong with my hearing, which caused me to stumble as I tried to slow when I heard my name again.

I skidded on the asphalt path, trying to catch my balance without completely embarrassing myself by falling on my face. With my hands on my hips to help me breathe, I kept walking to give my muscles a chance to recover from my sudden stop, searching the path and the nearby benches for a familiar face.

He was leaning against one of the benches that faced a small interior lake, watching me intently with his blue eyes, his expression unreadable. "Hello, Georgia."

I couldn't speak for a long moment, trying to find my breath, sucking air into a chest constricted with shock. I was glad to be concentrating on pulling air into my lungs, because otherwise I would have been thinking about what I must look like.

"Hello, James." An arm of sunlight through the leaves of the oak he stood under stroked his hair, making it gleam gold. His khakis were neatly pressed, his golf shirt devoid of sweat spots, giving an overall impression of a man unfazed by the heat. I put my hands out in a gesture of confusion, because I couldn't find the air to ask.

"Mr. Mandeville told me that you usually ran in Audubon Park on Saturday mornings. So here I am."

I walked around in a circle, feeling my feet hit the ground with each step, if only to prove to myself that I wasn't hallucinating, conjuring his face because I wanted to see it again.

"You live in New York." *Breathe. Breathe.* "It's not such an easy thing to just show up in Audubon Park on a Saturday morning."

He smiled. "I hope your gills are working, because you're really glowing."

I started to walk away, still too shocked for real anger, but needing air desperately. "If you wanted to insult me, you should have called my phone. I have one now, remember."

I heard his footsteps before his hand touched me lightly on the shoulder, making me face him. "I'm sorry. I've been here for an hour trying to think of what to say to you, and I'm afraid that was the best I could come up with."

His self-deprecating smile did a lot toward softening my attitude. I frowned, making him drop his hand. "You hung up on me."

"And you were being dismissive. I apologize, though. I was raised better than that." He smiled his *GQ* smile and I had to look away. "Please don't tell Caroline."

"Did she send you?" I narrowed my eyes with suspicion.

"Actually, no."

My heart thudded in my chest, but I wasn't sure whether it was just from the exertion of running. "If you wanted to apologize, you could have just called."

"I know." His eyes searched mine, but I looked behind him, not wanting him to find the answer he was looking for in mine. "But I wanted to see you again."

"Is this about the valuation?"

He blew out a breath in frustration. "No. But I'll say it is if that makes you more comfortable."

I began to walk away again. This was supposed to be my safe place, the home I'd created without connections. Yet here was James Graf, standing in Audubon Park as if he belonged there. "You should have just called me," I said.

"Why are you walking away? Do you do that every time somebody tries to get close to you, or is it just me?"

My eyes burned, but it wasn't from sweat. I stopped, but didn't turn around. "Why does everybody assume there's something wrong with wanting to be alone?"

"Because it's against your nature." His voice came from right behind me. I dipped my head and he lifted my ponytail, as if that could cool me off.

"You don't know me." I'd said that to him before, but it hadn't seemed to sink in.

"Yeah. I think I do. You're the girl with all the keys, knowing the right lock is out there somewhere. It makes you quite extraordinary."

I stepped away from him, aware of how badly I was still sweating. "I'm not what you need."

He took a step forward, closing the distance. "I disagree. You made me want to change."

I crossed my arms, remembering his parting comment before he'd left Apalachicola. "Even though I'm the most 'emotionally crippled' person you know?"

I had the satisfaction of watching him blanch. "I'm sorry I said that, even if it had some truth to it." He took my arm before I could run away. "I had no right to say that to you, mostly because I was swimming in the same pool."

I jerked my arm out of his grasp. "Well, I'm perfectly happy being emotionally crippled."

"Are you really? You don't miss Maisy? Or Becky? Or any part of the life you gave up when you left?"

"You have no right—" I began.

He interrupted me. "I called Brian. You challenged me to do

that, remember? I told him I was sorry. Sorry that I hadn't given him a chance to say to me what he needed to."

"And did he?"

James nodded. "He asked for my forgiveness. A simple thing, really."

"No, not really. And did you? Forgive him?"

"Yes. At least I began the process. But suddenly all that pain and hurt and madness—it went away. It no longer had the power to control my life. I felt free."

"I'm glad for you. I am. But if you've come down here to convince me that I need to ask Maisy to forgive me . . ."

"No. That's not why I'm here." That devastating smile lit his face again. "Caroline told me when I was a little boy that if I wanted something, then I needed to ask for it. That's why I'm here. I want to ask you to let us spend some time together. Let us get to know each other. And I wouldn't have come all the way down here if I didn't think you felt the same way." He reached up with one hand and cupped my jaw, using his thumb to wipe the moisture away beneath my eye.

"I can't . . ." I turned away again, Caroline's words swimming in my head. *There are no limits to starting over. That's why the sun rises every day. Unless you're running in circles, and then the outcome never changes.*

Maybe I liked circles. "No," I said, shaking my head. "It's too late. I'm happy here. I'm happy with my life."

I began jogging in the opposite direction, almost running into a bicyclist because I couldn't see where I was going through watery eyes. I'd taken only a few steps when my phone began to ring. I'd made the mistake of buying an armband for it, which meant people could reach me when I was running.

Maisy Sawyers. I didn't know why I'd typed in her last name, like I wouldn't recognize her name without it. Maisy was calling me, and the only reason I could think of was because there was a problem.

"Hello?"

I barely recognized my sister's voice. It was higher-pitched, like it used to get when she was small and scared of a storm. And it was thick, a cloud full of unshed tears clogging her throat. "It's Becky. And Birdie. They're missing."

I felt all the air leave my body. "Missing? What do you mean, missing?"

"They're gone. I went to get Becky up this morning to send her off to tennis camp, but her bed was empty. So was Birdie's. The sheets were cool, so they've been gone for a while. I don't think they went far, because Becky's suitcase is still packed and waiting by her door. Her bunny's gone—the one you gave her. With the little pocket in it. It's the only thing she took with her."

"Did she take her phone?"

"No. She turns it in to me every night at eight o'clock, and I still have it."

"Any idea where she could have gone? Did she leave a note or go to stay with a friend?"

"No and no. She's nowhere. And Birdie . . . something's changed with her. I found her in the attic yesterday. She had the teapot lid and had opened Grandma's cedar chest."

"Was Becky upset?"

"No. We just put Birdie to bed and I stayed with her until she was asleep. I checked on Becky, then went to bed myself. I don't think any of us ate dinner." A sob escaped. "I'd promised to take her out to dinner. Do you think she's punishing me for forgetting?"

"No, Maisy. That's not Becky. This is about something else." I took a deep breath. "Did you call Lyle?"

She seemed surprised. "No. I should have, shouldn't I? But you're always the first person I think of when I'm in trouble." I wondered if she'd realized what she'd just said, knowing that only severe duress would have made her admit to such a thing.

"I want you to hang up now and call Lyle. And I'm going to jump in my car and drive right down. Call me on my cell if you find her, or you get any more information. Okay?"

We said a quick good-bye and hung up, although it took me two tries to hit the red button, because my hand was shaking.

"Are you all right?" It was James.

I realized I was close to hyperventilating and allowed him to lead me to a bench and then keep his hand on my shoulder as I bent my forehead to my knees. But just long enough for me to catch my breath. I sat up, waiting for my head to stop spinning. "It's Becky. She and Birdie are missing. I need to go home."

"I'll go with you," he said, not waiting for me to ask. As if he already knew that I would. "I'd drive if I could."

Despite everything, I smiled. "I know. But you know how to use a cell phone. I'll have you checking in with Lyle and Maisy while I drive."

We began walking quickly toward the entrance to the park, but I stopped, putting a hand on his arm. "This doesn't change anything. Between you and me."

His eyes were cool. "I know. But I want to help."

I stood on my tiptoes and placed a quick kiss on his cheek, immediately regretting it the moment the heat stung my lips.

chapter 38

*"Don't you wait where the trees are, / When the lightnings play, /
Nor don't you hate / where Bees are, / Or else they'll pine away. /
Pine away—dwine away— / Anything to leave you! / But if you
never grieve your Bees, / Your Bees'll never grieve you."*
Rudyard Kipling

—NED BLOODWORTH'S BEEKEEPER'S JOURNAL

Georgia

We arrived in Apalachicola after a record-breaking four-and-a-half-hour trip that involved only one stop for gas and coffee. James ate something, but I couldn't bear the thought of food. My foot sat heavy on the pedal, my knuckles white as I gripped the steering wheel. All I wanted right now was reassurance, someone who knew how to offer companionship without stealing my solitude. James seemed to recognize this, and several times placed his hand over mine when I rested it on the bench seat beside me to get the blood flowing again. It made me think of Kate, his wife, and all she'd thrown away, wondering as I watched the miles pass whether she'd thought of him in her last moments, grieved what was already lost.

James kept up with Maisy and Lyle on my phone with updates, and shared them with me. Unfortunately there was nothing more to add than what Maisy had already told me. No witnesses, no notes, no sign of an elderly woman and young girl walking the streets of Apalachicola. No *reason* for them to be gone. At least as far as the rest of us knew.

During the last leg of the drive, as we headed down Highway 98 through Mexico Beach, my phone beeped. "Text?" I asked, feeling excitement, wondering whether it could be Becky since that was her favorite form of communication.

James looked down at the screen and shook his head. "No. E-mail. You get e-mail on this, you know. Someone must have set it up to send you alerts whenever you have a new one."

I remembered Jeannie the previous week commandeering my phone to set it up so I could use it "like a normal person."

"It's from Henri Volant."

In the stress and worry about Becky and Birdie, I'd spared no thought for the elusive china pattern or the beekeeper and his young daughter. I wasn't even sure that I wanted to deal with it now. But a niggling thought kept scratching at my brain. How Birdie and Colette were both the same age. How Colette had been given to another family to live with.

"Henri is the curator for a museum in Limoges," I explained. "He knows a lot about the area and Limoges china."

"Do you want me to open it?"

I swallowed hard. I wanted to tell him no, to deny the possibilities. Run away from anything that was unpleasant, because that was what I'd always done. Yet here I was, traveling back down the road I swore I'd never travel again. Maybe this meant I was through with running, was old enough now to face the truth, whatever it might be, and confront Birdie's past that was inexorably tied to mine and Maisy's, no matter how hard it would be to hear. Or forgive.

I turned to James. "Yeah, you probably should."

After waiting a moment, James read, "'So good to hear from you. I am very happy to continue to assist you with your research, and am very happy to send you information on Giles Mouton. He is a local hero, did you know? I must leave now for a conference in Geneva, but will be back in two days' time, when I will send more information. For now, here is a photocopy of a letter from my museum archives that I think you will find most helpful. I apologize that I could not be of more help with your first inquiry, but once you mentioned the name Mouton, I knew exactly where to look.'"

For a moment I almost forgot my worry and the reason for this trip. "Giles Mouton is a hero?"

"Apparently," James said. He was silent, staring at the screen. "Wow. This is remarkable."

He continued to read in silence, and I began to get uneasy. "Are you going to share it with me?"

"Yes, sorry. It's in French, so I had to read it a couple of times to make sure I was translating it correctly."

"And?"

"It's a letter from a Jean Luc de Beaulieu, dated January 1893. It's addressed to Pierre Mouton, thanking Mr. Mouton and his family for one hundred years of service as official beekeepers of the Beaulieu estate, and asking Mr. Mouton to accept a set of china as a token of his gratitude."

My hands felt slippery on the wheel and I had to grasp it harder. "Does it describe the china?"

"No. There's nothing else." He paused. "But I think we can make assumptions based on everything else we've learned."

I thought for a moment. "If that was 1893, then Giles might have been Pierre's grandson, and then the china was passed down until it was inherited by Giles from his father," I said, trying to focus on the road in front of me.

"And then to Colette, his daughter."

As if in mutual agreement, we were silent for the rest of the trip, each of us trying to slide the pieces into a puzzle that had lost all size and shape, the unspoken questions drowned out by the sound of the wind in our ears and the steady beat from the radio.

Maisy and Lyle ran out to greet us as soon as I pulled up into the driveway, Lyle's arm around her shoulders. For a moment I thought Maisy would hug me, or that I would hug her, and I knew she was thinking the same thing, the way we stood on our toes leaning forward. *You called me first,* I wanted to say, but didn't. The circumstances were wrong, and I wanted to think that we were both too old to keep score.

But Lyle hugged me and kissed my cheek before shaking James's hand. "Any news?" James asked.

Maisy shook her head, and I saw her red and swollen eyes, the hollows under her cheekbones. "No. We've set up a command central here, and there are teams working everywhere, but nothing yet. Nobody's seen a trace of them." She choked on the last word, unable to say it.

"The coast guard is sending a helicopter to search the bay, just in case they took a boat and ran into trouble and can't get back," Lyle said softly.

We moved up onto the shade of the porch. "How is Grandpa taking it?"

Maisy's brow furrowed. "I don't know—he won't say anything. And he won't leave the apiary."

I looked at Lyle. "Has he said anything since I left?"

"No. Nothing—although his speech and writing have improved enough that he can communicate if he chooses to." He glanced up at Maisy. "He's fighting some battle in his head, but he doesn't seem to want to ask for help."

Maisy's phone rang and she jumped to answer it, hanging up after just a few words. "One of the teachers from Becky's school, Susan Clementson. She's organized the teachers so that they're all driving around and asking people if they've seen Becky or Birdie. There's nothing. We're thinking they left pretty soon after midnight, and that they had a good head start in the dark so nobody would notice them." Her voice broke and I felt myself leaning toward her, wanting to hug her. But Lyle put his arm around her shoulders and allowed her to press her face into his chest. I felt more sad than relieved.

We moved inside and the house seemed so empty and soulless, the corners darker. It was almost hard to breathe. "Can we go up to

Becky's room?" I asked, not sure what I might be looking for, but knowing I had to start somewhere or go crazy.

I stood in the middle of Becky's bedroom, seeing how childish it was, with the small pink table and chairs, the ruffles on the bedspread, the stuffed honeybee mobile that danced in the corner in a draft from the air-conditioning vent. She'd told me she wanted to keep bees, too, that Florence had said she and Grandpa would help get her started as soon as Grandpa was feeling better. I stood under the mobile in the middle of all that pink and knew that I would have kept the room the same, would have wanted to keep Becky a little girl as long as possible. Maisy and I both understood that childhood was just a tiny blip in a person's lifetime, and that the rest of Becky's life she'd be forced to spend as an adult.

"Did she say anything to you? Give you any reason to think she would run away?" I asked.

"She did say something, but not for a moment did I think she'd run away," Maisy answered, looking at Lyle as if she needed corroboration. "Last night when she was packing for camp, she told me she didn't want to go. That she needed to keep an eye on Birdie. I told her that's what I was here for, that I would take care of Birdie. And Becky seemed to accept it, and was even excited about camp." She threw up her hands, as if she'd already gone over and over it all in her head and still couldn't find a plausible answer. But her eyes looked directly into mine and we were little girls again, and she was looking at me as if I held all the answers.

I turned away, then walked across the hall to Birdie's room. Her bed was unmade, all the drawers in her chest and dresser neatly closed, her nightgown carefully folded at the bottom of the bed.

"She changed into a dress, which would make her less obvious if she was walking around at night than if she were still wearing her nightgown," Lyle said.

Like she knew. Like she planned it. I wondered whether anybody else had thought the same thing. I walked to the closet and opened it, moving to the back as if my younger self were pushing me forward. The suitcase was still there, where Maisy said she'd returned it after finding the teapot lid. I pulled it out of the closet, then opened it on top of the bed.

"I looked through all the pockets," Lyle said. "I only found the lid."

"I know," I said. "But I always like to see for myself."

"You sound like Caroline," James said, and I had the impression that he'd meant it as a compliment.

Maisy left and came back with the lid. "I hid this in my drawer, just in case Birdie went looking for it again."

She gave it to me, allowed me to hold it in my palm and feel the heft of it, to see the pattern of the bees. "I'm pretty sure now that the entire set of china was made for the Mouton family—the beekeepers on the Beaulieu estate. It was a thank-you gift for one hundred years of service."

Maisy's eyes met mine. "And yet it ended up in James's grandmother's home, and two pieces ended up here."

"Actually, just one and a half," Lyle corrected. "We found the teapot lid, but not the teapot."

"Could that have been what she was looking for in the attic?" I asked Maisy. "Because you said she had the lid in her hand when you found her."

Maisy shrugged, her shoulders shaking, and I could tell she was trying very hard to keep it together. "Who knows what's in Birdie's head? Have we ever known?"

"Maybe she's gone looking for the teapot," James suggested. "That's just a guess, but it follows her discovery in the attic with the lid, and the empty cedar chest. Maybe she's on a quest to find it, and Becky decided to go with her to keep her safe."

"That makes no sense," Maisy said. "I can't believe Becky would just leave without telling me." Lyle put his arm around her, and Maisy let her head rest against him.

I continued to hold the lid, thinking. Remembering. I looked up at Maisy. "That summer I left—the summer when Birdie stopped talking. Grandpa found her in the attic—remember? She'd collapsed and was lying on the floor. Maybe she found something she didn't expect and it made her—I don't know—lose touch with reality."

Maisy's gaze met mine. "Or it made her remember something." She thought for a moment. "I'm wondering. . . . I found something that may or may not have anything to do with this. There's a possibility that Grandpa was sterile. He had mumps as a child—it's in his medical records. It could have made him unable to have children— like James's uncle. What if Birdie isn't his?"

Our thoughts ran in tandem, a blur of unexpected discoveries over the last few weeks: of the beekeepers on an estate in France, our grandfather's possible sterility, and of a little girl named Colette Mouton who came to America in 1947 and then disappeared.

I looked away, breaking the connection.

"Your grandpa found Birdie in the attic that first time?" James asked.

Maisy nodded. "Yes. He brought her down the steps and called the doctor."

"Did anybody else go up into the attic?"

I shook my head. "No. Grandpa said he didn't want anybody else up there. He said there were a lot of spiders."

Lyle and James shared a look. "So nobody went up there after Birdie collapsed, so nobody knows if something might have been taken out of the attic and put somewhere else?" Lyle asked.

"No. I left shortly after that and . . ." I stopped, realizing what I was about to say.

"And I was pregnant," Maisy said. "I didn't want to risk a fall, so I didn't go up. I don't think I've been up there since."

I stood. "None of this is helping. We've got to figure something out or I'm going to get in my car and start driving. Are we sure they didn't take a car or bikes or any form of transportation?"

"We've checked all of that—including Becky's friends. No leads," Lyle said.

"There may be one thing," Maisy said, almost apologetically. "I didn't think this was important. . . ." She stopped, waiting for encouragement.

I wanted to shake her, to tell her it was okay to speak out and be noticed. But I caught James watching me and instead I took a deep breath. "Nothing's not important when a child is missing. What is it?"

"Birdie may have spoken to Grandpa before they left. This morning, when I went to wake him and tell him about Becky and Birdie, his notepad wasn't on his nightstand where I'd left it last night. It was on the floor next to the bed, and when I picked it up there was something written on the top page."

"What was it?" I asked, forcing my voice to stay calm and trying not to imagine what she was feeling right now.

"'Is it a sin to love too much?'" She gave a little shrug. "That's why I didn't think it was important, until I realized I was the last one to speak with Grandpa last night, and this must have been from a conversation he'd had since then. I asked him about it, but he refuses to communicate. It's almost as if he doesn't want them to be found." Her voice hitched on the last word.

I ran my hands through my hair, wishing I could see more clearly, sure there was something obvious we were missing. "I'm assuming you've already spoken to Marlene."

He nodded, his arm holding Maisy tight to his side.

"What about Magnolia Cemetery, where my daddy is buried?"

Maisy's shoulders slumped. "A patrol car has already been sent to the cemetery and they are checking it routinely. There was no trace of them having been there."

"Is there another place? What about George's boat?" James asked.

"It was sold right after he died," I said. "The new owners took it to Biloxi. Marlene said it got destroyed in Katrina."

I rubbed my hands over my face, trying to clear my head of extraneous thoughts. I walked over to the dresser and picked up a miniature purple Nessie, a souvenir Marlene sold at her store for people she couldn't convince to buy the larger one outside. I tossed it in the air a couple of times. I stared at the small sea creature in my hands, as if it were a conduit to obscured memories. I looked up with a start, recalling trips I'd taken with Marlene to my paternal grandmother's home on Cat Point, where she and my daddy were raised. It was tiny, only three rooms and one bathroom, and smelled of fish and cigarette smoke. The memorable part of it was the almost wistful hugs from my grandmother, and the dock behind their house with an unobstructed view of St. George and a glimpse of Dog Island. I'd been fascinated with the name as a child, thinking the island was filled with all shapes and sizes of canines. My grandmother had died when I was still young, and I hadn't been back since. But George had grown up there, and Birdie had certainly visited while my father was alive.

"What about my grandparents' house on Cat Point?" I said. "Has anybody been there?"

"But that's six miles over a bridge," Maisy said, her voice rising, and I knew she must be picturing her daughter at night on the dark bridge.

Lyle took her hand. "True, but there are other ways to cross the bridge."

"Like hitchhiking," I said, feeling sick. I quickly found Marlene's stored number on my phone and hit the dial button. She answered after the second ring. "Georgia," she said, her voice thick with tears.

I didn't let her say anything else. "I need the address of your mother's old house. There's a chance Becky and Birdie may have gone there."

"The house has been abandoned for years, Georgie. It was on a dirt road right off of the old Pruitt property. But if you pick me up on your way, I can take you right to it."

"I'll be there in less than five minutes," I said, already rushing toward the stairs.

"We'll take my patrol car," Lyle said, following behind me. "I've got lights and sirens. I can call for backup to bring them home when we find them."

Feeling comforted by his optimism, I nodded my agreement as we all ran out the door to his car.

I sat up suddenly. "We need to tell Grandpa we're leaving, so he won't worry."

"I think he already knows," James said, indicating the side window.

It didn't open from inside the car, and before I could ask Lyle to open it for us so I could call out, he'd pressed on the accelerator and we were speeding out of the driveway. I stole one last look behind me and saw my grandfather watching us leave, his shoulders bent more than usual, his face etched with a kind of grief I'd never seen before and hoped never to see again. *Is it a sin to love too much?* I could almost hear him saying that into the empty air.

We picked up Marlene, then raced across the bridge over the bay toward Eastpoint. As soon as we got off the bridge, Marlene pointed out turns for Lyle to follow, bile rising in my throat from fear and apprehension as I imagined Birdie and Becky ducking under the bridge and hugging the shoreline in the dark. We hit a dirt road, and listened as the tires churned up sand and shells, billowing a smoke trail behind us.

"Slow down," Marlene said. "Everything's so different. I thought I'd recognize it, but it's been at least thirty years. . . ." She squinted her eyes, peering out her side window and then through the windshield. "Turn around," she commanded, and Lyle did as she asked.

We drove around what seemed like the same dirt road for nearly half an hour, each minute that ticked by dragging on longer and longer, the tension stealing our optimism.

Lyle began to turn left, but Marlene corrected him, pulling on his arm. "It's near the water—you have to head toward the water."

An unfamiliar road appeared on the right, and Lyle took it before coming to an abrupt stop. As if conjured, Becky appeared, running toward us. She wore shorts and a T-shirt and held her bunny with one hand while waving frantically with the other.

Hardly waiting for the car to come to a complete stop, Maisy jumped out and ran to her daughter. I tried to follow, but James held me back. Instead of hugging her mother, Becky grabbed Maisy's arm and began running toward the car.

"Birdie's hurt bad," she said, her voice strong, without a hint of a stutter, her face composed, as if an emergency had brought out her true mettle. "I'll show you where she is."

Becky sat on Maisy's lap. "That way," she said, pointing to a road we must have passed a dozen times already, the path mostly grass and weeds.

We traveled only a few hundred feet before Marlene sat up. "There—on the right," she said, indicating what could only be described as a shack on the side of the road, the glimmer of water behind it doing nothing to mask the desolation or sense of abandonment.

Lyle pulled up in front and parked the car, turning off his sirens and lights, the sound as intrusive as birdsong at a funeral. Cicadas whirred in the tall pines and cedars that surrounded the house on two sides, the sound almost obscuring that of a boat motor plying the waters behind them.

I recognized the remains of the bright green paint that had once covered the shutters and front door. I thought of the kinds of predators that could be lurking there, the snakes, and cougars, and other things I didn't want to think about.

"Is she inside?" Lyle asked.

Becky nodded as she scrambled off of Maisy's lap and led us to the front door. I could tell Lyle was trying to get there before her, to protect her from any danger, but Becky charged forward and opened the door, then ran into the dark interior.

"Birdie! I'm back. Mama and Daddy are here."

We followed her through a room that reeked of mildew and animal droppings, its sole piece of furniture an ancient sofa with most of its stuffing protruding from the remaining cushions that an unseen creature had made into a nest.

The room at the back of the house was what was left of a linoleum-floored kitchen, the cabinets and appliances long since taken, the flooring worn away in so many spots the floor looked more like the scales of a giant fish. We stopped on the threshold, looking for Birdie, then watched as Becky ran to a doorless pantry and knelt at an opening in the floor.

"Birdie? Are you still there?"

"Dear God," Marlene said. "It's where my daddy used to keep his moonshine. And where my mama let your grandpa store his honey a few times after a really good harvest." She put a restraining hand on Lyle. "Careful—it looks like the floorboards around the opening have rotted."

He asked Becky to stand back, then gingerly inched his way forward until he got to the opening. He took a flashlight from his belt and shined it inside. "Birdie? It's me, Lyle. Can you hear me?"

We heard a moan, and Maisy and I both stepped forward with tentative footing, peering into the darkness. Birdie lay on her side, on a brick floor that was covered in green slime. Her eyes were open, her chest rising and falling. Her right leg, the leg that lay under her, was bent at a wrong angle.

"You came," she said with surprise in her voice, as if she'd not expected us to. Our relief at finding both of them made it almost irrelevant that she'd just spoken to us for the first time in too many years.

"Careful," Lyle cautioned as he slowly lowered himself through the opening. "It's only a four-foot drop. I think she has a broken leg."

"You gave us a scare, Birdie," he said as he took her pulse, then carefully examined her leg. He placed a gentle hand on her arm before standing. "Maisy, I need you to step back into the kitchen and stay with Becky. I'm going to call for help and I don't want to move her until it arrives." He looked at me. "Can you come down here and wait with her?"

I nodded, and allowed him to help me into the hole. He handed me the flashlight while I sat down on the damp bricks next to my mother. I was surprised to find myself close to tears. It was as if in that moment I'd realized how close we'd come to leaving everything unsaid between us. Somewhere in the back of my mind I must have been thinking there would always be time to unspool the past. There wasn't, of course. If I'd learned anything in the last few months, it was that time was a tightly pulled cord, and life sharp, shiny scissors.

I reached out my hand and touched hers. "Mama," I said, grasping her hand in the darkness. It was cold and clammy, but she squeezed back, and I was a little girl again and all was right in my little corner of the world.

"You good?" Lyle asked. I nodded and he turned away from the hole. "James, I'm going to call for an ambulance—can you find your way back to the main road and direct them here?"

He must have said something, because I heard heavy footsteps heading away from me. And then another face appeared above us, and when I shined the flashlight I saw my sister.

"Becky's okay and Marlene's with her." She looked at me uncertainly, as if she was waiting for me to tell her to go away. "I didn't think you should be alone with Birdie."

I smiled at her and nodded, then watched as she carefully lowered herself into the hole, then sat down on the other side of Birdie, taking her other hand.

Birdie's eyes fluttered closed and then opened again, and I knew the pain must be excruciating, and that unconsciousness right now might be a blessing. She seemed to fight it, though, as if we both knew that there was too much to be said. Too many questions lurking in the darkness around us.

"What's this?" Maisy asked.

I swung the light in her direction. There were empty crates and piles of wet straw lying around the perimeter of the small space, perhaps remnants from the Prohibition years. Closer, there was a small empty box on its side, the masking tape that had sealed it ripped off and wadded in balls next to it. I searched the walls, trying to ignore the spiderwebs and praying I didn't find a pair of eyes staring back at me. The beam of the flashlight landed on something I thought I recognized, and realized I didn't. Not really. Just the pattern of bees flitting around the base. It was the elusive teapot, without the lid, its sides covered with a thin coat of dust but recognizable.

"My teapot," Birdie whispered, as if the discovery had unlocked her voice completely, and I imagined I could hear the turning of a key.

I leaned toward her, wiped her damp hair off her forehead. "How did it get here?" And we all knew that my question had little to do with how the Limoges teapot ended up in this hole used to hide moonshine.

"I went up to the attic," Birdie said, her voice so quiet Maisy and

I had to lean closer to hear her. "And I remembered. I remembered all of it." She closed her eyes and for a moment I thought she'd gone to sleep. But then she opened them again and drew a deep, shuddering breath. "I am Colette. Colette Mouton."

I met Maisy's eyes in the dim light, and I remembered something James had said to me. *Sometimes all we need to do to forgive our parents is to understand their own childhoods.* At that moment, looking at my sister, I knew that we were about to finally know what he'd meant.

We sat back against the wet brick floor and waited for Birdie to speak.

When I opened my mother's cedar chest, I saw everything with vivid clarity, in a kaleidoscope of color, flashing like a film reel that had fallen out of its moorings, the same scenes flickering over and over. And there I was, in the kitchen with George and Mama and Daddy and the stranger. Except I knew then that he wasn't really a stranger.

The first thing I noticed was Mama's garden spray bottle on the counter, something I knew was a mistake. She always mixed her chemicals outside, saying they had no place in the kitchen near food. The second thing I saw was that the trapped bee that had been knocking on the small windows in the door was now throwing itself at the light of the ceiling fixture.

Then, like one of her roses after being watered, Mama straightened in her chair, her expression calm, her mouth set in a single, firm line. "You must be hungry," she said to the back of the stranger's head as she stood and went to the counter, where two dozen biscuits waited under a dishtowel in a basket, then opened a jar of tupelo honey. She filled a glass from the tap and gave it to the man before turning back to the biscuits. Instead of placing the biscuits on the table, she prepared plates for everybody, giving a healthy dollop of tupelo honey on top of each biscuit before putting a plate on the table in front of us.

The stranger—Mr. Mouton, Mama called him—ate three biscuits very fast, as if he hadn't eaten in a long time and was afraid someone would take the food from him if he didn't hurry. I wondered whether it made Daddy angry to see someone eating his precious tupelo honey without savoring it.

Mr. Mouton licked his fingers, an odd look on his face. "This is your tupelo honey?" he asked.

Daddy nodded slowly, like a person left outside too long in the heat.

"Not so sweet as I thought," he said as he licked his fingers again, then smashed the crumbs on his plate, rolling them in the amber honey before bringing his index finger to his lips. He saw me watching him and the thick pool of honey and slid his plate over to me with a smile. I had the strangest feeling that we'd done this ritual before.

"Are you finished, sir?" Mama asked, snatching the plate away before I could dip my finger in the honey.

"Yes. I thank you. I have not had a meal in a while," he said, his eyes never leaving mine. "I would like to go back to France. Maybe I bring some of your bees with me, yes? To start over. It is never too late to start over."

He clenched his eyes for a moment, as if he were in pain, then rubbed at his throat. "May I have some more water, please?" he asked.

Without a word, Mama refilled his glass from the tap and set it in front of him. He drank it without stopping, gulping loudly. Mr. Mouton looked even more ill and frail than when he'd first arrived.

"You look tired, and we're not done with our conversation. If you don't have a place to stay, you may stay here tonight," Mama said, her voice not sounding like hers, her eyes hollow. Daddy sent her a funny look, but she pretended not to see. "I'll send you up with more biscuits and honey in case you get hungry. There are already fresh sheets in the guest room."

He swayed a bit in his seat, one hand clutching his belly. "I think I will do that. I am not so well right now." He tried to stand but his bones seemed soft, unable to hold him. George quickly moved to his side while Daddy moved to the other. The man began to cough again, his body shaking with each spasm.

"Get the doctor," Daddy said to Mama as he and George helped the man to the stairs before Daddy lifted him completely and carried him all the way up, Mr. Mouton's weak moans trickling down the stairs.

"Mama?" I asked, watching as she calmly carried dishes from the table to the sink, throwing Mr. Mouton's plate into the trash. I heard it break as it hit something inside, the sound loud in the quiet of the kitchen.

I rushed to the phone, not sure what number to dial but knowing something had to be done. Mama took the phone from me and quickly replaced it in the receiver. "I'll take care of him, Birdie. You don't need to worry." She was crying, the heavy tears slipping down her face, and that scared me more than anything.

The bee that had been flitting around the kitchen landed on the counter, and Mama smashed it with her bare hand. She stared at it for a long time, as if wondering how it had died.

"You shouldn't kill a bee in the house, Mama. It means a visitor will come and bring bad news."

She looked at me with those same hollow eyes. "Maybe he already has."

Mama hugged me and then kissed me on the forehead, and as she turned around to finish cleaning up the dishes she said something very softly that I couldn't understand. It wasn't until the next morning when I found out that the visitor had left, taking Daddy's truck with him, that I realized what it was. "Forgive me."

Maisy had moved to sit next to me while Birdie spoke and was sobbing silently. I put down the flashlight and placed my arm around her, my other hand still holding our mother's. My sister and I were children again, waiting out a storm.

Sirens rang in the distance and I pictured James, flagging down the emergency crew to show them where to go. I looked at the teapot, and a cool breath swept up the back of my neck, making me believe in ghosts.

chapter 39

*After killing the other queen bee pupae, the new queen bee must
eliminate the old queen. Usually the old queen will have already left the
hive, but if the old and new queen meet, there will be a fight to the death.*

—NED BLOODWORTH'S BEEKEEPER'S JOURNAL

Maisy

Georgia and Maisy stayed at the hospital with Birdie until she was
stabilized, her leg in a cast, and sleeping deeply, thanks to medication. She had a double fracture in her right leg, but no other serious
injury. They were exhausted, not just because they'd both been awake
for almost twenty-four hours, but also from Birdie's story.

They stood in the hospital parking lot, swaying on their feet, and
watched the sky shift from black to deep violet as a new day began.
"Entre chien et loup," Maisy said softly, understanding now how her
mother must have known the phrase.

Georgia looked at her in surprise. "Between dog and wolf,"
Georgia repeated. "You remember that?"

"Sure. Not everything Birdie taught us was bad."

Georgia smiled, pinching her lower lip with her teeth just like
Becky did. She glanced bleary-eyed out over the parking lot. "You
don't have a car, do you?"

Lyle had brought everyone home, then stayed to make sure Becky and Grandpa were all right. She didn't ask what bed he intended to sleep in. Georgia had then driven James and Marlene in her car to Marlene's house despite both their protests that they should wait with them at the hospital, and then Georgia brought Maisy with her to Weems Memorial.

"I can walk," Maisy said, wondering how she'd manage to get a foot in front of the other enough times to make it home. Despite their time together spent listening to Birdie's story—their story—there was still a distance between them. A distance filled by the presence of a small child who'd died and whose ghost still haunted them despite the space of years and Becky's birth.

"Don't be ridiculous," Georgia said, pulling on her arm and marching toward her convertible that unabashedly took up two parking spaces. "I need you to make sure I don't fall asleep while I drive."

"Then you'd better stay at the house. I don't want to be responsible for you hitting a fire hydrant on your way back to Marlene's. You can have Birdie's bed—I'll crawl in with Becky."

"Deal," Georgia said, apparently unable to add any more words.

Georgia pulled up in the front drive of the house, the gravel popping beneath the whitewall tires. She put the car in park and turned off the ignition, but continued to stare in front of her, unwilling to interrupt her thoughts by getting out of the car. "I don't know what to do. Who to blame. Who should be punished." She faced her sister in the dark. "That's what Grandpa meant—about whether it was a sin to love someone too much. Grandma did what she did because of how much she loved Birdie. And Grandpa kept it a secret all these years because of how much he loved both of them. Nothing can be gained."

Maisy turned to her sister, the dim light casting shadows over her face. "But it was murder, despite the motive. And he's an accessory for hiding it. I imagine Birdie will want justice for her father's death."

"You've always been so black-and-white, Maisy. But everything isn't always good or bad, and most things in life don't always fit nicely into labeled slots, no matter how much you'd like them to."

They both stepped out of the car, their gazes meeting over the roof. "You're wrong," Maisy said. "There is always someone at fault. Someone who deserves to be punished."

Georgia flinched, and Maisy knew they weren't just talking about Giles Mouton anymore. She slammed her door and began walking toward the house. "I'm going to get a few hours of sleep, and you should, too. Maybe it will help you think more clearly."

"You do that," said Georgia. "I'm going to check on Grandpa. And as soon as he awakens, I'm going to tell him what we know."

"Good. Somebody needs to, and I don't think I can face him right now."

Maisy slowly climbed the stairs, her relief at having Becky back home warring with her newfound knowledge. She automatically turned left to go to her own room, surprised to find the door shut. She pushed it open, pausing on the threshold at the form of a body lying partially under her sheets, a bare shoulder and broad chest visible. Maisy walked across the room and stood at the side of the bed looking down at Lyle for a long moment, loving the way his hair fell over his forehead, the way he still looked like the boy she'd married a million years ago. Before all the miscarriages. Before Lilyanna. Before her own insecurities made her blind, and stubborn pride made her mute. *Like Birdie*. An inability to speak had its advantages. No apologies were expected. And the horrors of a childhood couldn't be relived.

She sat down on the edge of the bed and listened to the familiar rhythm of Lyle's breathing, smelling the male musk she'd missed. She'd slept with one of his shirts for a long time after she'd asked him to move out, until self-preservation had forced her to wash it.

She could wake him up now and tell him what she knew. But she couldn't, not without Georgia. Like their childhoods, and their mother, the burden was something they shared, something they'd have to handle together. She just couldn't deal with it right now.

Without thinking about what she was doing, she leaned down and pressed her lips against Lyle's. They were warm and soft with sleep, and she left her mouth there, pretending everything was as it had been when they were happy. And then his arms were around her, pulling her to him, and he was pressing his mouth hard against hers.

She pulled back, met his gaze. "Stay," he said.

She watched his sleep-heavy eyes, her heart and head battling, needing more time to understand what she was feeling, and to say the right words. "I want to, Lyle—I really do. But I'm so tired right now, and my mind is in such turmoil I feel like I'm drunk. We can't just jump into bed together without working things out between us."

His eyes were serious. "You know how I feel—that's never changed. And all the talking in the world won't make any difference to me. I want us back together. Just tell me what I need to do, and I'll do it."

He lifted his head to hers and gave her a soft, lingering kiss. "You know where to find me," he said.

She nodded, then stood, feeling him watching her while she made her way back to the hallway, hearing a door shut somewhere in the house. The first thing Maisy noticed was the sound of rhythmic thumping and a warm stream of air, as if someone had left a window open. She stuck her head into Becky's room and found her sound asleep under her covers, her bunny stuffed between her arms.

The sound seemed louder now. With faster steps, Maisy made her way to Birdie's room, expecting to find Georgia sound asleep. But the bed wasn't touched, the only sign that anybody had been in there the blowing curtains from the open window, the bottom sash thrown up high enough for a person to lean outside.

The sound was louder here, undiluted by distance, as if the source were right outside the window. Pushing aside the curtain, she watched as the tentative light of dawn spread across the bay and the yard, where Maisy spotted Grandpa in the apiary. He wasn't wearing any protective gear or a netted hat, and carried an empty frame from a hive, struggling to walk with it, the bottom edge cutting into his leg with each step. He was walking slowly around the rear hive, where Maisy had set up the beach umbrella, and while Maisy watched he used his good arm to slam the frame into the hive.

"Grandpa, stop! What are you doing?" Maisy shouted. He didn't look up or stop.

She heard Georgia's voice, knew her sister was nearby but couldn't see her or hear what she was saying. Probably something about how it was too early to be working with the hives, that all the bees would be home, ready to protect it. It was something Grandpa had taught them both, something he would know.

Maisy stuck her head out further, and spotted Georgia near the front row of hives, as if she'd drawn a line in the sand and refused to cross it. Oblivious to his audience, Grandpa continued to bring the frame hard against the top box of the hive, as if he wanted to topple it over. It occurred to Maisy that with just one good arm, he couldn't lift it off the top by himself. He could have asked for help, but instead had resorted to this. He must have been stung, because he stumbled backward, his foot toppling over the can of gas that had been left beside the pile of yard debris.

"Stop!" Maisy screamed.

Georgia turned around to look up at her. "Stay away, Maisy, and close the window. The bees are agitated."

Maisy watched for a moment longer as Grandpa set down the frame and yanked his smoker off the hanging hook where he kept it, struggling to hold it in his damaged left hand while taking an igniter from his pocket. She looked at the upended gasoline can and thought she could smell the pungent scent of gas, realizing with horror that the lid might not have been tightly screwed on.

She ran downstairs to the foyer, where she'd left her purse, stuck her hand in the outside pocket and pulled out one of the two EpiPens she always carried with her. Dropping her purse on the floor she continued to the kitchen, pausing only when something crunched under her soft-soled shoes. Broken porcelain radiated from what was left of the teapot, the spout on its side, incongruously intact. She remembered Georgia bringing the teapot in from Lyle's patrol car when they were dropped off before leaving for the hospital. It had been left on the kitchen counter.

The toe of her shoe kicked something, and Maisy recognized the curved side of the teapot, saw the honeycomb of cracks that spread over it. The colorful bees winged their way around the base, their flight abruptly ended with a large break in the porcelain. She could picture her grandfather smashing the teapot, trying to hide all the evidence of what had happened in this very kitchen. One last effort to protect the wife and daughter he loved too much.

Maisy raced toward the back door. In that brief moment, she considered waking Lyle, then just as quickly dismissed the idea. Maybe Georgia was right. Maybe there was no right or wrong to this story. Just tragedy. Their grandfather had raised them, loved them, taken care of them as best he could, and they owed him now at least the chance to tell his side of the story. Maybe they had it wrong. Maisy loved Lyle, but she could never forget that he was a policeman.

Maisy burst through the back door, feeling the weight of her EpiPen in her skirt pocket, remembering to walk instead of run when there were bees present. Her grandfather had taught her that, along with the adage that bees sting only to protect their hive and queen. She hesitated briefly, aware that the air in the backyard was alive with the high-pitched bee song of hundreds of pairs of wings rapidly flapping. The backyard reeked with the overwhelming stench of gasoline.

Georgia heard her approach and turned, her face red and tear-streaked. "Go away, Maisy—he's stirring up the bees and you shouldn't be here. I can handle this."

Maisy threw up her hands. "Oh, yeah—I can see how well you're handling things. What is going on?"

"He was in the kitchen when I went to check on him. I told him what Birdie had told us and he smashed the teapot. He said he needed to talk to his bees, so I let him leave, thinking he needed to be alone, and I went upstairs. I heard the thumping, and that's why I opened the window and discovered what he was doing." She moved her hand over her face, deflecting a bee. "Now go inside."

A loud groan forced Maisy and Georgia to turn toward Grandpa, watching as he nearly tripped over the can, saw the contents slowly creeping toward the rest of the hives. He fell down on one knee, but managed to stagger to standing, slapping at the back of his neck as another bee found its mark.

He dropped the smoker, lifted the lid, and pulled out a strip of half-burned cardboard. His hand shook as he held it near the lighter, his fingers plucking at the ignition switch. He groaned in frustration, now using his body in an attempt to remove the top boxes from the hive. They were full of frames, heavy with honey and bees, his face sweating with the exertion and an unhealthy dark red, his eyes nearly bulging from his face. Still clutching the cardboard and lighter, he picked up the frame again and began to swing it at the boxes in a desperate attempt to dislodge them.

"Go get Lyle!" Georgia screamed.

Maisy's shoes slipped on the damp grass, her body landing hard as her knees and the heels of her hands skidded across the sandy soil. She grasped at grass for a foothold, aware of Georgia bolting down the row of hives. It took Maisy only a split second to realize why. He'd managed to ignite the lighter. Grandpa was attempting to light the cardboard with it when Georgia reached him, knocking the lighter from his hand, his other still clutching the lit cardboard.

"Let me do this," he shouted, his voice high-pitched and strident, a wounded animal in a trap. "I need to protect my family."

"Grandma's dead. And Birdie remembers everything. There's nobody left to protect."

A groan of pain and grief erupted from him, the sound sinking into Maisy's bones like a bruise. Grandpa picked up the frame and swung it back, ready to strike the hive box again, the hard wooden corner striking Georgia in the side of the head. She dropped silently, as if someone had suddenly taken away her legs, Grandpa unaware of what he'd just done. A scarlet circle spread wide in her bright blond hair.

"Stop!" Maisy screamed, aware of the bees that filled the air now, blocking her path to Georgia. She turned toward the house, remembering the open window, then screamed Lyle's name, hoping he'd hear.

Grandpa didn't acknowledge her, as if he had retreated to his own world where only he knew the rules. He tossed the ineffective frame on the ground, then held up the lit cardboard as he searched for the smoker that he'd dropped. His foot found the gas can again and he stumbled, dropping the flaming cardboard.

It seemed to float in slow motion, the bright flames dancing in its descent. "No!" Maisy wasn't sure whether she screamed the word or if it just reverberated in her mind. All she could think of was getting to him before the flames reached the gasoline-soaked ground. She knew she was running, was giving it all she could, yet her feet felt like lead, her legs slogging through water.

She was aware of bees stinging her on her exposed arms and legs and face, could almost feel the poison seeping into her bloodstream like the gasoline across the grass. The grass exploded into flames just as she reached Georgia, the heat wicking her ankles as she lifted her sister and half carried, half dragged her toward the house, away from the bees and the flames that had begun to consume one another.

Maisy stopped at the bottom of the back porch, unable to go any farther, her throat too tight to allow in any air. Her vision began to blur around the edges, like the moment between wakefulness and dreaming. She thought then of her daughter asleep upstairs, and how she didn't want to leave her, not now. Not ever. And of Lyle, and how she didn't want to die without telling him she loved him. And of Georgia, because too many things remained unsaid but no longer seemed important. But sometimes life didn't offer choices.

With her last burst of energy, she looked for her grandfather. He was on his knees in front of the hive, his hand grasping his chest. She tried to call his name, but no sound came. Her head sank into the grass next to her sister, who lay too still, the red blood dripping into her ear. Maisy felt the dew cool the welts on her neck and arms and legs as she stared into a bright blue sky that dimmed as she watched, the view from inside a box with a closing lid.

"Maisy!"

Lyle.

"Maisy—open your eyes. I'm here. Open your eyes!"

The effort was too much, the darkness descending too fast. She felt a pulling on her skirt, and then a jab on the side of her thigh.

"Maisy—breathe! Can you breathe?"

She took a deep gulp of air, feeling as if she'd been held under the water for too long and had just been allowed to surface.

"Thank God," Lyle said, cradling her head in his lap for a moment. She felt his kiss on her lips before he gently slid her back to the grass. "I've got to see to Georgia right now—help's on its way. I told Becky to call nine-one-one and run to the neighbor's."

Maisy nodded, the words unable to get past her throat. She felt Lyle leave her side, and heard the sound of approaching sirens. She stared up at the sky and saw her grandfather's face not as she'd last seen it, but how she remembered him: sitting in his chair under the old magnolia and watching his beloved bees. Closing her eyes, she thought of the teapot, its broken pieces reassembled, the cracks sealed and hidden, and the bees flying around its circumference in a never-ending flight.

chapter 40

*When there are too many bees for a hive to support, the old queen
takes off with part of the colony to establish a new nest—commonly
known as swarming. Before leaving their original colony, all of the
bees will fill themselves up on nectar—except for the queen, who is
deprived of food so she is light enough to fly.*

—NED BLOODWORTH'S BEEKEEPER'S JOURNAL

Georgia

I sat on the back porch in a chaise longue with my feet up, James on
the steps in front of me. Maisy sat next to me, her arms crossed over
her chest, staring silently over the bay. I wanted to ask her whether
she was thinking about how she'd saved my life and almost lost
her own. And whether she regretted taking such a risk for me. I didn't,
mostly because I wasn't sure of the answer.

A breeze billowed up from across the bay, bringing with it the
scent of salt air and the lingering scent of smoke. We all looked toward
the apiary, roped off now with yellow tape, the remaining hives
draped with black. I wondered whether Lyle had done that in a nod to
beekeeper tradition, to tell the bees when a beekeeper died. Not that
any bees were left. The ones that hadn't died the night of the fire had
gone, flying away to parts unknown.

A lone figure in a wheelchair sat under an umbrella on the dock, Birdie's head bent over the singed remains of Grandpa's beekeeper's journal, his first volume that started when he was a teenager and chronicled his travels through Europe, and ended in 1953. The final entry had not been written by him, the handwriting delicate and feminine, familiar to those of us who knew our grandmother. It had been a letter addressed to Birdie, unread and hidden away for sixty-two years.

The journal had been found inside the bottom box of the hive at the back of the apiary, emptied of frames and never moved, a mausoleum to a secret. Lyle had found it next to Grandpa's body after the fire had been extinguished. Even though the coroner said he'd died of a heart attack and not from the fire, we all knew that he'd died of a broken heart, trying to protect the memory of the woman he'd loved.

"Have you shown her the photograph?" James asked.

I shook my head, then wished I hadn't. My head still hurt under the white bandage that itched so badly at night I couldn't sleep. I remembered my grandmother telling me that when an injury itched it meant it was getting better. If only grief could be as easily gauged—weighed and measured in a finite quantity. I wished she were still alive so I could ask her when the grieving would go away. I knew she'd have an answer. Yet it was still so hard to reconcile the loving person who'd been my grandmother with the woman who could be driven to kill a man.

"Not yet," I said, staring into his warm, blue eyes. I didn't know why he'd chosen to stay here, but I was grateful that he had. While I'd been in the hospital and both Maisy and I were still reeling from everything that had happened, he'd taken charge and worked with Lyle and Marlene to get the funeral plans started for Grandpa and all the details involved with clearing the apiary and converting Grandpa's makeshift downstairs room to be ready for Birdie when she came home from the hospital. He said that Caroline had helped via phone, and had even threatened to come down herself and take charge, but I knew he'd done most of it on his own.

It was more than gratitude I felt, too. Maybe it had started that night on the dock when he'd dared to tell me the truth about myself.

And when he'd told me that I wasn't ordinary. Or maybe it was when he'd come back to Apalachicola with me for no other reason than that he thought I might need him. And I had. I smiled at him, unable to put my thoughts into words. But with James, we both knew that I didn't need to.

I picked up the folded piece of copier paper and my phone and stood, waiting a moment for my head to clear. "Now is as good a time as any, I guess."

I'd walked halfway to the dock when Maisy ran to catch up with me. "She's my mother, too."

I nodded, but didn't look at her. There was still so much unsettled business between us, reminding me of a game with sticks and marbles we'd played as children. Neither one of us wanted to draw out a stick and let loose the marbles, upsetting the unsteady equilibrium we'd clung to for so long.

"Birdie?"

She turned her head toward us and smiled. Despite what she'd gone through, she still managed to look like Grace Kelly on the Riviera, with the addition of a cast on her leg. Her face, still mostly unlined, seemed almost serene, her brown eyes clear and focused on us. It was surreal, as if we were meeting our mother for the first time. And maybe, in a way, we were.

We both kissed her cheek, then pulled up the two Adirondack chairs next to her.

"How are you feeling?" Maisy asked, always the caregiver.

"Except for the broken leg, I'm fine."

Maisy and I exchanged a glance, wondering whether our mother had just made a joke.

"I wanted to show you something," I said, unfolding the piece of paper. "James's sister Caroline e-mailed it to him, and Maisy printed it so we could see it better."

She held out her hand, slender and pale, but the blue veins and knobby knuckles indicated her true age. I handed her the piece of paper and she flattened it on her lap on top of the journal.

"The photo quality isn't great," I said. "Caroline took a picture of an old photo on her phone. It's a photograph of their grandmother, Ida, and Ida's husband, parents, and siblings when they arrived in New York in May 1947."

Birdie drew in a breath as I leaned closer. "Is this your Adeline?" I asked, pointing to the beautiful young woman standing in the back and a little to the side. A fair-haired man, just a little taller than she was, had his arm protectively around her shoulder. She was taller than her parents and siblings, her features carefully etched. Even though her hair and eyes were dark, both Caroline and James looked just like her.

"Yes," she said, her bony finger gently brushing the image of the woman. "My Adeline. So good and kind. I wish I hadn't forgotten her. I would have been a better mother if I'd remembered her, and what she taught me."

"That looks just like Becky," I said, pointing to a young girl with bright blond hair standing in front of Ida, Ida's hands on her shoulders.

"No," Maisy said. "I think it looks more like you, Georgia. But we both have that nose."

"That's Colette," Birdie said. "The girl I was and then forgot." Her brows knitted together. "And now all these years later I wake up and remember her, except I'm an old woman and I have no time to make any more mistakes."

The tears in her voice reflected my own, the truth of what we were looking at more of a corroboration than a surprise, but just as wounding. It was hard to reconcile in my mind that this little girl, Colette, was Birdie. The enigmatic mother whose presence in our lives we tolerated and survived. The beautiful woman who floated on our periphery like a brilliantly colored scarf.

Birdie folded the photo into one hand, then smoothed her other hand across the cover of the journal. "My father tried to destroy this, but I'm glad he didn't. I read what my mother wrote to me, and what my father spent a lifetime trying to hide. She made him promise that he wouldn't tell me until I was ready to hear it. But I suppose I was so good at pretending to forget what had happened that he decided to pretend along with me. All he ever wanted to do was to protect her. Love is funny that way, isn't it?"

The buzz of a motorboat skipped across the waves toward us, but none of us looked away from the journal and its faint smell of smoke. "She asked for my forgiveness," she said quietly. "But it was not my forgiveness she needed." She faced Maisy and me. "A mother's wounds are deep and permanent. I know this now. I hope in time you can forgive me, as I've forgiven her. It's not too late to start over."

Maisy looked away. She'd always found it hardest to understand Birdie. Probably because all she'd ever wanted was to please her and she'd always come out wanting. I simply hadn't cared enough to be disappointed. But I continued to stare at our mother, realizing with a start something I'd been wrong about. She hadn't been broken all those years. She'd been strong enough to keep her head down until she was ready to face the wind. My return home had been the change she'd needed. The change we'd all needed. And all because of a teacup and saucer that had sat in an old lady's china cabinet for decades.

"I want to try," I said, not needing to tell her about scarred childhoods. She already knew all about that. But maybe we'd built up enough scar tissue to lay a firm foundation to start again.

Maisy faced us, her eyes wet. "I feel so angry, but I can't even decide who to be angry with."

"Then don't be angry," Birdie said softly. "I have decided not to be. We have a choice. We can count the years we have lost, or we can count the years we still have ahead of us." She placed her hand on Maisy's arm as if to soften the blow of her words. "You've always been so easy to take offense, Maisy. And I take the blame for that. I had two perfect daughters, but I always felt that I needed to interfere, to make them who I wanted them to be. And I'm sorry for that."

Maisy wiped the back of her hand across her eyes. "Do you remember Giles? And your life in France?"

Birdie was silent for a moment. "Just small flashes. I was very small, but I remember the kitchen in our farmhouse. The black-and-white floor. I remember his hand, and how it felt when he held my hand in his." She looked down at her fingers, which clutched the black-and-white photo of a girl she no longer recalled. "I remember being happy."

"How did you know where the teapot was?" I asked, finally pinpointing one loose piece of the puzzle.

"I asked him—that night. He wanted me to think it had been destroyed, but I knew it hadn't. George had shown me that little room in his house years ago, and I knew my father stored his tupelo honey in there when he had a big harvest and he ran out of room. You'd already searched everywhere else, and when I asked him if that's where it was, all he did was write something down on his notepad."

"'Is it a sin to love too much?'" Maisy said quietly.

"Yes, that's what he wrote," Birdie said. "But is it?"

I shook my head, wishing I could make it hurt even more so I couldn't think. So I couldn't feel the desperation of a father trying to save his child. Or the desperate measures of another father and a mother believing they were doing the same thing. Or of a little girl caught in the middle of events she couldn't understand. I thought of how this all could have ended differently. Giles was a dying man, after all. It was a tragedy with too many participants to decidedly point the finger of blame.

My phone beeped and I reached for it to turn it off, but stopped when I saw that I'd received an e-mail from Henri Volant in France. I'd forgotten all about his promise to send me more information about Giles Mouton.

I met my mother's eyes. "The bee china was given to your father's family as a token of appreciation for being beekeepers on the Beaulieu estate. James's family would like to return it to you, since you're the rightful owner."

She nodded, her gaze focused somewhere over the bay, and perhaps over an ocean to another apiary and fields of lavender.

My phone beeped again, and I swiped my thumb over the screen and typed in my password, becoming one of those people I despised who couldn't ignore her phone. But it was from Henri, and he'd been looking for information about Giles. My grandfather.

I opened the e-mail and began to read. I read it twice, my eyes blurring so that I could barely see the words. And then I read it again.

"Georgia? What is it?" Maisy asked.

"It's about Giles. The reason Grandma and Grandpa couldn't find him after the war."

Birdie slowly turned to face me. "Read it," she said, and there was no hesitation in her voice. I'd never considered my mother brave, but I was beginning to understand that bravery ran in our family. I cleared my throat and began to read.

Dearest Georgia, I hope you are well. I also hope my previous e-mail was of some interest, as I am sure the following will also be of interest to you in the search for more information regarding Giles Mouton. As I mentioned, he is a local hero. The following excerpt is from a book published in France in 1968. It's a short biographical listing of known members of the French Resistance during World War II. I have taken the liberty of translating it into English for you. Please let me know if I can be of any further assistance.

My eyes briefly met Maisy's and then I resumed reading.

Giles Mouton, a beekeeper and farmer near Monieux in the south of France, hid almost one hundred Jewish men, women, and children in his barn over the course of two years from 1941 to 1943, before he was exposed by a German national who had recently moved to the area. Mr. Mouton was part of an underground railroad, hiding families fleeing from the occupied zone in northern France and other Nazi-occupied countries seeking refuge in nearby Switzerland and Italy (which did not deport Jews at that time). He was captured in 1943 and interred at the Natzweiler-Struthof labor camp in the Vosges Mountains in the Alsatian village of Natzwiller (German Natzweiler) along with many other resistance fighters. The camp was evacuated in September of 1944 by the Germans, but records do not indicate that Mr. Mouton was

evacuated, his death assumed to have occurred in the camp prior to
1944, although no death records are available. He has been
posthumously granted the title of Righteous Among the Nations
(Yad Vashem) by the State of Israel, and his name is
commemorated on the Mount of Remembrance in Jerusalem.

A gull shrieked in the distance, a melancholy sound full of anguish and sorrow, interrupting the silence that lay thick and heavy between us.

"Papa," Birdie whispered, tears etching their way down her cheeks. "He didn't abandon me. He saved me, too, didn't he? He gave me to another family so I could survive."

Maisy was sobbing loudly, shaking her head. "And when he finally found you . . ." She stopped, unable to finish.

Birdie bowed her head, the pale skin at the back of her neck looking as delicate as a child's.

"He loved you, Birdie," Maisy said. "Enough to give you up once. He must have promised you that he'd come back, and he kept that promise."

Birdie looked up, her eyes shining. "We make difficult decisions for our children, Maisy. You and Georgia know it better than most, don't you?"

Both Maisy and I stared at our mother. "What do you mean?" I asked.

"Becky told me. She found her birth certificate in all the papers you were going through in the china cabinet."

Maisy placed her hand over her mouth. "She's known all this time and didn't say anything?"

"Why would she?" Birdie asked gently. "I told her that she was lucky, because she had two mothers who loved her."

Birdie leaned her head against the back of the wheelchair, and the sun slipped in the sky, illuminating the face of an old woman. Her eyes narrowed into dark slits as she regarded us. "I like to think that you both have a lot of Giles in you, because when I look at my daughters, I see two beautiful women who turned out to be quite extraordinary despite their mother. And if it's too late to be your mother, maybe we can start again and try to be friends."

Sometimes all we need to do to forgive our parents is to understand their own childhoods.

I must have said it out loud, because I heard Maisy's sudden exhalation of breath, or maybe it was mine. It was as if all of our anger and hurt had been balled up and tossed away like so much garbage. I could still feel the phantom pain from where it had been, but it no longer lodged in the bottom of my airway, blocking my breath.

I leaned forward and took Birdie's hand in mine, feeling how small it was. How frail. How strong. I thought of the little girl Colette and all she'd survived, and how easily a person could shatter. Perhaps that was the meaning of strength—not the surviving, but the gluing together of all the broken parts to make a new whole.

You will never change your life until you learn to let go of the things that once hurt you. Caroline had said that to me what seemed like a million years ago. I just hadn't understood what she meant until now. "I want to try. *We* want to try." I looked over at Maisy and didn't see any resentment and recrimination at the word "we."

After a long moment, Maisy reached over and took Birdie's other hand and squeezed. "I'm still angry, Mama. I probably will be for a long time. But I want to try."

Birdie smiled tiredly. "Could you please ask James to bring me inside? I'm rather exhausted from all of this." She clutched the photograph and journal to her chest, and I knew she wanted to be alone for a while with her memories of people she had to learn to miss all over again.

I waved to James on the porch, and he took control of Birdie's wheelchair and began wheeling her toward the house. After a moment, Maisy stood as if to follow, but I called her back. I waited until they were on the front porch before facing my sister. I had no idea where to start, had not planned this at all. The only thing I'd been thinking about since being released from the hospital was how soon I could leave again. But now it seemed as if that person were somebody else I no longer knew. Somebody I didn't want to be anymore.

If you want things to change, you have to stop waiting for someone else to make the first move. I took a deep breath, no longer caring who went first. "I'm sorry, Maisy. For all the crap I did when I was a teenager that embarrassed you, or forced you to make excuses for me. But most of all, I'm sorry that I wasn't the sister you needed me to be. That I wasn't watching Lilyanna when I should have been. That I have been the cause of so much of your grief." I paused, searching for the next words, afraid to stop, because then I might not finish.

"For a long time I blamed my behavior on Birdie and how we were raised. But it's not about Birdie anymore. It's about you and me and where we go from here. I can't stand the thought of you not being in my life. And you can tell me to go away and never come back, but I'm just not going to listen."

Maisy was trying very hard not to cry, always the little sister trying to be stronger so she could keep up. "Why are you apologizing to me? You gave me the biggest gift of all. You gave me Becky. And all this time instead of thanking you, I've been punishing you for something I know wasn't your fault. You were always so good at taking the blame for everything, whether it was your fault or not. I was wrong, and I knew it, but you made it so easy, because I was hurting and I wanted you to hurt, too."

I didn't bother to wipe the tears from my face. "I loved her, you know. I still miss her every day."

She sat back in her chair and covered her face with her hands. "I know. And then when Lyle tried to defend you, I allowed it to drive this wedge into my marriage, let it fester all these years because I was too stubborn to admit I'd been wrong." Maisy looked up at me with reddened eyes. "Why are we so good at pushing everyone away? After a while it became the only way I knew how to be." She sniffed loudly and straightened her shoulders. "But you're right. This isn't about Birdie anymore; it's about you and me. I want you in my life. In *our* lives. I don't want another ten years without you."

She stood again and we faced each other for a long, silent moment, both of us sniffing loudly. Finally Maisy said, "Are you going to hold it over me for the rest of your life that you said it first?" I could tell she was only half joking.

"Probably," I answered, unable to stop the big grin that I couldn't hold back.

I hugged my sister without hesitation, and without wondering whether she wanted a hug or not, or whether I should wait for her to hug me first. She was my sister, the person I had always loved most in this world, and my name had been her first spoken word.

chapter 41

Although some varieties of bees can be aggressive and attack without provocation, the honeybee attacks only when it believes a legitimate threat to the colony exists. A honeybee's sting is the ultimate form of self-sacrifice—its single blow serving only to protect others, as its delivery means its own death.

—NED BLOODWORTH'S BEEKEEPER'S JOURNAL

Maisy

"**H**ow do I look?"

Maisy turned toward her daughter, who was dressed in her best church dress, the one with the satin sash and pretty sweetheart neckline. It had been Grandpa's favorite. Georgia had French-braided her hair, and Maisy had allowed her daughter to wear a short strand of pearls—the ones Lyle had given to Maisy as a wedding present.

"You look beautiful," Maisy said, biting back her resentment of the word. It didn't bother her as much now, not after the harrowing night when Becky and Birdie had gone missing. The night she'd discovered her mother's past, and the person her daughter truly was. They seemed to have both discovered it, since Becky had barely stuttered in the days since that night. She had proven to herself that she was brave and bold, that she was somebody who could save a life when she forgot how scared she was.

"You look beautiful, too, Mama," Becky said.

Maisy glanced in the mirror, feeling like a crow in her black dress and heels. "Thank you, sweetie. I'm sure Grandpa would approve of us both."

His funeral would be well attended by people in town he'd known his entire life, as well as several from the beekeeping community. She was sure the rumors swirled, but they didn't reach the family. The truth was hard enough to live with.

They would have a funeral for Giles Mouton in less than a month, burying him in the same cemetery near Ned and Anna Bloodworth. They had been inexorably connected in life, and Maisy and Georgia and even Birdie agreed that they should also be in death. Georgia and Birdie were avoiding reading the local paper, but Maisy assured her that Lyle had done a good job of disseminating the information regarding the circumstances surrounding Mr. Mouton's death. He made sure that everyone knew of Giles's heroism during the war, and how he'd sacrificed so much. And she, Georgia, and Birdie would make sure that his headstone commemorated his sacrifice.

The niggling thought Maisy and Georgia shared was how their gentle grandfather, whose sense of justice and goodness had guided them for most of their lives, could have allowed Giles's death to go unremarked for so long. They would never know now.

Becky tilted her head critically. "Are you sure you don't want to wear your pearls? Daddy likes it when you wear them."

"Yes, he does," Lyle said, surprising them from the doorway. He was off duty and wearing a dark suit and tie, looking a little uncomfortable but devastatingly handsome.

"I thought you were meeting us at the cemetery."

"I was. And then I realized I'd rather escort my two best girls."

Becky beamed up at him and Lyle smiled back. "Can you please go ask your aunt Georgia if she'd like to drive with us and then wait downstairs? Your mama and I will be down in a few minutes. We've got something to discuss. In private."

Maisy faced him. "Now just a minute . . ."

As if she hadn't said anything, Lyle said, "All right, Becky? Now go on. We'll see you in a few minutes."

"Is she okay?" Lyle asked after they heard Becky's footsteps running down the stairs.

"She's fine. She's amazing, actually. She misses Grandpa, and the bees, but she's talking about it. I called the counselor at school and she said that was a very good thing. And Becky's asked Florence to show her how to get new hives started." She felt nervous at the way he was looking at her, and she tried to back away from him. "I need to get my purse. . . ."

He took her arm and put his finger to her lips, silencing her. "Do you love me, Maisy?"

She pulled her head away. "Why are you . . . ?"

"Just answer the question."

Maybe if her heart hadn't been so emptied out from the events of the last few days she would have found the words to deny it, or speak around it. To find a reason she didn't deserve it. But she'd been scraped raw, down to the part of her that could see only the truth.

"Yes, Lyle. I love you. I never stopped."

"And you know I'll always have your back even when I don't agree with you."

She didn't bother to pause before answering. If she'd learned anything in the last few days, it was that life was about forgiveness, even when the one who needed it most was her. "I know that."

"That's what I thought." Without warning, he kissed her, a long, slow, deliberate kiss that he did so well and that he knew made her knees weak. She didn't fight it; she might have even kissed him back, but she was too busy feeling happy to care.

When he finally pulled away, he said, "I love you, too, Maisy Sawyers. I don't want to get divorced, and I want to move back in and live with you and Becky as a family. I've already got my bags in the car, because I'm not taking no for an answer."

"Aren't you being a little—"

He cut her off with another kiss so that she forgot what she was going to say.

A door banged shut downstairs and then they heard Becky's voice. "Mama! Aunt Georgia says she's getting tired of waiting!"

They pulled apart and Lyle's eyes smiled into hers. "You and Georgia will need to sit down with Becky and talk about things eventually. Probably sooner rather than later. There have been too many secrets in this family, and I think it's time to clear the air. And that's all I'm going to say on the subject. The rest is up to you."

He kissed her again before she could say she had no idea where to even begin, then allowed him to lead her toward the stairs.

epilogue

In many Middle Eastern and Asian cultures, bees represented the human soul and its journey on Earth. The bee is an emblem of rebirth and is also associated with determination and willpower, due to the fact that a bee's body is too large compared to the size of its wings, and it should not be able to fly.

—NED BLOODWORTH'S BEEKEEPING JOURNAL

Georgia

MAY 2016

I stood on the front porch steps, pausing to count the heads of people seated inside my convertible parked in the driveway. Three of Caroline's children were already strapped into the backseat, while the youngest—Adam, a five-year-old dervish—chased after Becky, who seemed to enjoy the game despite the melted chocolate chips smeared down his face and fingers. Now that Lyle and Maisy were planning on adopting at least one more child, I figured it was good practice for her.

We were on our way to the Tupelo Honey Festival in Wewahitchka—finally. When Becky had asked that we all go together, she probably hadn't imagined it would be such a large group. She and Emily—Caroline's oldest—had become BFFs (Becky's term) and were usually joined at the hip whenever Emily was in town.

Since Caroline and her husband had purchased a second home on St. George, the general chaos of a large family gathering had become a familiar sight. As had the occasional presence of Caroline's three sisters, their families, and James. Not that too much time separated the visits between James and myself. Mr. Mandeville had all of a sudden developed a huge interest in estate sales in the state of New York, and made sure that I was sent to all of them. And now that Caroline and I had started our own online vintage-clothing business, I was quickly accumulating a lot of frequent-flier miles.

I spent a lot of time in Apalachicola, too, visiting my sister and my mother and my niece, watching Becky change and mature into the extraordinary girl I was only just discovering. I never once regretted any decision I had made. As Grandpa used to say, regrets were like porch swings: They kept you busy but didn't get you anywhere. He'd been right about so many things. At least we had that.

Birdie emerged from around the corner of the house, where she'd been working in the apiary. Her netted hat was tucked under her arm, and she wore a blousy top and harem-type bottoms, making her look like Katharine Hepburn on safari.

The new hive boxes had been painted in bright colors—courtesy of Becky and Caroline's children—and Birdie and Becky were enjoying their new roles as beekeepers. They'd been such avid pupils that Florence Love, their mentor, had given them their own pairs of swinging bee earrings. It was good to see the bees flying around the hives again, to see the grass grow back and the scorch marks recede. It reminded me that all adversity was temporary, unless we insisted on clinging to it with both fists.

My hand found its way to the necklace that hung around my neck, a new habit of mine. It was an intricately carved silver padlock, probably sixteenth-century Spanish, with beautiful gold inlays around the edge and surrounding the keyhole. And behind it hung the matching key. James had given them to me, a serendipitous find in a shop-window on a small side street in Chelsea.

I'd been too busy over recent months to think about my collection of keys, or my endless search for locks they would fit. Maybe I didn't need to search anymore. Maybe there would always be questions without answers, and sins without forgiveness. But in finding James, none of that mattered.

I spotted James easily, the sun magnifying the red in his hair as he walked toward the car with Caroline's youngest—Alex—clinging to his back. Despite his claims to the contrary, he did burn easily. I turned around and began climbing the porch steps again to retrieve more sunscreen from the kitchen drawer.

I paused just a moment on the threshold to the dining room to admire the Limoges china that resided in the glass-fronted cabinet. The restored teapot, the elegant and proud honeybee perched on its lid, sat in its place of honor, front and center. A talented china restorer had done an amazing job with it, and only those of us who knew where to look could find where it had been put together. I sometimes thought that Maisy, Birdie, and I could identify with it. Our cracks were proof of our survival, evident only to those we allowed close enough to see where we'd been patched.

I was searching through the catchall drawer in the kitchen when I felt Maisy enter the room. Her face was drained of color, her lips slightly parted. I straightened. "Are you all right?"

"Florence asked me to bring her this today at the festival, to share with other beekeepers, so I went to go get it." She slid into a kitchen chair and placed a thick notebook on the table. I immediately recognized it as our grandfather's bee journal, the second volume that he'd used while we'd known him, chronicling his life among the bees. "I'd just shoved this on a shelf when Birdie came home from the hospital and we were trying to get the room ready for her. But just now, when I pulled it from the shelf, I dropped it. And something fell out. I don't know how I missed it before. It must have been stuck into the binding in the back."

She slid an envelope toward me, and I dropped into the seat next to hers when I noticed the foreign postage, the Hebrew lettering. The return address that was a P.O. box in Jerusalem. The addressee was Ned Bloodworth, Apalachicola. I stared at the envelope for a long time, not sure what I was supposed to do. Maisy opened it up along the top where it had long ago been sliced, and took out a letter and handed it to me.

The words were printed on embossed, official-looking letterhead, a bold black logo of six long triangles with a swirl in an "S" pattern beneath it, Hebrew letters followed by the words "Yad Vashem" beside it.

"Read it," Maisy commanded, as if we both realized I needed someone to force me to do so.

Dear Mr. Bloodworth,

In answer to your inquiry, the testimonies and accompanying documentation you provided to initiate the investigation into the case for Giles Mouton will be preserved in Yad Vashem's archives for perpetuity and serve the purposes of research, education, and commemoration. Yad Vashem is committed to pursuing the Righteous Among the Nations program for as long as petitions for this title are received and are supported by solid evidence that meets the criteria.

Yours very truly,

I looked at the name and signature, but couldn't read either because my vision was too blurry. "It was Grandpa who sent in Giles's name. Who gathered the documentation and testimonies needed to acknowledge what Giles had done during the war."

"In secret," Maisy said. "He must have traveled to France at some point for research—maybe one of his trips when he said he was visiting other beekeepers. And we never knew."

Maisy placed the letter on the table, smoothing the creases with her hand, and we read it for the second time together.

Neither of us spoke, our minds running in tandem, thinking of sins and atonement, and of the lengths a person will go to in an attempt to make amends for a wrong that could never be completely made right.

"Do you think Birdie knows?" I asked finally.

Maisy shook her head. "No. We'll have to tell her. Maybe it will bring her some peace."

"Maybe it will bring us all a little peace," I said, acknowledging the dark specter that hovered in the periphery of our sight lines, the ghost of a loss that could never be fully recognized.

We linked our arms and left the house, emerging into the bright sunshine and the shouts of happy children. We stayed linked together for a long moment, in tribute to our shared childhoods and the grandfather who had raised us and in the end taught us that love and forgiveness are like the moon and the tides, each dependent on the other. Each lost without the other.

James approached, and Maisy dropped my arm so I could go to him. He held my hand as we walked in the direction of the apiary, which no longer smelled of smoke but instead carried the green scent of summer grass and bright, blooming flowers.

James had once asked me what my price for flight was. I hadn't believed at the time that my decisions had a price. But of course they did. Every leaving, every good-bye, had a cost. So did reunions, the price paid in discarded pride and newfound forgiveness.

I thought often of Giles Mouton—not of his death, but of his courage in life. I saw it in Becky and felt grateful that his legacy continued. That he had not completely disappeared in a swamp and then been forgotten.

A bee buzzed past us twice in a circular flight pattern, reminding me of the bees on the china. James kissed me as the bee spun around us before flying up into the wide summer sky. I stared after it for a long time, thinking about journeys beginning and ending, the patterns of flight innumerable, the destination always home.

flight patterns

KAREN WHITE

questions for discussion

1. The title *Flight Patterns* has many layers of meaning that become clear only after you've read the novel. What do you think the title represents?

2. Many people collect china or have pieces that have been handed down in their family through generations. Do you have a china collection? If so, do you know its history? Is knowing its history particularly meaningful to you?

3. Georgia and Maisy grew up knowing that their mother, Birdie, was mentally ill, but it doesn't seem to be something that is openly discussed in the family, even between the sisters. Is there a stigma in talking about mental illness? Is it something you think you would be able to discuss with either family or friends?

4. One of the subjects of *Flight Patterns* is family—what people do in the name of family and to protect their families. Many of the characters have done extreme things to protect their families, such as Giles's sending away Colette, Georgia's gift to her sister, and Ned's protecting his wife even long after her death. Do you feel that this is realistic? Would you go to the same extremes for your family?

5. Bees and beekeeping are important elements throughout *Flight Patterns*. What do you think the bees represent to the different characters?

6. After caring for the bees almost religiously for most of his life, Ned does something destructive toward the bees, nearly burning down the house and killing his granddaughters. Why do you think Ned acted the way he did?

7. Birdie has acted for most of her life, despite not having a career on the stage or screen. Who do you think the real Birdie is?

8. Becky accidentally discovers a secret about herself. Is this something that Maisy should have told her about before? Why or why not?

9. We find out that Ned is the one who sent in Giles Mouton's name to Yad Vashem to be recognized and honored for what he did during World War II. Do you think this helps to mitigate some of the guilt he bears concerning Giles's death?

10. Birdie's inability to cope with her past and her emotional instability lead to her being a neglectful mother to Georgia and Maisy. Do you think she deserves forgiveness from her daughters now that they know the truth about her damaged personal history?

Merilee

SWEET APPLE, GEORGIA

2016

If there was one thing that Merilee Talbot Dunlap had learned in eleven years of marriage, it was the simple fact that you could live with a person for a long time and never really know him. That it was easy to accept the mask he wore as the real thing, happy in your oblivion, until one day the mask slipped. Or, as in Merilee's case, when it fell off completely and you were forced to face your own complicity in the masquerade.

No, she knew she hadn't made Michael have an affair with their daughter's third-grade math teacher. But she had allowed herself never to question any discrepancies in her marriage, content in her role as suburban wife and mother, until the props and scenery were pulled away and she was asked to exit stage right.

"Mommy?"

Merilee turned toward her ten-year-old daughter, Lily, blond and fine boned like her father but with a perpetually worried expression that was all her mother's. It seemed Lily already had a permanent furrow between her brows from the worry she'd been born with. The last months since the divorce and the stress from the upcoming move hadn't helped.

"Yes?"

"What if I don't meet any friends in my new school? And what if I don't have anybody to sit with at lunchtime? And I'm thinking I shouldn't be in the accelerated English class, because what if I'm not smart enough?"

Merilee carefully snapped down the lid of the plastic container she'd been filling with her collection of old maps. She'd been collecting them since she was a little girl, when she'd been in an antiquarian bookstore with her grandfather and he'd shown her an ink-drawn map. It had sketches of horses and cows and fences, and a cozy log cabin with smoke curling from its lone chimney.

"That's where you live," he'd said, pointing to the cabin.

It looked nothing like the white-columned brick house in Sandersville, Georgia, she'd lived in all her life and she had told him so, only to be made to understand that the cabin and everything around it had been plowed under to make room for her house and their neighbors' houses in the twenties, when he and Grandma weren't even born yet.

For a long time it had given her nightmares, thinking she could hear the cries of the people from the cabin, not completely sure they'd been removed before the demolition. It scared her to think of how temporary things could be, how your life, your house, your family, could be erased like a sand castle at the beach. And when her little brother had died, she'd known for sure.

Her grandfather had bought her the map, unaware he was fostering what would become a lifelong obsession. Merilee wasn't sure whether her love for old maps was because they reminded her of the grandfather she'd loved more than her own parents or because she'd needed proof that things changed. That no matter how good or bad things were, they were never permanent.

Merilee knelt down in front of Lily, silently cursing her ex-husband one more time. As if making her feel extraneous and unwanted wasn't bad enough, his inability to keep his pants zipped and his eyes from wandering had added an extra layer of vulnerability to their daughter.

Gently holding her bony shoulders, she looked into Lily's pale blue eyes. "You've never had problems making friends. You're a nice person, Lily, and that's why other girls like to include you. Remember that, okay? It's who you are, and if you stick with that, you'll be fine. And Windwood Academy is much smaller than your old school, which is a nice thing when you're the new kid. You'll know everybody in all of your classes pretty quickly."

"And if they don't like me?"

A little bit of the old spark lit her eyes, making Merilee inwardly sigh with relief. "I'm going to make them an offer they can't refuse."

Lily laughed her sweet laugh, a sound that evoked champagne bubbles popping, almost eradicating the guilt Merilee felt over having left *The Godfather* in the DVD player one night. It had been right after she'd learned of Michael's affair, when she'd felt the need to watch violent movies with lots of blood and bad language after the kids had been tucked into bed. Lily had flipped it on the next day thinking it was *The Princess Bride*, and in the five minutes it had taken for Merilee to realize what was happening, Lily had been exposed to more violence than she had been in her entire ten years. After much apologizing and lectures about the difference between movies and real life, it had become a secret joke between them. For weeks Merilee had watched her daughter for any signs that she might need counseling, glad for once that her daughter had always had the maturity of a forty-year-old rather than that of the young girl she was.

Merilee stood, her right knee popping, yet another reminder of why her husband had wanted to trade her in for a younger model. "As for the accelerated English class, they put you in there for a reason. You'll do great. And if you find you don't like it, we'll move you— just give it a try. That's all I ask, all right?"

Lily's small chest rose and fell with an exaggerated sigh. "All right. Should I tell Colin to finish packing his suitcase?"

"I asked him to do that three hours ago. Where is he?"

Lily twisted her mouth, unsure of her role. She wasn't a tattletale, but she also liked to keep to a schedule. "He found a hole in the back-yard and has been sitting in front of it waiting to see what might crawl out."

Merilee swallowed a groan of frustration. Her eight-year-old son had always moved to his own clock, content to study his world at its own pace. Merilee found it endearing and frustrating at the same time, especially on school mornings when Colin wanted to study how long it took for toothpaste to fall from the tube without his having to squeeze it.

"Would you please run out and remind him that I told Mrs. Prescott we'd meet her at three o'clock and it's almost two thirty? She's ninety-three and I really don't want to keep her waiting in this heat."

"Yes, ma'am." Lily ran from the room, blond hair flying, calling her brother's name with the harsh, authoritative tone Merilee recognized as her own. She bit her lip to prevent herself from calling out to remind Lily that Colin already had a mother.

She picked up the stack of plastic containers and moved to the garage, empty now except for the used Honda Odyssey minivan she'd bought with her own money. She'd let Michael keep the Mercedes SUV and his Audi, wanting the excision of him from her life to be a clean cut, even if it meant not having heated seats or a state-of-the-art stereo system. It was the principle of the matter. And at the moment, the only thing she had in abundance were principles.

Through the open rear door, Merilee spotted the jewelry roll she'd tucked into a back corner of the minivan. It was her brother's Lego figures. She'd taken them from his room without asking, know-ing her mother would never have let her have anything that had belonged to David. Deanne had wanted to claim the grief as her own, dismissing anyone else's as not big enough to count. So Merilee had taken them and wrapped them in her Barbie jewelry roll and kept them hidden, taking them out only on the anniversary of David's death, as if somehow that might bring a part of him back. It had been a while since she'd done that, but still she kept them, hidden in her sock drawer as if afraid her mother might find them and ask for them back. As if David were still the precocious boy of seven instead of the twenty-nine-year-old young man he should be.

After tucking the last of the smaller boxes and their suitcases into the back of the Odyssey, Merilee made one final pass through the rooms of the now empty home she'd lived in for less than two years. The rental house was already furnished, so it had almost been a relief to let Michael have all the furniture they'd accumulated over the past eleven years, and she'd felt a ping of regret only when their four-poster bed had been hauled into the moving van. It had been the bed where both of their children had been conceived. She imagined that if she ever had to see Tammy Garvey again, after the woman had been sleeping on that bed with Merilee's husband for a while, she'd mention that to her.

Having gone back inside, she listened to her footsteps echo against the bare walls as she moved from room to room. The house had never really felt like home to her, just as none of their previous four houses had. Michael thought they needed to upgrade every couple of years to keep up with his job success. They had moved into a bigger house in a nicer neighborhood each time, staying within the same school district to make it easier on the kids. And easier for Michael's affair, Merilee had realized much later.

Merilee thought she should be thankful for the frequent moves, knowing that leaving a beloved home would be almost as painful as leaving an eleven-year marriage. Or burying a favorite dog. Instead, this parting was as easy as pulling off a Band-Aid—it would sting a little but be forgotten as soon as they'd unpacked the first box in the new house.

The kids strapped themselves into the backseat of the minivan as Merilee headed down the driveway one last time and drove down the street without looking back. No neighbors came out to wave good-bye. She didn't know them well, having always worked and not had the time to build relationships in each of the neighborhoods they'd lived in, and hadn't expected any more fanfare when they left than when they'd arrived.

She waved good-bye to the guard at the front gate just as the first drops of rain began to pelt the dry asphalt and her dirty windshield, already splattered with the remains of dozens of insects. The rain and bugs were, Merilee thought, a fitting tribute to her old life, the one she couldn't quite let go of yet had no interest in holding on to, either. She thought of the boxes of old maps shifting around in the back of the minivan, reminding her again of the impermanence of things and how nothing stayed the same no matter how much you wanted it to.

Sugar

Sugar Prescott sat at her dining room table in the front room of the old farmhouse, tapping out a letter to her best friend, Willa Faye Macken-zie, on her 1949 Smith-Corona typewriter, her bottle of Wite-Out sit-ting nearby. She rarely had to use it but always wanted to make sure it was close by just in case. At ninety-three, she didn't have a lot of time to waste. And Willa Faye had all the time in the world to sit and wait for a letter. Her daughter had recently moved her to a senior living facility with the improbable name of the Manors. If there was one good thing about not having children, Sugar decided, it was being spared the indig-nity of being moved into such a place, like a box of old toys that a child has outgrown but doesn't want to get rid of completely.

She glanced outside, not wanting to miss the approach of her new renters. She hadn't met Merilee Dunlap or her children before, but the Realtor, Robin Henderson, who'd been handling the rental of the Craftsman cottage behind Sugar's farmhouse, had only good things to say about all three of them. Robin's children had attended Prescott Elementary with the Dunlap children, making Robin privy to the unsavory gossip surrounding the Dunlap divorce. Not one to gossip, but a good listener, Sugar had suggested the cottage as a good spot for the family to land while they decided what to do next. It wasn't as if she had any desire to befriend anyone, but Sugar had the feeling that Merilee Dunlap, whoever she was, was suddenly and unexpectedly on her own and in need of help. And Sugar was in a position to understand that need more than most. She suspected, but would deny if anyone asked, that she was getting soft in her old age.

She typed one last word, then drew the carriage back before standing and approaching the front window. The rain had tapered off, leaving a smoking, dripping landscape, her climbing roses on the front porch supports waterlogged, with petals opened as if gasping for breath. The small lake that sat in the front of the property, separated from the road by the white ranch rail fence, was thick like syrup, as brown as molasses because of the rain. She had a sudden image of her brother Jimmy sitting on the muddy bank, fishing for turtles, his feet bare and his freckled nose red and blistered. Although all four brothers were long gone, Sugar now found herself seeing them more and more, as if old age was nothing more than the past and present squeezing together like an accordion until no air was left.

She watched as a white minivan turned off the paved road onto the long drive leading around the lake to the farmhouse, winding between the stately oak trees that had been planted by her great-grandfather before the Civil War, their roots as wide as the trees were tall. The road was a ribbon of red Georgia clay, soft and muddy with rain, the minivan hugging the side, where grass gave the wheels some traction. Sugar smiled to herself, thinking that Merilee Dunlap knew something about driving in wet Georgia clay.

She moved to the front porch and waited for the minivan to pull to a stop. It wasn't ideal, sharing a driveway, seeing the comings and goings of her renters, but if there was one thing she wouldn't do, it was have one more strip of her property bulldozed for another driveway. Her brothers had done a good enough job of plowing under all the farmland the Prescott family had once owned, and she would not continue their legacy no matter how inconvenient it was for Sugar.

The woman who carefully stepped from the minivan wasn't what Sugar had expected. She was younger—mid-thirties, she thought—and much prettier. As if men didn't divorce pretty women. She was surprised to find that she'd thought she'd be able to spot a flaw in her new tenant, something that would explain how she'd ended up in the predicament she was in. As if Sugar didn't know better.

"Hello," the woman said, stepping carefully onto the flagstone walkway before sliding open the side of the minivan and waiting for two children to emerge. The children were as blond as the woman was dark. She had straight, no-nonsense brown hair, parted at the side, and hazel eyes that looked almost green. Her only makeup was a flick of mascara, a touch of nose powder, and a sheer gloss of exhaustion.

"I'm Merilee Dunlap," she said, extending her hand.

Sugar grasped the tips of her fingers, still unused to the way women shook hands these days, but didn't return the smile. She didn't want Merilee to think of her as anything more than her landlady. "And these must be your children, Lily and Colin."

"They are. Children, this is Mrs. Prescott, whose house we'll be renting." Both children extended hands as they were introduced, confirming to Sugar that their mother, despite other issues, had done a good job in teaching manners.

"Our old neighborhood was called Prescott Farms," said Lily, her eyes wide and earnest, her forehead creased as if she spent a lot of time trying to make sense of the world around her.

Sugar's mother had barely been cold in her grave before her oldest brother, Harry, sold the property for no other reason than somebody wanted to buy it. The memory still hurt. "Yes, well, that was part of my family's farm back when I was a little girl. Most everything around the county with the Prescott name on it used to belong to my family. But that was a while ago, when there were lots of Prescotts around these parts. Now there's only me."

Facing Merilee, she said, "Please call me Sugar. Everybody does. My real name's Alice Prescott Bates, but I've been known as Sugar Prescott my whole life and I see no need to change it now. I was married just a short time before I became a widow, so my married name really never stuck. And the children can call me Miss Sugar."

"I smell cookies," the boy said, looking up at her with a hopeful expression. His light blue eyes were the same shade as those of her youngest brother, Jimmy, making her forget, just for a moment, that he'd been gone more than seventy years. And in that moment of weakness, she stepped back to open the door wider. "Come on inside," she said. "They had sugar on sale at Kroger, so I had to bake a batch of chocolate chip cookies. If you don't want them, I'll have to give them to my friend at the nursing home, because I don't eat them."

"We really don't mean to intrude," Merilee said, a hand on each child's shoulder.

"Yes, well, the cookies won't eat themselves, so somebody has to."

The little girl's eyebrows knitted together. "Are they gluten free? I keep having tummy aches and my friend Beth says I probably have a gluten allergy."

Merilee put her arm around Lily and sent a pained look at Sugar. "She's never been allergic to chocolate chip cookies before. I think the upheaval of the last months has just given us all a bit of a stomach upset."

"My tummy's fine," Colin announced. "I can eat Lily's if she doesn't want them."

Sugar began leading the way back to the kitchen, then stopped as Colin paused at the threshold to the dining room and pointed at the typewriter. "What's that?"

Sugar took a deep breath, more concerned about future generations now than she'd been ten minutes before. "That's a typewriter. It's what people used to use before computers. I used to have a good-housekeeping column in the *Atlanta Journal* back in the day, and they gave me this typewriter when they retired both me and the column in 1982."

His eyes widened as if being presented with the key to Disney World. "Wow. That was way before I was born." With a quizzical expression on his face, he turned his head to look up at Sugar. "So you must be very old."

"Colin . . . ," Merilee began.

Sugar waved her hand in the air, stopping her. "You are correct, Colin. I am very old. Ninety-four in December, as a matter of fact. Thank you kindly for pointing that out."

Lily was frowning again, or maybe she hadn't stopped. Pointing at the typewriter, she said, "Does that mean we don't have Wi-Fi in the new house?"

All three new tenants looked at her with panicked faces.

"The young man I hired to update the house said he'd make sure it had all the modern conveniences. His name is Wade Kimball. I've got his card in the kitchen, which I'll give you so you can call him directly with any questions, as I do not involve myself with modern technology if I can help it."

"I've got to have Wi-Fi," Lily said, the frown back over her nose. "I need to access the school portal to check on assignments. I learned all about it in orientation last week."

Merilee's voice sounded weary. "I'm sure Mr. Kimball can get us set up right away if it's not there already."

"That's right," Sugar said matter-of-factly, taking the plastic wrap off the cookies and putting the plate in the middle of the large kitchen table. "No use borrowing worries."

Merilee smiled, her face relaxed for the first time. "My grandfather used to say that."

"Wise man," Sugar said.

"That he was." Merilee's face became strained again as she turned to her children and made sure they took only two cookies and placed their napkins in their laps. She didn't ask for her own cookie, and Sugar didn't offer her one. They'd already been there longer than Sugar had anticipated.

"Don't get any crumbs on the floor, children," Merilee said, hovering near the table, seemingly as eager to leave as Sugar was for them to go.

While Sugar poured two glasses of milk, Merilee moved to the large picture window behind the sink, a real farmhouse sink that had been installed in the house before they'd become popular as a decorating focal point.

"You can see our house from here," Merilee said.

Well. "Don't worry. I won't be snooping in your business."

Merilee's cheeks pinkened. "No, that's not what I meant. It's just, well, I guess I'm just used to living in a neighborhood with people on all sides. When Robin showed me the house I almost said no because it seemed too isolated."

The younger woman looked so young, so vulnerable, that for the second time that day Sugar forgot that she didn't want a relationship with her tenants. "What made you change your mind?"

Merilee didn't pause. "It's close to the children's activities and their new school and the right price. I didn't have a lot of options. And the house and all this land is lovely. Perfect, really."

After a moment's hesitation, Sugar put the glasses on the table and moved to stand by the window next to Merilee. The clouds wore streaks of pink as the late afternoon sun shredded them like cotton candy, and she saw all four brothers again as they'd been as children, bare chested and barefoot, running across the pasture toward the woods, hollering like stuck pigs. "I think your children will like living there. I grew up here in this house with my four brothers—I was the youngest child. My daddy built the house you'll be living in when I got married. Didn't live there long on account of my Tom getting killed in the war. But the house is good, solid construction—not like what they build nowadays. And there's a cellar for when there's a tornado. Make sure you know how to get in and out and how to latch it. Nearest tornado siren's about three miles away and you might not hear it."

"Thank you," Merilee said quietly, peering closely at the line of trees behind her new house. "Do those woods belong to you?"

Sugar kept her breathing even. "Yes, they do. But I wouldn't encourage you or the children to explore. There's a barn on the far side that might be a temptation, but that's also off-limits mostly because kids will think the woods are a good shortcut. They're not. They're very dark and deep if you don't know where you're going. And we still have black bears and more poisonous snakes than I can shake a stick at. It's just better if you and the children stayed away from the woods."

She felt the young woman's eyes on her but didn't turn.

"Look, Mommy—a rainbow!" Colin sprayed crumbs from his full mouth.

Before Merilee could say anything to him, his sister joined them at the window. "If I had an iPhone, I could take a picture."

Merilee's sigh was almost imperceptible. "Yes, well, you're ten. You don't need an iPhone. Where's the small camera I bought you for Christmas?"

"It's so inconvenient." Lily paused for a moment, as if to make sure everyone had heard her big word, which she'd probably picked up from her mother. "If I had an iPhone my camera would already be in my purse."

"You don't have a purse," her mother pointed out.

Lily frowned as Colin shoved another cookie into his mouth, undoubtedly hoping that the conversation with his sister had distracted their mother.

"I saw that, Colin," said Merilee without even turning her head. "Which means you're not leaving the supper table until you eat all your vegetables, regardless of how long it takes."

Colin swallowed thickly. "Yes, ma'am."

Merilee looked up at the sky, pale pink now, the clouds bruised with shadows. "Thank you for the cookies and milk for the children. The rain's completely stopped, so we should get going. I'd like to get our clothes hung and our suitcases unpacked before bedtime." She stared out the window for a long moment without stepping away. "How perfectly quiet and still those woods must be. Like time's being held back or something, you know?"

Without responding, Sugar turned back to the kitchen table and placed two paper plates and a box of plastic wrap in front of the children, with instructions to divide the cookies evenly. She'd never had children, but she'd had siblings so understood the importance of equal measure. Then she pulled out Wade's business card from a drawer and handed it to Merilee.

"Call him anytime. If there are any repairs, he'll give me a fair estimate and will actually show up when he's supposed to."

Merilee studied the card. "So, he's like a handyman? I'm looking for someone to build me more bookshelves for a collection I have."

"Just call him directly—I don't like to be . . . involved with any tenant issues. He's very handy because he's a builder, but he does work for me because his grandma is my best friend and I've known him since he was in diapers. Just let him know who you are and he won't say no."

"Thank you," Merilee said, taking the card.

Sugar gave Merilee the keys to the cottage before walking them to the door. "I had my housekeeper put clean sheets on all the beds. There are clean towels in the linen closet in the hallway and in both bathrooms. You'll be responsible for keeping it clean from here on out."

"Thank you, Mrs. Prescott . . . Sugar. You've been more than kind."

"I didn't do it to be kind. I did it because it's my job. And because I don't want a phone call in the middle of my shows asking where all the sheets and towels are."

Merilee's smile faltered as Sugar held the door open to let them pass, noticing the frown on Lily's face.

"Can you call Mr. Kimball now, Mom? I need to make sure we have Wi-Fi."

"Please stop worrying, Lily. I'll call him in just a minute." There was an edge to Merilee's voice that hadn't been there before. As if her last nerve had already snapped and she was grabbing at its threads.

Sugar turned to Merilee. "Just remember what I told you about the woods. They're fine to admire from a distance, but they're not safe."

"Got it," she said, sliding open the back door of the minivan. "With school starting and all their activities, I doubt we'll have much time for exploring anyway."

They said good-bye, then pulled away, Sugar watching all three heads strain forward in their seats as they waited for the sight of their new home to loom into view from under the canopy of the oak trees, baby birds looking for sustenance.

She listened to the drip of rain trickle off the porch roof and onto the old wood steps. Looking up at the sky, she stepped off the porch and into the drive, aware of the hum of the Honda's engine in front of her, just out of sight behind the oaks. Like so much in her life now, Sugar didn't need to see things to know they were there.

She allowed her eyes to follow the rainbow, noticing its colorful arches ending in the middle of her woods. She didn't need to go there to know there was no bag of gold or anything else a person would want to find. Her lips turned up in an unfamiliar grimace as she headed back inside, feeling the breeze from the opened windows teasing her with the scent of rain and old memories that seemed as permanent as the red clay that lay beneath her feet and under the tall pines of the dark woods.

Karen White is the *New York Times* bestselling author of more than twenty books, including the Tradd Street novels, *The Sound of Glass*, *A Long Time Gone*, and *The Time Between*, and the co-author of *The Forgotten Room* with *New York Times* bestselling authors Beatriz Williams and Lauren Willig. She grew up in London but now lives with her husband and two children near Atlanta, Georgia.

CONNECT ONLINE

karen-white.com
facebook.com/karenwhiteauthor
twitter.com/karenwhitewrite
instagram.com/karenwhitewrite